American Ghosts

American Ghosts

Edward J. Santella

Varykino Publishing | Stoneham

For Emerson, Marlena, Natalie
and all kids everywhere.

And while the cruelties of the white man toward the black man are among the heaviest counts in the indictment against humanity,
color prejudice is not our original fault,
but only one aspect of the atrophy of imagination
that prevents us from seeing ourselves in
every creature that breathes under the sun.

- Doris Lessing

CHAPTER ONE
MONDAY NIGHT

R ik read: "Gregor tried to suppose to himself that something like what had happened to him today might someday happen to the chief clerk; one really could not deny that it was possible".

A tap on the door.

The single, quiet knock was brother-sister code, the opposite of their parents' barrage of thuds and shouts, which preceded invasions. He checked his phone: it was nearly two. He wasn't surprised she was awake.

He closed the book.

He stretched.

He called, "In!"

The door opened six inches. Jessa peeked. "I saw your light on." She stepped in edgewise, as if the light leaking from her brother's room might wake their parents down the hall. She closed the door quietly behind her.

"Geez, little sister. Children your age are supposed to be asleep."

She looked down her nose at him from the corners of her eyes, a trick she'd learned as a two-year-old, and, as an afterthought, showed him her middle finger.

Inexpertly taped boxes, rescues from liquor stores, cluttered the room in stacks three or four high. A lamp duct-taped to the post at the head of Rik's bed cast distorted geometric shadows on the walls. The scent of newly painted walls and freshly waxed floors filled the room. The bed lay bare.

Rik wore jeans and a white t-shirt and had the slender strength of a young man. Jessa thought he could have been mistaken for a future movie star. His eyes gave his character away: they radiated acceptance and curiosity. His summer-dark tan had begun to fade toward a pale almond. Talking to him, others got the sense that he was prepared to step back in a deferential, even feminine way, to allow the other person more room. He did allow others room without judgment, though rarely did he do himself the same favor. Some misjudged him as weak. Jessa knew him as her protector, a role that had once gotten him a dislocated jaw.

Two curtainless windows looked out into the night.

He asked, "The stuff you're taking keeping you awake?"

"No. Not usually. Not tonight. Too much going on in my head."

Too much. Always too much, but more so tonight. This was their first night in the house, and tomorrow they began classes in a new school. Rik had a lot on his mind, too.

Jessa slid between the piles of boxes and stepped to the window beside the foot of Rik's bed. She wore loose gray jogging pants and a short-sleeved red tee. She was fifteen, almost two years younger than Rik. An air of vigilance hung about her. Her eyes held an intensity that said "whatever you give me I've already survived".

For the first time in a few months, the day had brought a serious rainstorm. All she could make out through the window were the large blurred shapes of nearby houses; moving lights in the sky, probably planes and security drones; and a few street-lights on the far side of the block. She heard the fractured wails of sirens, distorted by distance and the thickness of the windows. She heard other sounds, too. With her finger, she traced the erratic path of a raindrop down the glass. "You been listening?"

"To what?"

She tossed him an impatient glance. "Out there."

Rik cocked his head. He heard the rain and the background sound of engines. But he did hear something else. "Birds?"

"Yeah."

Jessa noticed things: a caterpillar crossing the walk, a hand-printed note caught in bushes, a change in an adult's mood. That was part of who she was, one of those traits that both amazed and irritated Rik.

"So?"

"It's almost two."

"Maybe a cat climbed..." He listened again. "You're right. Sounds like midday in a jungle."

"Weird, whatever they're doing." Jessa sat on the bed. She set her head on her hands.

Rik asked, "So what's going on?"

"Nothing. Nothing new." She lifted her head and looked at her brother. "I wish we hadn't moved."

They'd talked this through a million times to its inevitable rational inconclusion. "Probably right."

"The harder he works the unhappier he becomes."

"He" meant their stepfather, and now adoptive father, Gary, their mother's husband of nearly two years, though he'd been in their lives for three. "I hate it when he says he's doing it for us. He makes me feel so ungrateful. I don't even think the new school will be any different from our old one."

"We'll find out in, um, six hours, give or take."

Jessa said, "I liked our apartment. Why do we need this big house?"

"The manosaurus makes all the decisions, including the decision that the manosaurus makes all the decisions."

She glanced at Rik, turned away, frowned. "Do you ever feel that you're not really, I mean, I know he's not our birth father, but do you ever feel like you aren't really their child, maybe not anyone's child?"

Rik closed his eyes. Jessa could be a deep river. "God, we're their children, Mom and Dad, though we can't even remember him, then Meph, and now Gary. Our personalities are the sum of all the ways we defend ourselves from their craziness. Whoever else we might have been got lost." He stopped, thinking of their first father, who'd been killed in one of the African Wars when they were six and four. Were they like him? What had he been like? "No, that's not right. You didn't learn your art from them.

13

You found that yourself. That's yours. They didn't teach me to love words. That's mine. We have something that's ours. At least our own ways of escaping from them."

"That's what I mean. The person that's really me is lost inside my everyday self."

"You could do a sketch of you caught inside yourself."

"I could." Jessa pressed her tongue between her teeth. She harbored something she didn't want to tell him yet. Change the subject, she thought. "What are you reading?"

"Kafka. This poor guy, some sort of traveling salesman who lives with his parents and sister, wakes up one morning transformed into a giant bug. The family's terrorized. I think the guy who turned into the bug dies in the end."

"Ah, still into happy endings."

"I'm sure his sister had a lot to do with it."

"Really? Get me the magic spell."

Jessa leaned back, her arms braced on her brother's mattress. She had the profile and breasts of a young woman. Her skin was the palest copper, the result of having spent most of the summer inside. Rik thought her inquisitive and willing to meet others midway. At times, though, her eyes could harden like ice, and she would jut her chin forward as a man might. He envied her confidence...no. That was wrong. She didn't have confidence at all. What she had was the courage, or drive, or perhaps it was compulsion, to go forward despite the lack. She also had problems.

Jessa said, "You haven't begun unpacking."

"I will when I'm ready. Mom."

"And that will be?"

Rik paused for a second before speaking. "When I feel at home."

"Hah! I knew it. You feel as freaked out by this move as I do."

"I know it's worse for you than me."

"You're lucky the way things bounce off you. But, look at me!" Jessa stood on the bed and threw her arms out toward the bare walls. "I got up this morning! I've gotten up every morning for three weeks! I'm me!"

14

"A miracle of pharmaceutical science."

She dropped back onto the bed. "Able to confront the shit of modern life with a single..." Her voice drifted away. Not a single, she thought. Multiple. Multiple pills.

Rik sat up. His face was barely a foot from hers. "You'll do alright. We'll do alright. We're survivors. You've had a bad summer but you're better now. You've got me."

Jessa smiled, though her eyes grew damp. "And there's no cure for you."

They shared a thumbs-up. Mutual bolstering of spirits. Hope was something hoped for.

"Go to bed."

She stood and returned to the door.

Rik said, "Out, art demon!"

Jessa began closing the door, then said, "I think for your birthday I'll do a sketch of a man waking to discover he's a bug."

"You'll get the exact look of horror on his face, I'm sure. Up at six. Sweet dreams, sister."

Jessa closed the door.

She screamed loud enough to topple an empire. Rik had never heard anything as frightened. Or as frightening.

*   *   *

The ghost hated the girl and feared her.

They'd told him—they, the moon-faced ones—that hell lay below the earth. They'd lied. His mother'd told him that as a girl she'd had a home close to heaven. She said hell lay across the water from that home, days and days, horribly thirsty, hungry, can't-escape-the-smell-of-shit-and-piss-and-vomit-and-death-and-decay-and-fear days in steerage. Hell on an island where the weather blew so hot and dry it stole your sweat and filled your nose and mouth with sand. And that was just the first hell. Another hell, the hell he'd been born into, this hell, lay across more water,

15

not so many days, but farther still from home. Rain fell in this hell and so did snow, even up beyond a man's waist, and the cold so cold his mother could not, before they brought her here, have imagined it. The weather differed from hell to hell, but the whips, the foul, twisted men screaming orders, the ghost-whites with their snarly smiles and their pants down visiting your mother, your wife, your little sister, your own God-damned daughter, and the never knowing whether you or those like you would survive the day: those remained the same.

They'd learned him—not taught, learned him: that was the best their language could describe it—they'd learned him to work the bellows, to stoke the fire, to brew the inferno that softened metal that he would bend into the shape of a hinge or a tool or to fit a horse's foot. He spent unforgiving hours upon days upon years crafting metal shoes for animals while he himself did with what tossed-off boots the mistress might find him or he might scavenge. His only decent clothes he wore on Sunday to listen to the minister read from his holy book. They refused to teach him to read, or let him learn on his own. The moon-faced ones claimed he was unable to learn, then made rules to prevent him from learning. In their bones, they feared him. He tasted their terror, like rotten meat, on his tongue.

He'd come here, to where his mother's gods refused to go, to this strange house with his fire burning and restless horses and to this young white woman who must have been a queen—for, though she wore the clothes of a man, she was soft, soft as if she'd never carried water or beaten clothes or been beaten herself or turned a churn, and she was half out of her wits seeing him. I see your eyes, woman. I smell your terror. Scream, Queen, scream, for you have taken my life and I have nothing left to lose.

"Look at me, Lily Queen! Look into my eyes and see me!"

She did.

He looked into her depths. "I know who you are, Lily Queen. I know you better than you know yourself. I must, in order to survive."

The words hurt her. She covered her ears with her hands. Still, she saw him.

He probed her soul and recognized her wound.

The ghost recoiled from the horror.

They do this to each other!

Light exploded, as if the sun had broken through the roof, freeing him.

*   *   *

Rik was at the door in a second, opened it in two, had the hallway light on by three.

Jessa stood facing down the hall, hands over her ears, her eyes frozen open, shaking and crying.

He placed his hands tentatively on her shoulders, wanting to comfort her, but afraid to do more, for she shook with a wild agony. "What happened?"

He heard their mother and Gary rushing from their bedroom down the hall, Gary shouting, "What's wrong?"

Jessa panted, "Oh, my God; oh, my God; oh, my God!" This wasn't like the other times when she couldn't scream, when Meph wouldn't let her. Now she could scream and she'd put her whole soul and all her grief into it.

She held herself.

Rik put his arms around her arms. He tightened his hold to calm her shaking. "It's okay. Breathe slowly."

"Jessa, what's wrong? Is there someone in the house?" Gary's demand filled the hallway. He rushed past them, stumbling in his half-on slippers, to the top of the stairs.

"I'm sorry. No. I don't know. I saw... Oh, God..."—she caught her breath—"I mean, I thought I saw a man, a big man, almost naked, a black man, he had a hammer, a huge hammer, and there was fire. He looked me right in my eyes."

Their father marched back toward his bedroom. "I'm calling the police. Some thug broke in here and I want him arrested!"

Jessa laid panic on panic. Pulling free of her brother, she said, "No! Don't! It wasn't! Gary, don't! It wasn't...!" She wiped tears from her eyes.

"Don't? What do you mean 'Don't'? It wasn't what?"

"It wasn't real."

Gary stood like a boxer waiting for the bell beginning the round, eyes wide, hands clenched. "It wasn't real?" He took a step to the side, so as to face her more directly. "You screamed damn scared enough."

Jessa shook her head. "I saw horses behind him. There couldn't have been horses in the hall." She wiped her eyes with her sleeve.

"Horses," he said almost calmly. A step toward her, and he shouted, "You mean you're seeing things?" His voice ballooned. "You scared the living daylights out of your mother about something that wasn't there, that you didn't even see!"

"Gary, quiet. Calm down." Evelyn, hands clenched and shaking, approached Jessa. "Tell us the truth, Jessa." She reached out a hand, then drew it back, afraid to touch her daughter. She folded fingers and hands together as if in prayer. "We won't judge you if you saw something that wasn't there. We'll do everything to help you. Have you been taking drugs again?"

Rik rolled his eyes. "Oh, Mom."

Evelyn shot her son an angry look. "I'm worried about her!"

"It's probably the pills you have her take," Gary said. "I warned you!"

Evelyn snapped, "Well, that's what I'm asking. If she isn't taking drugs, it must be her meds. That's what I want to know."

"I don't use drugs. Not anymore. Maybe it is my meds, but I've been on them for weeks and I haven't seen...things."

Rik said, "Plus the stress of moving and going to a new school in the morning."

"What stress? She should be happy and all excited to have a new house and a new school!"

Evelyn placed a hand on her husband's arm. "Change upsets people, Gary."

"How can something better upset her?"

Rik asked, "Jessa, do you want to go to your room now? I'll go with you to make sure everything's alright."

"Damn, Rik, who put you in charge? I'm her father. I'll go with her. I'll calm her down!"

Gary grabbed Jessa's arm and marched her into her room.

Evelyn faced Rik and curled her lower lip into her mouth, as if she were biting it. "Rik," she said, "you have to learn to have a little concern for your sister. Get your head out of those books and pay attention to what's going on around you!" She stomped back to their bedroom.

Rik stood in the hall for a few seconds. His throat constricted, as if he were choking on himself. His teeth clenched. His eyes watered. His hands began to form fists, but stopped halfway, in claws. He couldn't make out all Gary's words but their tone came through Jessa's door clearly. He took a short breath. He hated himself because of his helplessness.

He walked back to his room and closed the door.

He turned, became like stone. His pupils grew large in the dark, large in amazement.

An ancient, breathless chill ran through this body.

A row of hedges stood where his wall had been, and a woman knelt, her back turned toward him, digging earth with her hands.

*　　　*　　　*

Tears clouded the ghost's eyes. The sun had long set and she could barely see her hands as she dug a hole in the earth large enough for the bundle next to her. She felt his eyes on her back as surely as she'd felt the master's whip, as surely as Nan would have felt the whip if the master had learned what the child had done. She'd had to lie, and lie expertly, to protect Nan.

Though her back was turned toward him, the woman spoke to the young man behind her.

"Did what I had to. No other way. I just buried the baby girl, just like this, digging in the earth with my hands. Was Nan's child. I told the master when he caught me...I told him she'd lost the poor thing...I told him she was only six months. Told him the child had come out like it had to escape. Told him I didn't know the father. That was the truth. No one cared which master used her. My Nan, she wouldn't say. No matter. No matter. The child an angel now." She paused. "Naw. It wrong. It matter. It matter.'"

She stood and faced the boy. Her facial features were African. She pointed with her left hand to two bound sticks on the ground beside the hole. "I have a cross for her. See, Master, there. A cross for the little one."

She squinted as if to gauge the boy's reaction.

"I said—I told him, 'Yes, Master, Nan was big for six months. Womens knows these things.' I afraid he suspected."

Again, she paused and cocked her head, as if listening.

"I told him, 'No, Master, you not hear a baby crying. That was Nan. She only twelve, you know. We not steal from the master.'

"He didn't whip me, God answered my prayers this time."

She slumped once again. "I thanked him. I told him, 'Yes, Master, I'll be up in the morning. I know you like my cooking.'"

As the woman faded, Rik mumbled, "I'm sorry."

*   *   *

What Rik saw was not a woman, but the ghost of what may once have been a woman, for parts of her were missing, as if holes had been carved into her with an ax and the spaces filled with ill-fitting stones. When she was digging the grave, he saw the curve of her back crossed by another curve, that of her shoulders, and her hands raking the earth, but soon he saw that she had but one hand, that her hair covered a gaping head wound, and part of her left side was gone, replaced with an oozing blackness. She spoke, but she had no mouth. It seemed covered by a hazy weave of cloth, though he heard her words clearly.

The vision held power. With the woman gone, he felt abandoned. He'd been shaken, a child shaken awake to a strange and darker world, only to have that new world stolen away. The transition made his head dizzy and his stomach unsettled.

He steadied himself, placing a hand against the wall.

Gary's voice still overflowed from Jessa's room, a rushing tide of the usual certainty and righteousness, but now, also, to Rik's ear, hollow, the words of a man who failed to grasp the complexity of his own home.

Rik fought to focus his mind. Too many horrors. Giving birth at twelve. A child. A rape. Jessa. The dead baby. The need to defend...

Stop it, he told himself. It wasn't a command but a plea.

What had he witnessed?

What had Jessa seen?

What was happening?

If he walked into Jessa's room and announced what he'd seen, Gary wouldn't believe him just on general principles. Jessa might think he was trying to protect her by deflecting Gary's attention. He had to wait to tell her when they were alone.

Who were they seeing? People who'd lived here before? Ghosts—good Lord, ghosts!—ghosts of...whom? Was their house haunted?

The wind had picked up, flinging rain into the windows. The birds continued their chatter punctuated with shrieks, as if arguing over what Rik had just seen. He felt cold. He put on his Sox jacket—an early present from Gary—and curled up beneath the burning bed lamp. The world contained multitudes he had not

21

suspected. Ghosts, of all things. He thought, we have a house with ghosts, ghosts of children who give birth at twelve, children who die or are killed at birth and women with pieces missing who bury the dead while fearing the living.

Too many thoughts. Too much sound from Gary's voice in the next room.

Ghosts. Rik had read stories about them. They haunted castles in England and, closer by, the old Victorians in New England. Years ago he'd memorized Poe's "Haunted Palace," and now a stanza came back to him.

> *And travellers now, within that valley,*
> *Through the red-litten windows see*
> *Vast forms, that move fantastically*
> *To a discordant melody,*
> *While, like a ghastly rapid river,*
> *Through the pale door*
> *A hideous throng rush out forever*
> *And laugh—but smile no more.*

"A hideous throng..." Jessa had seen something hideous. And the ghost woman had been hideous. Worse, her story, her life was hideous.

Poe's words played through Rik's mind like an old song that refused to be forgotten. He lay down, eyes staring at the ceiling. Hell, he thought, this was...hell, where the first commandment was "Fear."

*   *   *

After Gary left—after more than an hour—Jessa, still shaking, tried to comfort herself with her drawings. She took her journal from its hiding place. She hadn't trusted the movers with it. The book held five hundred nine-by-twelve-inch pages, just over two hundred of them filled with her drawings. She needed to sketch as she needed to breathe. Her grandfather, her mother's father, had understood that when he'd given her the journal. The covers were mahogany faux leather. The contents were honest. She opened it and studied what she'd last sketched.

Jessa had drawn a cavern with stalactites and stalagmites like giant teeth in the foreground. A young girl, a bit younger than herself, in the middle ground, sat on the cave floor, hunched, with her back turned to the viewer. A dark, watery expanse stretched before her to the bleak horizon. The sketch conveyed the young girl's need to cross that water, her inability to do so, and her lonely abandonment. Beneath, Jess had printed, "The Sea of Sorrow." The date written next to it was the day after she'd begun her meds.

If she could have, she would have redrawn the picture in her book differently tonight. The girl would have hallucinations. Cruel and unforgiving faces would appear in the stalactites and stalagmites; narrow, judgmental eyes would loom from the shadows; and a fearsome face full of anger would be rising from the water.

But since she'd finished that sketch, she'd been unable to draw. She felt no connection with her pencils or paper, no ability to convey feeling. That was what she hadn't told Rik. Her concentration tore itself to pieces running in circles. Her tears couldn't decide whether to fall or seep back behind her eyes.

Out of desperation, she took a pencil and piece of scrap paper. She attempted a sunflower. It was stillborn. Not a line showed life.

She was denied the single act by which she could calm her mind, concentrate and feel human.

What was real? she asked herself.

Something in her answered, Everything.

She hadn't told her family the worst of what she'd seen, and nothing of what she'd heard. She kept these things to herself. She could find no way to share such horrors.

Am I crazy? Am I so crazy I have hallucinations? Hallucinations that claim to know me better than I know myself? Am I so crazy I can't draw?

She wanted to hurt herself. Even on her meds she wanted to hurt herself, punish and reshape herself into a better person, a better daughter, someone she didn't hate, someone worth something.

She clenched her fists, snapping her pencil.

CHAPTER TWO
TUESDAY

R ik turned to make sure no one could see them from their new house.

He and Jessa each wore a backpack. Rik's contained his flex, his copy of The Complete Short Stories of Franz Kafka with its split binding, and a thin notebook. Jessa's held her flex and her sketchpad along with a pen and a half dozen pencils.

Patches of mist rose from puddles that had begun to evaporate as the heat of the day grew. Felt like the mid-80s, perhaps, and promised to grow hotter. Not a breath of wind. The neighborhood was quiet. The only indications that people might be home were cars parked in driveways. The birds, so raucous the night before, had gone silent.

"Jessa, you're not crazy."

With a bit of sarcasm, Jessa said, "I never thought I'd hear you say that." She added, "Just leave me alone. I didn't sleep much last night and nothing is going to make me feel better."

Rik held her arm. "I'm not kidding. I mean, unless we're both crazy."

She kept walking but said sharply, "What are you talking about?"

"After Gary took you to your room, I went back to mine."

"Yeah?"

"I saw something like you did."

She stopped in her tracks. "What? Like, you mean...?"

"Yeah."

When Rik had finished describing what he'd seen and heard, she looked away. "Twelve? She was raped." Her voice caught. For a moment she couldn't talk. "She was having a kid at twelve? And it died?"

"Died. Or someone killed it so it wouldn't have a life of misery. I couldn't tell. The woman said the girl, Nan, miscarried at six months. She was trying to convince someone. But then she said something about they wouldn't steal. I didn't understand."

"You're not making this up to make me feel better? Because it's not. Poor kid." She looked into Rik's eyes. She trusted him. He'd been the only one to protect her. "I didn't tell you everything. Like you said about the woman, the guy I saw had pieces missing. And he said something to me." She looked away.

Rik asked, "What? Unless you don't want to say."

She shook her head. "He said something like, 'I know who you are, Lily Queen. I know you better than you know yourself. I have to.'" As if New England still had winters, icy cold blew through Jessa's body. She shivered. "As soon as he said it, I knew he was right. I don't know why. I just knew he was right."

Rik sighed. His eyes caught a drone half a block down coming their way. "Let's keep walking." He kicked himself for not having realized that Nan would bring up Jessa's issues. "We can't be late the first day."

"Why did you apologize to her?"

Rik had felt sorry, still did, but he couldn't figure out what he was sorry for. That Nan had been raped? That she had miscarried, or...? That she wouldn't say who the father was? That we live on a planet where such things are allowed to happen? That the woman had conveyed to him such news? That they—his family—had moved into their—the ghosts'—house? All of the above? "I don't know."

Jessa felt her blood flowing. As confusing as it all was, she'd been suddenly and unexpectedly liberated, even though it was at another's terrible expense. At least, in a way. She shouted in a whisper. "Our friggin' house is haunted? I'm not crazy! Our friggin' house is haunted! Our new house that Gary almost killed himself working for has ghosts! Wait...why didn't you tell me last night?"

"Gary was in your room. I figured he'd never believe me. What was he haranguing you about anyway?

Her expression rolled through dismissiveness, disgust and hopelessness, as if, with Gary joining the family, she had not

26

gained a father but sustained another loss. "He's afraid I'm on my way to sluthood, you know, dreaming about half-naked black men with big hammers. He seems to think hallucinations are a kind of wish. Not to mention he apparently missed the part of my life where I went through puberty. He wants to believe I'm still a sexless little girl."

She grabbed her brother's arm and stopped him. "After Gary left last night I tried to remember everything I'd seen. I think the man I saw was making shoes for horses. What are they called?"

"Horseshoes?"

"Thanks. No, I mean the guy who makes them."

"Blacksmiths."

"Right," she said. "That accounts for the hammer, the fire and the horses. But that would mean the ghosts are real old. Sometime before cars."

"Or from Ipswich or somewhere they have horses as a hobby. The woman I saw...she acted like a maid or something. Really subservient. She was black, and if they'd had them around here, I'd have guessed she was a slave. Besides, the house was built in 1948. I saw the date on the copy of the deed the lawyer sent over."

They resumed walking.

"So our house is ninety-eight years old."

The drone Rik had seen earlier sailed past them at housetop height. It was one of the new ones that flew with the slightest high-pitched hum and looked like what people had once claimed to be flying saucers. You could no longer see if the cameras were pointed your way.

"But the woman you saw burying the child, that can't have happened recently."

"Why? If the girl didn't want people to know she was pregnant, then of course she'd try to hide it."

"She called you 'master.' When was the last time people went around talking like that?"

27

"Well, who ever heard of ghosts haunting a house that didn't even exist when they were alive?"

"Maybe their old house was torn down and ours was built on the same spot. Could we find out what was on our land before our house was built? Don't they keep records of who owned land and when?"

"There should be a way we could look it up."

Jessa asked, "How can we have ended up with a haunted house?"

"Apparently they forgot to put that detail in the real estate listing."

"What are we going to do?"

"We? You heard Gary. Who put us in charge? Sooner or later Gary and Mom will see them. I have no idea what they'll do after they calm down. Sue the people we bought it from? Where did they move to? I can see it now: The Happy Hollie Family v. The Sellers and Two Ghosts. There'll have to be a movie."

"But why?" Jessa asked. "Why is our house haunted?"

Rik said, "I don't even believe in ghosts." A step later, he added, "Or didn't."

Jessa felt more normal and a bit lighter with each step. Ghosts, she thought. Ghosts. "I feel good knowing it wasn't me being crazy, but..."

"That's how I feel too. But."

*   *   *

As soon as Rik and Jessa left, Evelyn called Dr. Dreier's office and made an appointment for Jessa for that afternoon after school. Then she watched the weather.

She'd seen it twice this morning. The station repeated it every fifteen minutes. Once in a while, something in the report was updated. The weatherperson always stood in front of a map of the United States arrayed with symbols that Evelyn didn't understand. She had little patience with things she didn't understand. She waited for the five-day forecast. If there were no big storms, no thunder and lightning and no tornadoes, she smiled. The world was as the world should be. Generally, she smiled.

She avoided the news. She hated the violence. They insisted on warning you not to look and that made you look at the dead bodies, even the dead bodies of children, or the children crying beside the dead bodies of their parents. Even the weather on the news was bad. Disasters everywhere: the government expelling states that had turned into miniature Saharas, or cities that had been flooded by the ocean; millions of refugees from those states smuggling themselves illegally across state borders, searching for a new place to live; and the state police and the National Guard capturing and arresting the refugees, trucking them off to reservations. No, she didn't see any reason to expose herself to that sort of thing.

Fifteen minutes of weather was about what she could handle. The weather forecaster predicted sun and heat, five days running.

*   *   *

The walk from their new home to Paradise High School took thirty minutes. Rik and Jessa slowed their pace as they reached the school property.

"Whoa," Rik said.

Three stories in most places, four in two, with rows of black windows all around, Paradise High was much larger and newer than their old school. It stood surrounded on three sides by sports fields. It was hard to take it all in at one glance. The flag, thirteen stripes and forty-four stars, hung limply in the heat in front of the main entrance.

Rik and Jessa went directly to the principal's office, as they'd been instructed.

"You must be the Hollies," the woman behind the counter said. "Welcome to Paradise High. I'm Mrs. Hemingway, the principal's assistant." Her mascara was smudged. "Let me see: Rik and Jessa. Is that right? Good." She took their pictures and a machine extruded metallic ID pins. She handed each of them their ID and a slip of paper with a number written on it. "Here are your security passes. New this year. They're required by Federal law." She pointed at her own badge. "You have to wear them whenever you leave your house. Your parents will be getting theirs soon. Everyone has to wear them. Rik, your home room is 314, that's Ms. Faudi. You'll like her. Jessa, you're in 217 with Mr. Cronin. He's very nice." She smiled at half sadly. "Oh! Wait!" She handed over two envelopes. "All notices are in the envelopes."

Rik looked at his ID. "What did you say these are these for?"

"Well, it means if there is any trouble, they'll know who you are. And where you are. They can track you if they need to. And, of course, the principal, or a teacher, or a parent, or the police could track your activities. If your parents should decide you shouldn't be allowed to read a certain book or see certain materials, that information would be transferred to your account and you wouldn't be able to take that book out of our library. Or if you took a book out or were seen reading a book that was suspicious, we'd call you and your parents in for an interview. It's part of ensuring your well-being and tracking potential terrorists." She added, as if they or she had a voice in the matter, "Is that okay?" Her eyes begged him to agree.

"You mean you can check what we're reading?"

"Oh, well, only if it's something suspicious. Or if someone should notice, they would let the authorities know."

"How do we know if what we're reading is suspicious?" Rik slurred the last word just a bit, in the interest of dramatic irony.

"That's decided after the book is reported. Eventually there'll be a list." She paused. "You must be so grateful your mother's new husband adopted you."

They responded with blank stares, a tactic they'd developed for use with their parents to convey no hint of a reaction.

"Well, then, if you need help with anything, just come on down and ask. Good luck!"

30

Walking up to the second floor, Jessa said to Rik, "I wonder if Kafka would pass their test, whatever it is. She looked like she'd been crying. In fact, a lot of kids here look kind of sad. Is the school that bad?"

After they parted, Rik walked into room 314. He made his way down the space between two closely packed rows of occupied seats, nodding to any student who noticed him, to an open seat in the back of the room. He sat, introduced himself to the boy on his left. The girl to his right didn't deign to acknowledge him.

That was fine with Rik. He felt awkward meeting girls, as if he had a duty to puff himself up like some kind of bird to impress them, the way most of the boys did. He sensed that the bravado rose from a fear of appearing incompetent. Or impotent. He refused to puff himself, did the opposite, then blamed himself for not doing it. Who were these young women who had once been classmates, friends and teammates and now had transformed into contested ground, something seemingly needing liberation by an outside intervener? Puberty had altered life, bringing with it erections, breasts, pubic hair, wants and needs. Puberty. The word itself sounded like a half-digested lump of rubber. He felt less uncomfortable being on the edge looking in on this unreality, watching and listening. He tried many times to romanticize his approach without success. He kept his passion and frustrations to himself.

Ms. Faudi came in.

"Good morning, class." Rik thought Ms. Faudi, too, looked drawn, tired, as if she had also been up all night. She spoke as if delivering surrender to a victorious invader. "Since the weather is so good, we're going to assemble in the stadium. Meet back here when the ceremony is over." She paused. "Alright. Let's go. Oh, wait. Wait! Sorry. We have a new student. Rik, would you stand? Rik Hollie? There you are. Zach, would you hang with Rik and help him get oriented? Thank you. Rik?" She pointed at her lapel. "Your security pass. Okay. Let's go."

31

He was still holding his in his hand.

Most of the other students dwarfed Zach. He looked part Asian, wore black slacks, a rugby shirt and glasses designed for a larger head. They shook hands.

Zach said, "Hey. Zach Wen."

"Rik Hollie. Where are we going?"

"The field. It's the only place that can hold the whole school."

"They do this every year?"

Zach looked at him sadly. "No. A girl in our class hanged herself. This is about her."

Rik closed his eyes. How much could he take? Decaying ghosts at home, and a girl hangs herself at school. Fuck this world, he thought. Fuck this life.

*　　*　　*

Mr. Cronin dismissed the class for the memorial service. Jessa, confused, looked around for someone to ask what was going on. She met a pair of brown eyes.

"Hi. You're new here, right?"

Jessa nodded and held out a hand. She introduced herself.

The girl said, "Celisa Adebayo." Celisa's bright brown eyes matched her deep bronze skin.

"I love the ribbons," Jessa said, looking at the girl's braided hair.

"Thanks—my mom fixes them for me." Celisa led the way, explaining where they were headed and why.

"Oh, my God. What happened? Did you know her?"

She nodded. "From soccer. We'd voted her captain this year."

"What was her name?"

"Ellen Scarpacia."

"Why did she do it?" Jessa caught herself after asking the question: how could anyone ever know? Maybe even Ellen hadn't understood why she was doing it.

Celisa shrugged. She stumbled over nothing and blinked back tears. Jessa took her arm.

Gary had achieved his dream—a decent house, two floors for living, a stand-up attic and a finished cellar, two and one-half baths, in a decent neighborhood in a decent city with decent schools. And he wasn't enjoying it. No one was predicting that he and his family would live happily ever after. No one had even thanked him for all the work he'd put into getting them here—not his wife, not his crazy stepdaughter who'd taken to dreaming of half-naked black men, not his I-don't-want-to-be-a-real-man stepson for whom he'd almost given up hope. No one had thanked him for getting them out of that cesspool of crime and failure that surrounded the boarded-up casino they'd lived near before. He tried to love them, but they kept making it hard.

Paradise was a "nice" town, several neighborhoods of single and two-family homes situated a few miles north of Boston between Somerville and Medford along the Mystic River. The town sported signs marking the present and former locations of historic homes and churches and its history as a shipbuilding port in the seventeen and eighteen hundreds. A large brick building, formerly a mill, had recently been rehabbed into a four-story, fashionably upscale shopping center named the Mill Mall.

Paradise, while not pricey, was expensive enough to keep out those who might interrupt your dream.

The former owners of their new home had been less than a year into a thirty-year mortgage when they'd been forced to sell quickly. Something about a parent's illness, the broker had said. They'd moved out before the end of July, and the Hollies had gotten the house for well below market. Otherwise, they wouldn't have been able to afford it. For being in the right place at the right time, Gary congratulated himself.

He sprawled in his recliner, the only place in the living room to sit. He hadn't slept much and his sleep hadn't been good, thanks to Jessa. He'd had to fight with his boss to get two days off and right

33

now he wished he were at work. At least there he knew what to expect. And how to deal with it.

For seventeen years he'd been a truck driver, delivering beer, wine and liquor, retracing the same routes and servicing the same stores every week. Drive a few miles, unload, talk with the guys in receiving: how they were doing, the Sox, the Pats, the Celts, the Bruins, the Revolution. But he'd found time to get his Bachelor's in management along the way, attending weekend classes. His break had come the year before, when the owner moved him to GM and Operations Director, a position where he oversaw not only the business and the drivers he'd worked with, but product ordering and promotions as well. There were also days when a driver didn't show and he'd have to do that route as well. As a driver, he'd been used to ten-hour days. His days still began at 6:00 a.m., but now they ran to twelve or fourteen hours, plus six to eight hours on Saturdays as well.

In reality, it was his show. His boss was a voice on the phone. Maybe he should have stayed in his old job, avoided the office crap where he was always disappointing somebody or other because he was responsible for keeping the ship afloat, but the raise had been enough for him to take a chance on the house.

Evelyn had assigned him to unpack the living room. She was upstairs doing something, God knew what, in the bedrooms. The kids were off to school. The sun flowed through the windows, and in Gary's state, he wanted only to sit and enjoy it.

But that wasn't the way the world worked.

Nothing gets done right unless you do it yourself.

He stood, sized up the couch, which the movers for their own mysterious reasons had left in the dining room, and then sized up the space by the living room windows where the couch should go. After fifteen minutes of shoving boxes around to clear a path, he maneuvered the couch into place. Carrying the end tables to their spots beside the couch proved easy enough. Still, he was

34

huffing a bit. Sitting at a desk all day had put near thirty pounds on him, at least the last time he'd checked.

Next he began examining the boxes, searching for the ones that the table lamps might be in. No luck in the living room. He finally found them in the dining room.

Of course, he had to pull the couch out so he could plug the lamps in. He'd just repositioned the couch and turned the lights on to make sure they worked, when Evelyn came down the stairs.

"Gary, you don't need the lamps on! It's daytime. You're wasting electricity!"

"Like I don't know that? I turned them on to see if they worked. They do. Now, with your permission, I'll turn them off."

"Well, if you'd only said so. You never tell me what you're doing. Look what I found." She handed him a square object, perhaps an inch and a quarter on a side, white with a blue design. "I found this on the floor of the hallway upstairs. After all the cleaning I've done up there! I don't know how I could have missed it. I can't imagine where it came from. It looks so old."

Gary turned it over in his hands. It had been worked, perhaps with a file, to even off the edges. He grunted. "Looks like a piece of tile. Must be one of the movers dropped it. Can't mean anything." He handed it back.

"What should I do with it?"

He shrugged. "Throw it out."

She put it in her pocket.

Evelyn worked in the office of a small insurance firm and had no hesitation asking for two weeks off. The office manager thought of her as dutiful and unimaginative and therefore a useful employee. The other office girls had been happy to pick up for her, and anxiously provided her with all sorts of moving advice. When she shared it with Gary, he did not pretend to listen.

35

In the four weeks between the real estate closing and the Hollies moving in to their new house, she and Gary had managed to have the floors stripped and polished, the walls and ceilings patched and repainted, the bathrooms redone and new kitchen counters and appliances installed. The house had been water-, wind-, mildew-, mold-, insect- and rodent-proofed. They'd added a generator in the cellar. This was their home. They thought it was worth it.

Evelyn knew she would need weeks, more than that, actually, to begin bringing the house to order. So far this morning she'd found, washed and hung the curtains in each of the upstairs rooms, and found and placed clean sheets and blankets on all the beds.

Whatever she worked on, at the moment, tears pooled behind her eyes. She'd thought Jessa had been improving. On a couple of recent days, in the excitement and rush of moving, she'd almost forgotten about her daughter's depression. The hallucination frightened Evelyn. Perhaps Dr. Dreier would have something to bring Jessa back from...from wherever she'd gotten lost.

Evelyn harbored a black hole behind her heart. The black hole came from having brought great harm to someone she loved. She accepted responsibility and blame, but, to be fair, she'd been in a difficult time in her life. Her husband had been killed in the wars, she had few earning skills, she had two young children and, well, Walt had seemed such a reliable, hard-working man. She'd tried to make it on her own but Walt brought home a real paycheck. She asked him to move in. He did.

He lasted four months.

Walt had taken Rik's existence to be a direct affront to his manhood. Rik was thirteen when Walt moved in and the beatings began. Rik said things about Walt that Evelyn couldn't believe. Then Walt dislocated Rik's jaw for saying them. The hospital staff had Rik write down what had happened. Eventually, and that was a very long eventually, Walt went off to jail for forty-six years on eighteen counts of sex with a child under twelve—Jessa—and multiple assaults and batteries on Rik.

It is a frightening thing to watch a twelve-year-old girl, sitting stone-faced in a witness chair, relate in clinical detail each of the times a grown man orally and vaginally raped her. Jessa had never completely unfrozen.

The kids had called Walt "Meph," even to his face. Evelyn hadn't understood that they used it as a shortened code word for Mephistopheles, a demon who served Satan. Neither had Meph.

Evelyn went to Rik's room and began opening the cartons. When she'd identified those containing his books, she stood and pushed one of his bookcases against the wall in what seemed a likely place. She grabbed several of the books and stopped to look through one. Rik had underlined and written comments on almost every page. After a moment's hesitation, Evelyn emptied the box, then another, then a third, filling the bookcase, arranging the books in no particular order. She looked at the bookcase.

Evelyn usually read several magazines, not thoroughly, and a few bestsellers over the course of a year, but books did not draw her. Random lines of poetry struck her as strange, as if the author had left things out to trick the reader. Anyone who lived by books the way Rik did had to be part stranger.

She knew he would want to unpack and stack the shelves himself, to put them in some order that made sense to him, and that he would never understand why she did what she was doing. She was doing it because she loved him.

She didn't even know how to describe to her friends what her son wanted to be. "My son is a poet." How did that sound? She tried it again, aloud, emphasizing "son." "My *son* is a poet." That wouldn't do. She changed inflection, putting the emphasis on the last syllable of "poet." "My son is a po*et*." No. She tried the emphasis on "po." "My son is a *po*et." Better. But what did that even

37

AMERICAN GHOSTS

mean? Better just to say, "My son? Oh, he's a writer." That could mean anything.

Next stop, Jessa's room.

Evelyn enjoyed housework. It provided a feeling of accomplishment, something office work did not. She labored under the conscious conviction that a neat, clean house meant a happy family, and, conversely, that family discord had its roots in unvacuumed rugs, dusty screens and uncleaned bathrooms. And unpacked boxes. Jessa's depression—how Evelyn hated that word—during the past summer had tested this belief. She could identify nothing she had failed to do that would justify her daughter's distraught sadness.

Evelyn had missed the beginning signs of Jessa's disease and felt guilty about that, too. Dr. Dreier had told her she shouldn't, because these things could begin slowly with symptoms only a professional would notice.

After Meph was arrested, Evelyn had spent more than a year in therapy. So had her children. She knew Jessa and Rik would likely suffer throughout their lives because of her choice of boyfriend. The therapists told her that child abuse actually changed the child's DNA, and that the child could even pass the damaged genes along to his or her children. She knew abused children didn't live as long on average as non-abused children. She knew they often suffered from depression. She'd known that she had to be vigilant, but she hadn't wanted to recognize the signs.

It was all too horrible.

Perhaps the first sign had been Jessa not getting out of bed. Evelyn had been watchful over Jessa for a year or so after the discovery that Meph had raped her. She'd noticed her daughter had periods of quietness, of wanting to be alone, but these had usually only lasted a few days. Jessa had always come out of her moods by herself. Evelyn realized now that she had become complacent. Toward the end of last school year, perhaps April, Jessa began getting up too late to make it to school on time. She napped instead of doing her homework. She claimed she couldn't do the simplest things. She ate less and less and always alone. She lost weight. She stopped taking calls and texting. She lost her summer job before she ever appeared for work, staying in bed for three days straight. Evelyn finally had to physically push Jessa out of bed so she could change the sheets.

In June, Evelyn decided to call Dr. Dreier, whom Jessa had seen before because of Meph, and who fortunately had an office in Paradise—partially as a way to protect her daughter from Gary, who could not understand anyone not showing up for a job. After trying various doses of various combinations of medications, Jessa had begun to return to a more normal life by the beginning of August.

Evelyn unpacked Jessa's clothing, more slowly and carefully than her son's books. She made associations with the clothing: where and when purchased; where her daughter had worn certain items; who had been there; times before the depression. Happier times. She packed them neatly away in drawers, so Jessa could look and see where everything was. Ordered.

Of course, Jessa, too, would empty the drawers and rearrange everything to her whim.

Evelyn opened another box and found it stuffed with art books. They made a colorful mess. She lost energy suddenly, interest, too, at the idea of sorting through more alien texts. Why did they have to like things she didn't understand?

Evelyn needed her world small, confined and cozy. She feared anything larger would overwhelm her.

Evelyn collected the medications her daughter had left scattered on her bed and lined them up on her dresser by the time of day she was to take each. When she had the plastic bottles in order, like little white-capped soldiers, she sat on Jessa's bed and cried.

39

*　　　*　　　*

The morning's remembrance service consisted of a series of principal, teacher, police officer and student speeches that strung superlatives together as if Wonder Woman had died. Such a marvelous individual, in fact, that no one could have predicted her suicide. Rik sensed excuses being made. Why not? he asked himself. Who wants to admit missing crucial clues that may have saved a life? Someone, at least in retrospect, must have seen some sign that she was troubled. Everything had a cause. Or so he wanted to believe.

He asked Zach. Zach shrugged. Yeah, he'd known her, had classes with her, been on a couple of projects with her and, no, he never saw any problem. Then again, Zach added, she'd killed herself during the summer, a week or two, he thought, after school ended, and he hadn't seen her during that period. Anything could have happened. Anything.

When the chance arose, Zach introduced Rik to other students. Rik worked at introducing himself when Zach wasn't around. Rik's old school had been full of the children of Mongolians from Central Asia and Midwestern drought refugees, called n'okies for new okies in remembrance of the Midwesterners who'd fled a lesser disaster in the 1930s—people bent on survival in the face of an uncertain future, people for the most part disliked by the people who had preceded them to Massachusetts.

Paradise felt different. Rik felt younger than the kids in this new school. He sensed, rightly or wrongly, an unearned self-confidence among them, as if mere existence justified their lives, no questions permitted. Not that they were rich by any measure, but they acted secure. Rik's flesh and bones, on the other hand, told him his life needed justification—and that, so far at least, he hadn't earned it.

On their way between classes, Zach nudged Rik. "That kid, there?" He pointed. "That was Ellen's boyfriend."

40

The boy he'd pointed out stood tall and broad-shouldered, though he hunched a bit as he walked, and had a chiseled, movie-star face and a mane of golden hair. Rik immediately thought "jock" and dubbed him "Thor, the Godlike." He was surprised when the boy later turned up in a couple of his classes.

*　　　*　　　*

Jessa left the memorial service hyper-alert, adrenaline pumping, vulnerable and needing to be alone. She imagined that her own recent feelings of exhaustion and worthlessness mirrored what Ellen had experienced before her suicide. Jessa hadn't felt suicidal, merely that she should have never been born. If she had been drifting toward suicide, the medications had cut off that route. Still, she and Ellen were sisters in depression, and Jessa felt the frustration of wanting to comfort the dead girl.

"You okay?" Celisa asked. "You look like a ghost."

The word "ghost" snapped Jessa between mental worlds. She met Celisa's gaze, then, quickly, looked away. "I'm okay. Just...not the way to begin a school year, I guess."

Never before had the dead been such a part of her life.

*　　　*　　　*

Gary was breaking boxes down and tying them into manageable piles when the doorbell rang. He checked his watch; it was just past two.

A thirtyish man in khakis and a checked sport jacket over a white dress shirt, open at the neck, introduced himself as Sandy Culver, a neighbor. He offered his hand. They shook. Then Culver pointed down the street. "We live in the white house there."

Gary was confused. All the houses were white.

"Look, I took my lunch hour to let you know that a couple of us, a couple of your neighbors, will be stopping by this evening to let you know, to sort of bring you and your wife up to speed on

41

what's going on here. We didn't want to interrupt your dinner, so we were wondering what time would be convenient."

Gary frowned. The guy seemed polite enough, but his announcement that the neighborhood would be descending on his new home before they'd settled in was impertinent. "You know, we're just moving in. We're anxious to meet everyone, of course, but next week would be better. We'll do next week."

Culver sighed. "We can't wait. This is too important. We did that once and things got out of hand. What time would be best tonight?"

"Something so important it can't wait till next week when we're all moved in?" Culver had Gary curious and a little worried.

"That's right. Look, there'll be four of us and we won't take much more than a half hour."

Gary thought for a few seconds. "Let me check with my wife." He yelled up to the second floor. "Evie, a few of our new neighbors want to come over to discuss something important with us tonight. What time would be best?"

"Tonight? Does it have to be tonight?"

"Seems so."

"Nothing's ready...I mean..."

"They say it's real important."

"Oh, I suppose around eight?"

Gary turned to Culver. "Eight okay?"

"That's fine. Real fine. That works well. It's good to see you'll be cooperative."

"You want the four of us?"

"No. No kids. You'll have to explain it to them later."

"Okay. See you at eight."

"We'll be here." Culver offered his hand again.

Gary took it and gave it a shake.

After he closed the door, he yelled up to Evelyn, "Eight's fine."

"How many are coming?"

"Just four."

"Well, I guess that's not too bad. What do they need to talk to us about?"

"He didn't say. Something important, he said. No kids. Just the two of us."

"Well, that's good. We'll send them upstairs to do their homework."

*   *   *

When the last class let out, Rik thanked Zach for playing guide for the day. They exchanged numbers. When Zach offered him a ride home, Rik thanked him but said he had to wait for his sister.

Rik stood alone on the walk in front of the school, the weight of new schoolbooks on his back, sweating and wondering how a world so hot, humid and sunny could harbor ghosts and suicides.

Two drones, one circling north along the street, the other south, lazily tracked students heading home.

Rik spotted Jessa walking toward him accompanied by four girls. He had hoped Jessa would be alone, but his sister made friends like the Fourth of July made hamburgers. Fortunately, from his point of view, three of the girls broke off to walk in another direction. Only the tall black girl remained with her.

Jessa had begun to make introductions when a car horn beeped and a voice they recognized as their mother's called, "Jessa!"

Jessa, her lips pursed, walked over to the car. After Evelyn explained she'd made an appointment for her, Jessa turned to Rik and her friend and shouted, "I've got to go! Mom says we'll see you at home later!"

"Thanks...?" Rik nodded and waved as Jessa got into the car.

As Evelyn pulled out into traffic, she asked Jessa, "Is that Rik's girlfriend?"

Jessa rolled her eyes. "No, Mom. It's not Rik's girlfriend. Rik's not capable of having a new girlfriend on the first day of school. Or the first month. He probably didn't even speak to a girl all day."

43

"That's not very nice to say about your brother. Well, then, who is she?"

"She's in my class. She's my friend. She helped me around today. She's very nice."

"Well, I'm sure she is, but you should be careful around girls like her. A lot of them do drugs. A lot. And they're loose, a lot of them, if you know what I mean."

Jessa rested her elbow on the car door and her head on her hand. She closed her eyes. This was no time for an argument with her mother. She had a decision to make. Her mother expected her to tell Dr. Dreier that she'd had a hallucination, while she now knew she'd seen a ghost. She doubted that either her mother or Gary would believe her and Rik. But how long could they pretend? She wished she'd had the chance to talk to Rik first.

*   *   *

"That's our mother."

"I figured." Celisa smiled.

A voice inside Rik said, It's alright to talk to her. He thought he knew that already, but the voice still made him feel better. As if he needed permission. He swallowed.

"I'm Rik."

"Celisa."

He saw why Jessa and she had become friends. Celisa had poise, she was attractive, her eyes bright, interested, inquisitive. A person with something to say. The kind of girl he might be attracted to if he were to someday become brave enough to want to spend time with a girl.

Rik said, "Hi."

"Hi."

"I'm walking that way. You?"

"Me, too."

They took their first steps in silence. Rik had read a fantasy novel about a shaman who believed every person had an animal

44

guardian. For Celisa, he thought it would be a small forest animal, something swift and agile and attractive when hiding behind its own stillness.

Despite this unthreatening vision, Rik panicked. He tried to find something to talk about. He felt responsible for entertaining her and already he was failing.

She asked, "I think I saw you with Zach during the day?"

"Yeah," he said, relieved. "Ms. Faudi had him show me around."

Celisa laughed. "Mr. Cronin would never think of that. He's sooo scattered."

"So how did you meet Jessa?"

"She looked lost when we broke for the assembly. I guess I just volunteered."

"That was nice of you."

Something about the phrase caused Celisa to glance at Rik and smile. "Well, wouldn't you have done the same, if you'd been the person who'd been here for years and someone else was new?"

"Probably. Really, thank you for helping her. You're right. It would have been worse going to the assembly and finding out about the, uh, suicide and having no one to talk to." He turned to look at her. "Did you know her?"

Celisa nodded. "Soccer team. We'd voted her captain this year. I couldn't believe it when I heard. Really, I'd have expected anyone more than her."

Rik thought. "You know, I don't mean this to sound cruel or anything, but after listening to those speakers I thought she'd have ascended into heaven like a proper saint."

Celisa caught the humor and smiled grimly. "She was fine to get along with. Something must have happened last spring. She spent more time by herself. Not sad so much as preoccupied. At the end of the year, she even showed up late for the sports award dinner. But still, no one ever suspected."

"There's something about a high school student's suicide that sucks away the air and leaves everything dirty."

They walked awhile in silence.

Celisa said, "You're very quiet."

He nodded. "I never know what to say."

"That's okay. It's better than saying a lot of stupid things just to keep the air vibrating."

A car full of students drove by. The driver honked repeatedly. Arms extended through the open windows, each with a raised middle finger. Words got lost in the noise of the car's getaway.

Rik stopped. Staring after the car, he asked, "What the hell was that about?"

"You don't know?" Celisa's eyes had narrowed, her posture straightened, her body tensed. No longer could Rik see her as a forest animal. More a hawk, hunting a forest animal. "White girls don't like seeing a white boy with a black girl." Her eyes did a three-sixty. A single drone flew up the street in the same direction as the car.

"They don't...?"

"They say it's unfair competition."

"Why? We were just walking together!"

She said sharply, "That's not the point, is it?"

Rik's jaw clamped shut. Celisa was right; that wasn't the point. But what was? Then he asked, "This happen a lot?"

He immediately wished he hadn't asked. He knew the answer. He couldn't remember how he knew the answer, but he did. The answer made him uncomfortable.

"Yes. You're not surprised, are you?"

"No. How do you put up with it?"

"Number one: I continue to exist. I be. Number two: I be right at them."

Rik felt like apologizing again. And once again, he didn't know why. He shook his head to clear his mind. "Jesus. The school we left you could get in some serious trouble for pulling shit like that."

Celisa caught the change of subject, the duck and hide routine.

Her mother had told her often enough that it was not her role to explain everything to every white person. They had brains. They could figure things out for themselves. So she rolled with it. "What kids were at your school?"

"Maybe twenty percent white, forty and forty each mongols and n'okies." He thought of the ghosts, of the blacksmith and the woman burying the child. He looked at Celisa, seeing her and sensing the outlines of her world for the first time.

She asked, "You still walking my side of the street?"

"Yeah."

They walked on in silence. Perhaps Rik kept at a slightly greater distance. Celisa had become radioactive. "I thought we all got along okay. But then, I rarely saw an 'inter' couple, you know, white and n'okie or white and mongol." And he'd had no n'okie or mongol friends, though there were some to whom he'd say hello. Wasn't much to pat himself on the back about.

"That's the second time you said that, that n'okies aren't white. But they're from Oklahoma and Kansas and places like that. They have white skin."

She'd forced Rik to think. "I don't know. I mean, you're right. We just always thought of them as...different. Like losers, or something."

"Whites used to treat the Irish that way. Everyone considered the Irish to be black. Then the Italians. Treated them the same way they treated blacks, too."

Something Rik hadn't known. That covered a number of his ancestors.

Celisa said, "Having white skin doesn't mean you're 'white.' You still have to qualify."

Rik felt a jolt of panic. Again, he had no clue. He changed the subject. Second time. "Are you interested in history?"

She laughed and grinned. "Not particularly. When you're black it's good to know stuff like that. Helps keep perspective

47

when a carload of white girls gives you the finger for walking with a white guy."

When they came to where Rik had to turn down another street toward home, he said, "I go down there. I'm glad you walked with me. Thanks for helping Jessa."

"Right. Glad to meet you, Rik." Celisa looked down the street where he was turning. Her eyes clouded over. "I can't say we were ever close friends, but I miss her. It's so sad."

Rik said, "We're not supposed to die this young." He immediately thought what he'd said sounded dumb. "See you tomorrow."

Celisa looked down the street again. She licked her lips and bit her tongue. She met Rik's eyes.

In her eyes, Rik saw an intelligence, an openness, a challenge, and a hope that her challenge would be accepted. He drew in a breath. Her face was marvelously attractive. She was marvelously attractive. "Thanks for walking with me."

"Thank you for walking with me."

When Rik turned down Antigua Avenue, he stopped to take it in. The neighborhood stood in a crook of the Mystic River, a section of relatively flat land barely above river level. Houses, predominantly two or three stories, stood along both sides of the street, separated by short spreads of water-deprived, brown-yellow lawns, bushes, perhaps a tree, and a driveway. The houses were all white. Cars sat parked here and there. All angles were right angles except the sloped roofs. No turrets rose above the trees for sentries to spy on attackers. No moat or drawbridge. No flags or pennants flying. No people save himself. Quiet. Nothing hinted of ghosts, hauntings, dangers or the remote possibility of romance.

Nothing reflected him either, his concerns, worries, woes. Nothing spoke to the turmoil of being seventeen, to his exploding sexual urges, to his love of reading, writing, and stories. Antigua Avenue stood indifferent.

48

I guess, Rik told himself, it's a nice place to be seen in, but I wouldn't want to live here. But he did live here, now. He knew, too, that he was one of the fortunate.

"Celisa." The word was a murmur of possibility. "Celisa." He frowned.

"Jessa, good to see you. Have a seat." A jovial elf of a woman, Dr. Dreier appeared a bit undersized for her professional desk and chair, as if her body was making an ironic comment on her supposed authority. Her hair fuzzed, and she had the eyes of a mother bird, sharp but caring. "How are you?"

"I don't know."

"Honest answer! I asked your mother to wait in the waiting area so that you and I could speak freely. I'm glad to see you will. Your mother told me that your depression has improved but you've had a hallucination. Is that true?"

"I think I saw something."

"You're not sure?"

"No, I'm sure I saw something." She warned herself to choose her words carefully. "It was over very quickly."

"Your mother said you screamed loud enough to wake heaven. I told her it would be nice if someone would wake heaven."

Jessa tried a smile. She wasn't in the mood for humor. She had never been comfortable lying and already she felt flushed and guilty.

"Why don't you tell me about it?"

"Sure. Well, I'd just left my brother's room." A bit of relief crept over her. She could tell Dr. Dreier the truth about what she remembered seeing.

"Do you remember the time?"

"After two sometime."

"In the morning? Had you been asleep?"

"Neither of us had been able to sleep. We moved to our new

49

house yesterday, and we were worried about starting school in the morning. Adrenaline, I guess. We talked about things. And we said good night."

"And then."

"The hall was dark. I wasn't sure where I was so I kept my right hand on the wall." She took a breath. "It came all of a sudden. A man, a large black man, built like a football player, naked from the waist up. There's something like a table in front of him." Her hands spread and moved back toward her center, as if running them across the table. "His right arm was raised and he held a hammer in his hand." Her hand hung above her head. Slowly she brought it down. "Behind him there was a fire. I couldn't see what it was coming from. On the other side of the fire I saw two horses. A blue light came from behind the horses so a lot of what I saw was in silhouette. Though the thing I remember most are his eyes. He looked at me. He saw me. He looked right into my eyes and he was furious.

"It was so quick, but he wasn't all there. I mean, he had pieces missing. And he said something." She repeated his words in a near whisper, as if performing a spell.

Dr. Dreier handed Jessa a box of tissue. Had Jessa's eyes not been blurring with tears, and had she been paying attention to the psychiatrist, she would have noticed that the doctor had gone pale and her hands shook. Jessa wiped her eyes.

"That's all I remember."

"That's very good." The psychiatrist worked to regather her professionalism. "You've a good eye for detail and a good memory. Can I ask a few questions?"

Jessa nodded.

"Did this person look at all like the man who raped you?"

"No, not at all. Not just that the man I saw was black and Meph was white, but Meph was small. Medium height and thin." She looked at the floor and closed her eyes against the memory.

50

"Did anyone else see this?"

"No."

"Did anyone find anything, an article, a fragment, that might have been related to this vision?"

"I don't know what you mean. How can a hallucination leave something behind?"

"Never mind. How long did this impression last?"

"A few seconds, I think."

"What caused it to end?"

"My brother turned on the lights."

"And it disappeared?"

"Yes."

"Had this ever happened to you any time before?"

"No."

"Anywhere else? Not just in this house."

"No."

"Had anyone told you they had such an experience or knew of someone who had?"

"No."

"Try to remember."

Jessa looked down and did try to remember. She looked up and shook her head. "No." She caught herself. "I mean, I've read of people seeing such things, like ghosts. I've read most of the Grimms, Hans Christian Andersen and Edgar Allan Poe. Some H.P. Lovecraft."

"Do you read a lot of horror stories?"

"I used to. The last novel I read was The Bell Jar."

Dr. Dreier nodded. "I remember reading that book." She typed something, then exhaled. "Were you very tired at the time you saw this man?"

"Yes. Like I said, we moved that day. I wanted to sleep but I couldn't."

"The hallway was completely dark?"

"Yes."

"Could you have fallen asleep and had a dream that woke you?"

After several seconds of thought, Jessa said, "I hadn't thought of that. I don't think so."

"Does this scene you described mean anything to you? Does it spark any memories?"

"No."

"Given your gender and age, dreams of large men and horses are not unexpected."

"This is the only time I've seen anything like this. It didn't feel like a dream. I didn't scream and wake myself. I was awake and I screamed."

"Would you like me to give you some medication that might prevent this from recurring?"

"I guess I'd like...I don't know. The meds I'm on have helped me feel much better. I get out of bed and do things. But..."

"But?"

Jessa looked at her.

"Jessa, dear, you look like you're going to explode. Tell me."

Jessa said, breathlessly, "I can't draw." She swallowed. "I mean, you said the medicine would take three or four days to kick in, well, that's when I couldn't draw anymore. And I have to draw."

"You have to draw." Dr. Dreier flipped through her notes. "Ah. Right. I see that here. I'd forgotten. What do you draw?"

"Pictures from stories I read. Sometimes from things that happened."

"An artist." She stopped, as if considering the issue. "Ah, so that's the problem."

"I'd rather feel depressed or have hallucinations if I had to, and be able to draw."

"Is that right? Drawing is more important to you than being depressed or having hallucinations?"

Did suggesting that make her seem crazy? "I don't know what to say." She didn't.

"I think it would be better if we found something that helped the depression and hallucinations that didn't interfere with your art." Dr. Dreier busied herself typing out the scripts, printing and signing them. "A 'best of both worlds' solution. We hope." She looked at Jessa. "Give me just a minute."

Dr. Dreier made entries onto her laptop and read the results. "We're in luck. You can stop all your current meds immediately and begin these as soon as possible. No need to ease you off. Get to the pharmacy and pick these up. Do you understand?"

"Yes. Thank you."

"I need to see you in one week. In the meantime, call me anytime if you see another vision or your symptoms of depression return. In fact, if you find you can't draw in two or three days, call me. This is very important. We need to stay in touch."

"Yes. I understand. Thank you."

"One more thing. Your first day of school was today?"

"Yes."

"Difficult way to begin the school year, I understand."

"Yes."

"You didn't know her, of course."

"No."

"You never heard about her...death before?"

"No."

"Had you met any students, or teachers, or anyone from the school before that?"

"No."

"Anything else?"

"No."

"One final thing. I asked you this before and I'm going to ask it again. Have you had any thoughts of suicide?"

"No."

"If you do, call me immediately. If you think of suicide at all. The first second, you call me."

"I will."

The doctor slowly exhaled. "Then thank you. And good luck with your art. And call me if you have any other experiences like that!"

Jessa had barely stepped through the door when Dr. Dreier called her name again.

"Jessa, you need to understand, if anything, anything, happens, you must call me right away."

Jessa nodded and closed the door. She felt like a felon, having deceived the therapist.

*   *   *

Dr. Dreier tapped her fingers on the desk until she heard the outer door of the waiting room close. She waited until she felt certain Jessa and her mother had gotten on the elevator.

Then she pushed two digits on her phone.

"Charlie?"

"What can I do for you?"

Dr. Dreier said nothing.

"Bonnie?"

"Charlie, bring me the Ellen Scarpacia file."

She heard a sound like a deep sigh before the line went dead.

A few short minutes later, the doorknob turned. The door opened ever so slightly. Then, with a series of thumps, the door blew open and a man equal in age to Dr. Dreier rolled his wheelchair into the room. The door closed itself behind him. On his lap, he carried a file. He handed it to the doctor.

"Can't you let this go? You think by reading this for the thousandth time you'll discover the key to her suicide?"

"Charlie, what would you say if I told you that the charming child, no, young woman who just left my office—she's an artist, would you believe!—told me she had a hallucination very similar, almost identical, to the ones Ellen Scarpacia had?"

Charlie's eyes widened. "Are you sure?"

"It could be a coincidence that two young women come to me complaining of similar symptoms. Coincidences happen. Or that she forgot she saw the story on TV, or heard some gossip, and imagines the same thing is happening to her, though Jessa denies knowing anything about that before the hallucination. Let me see." Dr. Dreier opened the files side by side. "Oh, my. Oh, my God. Charlie!"

"What's wrong?"

"Look!"

Charlie rolled his chair up beside the doctor.

She turned the files so he could see.

He saw. Once in each file, the address: 127 Antigua Avenue.

Charlie reprised the sound he'd made on the phone. "Bonnie, there is a rational explanation."

"Ellen killed herself, Charlie. She told me she saw things. She was my patient. She hung herself. In the same house where Jessa lives. I don't want Jessa...."

"I know, Bonnie. I know."

*   *   *

"Rik, the knives and spoons go on the right. Will you ever learn? And the fold of the napkins goes toward the plate."

When she had begun preparing dinner for four, Evelyn hadn't known which of the more than twenty miscellaneous brown boxes labeled "kitchen" contained the knives, the forks and spoons, the dishes, or the right pots and pans. Or the seasonings. That's what happened when you saved money by doing the packing yourself. At least she knew the food was in the fridge somewhere, wherever Gary had tossed it.

Somehow, with help from Rik and Jessa, she did it. Gary had dusted and polished the dining room set and moved the remaining boxes back far enough to claim a space for a meal.

Rik made a face but complied. Their mother's spark and

concentration made a better statement than words about how important this meal was for her. A roast in the oven; asparagus in the microwave; mashed potatoes—potatoes peeled, sliced and mashed by Gary—on the stove; and a cake on the counter for dessert: it wasn't a holiday, it was their mother's declaration that this house was their home.

Jessa finished setting the plates and glasses, wine for parents, juice for young adults. She smartly cracked open a bottle of Chardonnay and poured. Without being asked she turned on the music. Among the family the album was known as "assisted listening" because Evelyn had first heard it in her mother's assisted living apartment. She'd pestered the staff until they gave her the album name. The first notes of "Claire de Lune" floated in the air, so low they were barely more noticeable than the paint on the walls. Music and wine worked like vaccines against Gary's outbursts. Jessa edged up the volume.

"Gary, you can bring the roast in now!"

He carried the platter in to appreciative comments.

With a maestro's final flourish, Evelyn sat. "Isn't it great having supper together in our new house?"

Gary began eating. "Um. Good." He looked at Rik. "So, how was school today?"

Jessa looked at Rik and Rik looked back. They hadn't had a chance to talk together about the day.

Rik said, "It was kinda sad. They had a memorial service for a girl who killed herself over the summer. She was in my class."

Evelyn frowned. "Did you have to bring this up at dinnertime?"

Gary shot a suspicious glance toward Jessa and grumbled, "I thought I was sending you to a good school."

Jessa said, "That doesn't mean it's a bad school. These things happen." She added, "She'd been picked for women's soccer captain."

"Actually," said Rik, "I'm excited about some of my classes. I really like my teacher for American Novels. We're reading Fahrenheit 451 first."

"Um." Gary chewed. "What's that about?"

"A guy who burns books."

"Who'd pay him to do that?"

"It's set in the future. They made it into a movie."

"Oh, good. Must be a good book." Gary didn't read, had never acquired the habit, though in school he had to admit he'd actually liked a few of the assigned novels, at least until their endings. He didn't much trust or watch movies unless he knew ahead of time that the ending was good. He had enough experience in school to know that novels sometimes ended in ways you couldn't even tell whether the ending was good or bad.

Jessa said, "I have the same teacher for American Poetry. Mr. D'Ambrosio."

"What about your other courses, Rik?"

"I think I like Ms. Faudi," Rik said. "She's Modern American History and my homeroom teacher. The others seem okay. They give more homework here."

"Good," said Gary. "That's what I like to hear. So what other courses do you have?"

"Writing, Science for Non-Scientists and Basic Law."

Gary frowned. "What happened to job training? None of those apply unless you're thinking of going to law school. I'm paying good money on top of taxes and no one will want to look at you when you apply for a job!"

Rik's breath turned shallow. "Law is helpful in everything, I think. And writing helps with jobs that require reports and stuff. As for science, having a basic understanding of how technology works can't be bad."

Jessa mouthed, "Liar." Using the remote which she'd kept on her lap, she upped the volume on the music.

57

"I've completed all my requirements for graduation, so I got to pick all my courses."

"I don't understand," Gary said. "I really don't understand. You've got to work to get ahead. You've got to work as hard as you can and then some."

"Are you going to ask me about my courses, Gary?"

Gary looked at Jessa. "Of course. What courses are you taking?"

"Professionalism, Organizational Behavior, Early American History, and my favorite..."

"Don't know why they keep teaching history."

"...and," Jessa continued, her voice drifting toward inaudible, "my favorites, American Poetry and Art."

"The past is over. What is, is. That's all that matters." Gary continued eating. "This is good, Evelyn, real good."

Jessa's shoulders slumped. She kept her face down as if studying her plate.

Rik glanced briefly at Gary. He expected always to be disappointed by him. Still, every time Gary met his expectations, the blues swept in like the tide. Was it men, he wondered, or only the ones their mother chose?

Evelyn broke in. "Oh, before I forget. Some of our new neighbors are coming over this evening for a friendly meeting. They want to tell us all about our new neighborhood. So when dinner's done, help me clean up so we're ready when they come. They you two can run along upstairs and do your homework."

"Wait," said Jessa. "We can't stay?"

"Nope," said Evelyn. "Specifically for grown-ups."

"That's right," said Gary. "Homework, homework, homework. Work, work, work."

*   *   *

"Wow," said Rik. "An adults-only meeting. Must be about the local swingers' club." Rik went up the stairs to the second floor a half step behind his sister.

58

"Shut up, Rik. You're as bad as Gary."

"Now we'll never know what the big secret is."

"Oh, yes, we will."

He stopped and lowered his voice. "What do you mean?"

"When I turned off 'assisted listening,' I turned on the micro phone." She stopped at the top of the stairs. "We can listen on our phones via wifi."

"You're a little devil, you know that? By the way, what happened with your shrink?"

Jessa turned and started down the hallway. "She changed my meds."

"To stop your alleged hallucinations?"

Jessa nodded. "And hopefully to let me get back to drawing."

"I didn't know you'd stopped. What happened?"

They stood outside Jessa's door.

"The meds, I think. I couldn't think of anything worth drawing. I couldn't draw a good line, even. I didn't tell you because I was ashamed. If I can't draw, what the fuck is left of me?"

Rik sighed.

"And Dr. Dreier asked some strange questions. Mostly about the girl who hanged herself. I didn't get that at all."

*　　　*　　　*

Sandy Culver stood first in line beneath the porch light.

"Hey, Sandy, come on in. This is my wife, Evelyn."

Sandy wore the same clothes he'd worn in the afternoon and they looked as crisp and sharp as if he'd just put them on. Gary was jealous of guys like that. By noon he usually looked like he'd slept in his clothes for a week.

"Good to meet you, Mrs. Hollie."

"Evelyn, please."

"Your request is my command." Sandy introduced the second in line. "This is Officer Clint Adams of Paradise's finest."

Clint stood a few inches above six feet, wide as a roadblock, with a large unhappy smile, small eyes and graying hair. He wore a sport jacket, white shirt and red tie making no effort to conceal his shoulder holster. He offered a hand. "I'm the Director of the Paradise Intelligence and Surveillance Unit." His eyes ran from Gary to Evelyn and back to Gary, letting his importance settle in.

"We live right next door. Over there." He pointed.

Sandy continued, "This is Patrick—Pat—Swann. He lives diagonally across the street there and has a garden shop out on 16."

Swann, thin and with the craggy face of a New Englander, had an easy, relaxed smile. His large hand enveloped Gary's as they shook.

"And Nick Markakis, who lives the other side of Pat. Nick is retired and claims he plays golf every day."

Markakis had the muscled body and manner of a longshoreman. His eyes made a quick estimate of the newcomers. He didn't smile. His manner reflected his tendency to take everything, including his golf game, seriously.

When the introductions ended, Sandy asked, "Well, is there a place we can sit and talk a bit?"

Evelyn brought in a tray of drinks and served them like the waitress she once had been.

"So," Gary said as they passed around the sugar and milk, "How big is what you consider the neighborhood, and how did you guys get to speak for everyone? Was there a vote or something?"

Clint said, "Um, I think, oh, someone took a count, I think maybe thirty or so houses and fifty, fifty-two adults."

Nick said, "Something like that."

"And, yeah," Clint continued, "we were kind of chosen."

Evelyn brought in the goodies.

They thanked her and then began with the necessary compliments. "Nice place." "Did a nice job." "Looks homey." "I like the way you arranged the living room." "Nice choice of colors." "That picture: what's that of?" "Looks very comfortable. Lived-in, you might say."

Evelyn asked, "Is there anything else I can get you?"

They said they were fine.

She hesitated, then asked, "Can I join you?"

The guests looked at her.

"I mean, you're all men. I didn't know..."

They looked at each other, as if surprised to find that, yes, indeed, it was true they all were men.

Sandy smiled as if the joke were on him. "Oh, of course, please sit. We want to meet with both of you. Of course."

Evelyn gave the briefest of smiles and sat.

Sandy began. "Well, I'm glad we have this chance to sit down with you. Thank you for making yourselves available on such short notice. I think I'm going to ask Clint to bring you up to date on the problem we face here. He's lived here the longest of all of us and knows what the neighborhood was like before and—we hope, with your help—what it will soon be like again."

Clint said, "Thank you, Sandy." Though he spoke relatively softly, his baritone could have carried across an auditorium, the kind of voice you'd expect to narrate a war documentary. He took a breath. "We realize you moved into our neighborhood only yesterday, but we'd like to begin by asking if anyone in your family has seen anything strange or out of the ordinary?"

Evelyn looked at Gary. They each answered, "no," making the answer sound like a question.

Clint nodded his head. "Well, they don't always start right away. I think the best way to raise the problem we have is to say that we all, just like you, have made a huge investment in our homes. If we were to lose that investment, if our homes became unsalable, for example, we'd lose a huge chunk, if not all, of what we have. Right? You understand? I want you to think about that. What if no one would ever buy your home? Your home would be worthless after everything you put into it, but you'd still owe your mortgages."

Gary squirmed in his seat. He wondered why the neighborhood hadn't had this discussion with Evelyn and him before they'd bought the house. He thought he knew the answer.

Sandy said, "Not just us here, but everyone for blocks around would be affected. Like Clint said, thirty or more houses. Your kids wouldn't want you to leave them the house in your will."

Nick, with a voice like a pile of slag, said, "We, my wife and I, don't know anybody we hate enough to leave our house to." He laughed.

A feeling of uneasiness rose in Gary's stomach. He wondered if the below-market price they'd paid for the house had to do with this "problem," whatever it was. "Okay, I get that. I hear you. But what the hell are we talking about here? Are we sitting on a uranium dump or a toxic waste field? What the hell are we afraid of?"

"This has to be kept in the neighborhood." Clint leveled his gaze first at Gary, then at Evelyn. "You breathe a word of this to anyone outside this neighborhood and we will do everything, and I mean everything, necessary to defend ourselves, our families and our homes."

He took a deep breath. "The neighborhood is haunted."

Upstairs, Jessa gasped. Rik exhaled a low, "Oh, my God." They looked at each other.

Rik whispered, "The whole effing neighborhood!"

Jessa put a finger to her lips.

*   *   *

Gary roared. "That's a good one! They really had us going, huh, Evelyn? The neighborhood is haunted!" He laughed.

Gradually, Gary's mind wrapped around the sober expressions of the four visitors.

"Wait. You're serious? You can't be serious."

Clint said, "Very serious."

"There's no such thing as ghosts!"

"Not so long ago, everyone at this table would have agreed with you. But there are. We've seen them."

Gary breathed heavily. "Haunted." He shook his head to clear his thoughts. Random scenes from horror movies skipped through his head: mysterious floating lights; bodiless screams and footsteps; see-through shrieking skeletons wearing long gowns; screaming skulls; laughing, rotting corpses; claw-like hands reaching out from graves. Zombies. "By ghosts?"

"Ghosts," repeated Clint.

Gary turned toward his wife, sounding hopeful, as if not having seen them so far meant they'd never see them. Ever. "We haven't seen any. Have we, Evelyn?"

Unable to speak, she shook her head.

"What happened?" Part of Gary still insisted on believing this was a joke. He couldn't stand for the little bit of a world he had worked for and built for his family to be suddenly on the verge of disintegration. Fucking ghosts. Dead people lived in his house. His neighborhood. "When did this start? I mean...I don't know what I mean."

Patrick said, "Gary, you look like I felt when I first heard. It's unbelievable to hear for the first time. But it's true. And we have to take this very, very seriously. But we're here to work with you."

"What about your kids?" Clint asked, looking at Evelyn. "How old are they?"

Evelyn's voice sounded hoarse. "Seventeen and fifteen." She cleared her throat.

"They'd tell you if they saw anything?"

"Of course," said Evelyn. "Well, something like that, they would. I'm pretty sure." She thought, I think.

"Well," Clint began, "to answer the question you asked, the haunting began about a year and a half ago. It's an infestation. It's like a cancer. It's not something you ever get used to. At the beginning it was a real fright. Lucky one of us didn't have a heart attack. Still is, but now we expect the unexpected. One day you'll catch sight of one in the garage and a few days later in the kitchen."

Nick broke in, "Just their presence is enough to creep you out. You start feeling they're always around. You begin feeling cold and clammy all the time in anticipation. They're watching. Always watching us. Like they're judging us."

Clint took up the conversation. "We began to feel they're holding us hostage, which is true when you think about it. We're helpless. We can't do anything to them. We've tried. We've tried holding crosses and crucifixes in their faces—I never even knew the difference before—no response. We asked them to leave. We ordered them to leave. We tossed sage into boiling water, and when that didn't work, we threw cedar in, then garlic. Nothing. We prayed. We had Father Vic from the local parish perform an exorcism. We tried shooting them, first with bullets, then with lasers. Tear gas. Smoke grenades. What else? Oh, yeah, flame throwers. We've tried small explosives. We tried running them over. We've tried burning crosses. We stabbed them with knives and swung axes at them. We've thrown rocks at thm. We've called them names. We've run out of ideas."

Gary cleared his throat. "What exactly do they look like? I mean, are they like lights that shimmer or blobs of light or...or demons, or what?"

"Would you believe," Clint answered, "they look like people. They've got heads and bodies and they walk around and do things. I mean, the first time you see one you want to call the police because you think someone has broken into your house, but pretty quick you see it isn't a real person. It isn't so much you can see through them as much as it's like you see part of their world,

64

wherever it is that they come from. And it doesn't fit. And they have holes, like, I mean, pieces missing. That's when you know you're seeing something not so real."

Nick said, "And they look like they're rotting from the inside out. Really disgusting."

Pat picked up the conversation. "There's a lot to dislike about them. The way they stand so straight, like they're royalty or something, and they're so thin but with muscles, you know what I mean? Unnatural, too, the way they move, so deliberately, as if you're disturbing them!"

Clint said, "Sometimes they're dressed, the woman at least, all fine and frilly, and the next they look like they should be shipped off to a reservation with the n'okies."

"They're disgusting," Sandy added. "I think they must smell, but you know I sniff and don't smell nothing, and then I really hate them."

Clint said, "At night, even if you don't see them, you can hear them, singing, dancing, laughing. What have they got to dance about, I ask? What? And the moaning and groaning, their crying out in...." He glanced guiltily at Evelyn.

She asked, "In what?"

Sandy said quietly, "Clint is very protective of women."

Pat said, "That's why he put his wife on a pedestal."

Clint sat straight up, fury on his face. He didn't say anything; he just glared at Pat.

Pat looked away. "Sorry, Clint. I shouldn't have said that. My mistake."

Clint recomposed himself with several deep breaths. "I love my wife."

Sandy touched his elbow. "We know you do."

"Okay. Apology accepted." Clint looked down at the table. "And I apologize, Evelyn, for bringing this up, but you're going to hear it for yourselves and you might as well be prepared. It sounds like they're having a...a, uh, sexual ecstasy thing."

65

Evelyn blinked.

"I don't mean to offend."

Evelyn blinked more. She opened, then closed her mouth. A quizzical expression crossed her face. Then, she softly asked, "Are you saying that the ghosts are ghosts of black people?"

Clint looked taken aback.

Nick scowled.

Sandy's eyebrows arched.

Pat cocked his head as if considering an answer.

Gary stared at Evelyn with a frown on his face. "What made you say that?"

Evelyn, embarrassed by the five men staring at her, almost apologized for asking.

But then Clint spoke. "Uh, yeah. Exactly. What did you think we were saying?"

Gary glanced at Evelyn and then again at Clint. He said, "I didn't think... Is that what you mean? The ghosts are the ghosts of black people?"

Clint smiled and laughed, but quickly cut the laugh short. He began speaking in a lower tone, as if, for the first time, he feared being overheard. "Oh, man, I'm sorry. The answer to your question is yes, the ghosts appear to be the ghosts of blacks." Suddenly sober, he continued, "We're overrun by black mother-whatever ghosts. Man, I still shake when I think about the time I woke in the middle of the night. Totally dark. And in the dark I see this other darker darkness and it looks like a man but all I can really see are the whites of his eyes. Man, I shouted bloody murder. That's when I shot him, or tried to. It didn't do nothing. The thug just grinned."

Sandy said, "I didn't even know that black people could become ghosts. And I'm not a racist or anything like that. I just never thought about it."

Clint said, "Even if we didn't care about the value of our homes, think what would happen if people found out we were haunted by black ghosts? They'd think there was something wrong with us cause we live with black ghosts, that we weren't good enough. No one would want to associate with us."

"Like we were the ghosts," added Sandy.

Patrick said, "Don't get us wrong. None of us are prejudiced. Look at me. Some of my best customers are black. They come back year after year. Blacks are great at music, sports and gardening. You can't deny that. They have a real green thumb for plants. But, you know, no one would buy a house haunted by black ghosts. We're not prejudiced, but other people might be."

Clint said, "Just the fact that we forgot to tell you that they were black tells you that we don't see their race."

Patrick added, "I even had a cousin—he was maybe ten years older than me—he actually married a black girl. No one made a big deal. It's a free country. We went to the wedding, though after the first couple of years they never showed their faces at any family holiday celebrations." He asked, "Wonder what happened to them? Seemed to lose touch. Guess they weren't sociable."

Gary's eyes lit and his mouth fell open. "Oh, my God."

Clint asked, "What?"

Gary looked at Evelyn. "That must be...."

Evelyn put a hand over her mouth as words escaped her. "Oh, dear!"

"Oh, my God," Gary repeated. He sighed and said, "When you said ghosts, I thought of white sheet ghosts with mysterious blue lights crossing in front of windows, or bug-eyed demons. I didn't think... Well, now that you say the ghosts are black, it could be our daughter saw one." He swallowed. "We though she was having a hallucination."

"What did she see?"

"A big black guy. Mean and angry."

"That's one for sure," said Sandy.

Pat smiled. "Well, the good news is your daughter wasn't having hallucinations."

67

"Could see why you thought that, though," said Nick.

Clint's eyes narrowed with suspicion. "Wait. You didn't bring her to a psychiatrist, did you?"

Gary said, "Yes. Why?"

"Who?"

Gary asked, "Evelyn, what was her name, the shrink Jessa saw?"

"Dr. Dreier. She's in town."

The four men looked furtively at each other.

Clint said, "Get her away from that woman. Your kid didn't see a hallucination. She doesn't need a...a psychiatrist."

Evelyn, confused, agreed. She didn't want to reveal that Jessa had seen Dr. Dreier for depression before she'd seen the ghost. That would be too embarrassing.

"It's very important," Clint said, "very important you set limits with those kids of yours." Clint was in finger-wagging mode. "They cannot tell anyone about this. They have to understand the seriousness of our situation. They can't have friends over unless those friends already live in this neighborhood. No one from outside. We're in lockdown here. Never. No one."

"Sure. I mean, agreed," said Gary. "This is awful. The house means everything to us and for our kids. Who knows if they'll even be able to support themselves once they're done with school, the way jobs are now?"

Evelyn's forehead had shrunk into furrows. She asked worriedly, "Did the people who sold us the house leave because of the ghosts?"

Patrick and Nick both picked up their cups to drink. Sandy looked around the room.

Clint said, "You could say that. Yeah, they left because of the ghosts."

"They were nice people," Patrick added.

Nick grunted. "Too nice."

Gary asked, "Can we sue them? The people who sold us the house?"

"Not in a public court," answered Clint.

Lowering her voice, Evelyn said, "I don't blame them—I mean, the people who sold us the house. I don't want ghosts around me." She looked to Clint. "Who are they, the ghosts, anyway? Did they live here? What happened?"

Clint responded. "No idea. All I know is, when we say they're black, ma'am, we mean black. Some of them are African black. They dress like homeless people and look like death itself.

"Dead black people. Think about it. Black corpses we buried in the ground that God declared should never rise again. Straight out of hell. I can feel their touch on my skin."

Sandy said, "That's what I don't get: why they're here. The South was where they had slaves; we didn't. If they want to complain to someone, go back there and complain."

Nick tapped the table with his fingertips. "Parallel universe, I tell you. We should get some of those MIT people here."

"You know what?" asked Patrick. "I've read that being slaves wasn't all that bad. I'm not saying it was good, just not as bad as it's been made out to be. I mean if, you think about it, it makes sense. The slave owner wants them to work, right? The worse he treats them, the less they can work. If you want good work, you treat your employees well. That's all I'm saying."

Clint patted his neighbor's arm to reassure him.

Gary thought about the people he'd worked with over the years. A few of them had been black. He couldn't say that they'd worked less hard or harder than the others. They'd been edgier, perhaps, some of them, as if they'd expected something to go wrong, but they worked. All his coworkers worked harder than the owner. He himself worked harder than the owner. He thought all this in less than a split second, and finished knowing it would be out of place to say what he'd thought. So he forgot it.

Evelyn swallowed and asked, "But what did they say?"

Clint said, "I don't understand. What did they say about what when?"

69

"When you asked them why they're here?"

Clint scoffed, "We don't ask them anything. Who'd be foolish enough to believe them? We know why they're here: they're after our homes, our money, everything we worked all our lives for... and they're after our women."

Evelyn thought that was a lot to know without asking, but she kept quiet. Men, she knew, didn't like asking directions. They must not like asking questions either. Besides, these men were professionals. They knew what they were doing.

Pat said, "When you're in business, there's no black view or white view, no black way or white way. There's just the profitable way and that's what I go for."

Evelyn wondered why they went on. It wasn't as if she or Gary or anyone had disagreed with any of what they said.

"But they wouldn't be here if they weren't black," argued Sandy. "Clint, you said so yourself."

"Good point." Clint held his small plate on the table with both hands, as if it might fly away. "I think, and I know these guys and a lot of the people around here tend to agree with me, I think they're in league with the mongols and the n'okies."

Clint looked at Sandy. "It was just about the time the n'okies had that standoff at the state border, right after they opened that reservation in New York, a year ago this past spring, when we first started seeing these ghosts, right?"

Sandy nodded. "Just that time."

Clint continued, "And right after that the Canadians closed their border and the Californians started coming east. Just cause we've got water. When you think about it, they're the blacks' natural allies in trying to take this country away from us. Yeah, people think Oklahoma and Nebraska, even Kansas, but most of 'em are Mexicans. They don't look like Mexicans but they might as well be. Otherwise they'd have jobs. They'd own something. They wouldn't be crawling all over the map calling themselves refugees. The blacks come and haunt us out of our homes and the mongols and n'okies buy in cheap. Out of the whole world, why did the mongols have to come here? You see what I'm saying? We're the minority now. There's more of them than us. This is like a beachhead. They've landed here first, and once they secure this neighborhood, they'll move on to more and more neighborhoods till they have the whole country. That's what I think. It's up to us. We defeat them here and that's the end of it. If they beat us, then...whatever."

Sandy said, "I think Clint's right. We're on the hot seat for America and we can't tell anybody or ask for help."

"There's no other explanation," Nick said.

Patrick said, "If there is another explanation, I'd like to hear it."

Gary used a momentary break in the conversation's momentum to ask, "Is there anything else we can do to get rid of them? I mean, other than try to keep it quiet?"

"We've tried a couple of things," said Patrick. "We're on the river, so we're covered on that side. Then Clint got the city to designate most of our streets as one way. He had them put up lots of signs directing drivers to go away. We don't want people driving through and seeing ghosts. The whole world would know. Now outsiders can't drive through the neighborhood to get anywhere."

Gary said, "And now what? Is there anything else?"

Clint locked the fingers of his hands together in a ball. "Well, I'm not sure what to say. I've been in touch with this Christian shaman exorcist I happened to meet. I was at a police detectives' convention and they had a workshop about a case this guy solved. So I called and talked to him a bit. He seems interested. Should be here in a couple of days. I've asked him to come give it a try. I've also been trying to put together a, uh, sort of project which might be able to get us out of here without losing too much money. Nothing definite yet. Might fall through. We'll see."

Everyone became quiet, as if they needed time to absorb what they had said.

71

Clint spoke again, and he sounded almost reluctant, as if he were embarrassed, somehow not worthy of his own words. "We've gone too far." His voice seemed to dim the lights. "We think we're smart because we know so much. Trouble is we know too much. We know so much none of it makes sense anymore. You should read some of the stuff that's out there. They keep changing history. Think about that! They say the weather is changing. Well, I don't want the weather to change so they should just shut up! Scientists think there's more than three dimensions. Something can be two things at once. A thing can get from here to there without going in between. Evolution. Trillions of years. It's overwhelming! What's it mean? I'm not saying it's all wrong. I'm saying it's hideous. We can't keep track of it. It eats our minds. We can't control it. We learn something and think we're the more powerful for it. We don't look past the edge of what we learn and see the darkness that surrounds everything. We're surrounded by what we can't control, things we can't understand. The monsters of darkness push back at us. Sometimes the monsters break through. Well, they're here. The monsters have come to devour us. We've let too much in. It's time to close the doors."

The six of them sat in silence, each fearing to look into another's eyes. Evelyn feared that one of them, one of the four guests seated at her dining room table, might be a spy, might be a monster in disguise.

"Well," said Clint, clearing his throat and resuming his gruff persona, "What do we take away from this meeting? This. We belong here." He tapped a forefinger on the table. "Right here. We belong here. Where things are like they should be. That's what we've got to remember, that's what we've got to take away from this meeting. We're good people. We don't want anyone to get hurt. But we're not dealing with the ghosts of John Adams or Paul Revere. We're dealing with the ghosts of black people, people from Africa, damn it. We're losing American lives there right now! Twenty years now. More! We're dying in countries we've never heard of! My cousin lost a kid two years ago. We've got to teach them to leave us alone! We know what we're up against.

"Welcome to the war."

Before he let himself be ushered out the front door, Clint pulled a stack of business cards from his pocket. "Here's my card. Take a bunch of them. One for the whole family. This is my neighborhood. You got a problem, call me. I've told the other officers that this is my territory. Anything. Call me."

* * *

As the sounds of chairs scraping on the floor and words of parting replaced the discussion, Jessa switched off the sound.

Rik lay on his sister's bed staring at the ceiling. He exhaled, "Our neighborhood is haunted by black ghosts."

"I think they said 'infested with a plague of,' if you wish to be specific," said Jessa. "The living sound as scary as the dead."

Rik said, "The conspiracy of black ghosts, mongols and n'okies. All coming together on our beachhead. Who's writing this screenplay?" He thought about the incident with the carload of girls tossing Celisa and him the finger, turned it around like a puzzle piece, tried to fit it together with the meeting they'd just eavesdropped. Sirens and warning buzzers went off in his brain, as if it were morally wrong to link the two, as if he'd be putting himself in danger. He couldn't handle it. At least, not now.

Jessa worried, "What I don't understand is what they have against Dr. Dreier."

"They didn't explain, but they sure don't like her."

"What am I going to do without her to prescribe my meds? Crawl back into bed for the rest of my life?"

"At least Mom didn't give them your whole medical history. I don't want that group knowing anything about us. I can't feel too threatened by the ghost of a woman burying a dead baby. She practically cowered before me."

73

"Yeah, well, my blacksmith with his fire and horses and his hammer sure scared me."

"Point to Jessa. Besides, I did feel...I don't know what. Creeped out, I guess, by that woman. What do they want?"

Jessa spoke as if her words had already been engraved in metal. "I'm going to find out why the ghosts are here and what they want."

Rik's eyebrows went up. "You mean 'we' are going to find out."

"Sure. You can come along."

"Do you know how, uh..."

"Presumptuous?"

"Yeah, how presumptuous you sound?"

She asked, "You think I am?"

"Are you Sherlock Holmes? Well, neither am I. The way I see it, we don't have a choice. The neighbors could care less. Clearly they don't negotiate with ghosts. I don't trust those guys and I'm not so sure about Dad and Mom if the house or its value is threatened." He paused and looked at Jessa. "You know, I was worried about Mom and Dad if the house was somehow in jeopardy, but I just realized that we have a huge interest in this."

"What do you mean?"

"If the house becomes worthless, our chances of going to college are zero."

That sobered Jessa. "Shit. You're right. What the ef."

Rik thought of the woman burying the child and the child being kidnapped. "The other thing is the ghosts have made it our business."

Jessa nodded. "Really? How?"

"The woman who buried the child: she really felt, I guess, a lot of pain."

"So, it's our business if a ghost shows up in pain?"

Rik looked at his sister. "I get all these protective feelings over mistreated women. And anger. Lots of anger."

*   *   *

Evelyn closed the door behind the last guest, turned and leaned her back against it. Clint's remark about the soldiers who had died in Africa had triggered bad memories. She said aloud but uncertainly, "My house is haunted." She listened to the sound of her words. With a desperate firmness, she repeated, a bit louder, "My house is *haunted*." She did and did not believe herself. She asked herself: How hard do I have to clean to get rid of ghosts?

She noticed Gary standing in the living room.

"We've got to tell the kids."

Gary said, "You do it." He held onto the living room mantel to steady himself. "Make sure they understand. Really understand."

*   *   *

Evelyn knocked and knocked as if Jessa were half a mile away. "Come in! Geez."

"Oh, Rik, you're here, too. Oh. Oh. Good. I have to talk to both of you." She sat on the bed. Her hands seemed caught in indecision, torn between resting on the bed and folding in her lap. She tried for no good reason to smile. "I have something important to tell you, so please listen."

Rik lay back on the bed and stared at the ceiling. Jessa looked at her mother as if a Martian had crept through the window.

"Some very nice men from the neighborhood came over this evening."

"Right, Mom. You told us they were coming. We weren't good enough to participate. Remember?"

"Rik, be quiet. I'm talking. They had something to tell us." She paused. A puzzled expression came over her face. "There's good news and there's bad news, except that it's the same news. If that's possible. Jessa, you did not have a hallucination."

"I didn't?" She forgot to try to sound surprised. Her mother didn't notice. "What did I have?"

"You didn't have anything. You saw a ghost. And I suppose if I had been in the hallway at two in the morning instead of sleeping I would have seen that man, too. Our house is haunted. The whole neighborhood, as a matter of fact, is haunted. And they're all black."

"The neighbors are all black?"

"Rik, you know that's not true. The ghosts are all black."

Jessa, trying now to appear surprised, asked, "How could such a thing happen?"

Evelyn looked at her daughter. "How would I know? I don't know anything about black men."

"I meant, where did the ghosts come from?"

"No one knows. But we're trying to get rid of them so we can be happy. And, Jessa, you're not going to see that Dr. Dreier any more. We're going to have to find you another psychiatrist."

"Why?"

"Why? Well, I don't know exactly. The neighbors don't like her. That's all I know."

"Did they say why?"

"No, Rik, they didn't. But these are experienced men and they should know. One is even a police officer. The head of some sort of security department. So we'll do what they think is best.

"And," she added, emphasizing, "it is very important that you don't tell anyone about this. No one. Ever. And no bringing friends from school here. If they saw something and word got out about the ghosts we could lose everything we put into the house."

"Because no one would buy a house haunted by black ghosts."

"Now, Rik, you know how I feel about that. Everybody deserves the same. We don't treat people different. But others sometimes do. And we can't afford to lose...everything."

"Mom, do you remember when I was a little kid I saw a black guy and asked you why he was brown and you told me because he was made of chocolate? You remember that?"

"Yes, I do. And I meant it. I mean not that he was made out of chocolate but that there was nothing wrong with him."

"And that the mongols were made out of margarine?"

"Butter. I'm sure I said butter. For the same reason."

She rose from the bed and walked to the door. "Remember." She placed a raised finger over her mouth. "No one. It's our secret."

Evelyn left.

Jessa turned to Rik. "Did Mom really tell you that about the black man? He was made out of chocolate?"

"She sure did. And I said, 'Hi, Mr. Chocolate Man.' He thought it was funny. He laughed. I think I made his day." Rik's expression turned puzzled. "It's like out of a kids' book. Some people are made out of chocolate. Others out of butter."

"Native Americans are made out of strawberries and little green men from Mars are made out of broccoli. And you, brother, are made out of painfully boring vanilla." Jessa shook her head. "I can't imagine what I did in my past life that I should deserve this family."

"Mom told me once that the mongols and n'okies are the same as everyone else but she didn't want me playing with any of them. I still don't understand. Oh, Celisa and I were talking..."

She spun around, eyes wide with surprise. "You talked to Celisa? I figured she'd grab my arm tomorrow at school and ask why my brother can't speak."

"Shut up. She said Irish and Italians and, I guess, some others, weren't considered white people at first."

"Really? That's...sort of us."

"Sort of? That was after I referred to the n'okies as if they weren't white."

"They have white skin."

"Of course, but Celisa's point was that sometimes that's not enough. Just like those guys downstairs talked about the n'okies as if they weren't white."

77

"This is weird."

"What?"

"I just told Mom in the car that it would take you at least a month before you had a girlfriend."

"She's not my girlfriend! What? Did you want me to be rude and not talk to her?"

"When did you stop being rude? This afternoon? For you, talking to a girl the first time you meet her is practically a proposal."

"I talk to lots of people."

"You talk to me. That's about it"

"I have to. It's in my contract under 'brother.'"

Jessa sighed. "I lied to Dr. Dreier and now I'll never see her again."

"You told her you had a hallucination?"

"Should I have told her the truth? That we both saw ghosts?"

"No. She'd have had me on meds, too."

"She asked a lot of questions at the end about the suicide."

Rik lay on his back on Jessa's bed using Fahrenheit 451 as a pillow. "Why did she do that?"

"I don't know and I don't want to talk about it anymore. Get out of here. I've got work to do."

"So do I."

"Do it in your own room."

"Can't. Too messy. Mom really messed it up." Rik opened the book and read, "'It was a pleasure to burn.'"

"Wow, you memorized all that in one night?"

Rik mimed throwing the book at Jessa, but held it and began to read. The words blurred. The print was lost in a deepening gloom.

Rik sat up. He and Jessa looked at the door their mother had just closed.

The door and interior wall faded, replaced by a muted tropical scene, a path among trees, men with burning lights and people mostly hidden by the dark.

     *   *   *

The ghost girl heard voices without understanding words.
They dragged her facedown but she knew they were the men
with moon faces. She felt the pinch and scrape of wrist and ankle
chains. She felt the backhand slap across her face all the way
down her spine. Hands grabbed her bottom, pulled her toward a
foul body, a man pulled his... But other hands dragged her away,
shoved her hard toward the path. Loud, insistent words full of
anger all around her. She fell on the grass and couldn't get up. Her
ankles, knees and wrists bled. A kick caused her to gasp for air.
Other hands, so many hands, stood her up, chained her chains to
the long chains of others.

Out of breath, she sobbed in the only language she knew,
Yoruba, the language of boat builders, fishermen, woodworkers,
sculptors, and musicians. "Orisa! Orisa! Mother! Father! Help me!
Save me! Don't let them take me! Please save me!"

Those like Jessa and Rik, who did not understand her
language, understood the sound of her fearful plea that carried
more agony and pain than any translation might have.

She focused and saw two faces: a young man, a young woman,
both moon-faced, shocked, staring at her in horror.

"Orisa, tell me: why must I suffer?"

     *   *   *

Jessa and Rik sat in the midst of the vision. They sat
surrounded by white men and black men clothed, some in
uniform, dragging the others, the naked black men and women
in chains, the children in chains . They saw the young girl's face,
the chains being snapped on her hands and locked behind her.
Her legs pumped, trying to run, slipped on the path as she tried to
pull away. They saw the larger, whiter hands that locked her to
the chain of other captives.

Parts of the ghost bodies of both victims and slavers looked
gouged out.

                                                                 79

AMERICAN GHOSTS

Jessa screamed as one of the white men grabbed the girl's body and unbuttoned his pants. She dove, as if she could tackle a ghost. Rik caught her. A white ghost stopped the intended rape with a fist to the other ghost's head.

When the vision faded, it left Rik and Jessa panting, as if they'd run, as if they'd breathed the dirt kicked up by the caravan, as if their own lives and freedom had been at stake.

Jessa's mouth opened to speak, to cry, but she saw her brother already tearing up. "Oh, my God. What are we going to do?"

"We need help."

"She needs help."

*   *   *

"Did you explain it to them?" Gary stood with a hand on the kitchen counter. He held a small glass in his hand. It contained two ice cubes and whiskey. The bottle stood open for the next pour.

Evelyn nodded. "Yes. They understand." She paused. She'd heard something. "What was that?"

"Sounded like Jessa laughing." Gary swirled the whiskey and ice in the glass. "They'll probably forget by morning." He sipped. He wasn't one to throw down a glass in one gulp. "Airheads."

"They're not airheads! Sometimes you..."

"I what?" He waited for her not to answer. He knew she wouldn't. "I worked hard for this house. I worked real hard. They're trying to take it away from me! Ghosts! Fucking ghosts!" Another sip. "Well, they can't fucking have it. That's all. They can't have it." Another sip. "It's mine."

Ours, Evelyn thought. Ours. And Gary was right. The kids would forget. They were kids. They'd screw up. That's what kids did. She would remind them. Again and again.

*   *   *

Back in his room, Rik moved his lips, as if to taste the words, as he silently reread a sentence from Fahrenheit 451, "It was a special pleasure to see things eaten, to see things blackened and changed."

Was that possible? Was that true? That a person might find pleasure in destruction? In burning books? In kidnapping and chaining children?

Taking out the photos was something Rik rarely did, something he reserved for times he felt he faced problems that required the advice and support of an adult. A father, for example. He opened the cover of his boxed, red-bound volume of Tolkien's The Lord of the Rings. He kept six photographs hidden inside the pages.

He lay the book down and lined the photos up across the bed his mother had made earlier in the day.

They'd all been taken during his father's final leave. Though he had been in the army, he didn't wear his uniform in the pictures. Rik wanted to believe that his biological father had been a better father than Gary, not to mention Meph...but Evelyn had chosen them all. It was likely they'd been alike, or at least not too different. But in the pictures, his first father held Jessa and played with the young Rik, acts Rik had trouble imagining Gary doing.

Rik wondered what kind of father he would make. Perhaps the key was to ask what would Meph or Gary do and do the opposite. Was that enough? If something more was required, what could it be? How could he imagine it? Who taught such things?

He went back to studying the pictures, the ghosts of his first father. Had he blown things up? Killed people? How had he died? Had someone felt pleasure that they had killed him? Had his father felt pleasure in seeing things eaten, blackened and changed? Rik had questions but the pictures had no answers.

His father, an American, had died in Africa. African-American ghosts lived in their house. As if the war had come home.

Outside in the night the birds called and shrieked.

Gary sat at the kitchen table. The whiskey level in the bottle had dropped like a tide. A plastic bowl of ice cubes sat next to the bottle. He knew himself. He knew he'd gone long past where he could drive, but he thought he could still walk upstairs to bed.

He thought he knew himself. Of course, he knew himself.

Even as he drank, his eyes wandered over the kitchen. He began imagining movements of light and dark, as if by staring his vision could bore through to the land of ghosts. No, he knew better. When he saw one of these ghosts, he wouldn't mistake it for anything else.

He felt fear, but not so much of the haunting.

He felt that special fear, that feeling he thought he'd left behind when he bought the house, the feeling that he would never amount to anything, that the world had been rigged against him, that the situation was hopeless, that everyone would see the piece of shit failure that he'd always felt he was. He drank deeply, trying to mouth the ice, but the cube was too big. His emptiness, his lack of worth brought him more poison than any ghost could.

He dropped two more cubes and poured, nearly to the brim.

He'd show them. He began to tear up. He wiped the tears away with a sleeve. Damn, he was such a fucking pussy.

In his head, he ordered himself, "Pull yourself together, you fucking asshole!"

His answer was to drink.

He drank.

He drank.

He wavered. Gradually his head dropped nearer and nearer to the table.

There. His head rested on his arm. Whiskey remained in the glass. He slept.

*   *   *

Jessa was at the door.

Rik had begun to drift into sleep.

She entered with an object in her hand. She gestured for her brother to take it.

He turned the light on and took the object, a small, very worn piece of translucence.

She said, "I think it's glass."

He said, "Probably a broken bottle. Murky color. It's scraped a lot, like it's been in the ground for years."

"It says something."

"Like a logo in a circle, but I can't read the words."

"I couldn't either."

"Where'd you find it?"

"The place I hide my sketchbook."

"Find a better place to hide your beer bottles."

"Funny. The reason I'm showing it to you is because Dr. Dreier asked me if I'd found anything after I had my 'hallucination.'"

"What? She asked that? Why would she...?"

"I think she knows some things she didn't tell me." Jessa's eyes moved toward the newly curtained windows.

"You listening to the birds?"

She nodded. "Sometimes I think I hear sounds of something more than birds."

*   *   *

Clint's dream visited him nearly every night.

In the dream, he clung with the fingers of his left hand to the crumbling edge of a rocky precipice. His right hand performed work, though he could not tell what that work was. Above him, on the ledge, were men he could not see. They talked about him, judging whether he was worth saving. Winds punched and knocked him, doing their best to pull him away from the earth. He didn't fear falling. He feared flying.

He panicked. He stopped working and grabbed for the ledge with both hands.

The rocks beneath both hands broke.

His fingers grasped only loose pebbles.

The wind carried him up and out.

Connected to nothing, with nothing but pale sky in all directions, he sailed like an autumn leaf.

Terror gripped him.

Panting and sweating, Clint woke. The back of his pajamas was soaked with sweat, as was the sheet beneath him. His hands shook.

He sat and, eyes wide, looked around his bedroom. He always kept a small light on. No ghosts, thank God. Not tonight. He drank water from the glass he kept on the bedside table.

Gradually, his breathing returned to normal.

To the figure that lay beside him, he whispered, "Don't be afraid. I'm here to protect you."

CHAPTER THREE
WEDNESDAY

Holding a hot coffee and bag with a bacon-juice-dripping breakfast sandwich in one hand, Gary turned the knob on the door to his office and kicked the door open.

It was 6:02 a.m. He wasn't the first one in this morning.

"Art," Gary said, with totally flat inflection despite the surprise. His brain switched from ghosts to his boss.

"Hah! What, did I scare you? Here, sit down." Art sat in Gary's chair behind the desk. He cleared a portion of the desk for Gary's breakfast.

"You could have let me know. I would have been here earlier."

Art Malloy looked as if he spent every morning working out and every afternoon on a beach, a fairly accurate description of most of his days, if you set aside an hour or so for rapid-fire phone calls to Gary and the other men and one woman who ran his businesses for him.

"How's the new place?"

"Great. Love it."

"Good. Not such a long drive now? Right?"

"Fifteen minutes at this time of the morning."

"I'm not going to take up much of your time. I needed to let you know that I met with my lawyers yesterday and, well, there's been some real exciting changes in the law recently, changes that we can use. We're catching up with the rest of the world.

"I need you...wait, here's a pad, write this down...I need you to handle this. We're laying off all the drivers. Every one of them."

Gary stared at the man. He blinked. Art was still there.

"Not you, of course. Everyone else. We'll carry you on as our employee. Now listen, you look like a fucking deer caught in some headlights. You're a doer now. Your job is to make the takers make more money for us whether they like it or not.

"All this is worked out. The lawyers have drawn up all the

documents and one of them will come out from Boston to be with you when the signing happens.

"After they're all laid off, we offer them contracts as independent contractors. It's mumbo jumbo, but it's legal. The drivers do the same job, of course, but they'll be owners of their own businesses. They'll have to do their own taxes, their own withholding, lease the routes and trucks from us, pay their own gas, get their own comp insurance, their own auto insurance, the whole nine yards. We pay them per items delivered, from which we deduct what they owe us for costs, the trucks and the routes, plus certain administrative fees. They have to provide certificates of insurance and proof they made the deliveries and other stuff. But they get to run their own businesses." Art grinned. "It's win-win."

"So," Gary said, beginning slowly, "They continue doing the same work, but they have to pay for all the things, like the five kinds of insurance, for which you now pay."

"We, Gary. We. We're management. You and me. We tell them now they're in business for themselves. Congratulations! Now pay us. We've been waiting for a long time to be able to do this. It's beautiful. Just too beautiful. Well, got to get out of your way."

Art began gathering up a few papers and shuffling them into his briefcase. "The lawyer, wait, I've got his card, here it is, he's set for the signing. You call him and tell him when to be here. He's arranging for police protection. Can't be too cautious."

Art left and Gary got his chair back. He sat staring at the files containing the new contracts without moving until he heard Miriam come in. He gave her a few minutes to settle in, then called her in. "Miriam, hi. Look, I need you to text the drivers that there is a six a.m. meeting Friday morning. Mandatory. And call the lawyer on this card. He has to be here at the same time. Thanks."

Gary emptied one of the files and read through the provisions, making notes with a pencil. Then he did the math.

When he'd figured it out, he sat looking at the wall.

A vague uneasiness settled in him. As a management employee he had to do what the boss told him to do, simple as that, but there remained a sour note. Almost a sour smell. Nearly a stench. The drivers wouldn't like it, of course. He knew what it would be like. He'd been one of them. But they knew the name of the game. Would he be able to look them in the eye? Of course. It wasn't his decision; he was merely relaying a message. He was just the messenger. Didn't someone once say, "Don't shoot the messenger?" Or was that the piano player? Either way, wasn't his idea.

He had no choice. This was nothing new. Since the beginning bosses made decisions employees didn't like. The employees had no choice. They did what they were told. So would he. Of course.

But he wanted to talk it through. With whom? Not Evelyn. She wouldn't understand. No one here at work. Couldn't do that. He remembered an old high school friend he'd hung out with for years. Hadn't seen him in how long? Didn't he work not far away?

*　　　*　　　*

Rik stepped onto the porch into another hot late-summer day and found a woman coming up the front walk. Jessa came out behind him.

"Well, hello!" The woman waved. "My name's Annie Jessop and I live right there"—she indicated with a forefinger the house next door on the left—"with my two lovely children whom I've just put on the bus to go to school. What are your names?"

Rik and Jessa introduced themselves.

The woman wore her dark blond, curly hair over her shoulders, accessorized with circular earrings a bit larger than her ears. She wore a red dress that floated over her thinness, as if her body had recently contracted. She carried a matching red bag and wore red heels. Her smile failed to balance the anxiety in her eyes or the nervousness of her hands.

"Well, welcome to the neighborhood. I'm certain you'll love it here. Everyone is so friendly. We live to help each other. You'll

87

have to meet Sophie and Issa. Those are my children. They're a bit younger than you but I'm certain you'll be great friends. Are your parents at home?"

Rik walked back into the house and shouted, "Mom, the next-door neighbor wants to meet you. She's here."

Evelyn yelled that she'd be right down.

"So, do you like your new house?" she asked them. "I bet you love it. Enough space so you each have your own room. I hope everything is going alright. It is going alright, isn't it?"

"Fine," said Jessa.

"You haven't seen any more little ghosties, have you?" She giggled.

Before they could answer, Evelyn appeared on the porch. "Children, you run along." She invited Annie Jessop in.

As Jessa turned the corner onto the sidewalk, she whispered to Rik, "Where do you think they find these people?"

"Got me. Your shrink should know. But, then, you can't ask her, can you?"

"I can't but I will." She'd found that telling her brother she would do something was often the best way of getting past her crippling fear of doing it.

*   *   *

"How long have you lived here?" Evelyn poured her guest the last of the coffee. The TV reported on the weather.

"Thank you."

Evelyn pointed out the milk and sweeteners on the table.

This time Annie answered the question. "Since before the children were born. Fifteen years, I think." She spoke tentatively, as if memory took more energy than she had at the moment.

"That's a good long time. You like it here?" Evelyn rinsed the carafe. When she finished she turned and looked at Annie, who was looking around the kitchen, not forgetting to survey all its parts, including the ceiling. Evelyn repeated, "You like it here?"

Still looking around, Annie said, "It's a very nice house."

"Yes, I think we'll be happy here. That's important, don't you think? To have a place to be happy?" She began filling the carafe to make another pot.

"Yes. The coffee is very good."

"What does your husband do?"

"He lives with his girlfriend."

The carafe filled and overflowed. Evelyn caught herself and poured the excess water out so enough remained for six more cups in the coffee maker.

"I'm sorry. About your husband, I mean. That must be hard, especially with two young children." She set the machine to brewing and sat down across from Annie. "Can't trust men."

"No. Oh, no, you can't." Her eyes widened like a little girl's. "He says he won't get married again. He's had his fill of that. And he doesn't want more kids."

"And you?"

"Oh, I guess I'm not very good at choosing men. I always pick ones that can't be trusted. They grow tired of my body so quickly!" She sniffed twice, rubbed her nose, then began crying quietly. She pulled a sheaf of Kleenex from her purse, separated a single sheet and dabbed her eyes. "Even though I always let them do whatever they want."

Evelyn saw there was almost enough coffee for a cup. "So, do you work?"

"Bob was good to me though. I never slept with him. He never even tried. It was terrible."

Evelyn poured the cup for herself and sat across from her neighbor. "Who was Bob?"

"Oh, Bob and Patty. They helped me a lot. It was awful what I did to them."

89

"What did you do?"

"What did I...?" Annie startled, as if she'd woken from a dream. "No. My doctor won't let me."

"Won't let you...?"

Annie cocked her head, surprised. "Work. You asked me if I worked."

Evelyn had to think to remember. "Oh. Right. I did."

"He tells me I might be able to in the future but not now. He says I'm too unstrung."

"I have a muffin—blueberry, I think—if you'd like."

"No, thank you. I need to lose weight if I'm ever going to attract a man again. I don't really like men, but when all you've got is three years of high school, you kind of need them."

"So...Annie...how do your children like the schools?"

"Oh, good. They go to Saint Benedict's. It's a good school." She stopped moving. She began to smile. "I'll bet you didn't know this."

"What?"

"St. Benedict."

"Yes?"

"He was terrified of women. Every time he was walking down the road and he saw a woman coming from the opposite direction, he'd..." Annie couldn't keep from laughing. She placed a hand over her mouth, as if to keep from spitting her coffee out. "He'd throw himself into bramble bushes." She laughed out loud.

"What?"

"It's a true story. Father Vic told me. He even showed me in a book."

Evelyn repeated. "St. Benedict threw himself..."

"And you know where we were when Father Vic told me this?"

"I'm afraid to ask."

"In bed! Really! Oh, I know, he's a priest, so we can't have sex. But he goes down on me. You know really, he's the only man who ever cared if I got off. The only one! And he always gets me off. I suppose it's kind of sad in a way, if you think about it.

You begin looking for love and then you settle for sex and then you end up settling for you helping someone else have sex and after that there's just boring. Father Vic, he's the only one who cares about me."

Evelyn stared at Annie, an expression of amazed and disgusted concern on her face.

"Oh, of course, the girls are on scholarship. Father Vic saw to that. Sometimes I think he likes me. I have moments when I've had too much to drink I think he loves me. I can't imagine why. But he's a priest. He probably understands things I don't. Maybe he knows things other men don't know. You know?"

"I really don't know much about..."

"Yes. So how's the upstairs?"

"The upstairs?"

"Uh huh. The upstairs."

"Good. I like it. We had the whole thing painted and the floors done."

Annie's eyes narrowed and she leaned toward Evelyn. "You didn't find anything there, did you?"

Evelyn blinked. She answered with a cautious, "No. What were you thinking of?"

"Nothing. Oh, nothing. You know how these old houses are. Clint and the boys told you about the ghosts, didn't they?"

"Yes. That they did do."

"Well, sometimes the ghosts leave things. You might find anything." She giggled, as if the ghosts might have left old pornographic magazines in the attic. "You haven't seen a ghost yet?"

"No." Evelyn glanced at the top drawer next to the sink where she kept odds and ends, where she'd put the piece of tile she'd found, the one that Gary had said to throw out.

"Don't worry. You will. Everyone sees them. Don't forget to act frightened. The ghosts like it when we act frightened. That's what ghosts do, you know, frighten people."

"I never heard of them doing anything else."

"Sometimes I turn on a horror movie and turn it up loud, just to let them know we're on to them. Well, this coffee has been real nice. I have to get your recipe sometime." She began rummaging in her pocketbook. "Actually, the boys asked me to deliver these to you." She handed Evelyn two small manila envelopes across the table. "These are your new IDs. The things they come up with these days are amazing, let me tell you.

"Look," she said, sliding one out of its envelope, "how tiny it is! It's like a button! It'll stick to anything you're wearing." She illustrated by putting it on her blouse, then on her skirt. Annie was right: the disc was just a bit larger than a coat button, but very much thinner and lighter. "See. It even fits under a collar." She hid it and took it off again. "You know what else? If, say, for instance, you should fall. Like down the stairs or even on the floor? This notifies the ambulance to come save you! Yes! It monitors your body, so if you have a heart attack, they're on their way! Here. One for you and one for your husband."

Evelyn took the ID. The card it was attached to was, in fact, labeled with her name. She stuck it beneath her collar. "This isn't like the ones the kids got. They're picture IDs."

"You know what! They did that for a purpose. They did research, would you believe, and found that kids, like, under twenty-one, I think it is, commit fewer crimes if they have to carry the large badges. Really! Amazing, huh?"

"Where did you find all this out?" Evelyn avoided news of all types. She felt she had a brighter outlook on life that way, so before the kids had received their IDs, she'd had no idea about the new requirements.

"Oh, I know people. Men, you know, they'll say anything in bed. They just love to prove they're important." Annie went back to rummaging in her pocketbook. "I'm sure I brought my pills. I never go anywhere...oh, here they are! Take two. Do you have a glass of water? I finished the coffee."

"Yes." Evelyn brought her the water.

Annie popped two pills in her mouth. Before she completed swallowing, she tried to talk. She put her hand over her mouth and coughed. Again she swallowed. "Oh, dear. I still have episodes, but I don't shake any more. Like I did." She gave Evelyn a smile. "I just cry. You know, the ghosts never bother me when I'm crying. I think they may feel sorry for me. Remember, I'm here to help. We're all here to help. Well, gotta go!"

Evelyn sat alone at the table. Her face crinkled with puzzlement. Was Annie really having all that sex? Was Annie what happened to a person who had too much sex? "Annie Jessop," she said. "Annie Jessop. Annie Jessop." The name tasted funny.

Knowing that Annie was home all day long with the ghosts made her feel a bit more confident. If Annie could live with ghosts, she could, too.

She looked up at the TV where the weather woman swept her hand over a map, seeming to push a warm front up and over all of New England.

*　　　*　　　*

Two minutes before class, Jessa called Dr. Dreier's office. She reached the answering machine.

"Dr. Dreier, this is Jessa Hollie. I can't explain everything over the phone but my mother is going to call you to fire you, I guess, as my therapist. I want you to continue, but more important than that, I need to see you today. My brother, too. We need to see you. As soon as you can after school. Even if I can't be your patient anymore."

*　　　*　　　*

Celisa worried. Nothing good ever came out of being told to go to the sophomore class vice principal's office, or to any other school office. She couldn't imagine what she'd done that had gotten his attention.

93

The secretary had her wait a minute until he was off the phone. Then she told her to go in.

Celisa left the door open.

Vice Principal Urbanowicz walked around her and closed the door. Though he sat, he didn't ask her to sit.

"I don't know what to do about girls like you."

"Perhaps you can tell me what's wrong."

"Don't lie to me. You, my dear, know what's wrong."

"Don't call me 'dear.' I do not know what's wrong." Celisa was careful to maintain a very low, calm tone.

"Eight of your fellow students, all of whom are in good standing with good grades and who have never been the subject of any sort of disciplinary action, have provided me with statements that you and your boyfriend, that new transfer student, did give them the finger and shout obscenities and made racial remarks at them yesterday afternoon after school as they rode by in a car. Such a public display of juvenile disrespect for your classmates requires a judicious response."

So, that's it, thought Celisa. "Perhaps a judicious response might include asking me what happened. It might also include asking the person I was with, who is not my boyfriend, what happened."

"Don't give me that. I have no reason to doubt the statements of eight, *eight*, students whom I respect."

"May I see the statements?"

"Of course. Here are your copies."

"May I have time to read them?"

"Yes. A minute or two. They're not long."

Celisa finished quickly.

"The statements closely follow one another."

"That makes them believable."

"Almost word for word. That means they copied from each other. And they all claim they were in the same car. Eight girls in a single car is a stretch."

"The kind of vehicle they were in is not relevant."

"I know what kind of vehicle they were in when they gave us the finger and shouted obscenities at us. It doesn't hold eight unless a couple were riding in the trunk, which I doubt, because it would mess up their clothes."

"I'm suspending you for a week, beginning tomorrow."

"For what reason?"

"Instigating a racial incident."

"I appeal. I'll serve my suspension, if there is one, after my appeal is heard."

"There's no appeal."

"The appeal is described in the school handbook."

The VP smirked. "Make that two weeks. The second week is for acting like a bitch to your vice principal."

"You'll have to rephrase that when you write the formal charges. I've read the rules. 'Bitch' is one of the words the handbook says we can't use."

She walked out.

Once she had calmed her breathing and wiped her tears, she turned her recorder off. Her father had said she should carry it at all times and use it if she were stopped by police or had trouble in school. She'd said she didn't need it. He'd insisted. He had also insisted she read the handbook. She'd argued he was overreacting because he was an attorney.

She felt frightened and out of control when her parents were right about white people.

She'd been raised to be proud of her race and she was. Still, times like this, part of her wished she could wash the brown in her skin away. The color of her skin seemed like a wall that stopped white people from seeing her. She hated living this way.

She would ask Rik to testify for her at the hearing, but he wouldn't. They never did. Didn't want to get involved, they said, and looked sad as they apologized.

Evelyn sat and slowly drank another cup of coffee. Then she called. She, too, left a message. "Dr. Dreier, this is Evelyn Hollie, Jessa Hollie's mother. Um, I'm not sure how to say this, but we have to terminate your services. Nothing personal. Jessa really likes you and so do I. It's just that something has come up. I'm sure you understand. This must happen a million times in your work. Also, if you could recommend another therapist in this area, we'd really appreciate it. So if you could call back. Thank you."

*　　　*　　　*

Rik wolfed down his lunch and told Zach and his friends that he had an errand to run. Zach raised his eyebrows as his new friend ran off.

Rik hurried to the school library. As the sensor by the librarians' desk allowed him entrance because of his new ID card, he realized that the sensor would record any books he checked out. He did his best to push the resulting queasiness aside. He accessed one of the laptops and searched his topic. He found the reference numbers he wanted.

He walked nearly the length of the library, scanning the numbers on the shelves, until he turned down an aisle.

About where the books he was looking for might have been on the shelves, a student sat cross-legged on the floor. Rik recognized him as Thor the Godlike, the boy Zach had pointed out as having been Ellen Scarpacia's boyfriend. Now that he had a closer look, though, Rik saw the dark lines beneath his eyes, his pale complexion and his hunched, defensive stance against the world. Thor was beset by great anxieties, he thought.

They looked at each other.

Rik said, "Hi. I'm Rik Hollie. Just started here."

The boy said, "Yeah. Hi." He stood. "I'm Steve Ostrum. What are you doing here?"

96

"Looking for books."

"Really." Steve knew how not to overplay sarcasm.

"I mean, history books. On Paradise."

Steve nodded. "And I've been using my lunch time sitting here waiting for someone to come looking for books on the history of Paradise."

Rik felt an uneasiness in his gut. "Why?"

Steve took a step back. With his left hand, he swept past a section of empty shelf.

Rik checked the numbers he'd written down and confirmed that that shelf should have held the books.

"Where are they?"

"Gone. So are the books on Paradise's history in the city library. No one knows what happened."

Rik ran his tongue along the inner edges of his teeth, attempting to incorporate this information. Then he asked, "Why have you been waiting here?"

Steve nervously tapped a foot. "A hunch. A hope."

"That I'd show up looking for the books?"

"That someone would."

"And then?"

"Well, yeah, uh, I don't know. Maybe you could tell me why you're looking for them."

Rik's eyes looked away from the boy's face. "Like I said, we just moved here, and I figured..."

"You figured you'd become the resident expert on local history."

Rik shrugged.

The boy's eyes began to tear up.

"Hey, look, someone told me that you and..." Rik had to think a second to recall her name, "...Ellen had a relationship. I'm sorry. She must have been a wonderful person."

"Yeah, thanks. Sympathy noted. But you can't or won't tell me the real reason you wanted those books, is that right?"

"Right."

"Well, even so, I'll do you a favor. Don't bother trying to order any of the books online that should be here. You won't get them."

Rik began to feel his skin crawl. "What do you mean?"

"They won't come."

"Why?"

"Don't know. You can order other books. They'll come. You can even order porn and it'll arrive right on your doorstep. The boxes will have been opened and resealed, but they'll come. But order a book on the history of Paradise and you'll never get it."

"Wait. No one could...stop...or open the mail."

"My understanding as well. Say, that girl you walk with to school?"

"My sister. You leave her alone."

"I'm not going to hurt anyone. I won't even talk to her. I just needed to know who she is."

"Why? What are you after?"

"The answer to the question...why did Ellen kill herself?"

Rik nodded. "I can understand that. I'd probably need to do the same if...it was me."

"Except, if then I was you, I'd tell you what...whatever it is you know."

Rik frowned. "No, you wouldn't. In fact, until just now it never occurred to me that there was a connection between wanting to see those books and Ellen's, uh, suicide."

Steve looked at the ceiling, then up and down the rows of books. "Well, I think I'll get my ID card back. I put it behind a book at the front of the library. You might think of doing that yourself. Someone might get upset if they knew we'd talked."

"Good thinking." Rik said the words slowly, as if he was discovering new information in each sound.

"Well, see you around."

"Yeah."

Rik still had a few minutes before he had to return to classes.

98

He used the library terminals to search for Paradise's history on the web. As a high school student he had only general, Level A access. Level B was for college students and Level C for college grads. Higher levels went to those who were "qualified" and willing to pay the premiums. Rik wasn't surprised when the responses he got were limited to the official websites of the city and its departments.

On a hunch he returned to the computer catalogue and redid his search. This time he scanned down the names of the students who had taken out the books. His heart fell when his hunch proved right. The last student to take out—and return—the books on Paradise's history had been Ellen Scarpacia.

*   *   *

Jessa found Rik right after school. "Come on. We have an appointment with Dr. Dreier."

Rik stopped her. "Listen, before we go, I have to tell you. I had a thought at lunch and I went to the school library. I wanted to see what they had on Paradise's history. The catalogue said they had a dozen or so books. When I get to the place they're supposed to be, the shelf is empty. And guess who's waiting there for me?"

Jessa shrugged.

"Ellen Scarpacia's boyfriend. Waiting for me to show up, like he's haunting the place"

"The tall...?"

"Thor, the Godlike. Yeah. Except his name is Steve. And he doesn't look godlike up close. He looks beaten and scared. He tells me the books have gone missing. Not only the ones in the school library but the ones in the main library, too. And when he tried to order them online or from booksellers, they never came."

"Wait. Too much information. What are you saying?"

"All the books about Paradise's history are gone from the school library and the main one. When Steve ordered them, he never received them."

99

Jessa thought. "Anyone can walk into the library and steal books, I suppose. But you'd have to know someone to stop mail deliveries."

"Right. Then I checked back with the catalogue... Ellen Scarpacia was the last person to check the books out. She brought them back, too."

Jessa stood like a puzzled sphinx. Slowly she wrapped her arms around herself and said, "My God, what the fuck's going on?"

"I don't know. You don't know. Steve the Godlike doesn't know."

"Did Ellen Scarpacia know? Is that why she killed herself?"

Rik closed his mouth firmly and thought. Whatever she saw on his face caused Jessa to keep silent and watch him intently. Almost whimsically, he said, "You know what I wouldn't be surprised to find out?"

"What?"

"Do you have Celisa's number on your phone?"

"Yeah."

"Let me have it."

She handed the phone to him.

He found her number and dialed. "Hi, Celisa? Hi. Yeah. This is Rik, Jessa's brother. How'd you recognize my voice? Really?" His eyebrows rose. "Look, sorry to bother you, but Jessa's here with me and we have a question. Yeah. If you wouldn't mind. Do you know where Ellen Scarpacia lived? Her address? Oh, okay. Sure. Take your time. You're certain? Absolutely certain? One hundred twenty-seven Antigua Avenue. Are you sure about the number? Sure. You guessed it. Oh. Yeah, that's what I was wondering. No, it's fine. Don't worry. Really. Thanks. Bye."

Jessa's eyes began to tear up. "We bought Ellen's house?"

Rik nodded.

"We live in Ellen's house?"

Rik didn't move.

"Where did she hang herself, Rik?"

Rik looked away as he spoke. "Your bedroom."

*   *   *

They lucked out. Zach was just pulling out of the school parking lot when they left the building. Rik recognized his car and flagged him down. Zach dropped them in the Square.

They arrived on time for the appointment.

Just before they entered the building, Jessa grabbed Rik's arm. "Wait." She took a deep breath, then another. She swallowed and smiled weakly. "Okay. I'm ready."

Dr. Dreier found herself confronted by two somber teens.

"Your mother left me a message that you would be seeing a different therapist."

Jessa was still trying not to visualize Ellen hanging in her bedroom. "Some people told her that I shouldn't see you."

"You don't agree?"

"No, but that's not why we're here."

"Okay." Puzzled eyes cautiously explored their faces. "Why are you here?"

Jessa said, "Information. We know some things you may want to know. We think you know things we need to know."

Rik broke in. "But everything we talk about must be kept secret. Everyone is afraid what will happen to the house values if word gets out."

Dr. Dreier wondered why he was here. He'd barely mumbled a hello and looked, well, frightened. "I agree. Everything we say is to be held in strict confidence."

"Good," Jessa said. "Why did you ask if we'd found anything strange in the house after I saw that hallucination?"

Dr. Dreier held her silence for several seconds. "A patient who told me of similar hallucinations. She'd found somethings."

Rik and Jessa exchanged glances. Jessa asked, "Why don't our neighbors want me to see you?"

Dr. Dreier tapped on her desk. "I think I know, but why don't you tell me about these people first."

She looked surprised when Rik answered. "It's our neighbors or at least some of them. Four of them, men, met with our parents last night after supper. Our neighborhood has a problem."

"An infestation is what they called it," added Jessa.

Rik continued. "Jessa didn't have a hallucination. She saw a ghost. I saw a ghost right after she did. A different one, a woman burying a child. Last night we both saw a ghost, a young girl being kidnapped. The whole neighborhood is haunted."

Dr. Dreier closed her eyes. "They said that the whole neighborhood thinks it's seeing ghosts?"

"Yes."

Jessa said, "All the ghosts are black. I mean they are the ghosts of African-Americans."

The doctor nodded.

"You knew that already?"

"No." She sighed. "But I'm not surprised."

"Why not?"

"For the same reason your neighbors don't want you talking to me, which, I presume, is because Ellen Scarpacia was my patient. She came to me because she thought she was having hallucinations of black people. When her parents found out she was seeing me, they stopped her from coming. I also know you live in the Scarpacias' former home."

Jessa asked sharply. "Since when did you know that?"

"After we met the last time, I had both your folders on my desk."

"And you put us together then? Not before?"

"Not before. But I'm not as convinced as you are that what everyone is seeing are ghosts. I'm inclined to the scientific approach, which would be to treat this as a group hallucination."

Rik was surprised. "There are such things?"

"Yes. They're not all that common, but they do happen. Dancing mania, for example," she said firmly, as if establishing a fact. "Fainting clusters, visions of the Virgin Mary, UFO sightings, cargo cults, men claiming their penises are shrinking. A couple of decades back we had people saying aliens were communicating with them through the fillings in their teeth."

"You mean," Rik said, "that men think their penises are shrinking but they're not? How can they think that? They can see them, can't they?"

"People have uncomfortable experiences they are unable to explain or deal with. The pain of the experience gets translated into bizarre symptoms. Think of anorexia, in which, usually, a young woman looks in a mirror and sees herself as if she weighed much more than she actually does. Seeing isn't always believing. Imagination is believing. That's why we have psychiatrists."

"But how can different people have the same hallucination?"

"We don't really know, but we have several theories. Conversion hysteria, Smelser's social strain theory, convergence and emergent norms. Mixed evidence exists for each of these explanations. I'm not going to try to explain them to you because the problem here is that our information is too limited to fit into any of these possible theories.

"And, if I remember correctly, all these theories require the people having the experiences be part of a group. All the others who claim to have seen these ghosts, including Ellen, can be considered to be part of a group, the neighborhood. You two, it seems, cannot. You saw ghosts before either of you had any reason to expect that others had such visions. Thus all the theories seem inapplicable."

"So we are seeing ghosts."

"I don't believe in ghosts."

"Neither did we. Rik, tell her about the books."

"Right. Well, we thought the ghosts seemed old. I mean historical. The blacksmith. But we know from the legal papers that our house was built in 1948. We wondered why ghosts from early times would be haunting a house built barely a hundred years ago. So I went to the school library to check out some books on Paradise's history. When I went to the shelf where the books were supposed to be, someone was waiting for me: Ellen Scarpacia's boyfriend. He said all the books on Paradise's history had disappeared, and not just the ones in the school library but the ones in the main library as well. When he'd tried to buy some books online, he said they never came. I checked the school library records and Ellen was the last person to take the books out. She brought them back."

Dr. Dreier looked at the brother and sister for several seconds. "Is it possible that this 'boyfriend' took the books?"

"But why?" asked Rik.

Jessa asked, "Do you know anyone who would be familiar with Paradise's history?"

She thought. "No." She shook her head. "No, I don't. But I'll ask around. I'll let you know."

"But you're telling us," Jessa asked, "that Ellen Scarpacia reported seeing ghosts, or whatever you want to call them, just like we're seeing now?"

"Yes." She opened the top, right-side drawer on her desk. "Let me show you something." Inside the drawer lay an automatic pistol. The gun was loaded and the safety was on. It was held in place by a mechanism which she could free immediately, but which would require several seconds of experimentation for a person unfamiliar with it. Beside the gun lay an odd, older object. It was this she wanted to show the Hollies.

"Ms. Scarpacia gave me this at her last visit."

The doctor laid three intertwined chain links attached to a broken circle of metal on her desk for them to examine. "I'm told by an historian I contacted at BU that these date from the early-to mid-eighteenth century. It's part of a leg iron. Ms. Scarpacia found it in your home."

Rik asked, "A leg iron? What...?"

Dr. Dreier shrugged. "Used for slaves. All I know is it's troubling. It's not an illusion, individual or group. It's real."

For several seconds the brother and sister examined the article. Rik reached out and ran his hand along the cuff. He turned to Jessa. "That piece of old glass you found."

To Dr. Dreier, Jessa said, "I found a piece of glass that seemed old and very worn. That might have been something the ghosts left."

Dr. Dreier asked, "Do ghosts leave objects around like souvenirs? Can they move or carry objects?"

"You still don't think they're ghosts."

"No, Rik, I can't. I'm going to need a whole lot more before I toss out my scientific worldview."

Rik nodded. He didn't want to argue with the woman, but he wondered if it all could be scientific but we just didn't know how yet.

Jessa said, "We just found out that Ellen hanged herself"—she paused to look at Rik—"in my bedroom. I don't want to sleep there anymore."

"Don't."

"One more. Which pills are for depression and which are for hallucinations?"

"You're not going to take your meds for hallucinations?"

"I'm sorry we disagree, but I don't need them."

*   *   *

When they left the office building, Rik grabbed Jessa's arm. "Act casual. We're being watched."

"Hey, you two! You're the Hollie kids, aren't you, Gary Hollie's kids?"

They turned and saw a policeman leaning his butt against a police car parked beneath a "handicapped only" sign. He looked as if he'd been waiting for them to come out of the building.

They nodded.

"Thought so. I'm Officer Adams. Clint Adams. Your next-door neighbor. Hey, you kids like a ride? I'm on my way home right now. Come on, get in." He held the back door open for them. "Get in."

They couldn't think of an excuse with that uniformed authority staring them in the face.

*   *   *

Rik and Jessa realized as soon as they settled into the back seat that Clint's invitation had been a trap. Neither back door had a lever to open it or a button to open the window. A metal screen separated them from Clint in the front seat, though it had been designed to protect him from them, not them from him. The seat belts seemed a bit too tight and secure.

Clint started the engine and pulled out into traffic. "You down here doing some shopping?" He knew they weren't. He knew they'd been to see Dr. Dreier against his orders. Clint had programmed his resources to track everyone in the neighborhood and report suspicious contacts. He could track phone calls, texts, messaging, information queries, everything. That, after all, was the main purpose of the new Federal IDs. "You should try the new mall. They've got some great stores."

He took violations of his orders personally. He had feelings of abandonment when people disobeyed him, the feelings of a lost child, and feelings of persecution.

Jessa answered the officer's question about why they were downtown simply, saying, "We needed to make a stop. Thanks for picking us up."

Clint's ancestors, Asnavur Hovhanessian and his wife, Margarid née Kazarian, were born in the mid-1870s in Armenia, then part of the Ottoman Empire. They fled hundreds of years of oppression with their two children. The Turks held the Armenians in total contempt and treated them as noxious animals good only for the slaughter. When they fled Armenia, neither Asnavur nor Margarid had any family members left alive save their two children.

They arrived with their children, five and two, in the US in 1896. It was the year of Plessy v. Ferguson, the separate-but-equal decision, and of the arrival of increasing numbers of Italian, Greek, Hungarian, Polish, and other immigrants speaking Slavic languages. Many of the descendants of the English, Irish Protestant and Scotch immigrants who had penned "all men are created equal" refused to include the new immigrants and didn't like any of them.

Asnavur did not want his family to be mistaken for Hungarians or Italians. He did not want to be identified as an Armenian. He'd seen more than enough of the horrible results of being an ethnic or political minority. He refused to settle among the many other Armenians who lived in or had recently arrived in Boston, fearing that by living together they might draw attention and the larger society would try to kill them all again.

He settled his family in Paradise.

His daughter brought home a reader from school. Asnavur searched the book and found the names "Will" and "Kate." After a visit to the public library and a broken-English discussion with a librarian, he settled on the surname Adams.

He and his wife became Will and Kate Adams.

He changed the names of his two children to Martha and George. The three children who followed he named Abigail, John and Lincoln.

The family joined the First Presbyterian Church.

Will forbade Armenian, Italian, Russian and all other ethnic foods in his kitchen and dining room. Meat, potatoes and the vege-table of the day, preferably all boiled and unseasoned, became the family cuisine. He banned folk dancing, folk songs, traditional clothing, the display of parents' or extended family photos, the speaking of Armenian and any other reminder of the Old World. No alcohol, card playing or gambling allowed.

Though at first they had hardly any money, he hired an English tutor for the whole family. He explained his and his wife's remaining accents as speech defects they'd been born with. They'd met, he explained, in a school for children with speech problems.

He joined the Republican Party and the American Protective Association.

Despite his conversion to American, Will frequently woke in the middle of the night, certain he'd heard the sounds of gunshots and marching Turkish boots. Kate faded to the point at which she was half present, a half-mother, a half-wife. Her other half lived back in the place of death, the place of unburied bodies and anguished memories, the place she still called home. Sometimes at night she cried out in Armenian. Will silenced her with his fists.

Will and Kate's life became a disguise, an effort to measure up to standards not their own, an attempt, born out of fear, to deny history. Other immigrant families made the same adjustments over generations. Will and Kate were unusual only in that they made the leap consciously, by themselves.

Will found a job at the local mill, where immigrants and the children of immigrants ran machines that turned black-grown cotton into cloth. The owners fired the former manager, who had failed miserably at keeping the workers under control. They hired Will. The first thing he did was end rum privileges. The workers walked out. Will called in the police. He fired workers who came in late or left early or who dallied at any time. He fired those who extended their lunch break running to a bar or playing bocce ball. He fired anyone who smelled of alcohol. He fired all who smoked or gambled. Twelve-hour days and six-day weeks kept the workers from participating in what he termed "amusements." Then he cut the workers' pay by twenty percent.

It didn't matter how many he fired. There were always more. Immigrants swarmed into the country like a biblical plague from Godforsaken places across Europe and the Middle East. Will realized from experience that he could control their women more easily than the men, so he hired more and more woman. His strategy worked well for several years, until the women began organizing. Once again he had to call in the police. He made certain the police beat female union organizers as hard as they beat the males.

In May 1911, William Wood, then the manager of Ayer Mill in Lawrence, Massachusetts, arrived in front of the Adams' residence on Washington Street in Paradise in his 1910 Ford. Wood, the son of a Portuguese immigrant who had changed his name from Guilherme Medeiros Silva to William Wood Sr., sought advice from Adams regarding worker dissatisfaction in the Lawrence Mill. Wood used what he learned from Adams the following year to fight his workers in what became known as the Bread and Roses Strike.

He and Will agreed that these subhuman people, especially the Italians and more especially the women, had to be taught to adapt to the rhythms of the industrial age if they ever hoped to be accepted as Americans.

Secretly, Will began to think of himself as "The Turk," a joke that brought a knifelike smile to his face. He had made it. He had destroyed his language, his customs, his religion, his memories. He had become an American. He had awards from the mill owners to prove it. When Congress passed, and the president signed, the Immigration Act of 1924, which limited immigration of people like his family, he cheered.

He failed to notice when, in 1925, a Federal Court ruled in the case of United States v. Cartozian that, indeed, Armenians were white.

Will and Kate's children grew up to be white Americans looking toward the future. Unknowingly, they carried in every cell of their growing bodies DNA altered by their parents' traumas, alterations they would pass to their children and generations after.

One of Will and Kate's grandsons, Alexander, became an Evangelical minister. Among his fondest sermon themes, one he drew from reading John Winthrop, was, in Alexander's words, that "the sins of the father, the evils that men do, persist in time, attach to their offspring, bring low the generations." He lived before theologians and psychologists figured out the same could be said for evils suffered, for having been sinned against.

Clint said, "Good. Nice weather for it. Supposed to stay nice through the weekend."

Rik asked, "How did you know it was us?"

Clint didn't like people who asked questions. He activated his flashing red lights and eased through a traffic light. "You see all this stuff up here?" His right hand swept over the dashboard and the area between the front seats. "More electronics than a NASA rocket. You know, the average person on the street these days doesn't understand the assets we have to catch criminals. Including your new ID badges. We know who you are and where you are and can protect you from others and from yourself. Once we're onto somebody, we know every single thing that person does and says. We cover phones, texts, emails, everything. You just can't get away with crap like you used to be able to. And the criminal types always start small, with one thing that they think is too small for us to notice. Nothing's too small. We notice. And if we don't move in on them when they do something they think is small, they move on to bigger stuff right after that. Crime is like a drug. Once you start, you can't get enough. I take a particular interest in the people in our neighborhood. Like you two.

"So here we are."

He pulled into his own driveway and parked behind his personal car.

Rik asked him to open the doors for them.

Clint turned. He stared at Rik, no longer playing the role of accommodating next-door neighbor. "Boy, you can't get out until I let you out. You sit there and listen to what I have to say. I'm letting you off easy this time cause you're Gary's kids and I like Gary. I understand him. He's a nice guy. Evelyn's nice, too. Kids like you two don't deserve good parents like them. You hear me? When you're told to stay away from someone, you stay away. Consider yourselves warned. The next time won't be so easy."

The doors clicked and opened.

"Get out. And say 'thank you.' I did you a favor."

"Thank you." In unison, as Jessa slid out first.

"Boy!"

Rik turned.

"You see this? You know what this is?" Clint held up his handgun.

Rik nodded.

"This is what it's about. You want one of these, you'd better learn to do what you're told. Don't fuck with me."

*   *   *

Jessa found the humid air outside fresher than the air-conditioned air inside.

When they got inside their house, she said, "What a..." No word fell into place for her.

"Maybe we should paint over all the windows on his side of the house."

"And Rik, don't run upstairs and measure your dick to see if it's shrinking or Clintie will know how long it is."

"No joke, Jessa. We've got to be very careful from now on." He told her how Steve had hidden his ID in a book in the library.

Jessa frowned. "You're right. I have to let Dr. Dreier know what happened. How can I get a message to her without the all-knowing Officer Adams intercepting it?"

*　　*　　*

When she arrived upstairs, Jessa stopped at the door to her room. She turned and went into Rik's room and dropped her books on his bed.

"What are you doing here?"

She began to answer, then stopped. Finally, she said, "Oh. I didn't notice...I have a call from Celisa." Her eyes widened and the sides of her mouth fell as she listened to the voicemail, then handed him the phone. "You'd better listen to this yourself."

Celisa's message was about the class advisor and her suspension. Rik called Celisa immediately.

"I will. Really," he said, promising he would testify at the hearing. He was sure she was exaggerating. No school official could act like that toward a student. She was overreacting. Had to be. "I will testify."

Celisa said she would understand if he didn't want to get involved. Her tone suggested she knew she couldn't rely on him.

With a trace of irritation in his voice, he said, "No, listen, I said I will and I will."

"You don't have to," she said. "I don't expect you to."

"I do have to. I really do."

*　　*　　*

Jessa didn't want to be in the room where Ellen had committed suicide. She asked Rik if she could move into his room. Neither thought to tell their parents. He said she could have the bed. That night, when he lay down on an old sleeping bag on the floor, he couldn't sleep. His mind tripped and spun as if each thought were part of a fireworks display.

Half fearing he'd run into a ghost, he got out of bed and cracked open his bedroom door. He heard snores coming from his parents' bedroom. Jessa didn't stir.

112

He opened the door to Jessa's room and turned on the light. He stayed in the doorway, too respectful to enter the room where Ellen had died. The room seemed eerie to him now. Foreboding hovered in the air like fog. But what had she hung herself from? The ceiling light was the obvious choice, but it was difficult to judge how much weight it would bear. Besides, he and Jessa's parents had had everything redone. Had she screwed a hook into a ceiling beam and used that? It was impossible to tell.

He stepped back and closed the door.

As quietly as he could, so as not to wake the living or the dead, he headed downstairs. He opened the refrigerator. Nothing in there seemed to inspire him.

He poured himself a glass of orange juice and settled at the kitchen table. He was wide awake.

*   *   *

Rik saw the horizon, a line dividing a stretch of summer-blue sky from an earth covered with the yellows and greens of plants. A light wind from the east carried the scent of ocean and caused the plants to sway slowly. Crows, playing and showing off, circled and swooped at a black-faced scarecrow. Among the plants, roughly dressed black men and women stooped to their work, their backs rising and falling, visible just above the plants' tassels. They did not pause to notice the day or enjoy the breeze.

At the edge of the field, a more neatly attired white man wearing a broad-brimmed white hat stood in the shade of a tree, drinking from a cup, surveying the dominion. He held a rifle casually, as if expecting a pheasant might poke its head out among the corn. Behind him was a coach with a single horse. In the far distance, stood another white man wearing a similar hat.

It was a peaceful scene. It was a scene of violence.

No sooner had the vision faded than Rik heard the sound of Gary at the front door. Too late to run upstairs and avoid him. Rik remained at the table drinking his orange juice.

Gary entered the kitchen like a late train into a station. He rinsed his face in the sink, dried himself with a dish towel, then went to the fridge for a beer. He went off to the living room.

Rik heard the faint sound of the TV.

Outside, birds began to announce their waking.

CHAPTER FOUR
THURSDAY

Evelyn caught her children as they were leaving for school. "Jessa!"

"Can't now. We're late for school."

"Why'd you sleep in Rik's room last night?"

They stopped.

Jessa asked, "Did Clintie call you?"

"What?"

Jessa walked back to her mother so she wouldn't have to shout. "My room's haunted."

"You saw another ghost?"

"No. It's not one I see. It's worse. It's one I feel."

*　　　*　　　*

Rik said, "I think I know why Gary hasn't seen any ghosts."

"Why?"

"Because they're not on TV."

As if she feared she was being watched, Jessa repressed her laughter. She shook her head. "That might be the truth."

A drone followed them fifty yards behind and twenty off to the side all the way to school.

*　　　*　　　*

"I'm tap, tap, tapping at your door." The voice giggled.

Evelyn recognized the voice and closed her eyes. She'd hoped this wouldn't happen. "Come in." Evelyn didn't cross the kitchen to welcome Annie because she wasn't.

Annie sang, "Another beautiful morning! My lovely doppelgangers are off to school and I have the day off."

Evelyn stopped in mid-pour, leaving the carafe in her hand hovering above the coffee cup. "Your lovely what?"

"What?"

"You said your lovely something or others had gone to school."

"I did? Oh, right. Doppelgangers."

"What does that mean?"

"Doppelgangers? Oh, it means, it's like, I think it's German, things that kind of sort of look alike? That's it. Things that look alike like my daughters. They look alike. They do, you know? It's a word my ex taught me."

Evelyn thought, wonderful, here we are, back together, Annie, her husband, and herself, just like yesterday. No doubt Father Vic was on his way. She served her guest coffee then poured her own. She thought she should perhaps bring one of the liquor bottles from the cabinet and leave it behind the coffee maker in case she needed it in the future.

"So, why do you have the day off?"

"Oh, I was joshing. It's like every day. Put the little doppelgangers on the bus and then wait for them to come home."

"Don't you have housework?"

"No." Annie waved the idea away with her free hand. "My ex pays to have the house cleaned professionally twice each week. He doesn't trust me, you know."

"He doesn't trust you to clean the house?" She thought, but he trusts you with his children?

Annie shook her head no as she sipped her coffee. "This is, you make the most wonderful coffee. I could sit here and drink it forever."

"There's more if you'd like...more." The word "penance" rose out of Evelyn's mind from behind the door labeled "Catholic Childhood."

"Oh, thank you, you're so nice. I'm so glad you're the new neighbor. But I can't stay. Really. I'd so much, I mean, I'd really love to. But you know."

"I do."

"I just came over to tell you the news!"

Annie's tone caused Evelyn to think "pregnancy." "What news?"

"Now don't be angry. They're children after all. They don't understand things the way we do. But still, what they did was so dangerous!"

"Are we talking about Rik and Jessa?"

Annie nodded. "Our neighbor and very good friend Officer Clint Adams caught them, yes, caught them, as he said, emerging from the offices of the infamous Dr. Bonnie Dreier." She nodded her head affirmatively for punctuation.

"Infamous?"

Annie nodded exaggeratedly.

"Why is she infamous?"

"She asks too many questions."

Evelyn slowly closed her mouth.

Annie waited. A sly smile crept over her face. "You're catching on. Go ahead. Ask. I came to tell you."

"When was this?"

"No later than yesterday."

Evelyn spoke mostly to herself. "After I told them not to."

"That's right. And Officer Adams gave them a thing or two, too."

"Gave them?"

Annie nodded again. "Gave them warnings."

Evelyn rubbed her forehead. "I'll talk to them. It won't happen again."

After Annie left, Evelyn cleaned up the kitchen. As she swept her sponge behind the toaster, she felt something and heard a muffled clatter. She moved the toaster out and found the object.

She didn't know what it was. It was old. That much was clear. Most of its length seemed to be tooled leather, but one end was of a more solid material. She turned it over in her hands, then, instinctively, pulled the ends apart.

A dagger. And scabbard.

*   *   *

At Rik's request, his third-period teacher gave him a pass to see the vice principal. It was an unusual request since VPs dealt primarily with discipline, but she asked no questions. He didn't tell her he intended to see the sophomore vice principal. He wanted to avoid having to explain his reasons.

"Why," the secretary asked, "do you want to see him? He has nothing to do with you."

"I'll explain it to him."

She didn't exactly roll her eyes, but her pupils moved in that direction.

Rik closed the door behind him.

The VP smiled when he saw Rik. Of course, he knew why the boy had come.

Rik thought the man's smile vampirish, but chalked that up to his own imagination.

"Well, the knight in shining armor rides in to save his ladylove."

"Mr. Urbanowicz, I just wanted to tell you..."

"Speak up, boy. I hate whining."

Rik swallowed. "The girls in the car that went by gave us the finger. And they swore at us. We did not give anyone the finger. We did not swear. And if Celisa's going to be punished, I should be, too."

"A real hero. So what favors did that uppity little piece of whatever of yours perform to get you to come in here and lie to me?"

Rik felt sucker-punched. He'd thought Celisa had exaggerated and he'd come to try to be reasonable. Suddenly he didn't know what to do. He was speechless.

Mr. Urbanowicz said, "Let me tell you something. This is a world of laws and rules. The rules were made to help you. But if you go around with your little black girlfriend because she knows the tricks of the trade and sells you drugs, then you're likely to find the rules that once favored you no longer do. Do I make myself clear?"

Rik understood too many things all at once for him to cope. A dozen different responses, each half-formed, fought to be the first one from his lips. What he finally said was something entirely different.

Rik hadn't planned it, hadn't thought about it, and probably wouldn't have said it if he had. But since he hadn't, his question emerged directly from his gut.

It was Kafka's question.

The words didn't come out smoothly and, though his voice had a hoarseness to it, he spoke distinctly.

"What did you think when you woke up that morning and found you'd turned into a giant bug?"

He left as the VP, quickly out of his seat, demanded to know what he meant by that question.

Once safe in the hallway, Rik turned off his phone recorder. Celisa had been right. He smiled, but just a little. He hadn't expected such a test, but he felt he'd passed it. He was certain more tests, just as unforeseeable, would be coming.

But Celisa had been right. Urbanowicz had been as bad as she'd said. Celisa had told him this kind of stuff didn't happen all the time, certainly not in school, but it happened more than enough, four or five times a year perhaps, to keep her constantly on guard.

Celisa and he lived in the same world and yet it took an act of imagination for him to begin to see her life. She understood his, of course. Just like Jessa's ghost claimed to know everything about her. He had to. She had to. They had to. Self-defense.

What about the mongols and the n'okies, those non-white whites?

Rik no longer recognized the world he lived in. As a consequence, he no longer recognized himself. Whoever he was, he was angry.

*   *   *

"Hey, Gary, my man, good to see you." Firm handshake followed by pat on the shoulder. "Put on a few pounds, old boy."

"Good, Ken, good. Yeah, got a desk job now. You look great. Don't you age?"

"Course not. I'm single."

They sat.

"So you got a desk job! Promotion?"

Gary nodded. "I fucking run the place. The boss calls in from a Florida beach."

"Florida. Geez. Wish I could get myself fixed up like that. So how's the wife? You still married?"

"Seem to be."

"How are your kids?"

"They just started at Paradise High."

"Whoa! You moved! I hear that's a good school."

"They're both smart; I'll give them that. Unrealistic as hell, but smart."

"What? They want to be astronauts or something?"

"Something."

"They'll learn. The world has a way of beating common sense into you. Hey, how's that, what's her name?"

"Jessa."

"Yeah, Jessa. How's she developing?" Ken grinned and lifted both hands in front of his chest, as if lifting breasts.

"Ken, she's my daughter, for Christ's sake. You haven't changed."

"Just joking, man. No offense."

"You never thought of getting married?"

"Naw. Hey, look at what's coming. Hi, sweetheart!"

The waitress glanced aside at his words, and then took their orders, her eyes never leaving her order pad.

"Woof," Ken said as his eyes followed her. "Marriage? No. Who'd want me? I'm just middle management. Could lose my job any second. They're smart these days. Women demand security, a guy who's made it, who you can count on to bring home the bread. It's a new age. Women are perfectly capable of losing their own jobs, they don't need to be shackled to a man who loses his."

"Actually, Ken, I called you to run something by you. Something to do with my job. The boss is switching all the drivers from employees to independent contractors."

"Ouch. Yeah, a lot of places are doing that. Saves money big time. They're not trying to do that to you, are they?"

"No. But the boss wants me to break the news to them."

"Coward. When is this supposed to happen?"

"Tomorrow."

"Who else is going to be there?"

"Lawyer from Boston and some cops."

"How many?"

"Four."

"Well, sounds like your boss is handling the situation in a professional manner, except his ass is out of town. What's the problem?"

That stumped Gary. What was the problem? Shit happened. Everyone knew that. "I guess I'm wondering how to approach it."

"Oh, Gary. One way and one way only: professionally. Head-on. Up-front. Don't try to soften it or make excuses or those guys will eat you up. Whatever they call them, you're still their boss. Got to maintain that respect, know what I mean?"

The waitress brought their orders.

Ken said, "Thanks sweetheart."

She failed to acknowledge him.

"And they expect a tip for service like that. My God." He opened his napkin across his lap. "Gary, the one thing you got to remember: stay profitable. As long as they're making money off you, you're safe."

Gary nodded.

"Hey, you remember the time we..."

As they got up from lunch, Rik asked Zach if he would do him a favor.

"Sure. What?"

Rik handed him an envelope. "Can you get someone to deliver this to the address here?"

Zach took the envelope. "You ever heard of the post office?"

"Too dangerous," Rik said. "That's why I don't want you to deliver it. Get someone else to do it. Someone who doesn't know me or Jessa."

"When are you going to tell me what's going on?"

Rik winced. "Yeah. Wish I could."

*   *   *

As usual, Gary worked through dinnertime. Evelyn felt relieved he wasn't there. No telling how worked up he might get if he found out the kids had seen Dr. Dreier against specific orders.

Evelyn began even before anyone at the table had a chance to start eating.

"Annie came over this morning. She told me something that upset me a lot."

Jessa and Rik looked at her and waited for her to explain.

"Annie said that Clint, I mean, Officer Adams, who lives right next door, caught you two seeing Dr. Dreier yesterday afternoon after I told both of you not to see her anymore. I even called her during the day and told her we wouldn't be seeing her anymore. I'm going to have to punish both of..."

"Mom, wait."

"Rik, don't interrupt me. I'm not finished talking."

"You don't understand," said Jessa. "I had to go there."

Evelyn pursed her lips. "Alright. Why did you have to go there?"

"Because, you remember, when we were there the day before, Dr. Dreier gave me three prescriptions for depression and two for hallucinations. Remember, we had to stop at the pharmacy to pick them up? Since I wasn't seeing hallucinations, I needed to stop whatever I was taking that was for that. I didn't tell her why, I just said I wanted to know which medicine was for which thing. I had to find out what was for the hallucination so I could stop taking it."

"And I had to go with her so she'd have a witness that she didn't talk about anything else. As far as that Officer Adams is concerned. He's a jerk."

"Rik!"

Jessa said, "He is, Mom. He didn't give us any chance to explain. Not that I'd want him to know I'm depressed."

Evelyn watched her children eat. This was all too confusing for her. Why wasn't Gary home? He should be home at dinnertime. But that would have been worse. He wouldn't have waited for an explanation.

*   *   *

Evelyn was finishing cleaning up the kitchen when Gary walked in. She began assembling a reheated dinner for him.

"Gary, come here. Look. I found this behind the toaster this morning."

She unwrapped the object from paper towels. She'd tried to clean it, but it still looked like burned and tarnished metal, scoured and misshapen. Just less than a foot long, it had a cutting edge, ended in a sharp point and had an ornate handle, more like she'd have expected on a sword than a little thing like this.

Gary studied it. "What is it? An old knife?"

"Maybe."

"It's black. It's a piece of trash," Gary said, handing it back to her. "Game's coming on. Oh, by the way, I had lunch today with Ken. You remember him?"

123

"Ken?" Something familiar but long placed aside rose in her. "Ken! You met with that creep! He tried to turn Jessa being raped into a joke! Right to her face!"

Gary rolled his eyes. "So what? He's that kind of guy. Just who he is, that's all."

Evelyn turned furious. "You think that my daughter being raped is some kind of joke?"

"No. And she's my daughter, too, now. Of course not. Calm down. Jesus. Jessa didn't even get the joke."

"What do you mean she didn't get the joke?"

"She didn't laugh. If she'd understood what Ken was talking about, she'd have laughed. All Jessa knows about sex is what your boyfriend taught her."

"What...?" For several seconds Evelyn was too exasperated for words. "That was cruel, what you just said." She burst into tears.

She started to leave. He grabbed and held her.

"Evelyn, Evelyn, calm down." She pulled away but remained in the kitchen. "I'm sorry I said that. It just came out."

"I don't care. You're not bringing him here. He's not coming anywhere near this house. Do you understand? That man is a psychopath!"

Gary nearly laughed. "A what?"

"A psychopath. Someone who thinks only about himself and has no feelings."

Gary shook his head in disbelief. "I'm not inviting him here. Don't worry. I just wanted to talk to him about my job."

"What about your job?"

"The boss has made some decisions the guys won't like and I've got to tell them about it tomorrow. That's all."

"And what did Ken tell you?"

"To do my job."

"A real genius it takes to figure that out." She threw down the dish towel and stomped out of the room, the battered knife still in her hand.

124

Welcome to the real world, he told himself. A psychopath. Wouldn't that be something: to be able to do what needs to be done and not care who got hurt. Did you have to be born that way or could you learn it? Out loud he said, "I can do this."

What he couldn't do was explain it to Evelyn. Women only wanted to know that the check was deposited every two weeks. Other than that, they cared little about men's work and what they had to put up with. She wouldn't have understood even if he'd been able to explain it. Which he was fairly certain he could not.

*   *   *

Jessa kissed Rik on the cheek when he told her what happened. "I'm proud of you, big brother."

"Will you support me all my life because I can't get a job after being thrown out of high school?"

"No, but I'll do a sketch that makes you look noble. Did you tell Celisa?"

"Yeah."

"And?"

"At first she was angry."

Jessa, taken aback, asked, "Why?"

"She said this was her fight, not mine. I said, maybe it was more her fight but it's my fight because I was with her. Apparently stuff like this happens a lot. She said we don't see it because we're either not affected or we're helped by it. I said she showed it to me and I hated the way he treated her and I had to do something about it."

"Then what?"

"She started crying."

"Then what?"

"I started crying."

"Interesting discussion. Anyone try using words after that?"

"She thanked me. Said she hoped I didn't get in trouble."

"Good. I'll ask her more tomorrow."

"I... this affects you too. The girls who gave us the finger?"

"Yeah?"

"And the sophomore vice principal?"

"Um."

"Celisa says they aren't the only people like that at school."

"Probably."

"We'd have a pretty horrible time if people like that found out we live in a house haunted by blacks."

Jessa paused to think this through.

Rik said, "There's something else."

"Oh. Are we getting deep now?"

"Yeah. When I asked Mr. Urbanowicz about turning into a giant bug: that was the first time I remember feeling..."

"Feeling what? Come on, boy."

"It's hard to explain. It was like I wasn't there."

"Right. You were doing this for Celisa."

"No. I wasn't thinking about her either. I think I'd stopped thinking." Rik made a disgruntled face. "Go ahead, Jessa, roll your eyes. Forget it."

"No, Rik, go ahead. I'm sorry. Just a habit. Sort of."

More for his benefit than hers, he tried again. "The best I can say it is that the words came from a part of me I hadn't met before and I just passed them on."

Jessa looked at her brother while various possible responses debated each other in her head. She'd always believed she understood things in ways he couldn't, even though he was older. Now she wasn't so sure. "Okay. All I have to say right now is: you're weird, but in sort of an interesting way."

*   *   *

"Listen to this. Something new I learned about the world. People in Boston owned slaves." Jessa lay on the bed in the midst of an aggregation of schoolbooks.

126

"Really?" Another tectonic plate shift.

"Guess we owe some apologies to the South."

"This from your history course?"

"Nope. Poetry. Listen. I'll tell you the good parts. Her name was Phillis Wheatley. She was born in the 1750's somewhere in West Africa. She came to Boston on the ship the Phillis."

"Wow. Some women have ships named after them. Some get named after the ship."

"John and Susanna Wheatley bought her, that explains her last name, though it sounds like more of an experiment. They taught her and had her taught. Everything. Including Latin and Greek. She soon began publishing poetry in the Boston papers."

"Whew. I've been wasting my life."

"We already knew that. She became famous in England, though she was pretty much ignored here. She died and was buried in an unmarked grave with her youngest child."

"Sad ending."

"Thought you'd like it. Listen."

"I always listen to you, Jessa."

"Listen!

Should you my lord, while you peruse my song,
Wonder from whence my love of Freedom
sprung,
Whence flow these wishes for the common
good,
By feeling hearts alone best be understood,
I, young in life, by seeming cruel fate
Was snatch'd from Afric's fancy'd happy seat:
What pangs excruciating must molest,
What sorrows labor in my parent's breast?
Steel'd was that soul and by no misery mov'd
That from a father seiz'd his babe belov'd:
Such, such my case. And can I then but pray
Others may never feel tyrannic sway?"

127

Rik sat quietly. "You don't think she was girl we saw being taken, do you?"

"Geez, I hadn't thought of that. Maybe she was. Well, what did you think?"

"About people around here having slaves?"

"Yeah."

"It means the ghosts we've seen could have actually lived around here. And..."

"And what?"

"And can I take some of your antidepressants?" Rik held up his copy of Fahrenheit 451. "Bradbury mentions something called the 'Library of Alexandria.' I looked it up. It was huge. Tens of thousands of scrolls. Bradbury says it was burned, but that's not the exact truth. It was burned and burned and burned and burned, reportedly by Caesar, by the Christians, by the pagans, by the Muslims and by the Jews. Apparently, wanting to be in charge means burning books. One of the great philosophers of the ancient world taught there: Hypatia. A woman. The Christians murdered her. The human race is really fucked up. Talk about dominant species. We're dinosaurs with technical skills.

"Little sister, maybe Ellen just saw everything for what it is and had to get out."

CHAPTER FIVE
FRIDAY

The drivers sat cold-stone still for several seconds, as if waiting to catch the final echo of all that Gary had said. Eighteen pairs of eyes focused on him. After a bit, one driver shifted slightly in his seat and leaned a few degrees to the left as if the tilt would provide a more meaningful view. Another driver cleared his throat.

The four police officers, standing two on each side of the room, didn't move.

"Well, if there are no questions, then you can read through the contract. If you have any questions, Attorney Perocchi is here to answer them. If I can help I'll be glad to. It's your decision whether or not to sign. If you do, you become businessmen. From then on you get to make all the big decisions."

Gary started to stand.

A hand shot up.

He sat back down. "Yeah, Carla."

Carla was white. She held up the contract as if it were show-and-tell. "Gary, what does this mean?"

Gary frowned. Hadn't she been listening? "If you sign, you will own your own business. You will..."

Carla cut him off. "No, Gary, I mean the bottom line. What does this contract mean for us, for what we take home?"

She'd pinned him. He tried to wiggle out of it. "It depends..."

"Gary, damn it, stop being a shit." This was Frank, white and usually laid-back, but now sitting on his haunches, eyeing his manager the way a lion eyes a gazelle. "We know you. Most of us have worked with you for years. We know the first thing you did after the boss left was to do the math. What are the numbers? What's this going to cost us? Give us the numbers!"

Gary had no way out. He reared himself up like a bear defending its cub. "Twenty-seven percent."

The room erupted with incoherent shouting, but words like "family," "wife," "husband," "children," "rent," "bills," and "loans" came through. "Hopes."

"Wait! Wait!" Gary stood, both hands in front of him, palms out, trying to quiet the drivers. "It's not like that. Listen!"

"It's not like what, Gary?" shouted Ben, who was white. "Are you taking a third cut in your pay?"

"No. And neither are you. Stop exaggerating. It's barely over a quarter. You're free to expand your business. You work hard now. Work just a bit harder and you'll make the difference back, maybe even more. Think of this as an opportunity to do better."

Ben erupted. "Bullshit! The only way to expand is to steal from someone else here. You want me to underbid Frank or Debbie or Ahmad for their customers so they make even less? Is that what you want us to do? Cannibalize each other?"

The drivers applauded.

"Wait! Wait! Quiet down. Listen. This is business, Ben. It's the way the world works. Hard work. Competition. Innovation. Efficiency. May the best man win."

Debbie sniffed in indignation. Gary wondered what her problem was.

Silence once more.

"This isn't survival of the fittest." This was Harry speaking, softly but with authority. "This is survival of whoever doesn't give a shit."

Then Paul, one of the black drivers, spoke up. "Gary, I need a job, not a mountain to climb. I've been doing this for thirty-eight years."

"Stop." Attorney Perocchi stood in front of Gary's desk, blocking his view of the drivers. "That's enough whining. You all sound like bunch of geese. Gimme! Gimme! That's all you care about: the easy life. Getting a free ride. Well, that's over. You," he said, pointing at Paul, "you don't want a mountain to climb?

Fine. Dig your hole where you are for all anybody cares. It's your choice: you climb the mountain to the top and make something of yourself or die in your hole, but nobody is going to listen to your complaining. We have high school grads out there anxious to take the work if you don't want it. We don't have time for quitters. You don't even know what real work is! We're all working on our own mountains. You have no right to question what we do. So, shut your mouth! I don't have time for your crap. You sign or don't sign!"

Paul stood. His voice shook, and seemed all the more a challenge because of that. "I'm not going to shut my mouth. Sorry if I spoil your day, Mr. Three Piece." He knew he was burning bridges, making a romantic but useless gesture. What did he have to lose? He had nothing, or, more correctly, he had been set on the road to losing everything. He felt hot, sweaty. "How much did that tie cost? More than I make in a week, I bet." He took a step forward. "Come on, tell us, we're listening for news from the gods. I've worked..."

At a sign from the attorney, the police, all four of them, closed in on Paul.

Paul backed away into Kuan. Kuan placed a hand on Paul's back to steady him. In order to clear himself from the other driver, Paul moved forward, toward the police.

The police took the movement as a charge.

Immediately, two of the police fell on Paul, twisted his body, forced his face down on the seat of his chair and handcuffed him. "Wait! What are you...you can't..."

Carla half stood. One of the police not involved with Paul turned toward her. She froze. She clamped down on her tongue with her teeth.

Frank leaned forward, his hands held out in a wrestler's stance, but his butt never left the chair.

Tensen's face hardened into stone, his eyes wide.

Waylon pushed his chair back, away from the confrontation. Heather vibrated with barely contained rage.

Gary watched the police as if he were watching a crime show on TV.

While the police wrestled with Paul, the attorney went on. "Thirty-eight years! You been at the same job thirty-eight years and you couldn't find something better to do than be an errand boy? You don't even deserve the job you have!"

Paul roared in pain as the two police maced him. The other drivers fell over their chairs and each other trying to get away. One of the cops shoved Paul to the ground. Another kicked him in the kidney. The police hauled him out of the room.

Attorney Perocchi smirked. "I don't suppose anyone else has anything to say? No? Very good. Excellent. Now, sign or don't sign, and get back to work. This isn't a vacation."

Paul's screams and a few heavy thuds echoed back into the room.

Perocchi turned to Gary. "You'd better learn how to handle these people. You're supposed to be the guy in charge, the man who gets things done, not some hand-holder." He left.

Through the window, Gary watched the police shove Paul into the cruiser.

Slowly, the drivers stood, walked to Gary's desk and handed him the papers. Everyone signed.

Gary stood alone, holding the stack of contracts, unable for several minutes to move. He wasn't thinking about what had happened. He was too shocked to think.

Carla's voice broke the spell.

"What? What, Carla?"

She stood in the doorway with her arms crossed. "Why didn't you stop the cops from taking Paul?"

"What could I have done?"

"Stopped them. You're the boss here."

"I can't interfere with the police!"

"So, you'd have let the cops take me?"

"No!" That was the truth. He didn't know why, but he immediately wished he hadn't said it.

"Because I'm a woman?"

"I don't know! How would I know?"

"What if they'd taken Ben? You'd have let them take Ben?"

"No! Of course not."

"But you let them take Paul. Why? Why did you let them take Paul?"

"He was asking for it."

"Was what he said worse than what I said or Ben said? Did he threaten somebody?"

"You're confusing everything."

"You could have acted like the boss and told them to let him go. They would have had to do what you told them. You're the boss. You could have acted like a man and not some wimp. But you couldn't do it, because you didn't have the balls."

Gary felt relieved it had become a question of his manhood. "There's nothing, nothing, I could have done. It's the boss's decision. You have to stay profitable. If you're going to survive, you have to stay profitable."

Carla didn't look impressed.

He thought of what Patrick had said a few nights before. It suddenly made absolute sense. His mind replayed it, closed in on it like an echo chamber until the words sounded almost like genius. "Besides, we want you to do good work. You have to be happy to do good work. It's just something new. You'll get used to it. You'll be happy."

Carla stared at him. She unfolded her arms and put them on her hips. "Did you learn that in college? Did you? Because that's the single fucking dumbest thing I ever heard in my life. It's about the money, you jerk, it's about the money and the fact that Paul is black."

133

She left.

For the rest of the day, Gary moved like a mechanical device, going through motions and repetitions of those motions. He was incapable of anything more.

*   *   *

Just as first period began, Rik received a call to go to the senior class vice principal's office. He felt the eyes of his teacher and the snickering among the class.

"So," Ms. Gorski said, "I received this report from the sophomore vice principal."

"Yes?"

"It's a bit confusing. He seems to want me to discipline you. Tell me if I'm understanding this correctly. You went to see him about a complaint made against a friend of yours?"

"Yes."

"And this friend of yours is a black female sophomore?"

"Yes."

"You did not think the vice principal was helpful?"

"No, he was not."

"And before you left you asked him a question which had to do with how he felt the morning he woke to find he was a bug?"

"Yes."

"Did you come up with that question yourself?"

"No."

Ms. Gorski cocked her head, shrugged, waited to hear more.

"I'd read it. In a short story by Kafka."

She nodded. "Did you know that Mr. Urbanowicz never taught literature?"

"No."

"Aha. Well, that clears things up for me. That will be my report: you approached him concerning an issue; you asked a question which he was unable to help you with; and you left."

"Thank you."

"That's all."

Rik began to turn to leave.

"Oh, something you might be interested in. I visited the house where he was born."

Rik didn't get it at first, thinking the reference was to the sophomore vice principal.

"In Prague."

Rik understood. His eyes widened. He smiled. "Kafka."

"Yes. He died before it happened, of course, but his three sisters were murdered with their families during the Holocaust. Racism is a terrible thing."

"Yes."

"I'm glad you know that."

Rik turned to leave, but stopped.

"Ms. Gorski?"

"Yes, Rik."

"Thank you. I was wondering. Is there anything you can do to help Celisa?"

The vice principal dropped her head. "Not that I can think of right now. I'm sorry."

*   *   *

Annie sipped her coffee and said, "Ummm." She placed her cup on the table. "Well, how did things go when you talked to your kids about seeing the doctor?"

Evelyn became conscious of a question that had been tugging at the edges of her curiosity since the day before. "Annie, who am I talking to when I talk to you?"

Annie spurted coffee as she tried to control her laughter. "Oh, Evelyn, you are something. You're talking to the neighborhood, of course!" She raised her right arm and pointed her index finger at the ceiling. "You know! One for one and all for all!"

"I thought so. Well, you can tell the neighborhood that the doctor had prescribed more than a single medication for Jessa and she had to know which one was for hallucinations and which was for the other thing, which is none of your business. Rik had to be with her so he could confirm they talked about nothing else."

Around mid-sentence, Evelyn realized she was covering for her children's disobedience and lies, then decided that wasn't so bad.

"I see. I see. But they didn't call her?"

"They did. Jessa got the answering machine and said they'd be in after school. They didn't need an actual appointment."

"But..."

"They're kids, Annie. Kids don't always make a lot of sense. I'm surprised Jessa even thought of it. I didn't."

"You know, I see your point. I do see your point."

"Thank Clint for us for bringing them home." Evelyn smiled extra broadly. "He did teach them a valuable lesson!"

"I'm so glad." Annie gazed toward the heavens, then returned her eyes to Evelyn. "So how is your husband doing?"

"Oh, I'm afraid he's having a bad day. He wouldn't explain exactly, but something is going on at his work. I think he has to be unpopular today."

"That's hard. You haven't seen any ghosts?"

"When I do, or my husband does, you'll be the first to know."

Annie smiled. "Thank you. And your children haven't..."

"If they had, I'm sure they would have said something. Well, I'm pretty sure."

Annie finished her thought. "But kids don't always make a lot of sense."

They laughed.

Rik felt a touch on his sleeve as he hurried to class after lunch. The hand belonged to Steve the Godlike.

136

"Hey."

"Hey." The god could blush. "Look, I was thinking..."

Rik read Steve's seriousness.

"I like to hike in the Fells. You ever been there?"

"Never heard of it. What's it called?"

"The Fells. A couple-thousand-acre wooded area not far from here. Lots of trails for hiking. I'd like you to come. I'm going tomorrow morning. Your sister could come, too."

Rik thought about it. "Sure. I'll ask Jessa. She'll probably want to come. I don't know where this place is."

"Don't worry. I'll pick you up." Steve paused. "Is it okay if I pick you up?"

"Yeah."

"I don't want to get you in trouble."

"No trouble."

"So I can pick you up at your house?"

"Oh, no. I forgot. No, don't pick me up there."

"I thought so. Ellen always had to meet me somewhere else, too. Look, you know where Main and Washington meet? That's not far from where you live. I'll pick you up there."

"Sure. Main and Washington."

"You look puzzled."

"Just surprised. How did you know we moved into Ellen's old house?"

"Couldn't think of any other reason you'd be looking for those books. Besides, I talked to Celisa last night and she confirmed it." Steve broke the narrowest of smiles. "Lots of things round here are surprising. It may help if we stick together. We'll talk tomorrow.

"Oh," he said, "Long pants, long-sleeve shirts and insect repellant. There's ticks. And mosquitoes the size of doorknobs."

*   *   *

Evelyn thought she heard a door slam, but she recognized that the sound did not come from one of her doors. She looked around, thinking, perhaps, that something had fallen. She glanced at the TV where the weatherperson was preaching sun, sun, sun. She returned to wiping the top of the stove.

The muffled sound of tiny bare feet made her turn.

Two children—an older girl, perhaps five, and a younger boy—both wearing tattered clothes and shoeless, both black but not "African black," both in the midst of shedding smiles, stood at the door from the hall. They stood stock-still, eyes down.

The little girl snuck a glance at Evelyn's face.

"Go play," she said, waving a hand at them.

They spun and disappeared.

She called Annie to let the neighborhood know.

*   *   *

Charlie wheeled himself into Bonnie Dreier's office. He had an envelope on his lap. He gave it to the doctor.

She looked a question at him.

"A woman brought it. Never saw her before. She said it was important."

Dr. Dreier opened it and read. She grew more and more serious as she finished the message.

"Well. The police were waiting for our young friends when they left after our last meeting. Got a verbal reaming for seeing me. Seems we have to be very careful how we communicate."

*   *   *

"You tried any sketching?"

"No."

"It's been three days."

"I know. I'll draw as soon as I feel well enough. It's coming back, I think."

"It will. I envy you. You know who you are."

138

Jessa worried over Rik with her gaze. "You don't?"

"No idea."

"You never told me that."

"Urbanowicz filed a report on me."

"That jerk!"

"I don't have to worry about it. Ms. Gorski got me off the hook."

"Great!"

"She couldn't do anything to help Celisa."

"Well, she's your vice principal."

"Exactly. We take a job and it makes us smaller. She can help a white male senior but not a black female sophomore. It's like your job suffocates you. I'm trying to understand. Should I be the man Gary wants me to be, the man Mom wants me to be? The man this or that teacher wants me to be? Or should I graduate and enlist, and be the man the military and society want me to be? Are there any other alternatives?"

"Fuck being a man. Be yourself."

Yes, he thought: whoever that is. "That's treason, my lady, and you're a seditious little sister."

"You've told everyone you want to be a poet or writer."

"No, I don't want to be a writer. I want to be me and only me and sit in a little, barely lit room where parents and all sorts of adults are banned and write things that topple battlements and destroy empires."

"Do it."

"There are no pre-approved voices in me that approve of that."

Jessa spoke sharply. "I hate to see you like this, Rik. Look, try writing. Do it."

"I've thought about it."

"Really. Imagine. And what have you thought about it?"

"I'd try, except for two problems."

"Go on."

"I'm scared I'd fail at it and I'm scared I'd succeed."

"That pretty much covers the possible outcomes."

"I...I think I want to write. I do. I don't know how I'd handle it if I wasn't real good at it because I can't think of anything else I want to do. Except read. And if I succeeded, then the heavens would open up and destroy me."

"Shake your fists at the heavens. Write."

"Actually, I have. I've been keeping a notebook for a while. Sentences and things. Notes for stories."

"Good. What's this 'man' thing about, anyway?"

"Got me. Ask the manosaurus. You know the one thing I learned from Meph and Gary?"

"I'm holding my breath."

"Never ask a man a question if the answer is important to you."

Jessa frowned. "Rik, I think we're beginning to grow up."

*   *   *

"I saw one. Two actually. Children. Here, in the kitchen."

"Who?" Gary looked around as if a bit surprised to find himself there.

"Ghosts. I'm talking about ghosts.

"Oh. Nothing happened?"

"No. Gary!" Evelyn was exasperated. "What's wrong with you!"

He kept his eyes lowered. "I'm fine."

"They were children. That's all they were. They weren't scary. I shushed them away and they ran."

"Good."

"They weren't black like Africans. They were half black."

"Half black? So what? What does that even mean?" He looked at her for the first time. She saw his eyes and they frightened her. "Evie, why the hell are you bothering me with this crap?"

"What happened at work today?"

"Nothing. Nothing happened."

He went upstairs.

140

*   *   *

Jessa had discovered early on that sketching was a full-body activity, and her body now signaled its need to hold a pencil in its fingers and draw. This familiar sense of herself arrived like a flash of adrenaline that removed whatever had blocked her nervous system for the past ten days. Sitting at her desk, she took a dozen sheets of scrap paper and, using one of the sharpened drawing pencils she always kept there, tested various approaches to a scene she held in her mind: the blacksmith ghost.

She drew. A miracle of molecules. She'd been freed.

She tried his eyes dozens of times before she began to catch his anger.

After two hours of preliminary work, she retrieved her bound journal. The smith's black skin, which had seemed to radiate feathers of color from within, proved nearly impossible with pencil. Slowly, carefully, frequently changing pencils, she transferred the scene of the muscled, sweating man, naked from the waist up, wielding a Zeus-sized hammer, flames shooting up and two nervous horses behind him, from her mind's eye to the paper. The man's eyes stared directly out, full of anger, fear, confusion, and vulnerability. Close, but not quite right yet. Something was missing.

By one she was exhausted. She would need another evening to finish the sketch, but the basics had fallen into place. She pushed her unopened homework off the bed and onto the floor. Without pulling the covers back, she threw herself down to sleep, a smile on her lips.

The smile dissolved. Who would care about her sketching? Rik. Not her parents. When she talked about drawing they both acted as if the discussion were about some unconnected, distant universe. That left Rik. And herself.

A M E R I C A N   G H O S T S

141

EDWARD J. SANTELLA

CHAPTER SIX
SATURDAY

G ary arrived at work just before six a.m. At nine thirty, he drove downtown. He pulled into a visitor's slot in front of the Paradise Safety and Security Building. For ten minutes he sat listening to a sports talk show, wondering whether he should do what he intended to do. He was frightened as a child.

The Safety and Security Building was a five-story structure housing the Paradise Police, the local Massachusetts State Police, the Massachusetts National Guard and the local office of the Federal Bureau of Investigation. Unknown even to many of the employees who worked for those agencies, the building also contained offices of agencies with names unfamiliar to all but a few people, most of whose employees commuted frequently to the District of Columbia or Virginia.

While Gary sat in his car, he was watched by several people inside the building, three people in D.C., one in Virginia, and several in as many countries who had hacked into the numerous security systems. Since Gary wore his ID as required, his education and work histories, personnel files, criminal and medical records were open books.

When the radio segment ended, Gary got himself out of the car. Without looking around, he walked up the disabled ramp to the front door. It was locked.

A long, slender device which ran from the top to the bottom of the door lit. Five red stars ran up and down its length. After a few seconds the stars disappeared. The screen stated: ID LOCATED. After two more seconds, it read: ID SYNC.

A voice from a tiny speaker beside the door asked, "What do you want with us, Mr. Hollie?"

"I'd like to see a prisoner."

Following a series of clicks that sounded like small bolts being withdrawn, the door slid open. Then it closed behind him.

Two officers ushered Gary through a metplass scanner while two German shepherds eyed him indifferently.

The reception officer sat behind a counter similar to what Gary had seen in banks: a metal divider at chest height, and above that, bulletproof glass to the ceiling. A metal drawer provided a way to exchange small items.

"Yes, Mr. Hollie. What brings you here today?"

"I'd like to see one of the prisoners: Mr. Paul Lasxeau."

"The purpose of this visit?"

"I...he's my employee. Well, not anymore. But we worked together for many years. He's here because he tried to attack...the company lawyer."

"Why would you want to see him if he tried to attack your lawyer?"

Gary's fingers fidgeted with the narrow metal ledge that protruded from beneath the glass. "I suppose...I guess..."

"You seem very nervous, Mr. Hollie."

"Yes. I do. I am." He began speaking rapidly. "I've never done anything like this before. I don't know exactly, I don't have any idea really what to say. I don't know what to expect. I felt I had to come."

"This is not a place where miracles happen, Mr. Hollie."

"Oh, I know that."

"You can visit Prisoner Lasxeau. Fifteen minutes. You will not be able to touch him, give him anything, or take anything from him. Everything you say will be recorded. Your visit will be taped by the security system. Do you understand?"

"Yes. Yes. Thank you."

"One further thing."

"Yes?"

"Prisoner Lasxeau has not been fully cooperative. His physical condition will reflect that behavior."

Gary nodded.

Two officers led Gary down a corridor and onto an elevator. They descended several levels. When the elevator doors opened, Gary followed his escorts down a corridor oddly narrow for such a new and expensive building.

When they reached a small concrete-block room painted a disturbing shade of green, they told him to have a seat on one of the metal folding chairs. Seated, he looked though a double row of jail bars. The rows were about six feet apart.

He waited. The room was chilly and damp. Cameras hung from the walls.

Finally Gary heard the sound of a door he could not see opening and closing.

Paul limped in from the left and awkwardly sat himself opposite Gary in a similar folding chair.

Gary couldn't stop himself. "Paul, what happened?"

Paul had two black eyes, bruises on both cheeks and a lip with a long curve of dried blood. Something was wrong about his nose.

"Nothing," Paul said. "Nothing happened. Why do you ask?"

Gary began to understand. "No reason. Just wondering how you were doing, that's all. I, uh, came to see you."

"Really?" His response was dull. "That's nice."

"I'm sorry about yesterday."

"Me, too."

"I, uh, I'm going to talk to the prosecutor next week. See if we could work something out."

"I'd appreciate that. Not sure it would help. New charges."

Gary didn't know what to say.

"They say I beat up some officers pretty badly." He held his hands out in front of him next to each other, backs toward Gary. In an awkward cadence, and speaking louder, as if he wanted his voice to reach more people, he said, "My life is over, Gary. I have no hope."

Gary said, "I don't understand."

A voice over a loudspeaker he couldn't see said, "That's enough. Prisoner Lasxeau, return immediately to your cell."

As quickly as a scared rabbit, and without a goodbye, Paul rose and limped away.

The officers reappeared and returned Gary to the reception officer.

"Mr. Hollie, I have a few questions for you before you leave."

"Yes, sir."

"Do you swear to answer these questions truthfully under pains and penalties of perjury?"

"Yes, sir."

"At any time while you were in this station, did you see, hear or otherwise sense anything which you believe to be suspicious?"

"No, sir."

"At any time while you were here, did you see, hear or otherwise sense anything which disturbed you?"

"No, sir."

"Is there anything that you saw, heard or otherwise became aware of which you believe should be brought to the attention of supervisory police authorities?"

"No, sir."

"Thank you, Mr. Hollie. Nice seeing you today."

"You, too."

Gary had trouble coordinating his feet down the handicap ramp to his car. He fell into the driver's seat. The vision of Paul sitting there with his hands out, speaking like a mechanical parrot, pulsed and hammered at him. His eyes filled. What had he said? New charges. He'd severely beaten police. His life was over. What did that mean? What...?

Paul's bloody face. The skin on the backs of his hands, unbroken. He hadn't beaten anyone with those hands.

Three voices shouted over each other on the radio. Tomorrow would be Sunday. Games to watch, games to help forget the pain.

In the middle of making up the bed, Evelyn lifted her pillow to fluff and smooth. She stopped. On the bedsheet where the pillow had been seconds before, on the bed where she'd lain her head the night before, she saw an object.

This time she recognized it right away. She eased the blade from the scabbard. It wasn't a twin of the first dagger. More a cousin.

She felt a strong sense that the dagger had been given her for a reason. She wanted to drop it, shake it from her hand, but she couldn't. Her fingers had closed on it too tightly.

*   *   *

Steve drove while Rik rode shotgun, his head turned toward the window as he wondered how to relate to death. How to relate to someone who'd suffered the death of a friend or lover? How to relate when that death had been a suicide? How would he feel if he'd loved someone, had sex with her, and then she had killed herself? Something moved in his stomach. His throat constricted. He wanted to fold up inside himself. Hints of the full horror. Yes, it was both full of awe and awful that he could, he might, be able to find words to describe such a thing, at least partly.

Jessa sat alone in the back seat, listening to the infrequent conversation up front and watching houses go by.

Steve didn't talk much as he drove, only speaking to point out landmarks for Rik and Jessa's benefit. The houses gave way to woods on both sides, though they could still catch glimpses of the highway here and there through the trees.

Eventually, Steve pulled off the road and parked the car at a small roadside cut beside two other cars. They slipped backpacks on, took sips from their water bottles, sprayed themselves with bug repellant and began to follow the trail. Within the first half mile of their walk they exchanged greetings with two dog-

147

walkers coming in the opposite direction. After that, Steve led them off on a narrower and more difficult trail.

Every several steps Steve stopped to point out a species of tree or shrub. Twice he pointed out tracks: an eastern coyote, he said, and a fisher cat, whatever, Rik thought, that was. They glimpsed a pair of wild turkeys and an electric-green garden snake slithered out of their path. But Steve grew quiet, and the walkers eventually settled into a silence only sporadically interrupted. The path climbed and fell over ragged outcrops of rock that required a good deal of concentration to climb and even more to descend.

Their path eventually led to the top of a hill, where the rock, dotted by sandy patches of soil from which impoverished weeds grew, lay open to the sky. A stone tower stood at the edge of the hill, providing a clear view of the Boston skyline. The tower entrance had been long blocked off with an iron gate. Steve squatted and showed them striations left by glaciers. While Rik and Jessa explored the area a bit, Steve sat with his back against the tower.

A few minutes later, the brother and sister joined him. "Thanks for bringing us up here."

Steve didn't speak for a bit. "We used to hike the Fells a lot. She's the one who taught me to identify the trees and stuff. Her mom was a botanist. They moved here because her mom got a teaching position. Last winter, that time it snowed, we came up and snowshoed."

Jessa asked, "It must be sad, I mean, coming back like this?" Steve nodded.

"Why?" asked Rik. "Then why did you bring us here?"

"So you'd know...that this was her place, the place she showed me, the place she loved. And so we could talk.

"I'm being selfish. I know that. I have to know. Something inside me absolutely needs to know. Every morning I get up I get lost because nothing is in the same place it was last year. It's the same place but it's not the same place. Does that make any sense?"

Rik said, "Of course." He tried, for a few seconds, to live in Steve's perspective.

Steve briefly formed a frown. "A thing that bothered me a little is Ellen never let me pick her up at her house. It wasn't just me. She never invited anyone over. So I wasn't surprised when you guys didn't want me to pick you up at your house.

"Conclusion: there's something about the house the owners don't want other people to see. Is that fair?"

Rik began, "I see how you might think that, but..." He had no explanation to follow the "but."

Jessa said, "No comment. Steve, we know how you feel..."

"No, you don't! You do not know how I feel. You don't know what it's like for me to wonder if I did something to cause Ellen to... to kill herself, or if I could have done something to prevent it.

"But there's something else I don't know. I don't know how you can live in the same house she did—keep people away from that house like she did, show the same kinds of evasiveness and nervousness; see the same psychiatrist she saw... How could you know that she killed herself, and somehow expect that you living there and doing the same things she did is going to end with a different result?"

Rik let his eyes close for few seconds. "I hadn't thought of that." Steve was right. They hadn't dreamed either of them would follow Ellen's path. "I don't think we think of our situation like that."

"You should."

Jessa said, "Steve, we, I mean, neither of us are close to doing anything like that. And we've got each other."

"Ellen wasn't close to killing herself until she did. And she had me. Nothing helped."

Rik and Jessa sat silently.

"Steve, wait." This was Jessa. "We've repeated a lot of the things in Ellen's life, and yet neither of us feels a bit suicidal. What is

149

different in our situation from hers? What did she do that we haven't?"

Rik answered. "She read the history books, the ones about Paradise."

"Steve? Is that it? Or is there something else?"

"I need to think, to remember, try to remember everything. Even what doesn't seem to matter."

Rik added, "And we need to discover the history of Paradise."

Jessa said, "We'll be cautious. The three of us together. We'll have each other's backs."

Steve dropped his head. His body shook the slightest bit and they saw that he was crying.

Rik put a hand on the boy's back and moved it awkwardly. Steve drew in a deep breath to control his sobbing, but all it did was make him sneeze. Rik left his hand where it was.

Jessa had to look away. Of course, she was all for men showing their feelings. She had seen Rik cry many times. Still, watching a six-foot-something, blond-haired, blue-eyed, movie-star-looking he-man sob seemed to undermine the structure of the universe. At least it was over love.

Slowly, Steve crawled back under the cover of composure.

"I suppose she didn't love me after all. She said she did, but people say that all the time. Right?"

Jessa said, "I'm sure Ellen loved you."

"Really? Then why did she kill herself?"

"None of us can answer that," said Rik. "Not now. But we could think about why the books on Paradise's history have disappeared. It's hard to think of this as a coincidence. Someone must know something."

Steve spoke through his tears. "So there is a connection between..." He stopped because he didn't know which things might connect.

"There might be a connection," said Rik. Things had to make sense, he believed, even if the sense was irrational.

Jessa said, "We could help you there, tracking down who took the books and what it is they're trying to hide."

"We could call the area college history departments," Rik suggested. "We could divide them up and each call three or four. Get some names."

Steve, still red-eyed, nodded. "Okay. Let's do it."

*   *   *

"I think you'd like this book. You should read it."

Jessa looked up. "Fahrenheit 451?"

"Yeah. This fireman, whose job it is to burn books, has stolen some and now everyone is after him.

"Listen to what Bradbury wrote. 'We need not to be let alone. We need to be really bothered once in a while. How long is it since you were really bothered? About something important, about something real?'"

"Maybe that's why the ghosts are here. To bother us." Jessa paused, then said, "I've got a crazy idea. I'm going to call Celisa."

"What for?"

"She told me something about her mother's family. Said they'd lived around here a long time. Maybe her mother knows something about Paradise's history."

"Worth a try."

"Or do you want to call her?"

"Why me? She's your friend."

Jessa stared at him in silence, the slightest bit of a smirk on her face.

"What?"

"Men are so...oblivious."

"Wow. Big word for a sophomore."

She tossed her phone to him. "Call her."

"Alright. No big deal."

Celisa answered. "Hey, Jessa. What's up?"

"This is Rik. Jessa's too busy giving me orders to call you."

151

"Oh! Hi!"

"Yeah, how you doing?" Rik thought he should ask.

"Good. Good. You?"

"Okay. Uh, we have a question. We are, uh, trying to find out about the history of Paradise? Way back, I mean. Jessa said your family has been around here a while. Do you know anybody who might know about Paradise's history?" He was certain he'd used a laughable number of words getting the question out.

"I don't, but let me ask my mom. She grew up in Malden and she's still friends with one of her history teachers. I'll let you know."

"Great. That could be a big help."

Pause.

"Is that all you're calling about?"

Panic swept through Rik. "Yeah, uh, I think so. I mean, it's been good talking to you though. Maybe we could get together some time, though."

"That would be great." Celisa paused, waiting for Rik to fill the void with a suggested date and time. "Well, I'll get back."

"Thanks."

He tossed the phone back to Jessa.

"My brother, the mover."

"Shut up."

Jessa stared at him, as if she'd lost a child.

"Why are you looking at me like that?"

She glanced away. "Didn't mean anything."

"Really? You wanted me to call her, I did, and then I thought you were frightened, then I thought you might murder me."

"I've always wanted to do that."

"Come on, Jessa, what's wrong?"

She shrugged her shoulders, as if to say, "nothing." "You're going to leave some day, that's all."

"What do you mean? Why am I going to leave?"

"You're going to find some girl and fall in love and leave me."

Rik paused to pull his thoughts together. "Yes. Maybe. But you'll find a guy and leave home, too."

"No, I won't."

"Jessa, you're a great person and good-looking woman, not that I'm supposed to have noticed, but you are. Guys will line up..." Her voice snapped like a whip. "They do already, Rik. I've been asked out a dozen times since freshman year. I can't. I can't do it. I don't like men."

Rik blinked. "You mean you like women?"

"No! I mean, I like women but I'm not attracted to them."

"So, you're attracted to men?"

"Yes. But I don't like them. I fear them, I'm afraid of what they want to do to me. I don't want them to get close. When some kid asks me to do something or go somewhere, and he leans in close, almost as if he's about to kiss me, all I feel is panic. I don't want my lips to touch his lips, or my hands his hands, and the whole idea of my body touching his, of having sex, makes me want to throw up, and a couple of times when guys as asked me out I almost did throw up. I want to run so fast and so far!"

"Jessa, come on, calm down. Is this because of the Meph?"

She nodded. "What the hell else could it be? So is my fucking depression."

Rik closed his eyes. The seconds of silence added up.

For perhaps the first time in his life, Rik stuttered. "I-I w-wish he'd done that to m-me, n-not you."

She turned on him, fury in her eyes. "You do not wish that!" She bit off her words. "You do not wish that at all. There is no way in fucking hell you wish that. You don't know what it's like. You have no idea. You have no fucking idea."

Rik looked away. She was right. He had no idea. He didn't want to know.

"I'm sorry." This time he knew why.

Their mother's voice came from downstairs. "Hey, you two, stop arguing!"

154

CHAPTER SEVEN
SUNDAY

Gary had picked through the refrigerator, made himself a sandwich and was halfway through it when the doorbell rang.

"Shit. I'll get it."

No one else was in the kitchen or even on the first floor.

Clint, in civvies, said, "Gary. Come out on the steps. We've got a few things to discuss."

Gary closed the door behind him. He felt small standing beside Clint. "What's up?"

"I got the word that you were down at the station yesterday to see the prisoner who tried to kill you. There's..."

"Paul?" Gary blurted. "He didn't try to kill me!"

"Gary, calm down. Listen, the police have ways of getting more information than you'll ever know. Believe us, if we say he was trying to kill you, he was trying to kill you. He did a pretty good job beating up two of our officers, too. One is out indefinitely. Okay? You calm? Because there's even worse news.

"He hanged himself last night. He's dead."

Gary's frightened eyes looked into Clint's. "What? What did you say?"

"I said that Paul's dead. He hanged himself."

"Paul's dead?"

"Yeah, look, I'm sorry, but these things happen. All the time. Guys get in trouble, they realize it's over for them, they take things into their own hands. Happens all the time. You wouldn't believe how often this happens. It isn't your fault."

"No, it isn't...my fault." Gary felt it wasn't and it was.

"Look, the past is over. All that matters is the present. What is, is. We've got to move forward together. Right?"

Gary nodded.

"Heh, I put in a good word for you down at the station, okay?" Clint's arm was over Gary's shoulders. "I don't forget my neighbors. Right?"

"Right."

"Hey, cheer up." Clint slapped Gary's back. "The game's almost on."

*   *   *

Evelyn noticed Gary standing still and stiff in the living room. "Gary? Are you alright?"

Gary turned away. He walked into the kitchen and opened the cabinet where they kept the alcohol. He poured and drank three glasses of whiskey in thirty seconds. His mouth and throat burned. He coughed like he was choking. He became vaguely aware that Evelyn was beside him, saying something. He should have used ice, he thought. Ice would have helped. Cold, clear ice.

*   *   *

Rik pulled away the towel he'd used to dry his face and saw himself in the bathroom mirror. He'd just brushed his teeth and washed his face before going to bed. He stared at the revealed face. The face he saw was somber, defensive, the face of an aging young man who kept one foot braced behind the other to steady himself against whatever was next to hit him. His eyes were half dead, shorn of hope, long on desperation.

And he was one of the luckier people in the world.

He hung the towel and returned to his room. For half a minute he stared at the binding of Lord of the Rings. He took it off the shelf, opened it and spread the photographs. This time he wasn't looking at his father. He looked at himself. And Jessa. Back through time.

Open, wide-eyed faces with fearless smiles. Freely laughing. Awake. Living.

He called Jessa. She answered. "What?"

"Where are you?"

"In the kitchen stealing food."

"Look. This is important. Come upstairs. Look at yourself in the mirror then come in here."

"You know how to hurt a girl, don't you?"

"I'm serious."

"Sure. Anything for my big idiot brother."

A minute later came the single knock.

"Alright. I'm depressed."

"Look at these."

She leaned over. "Geez. Hey, you never told me you had pictures of Dad. You scum."

"I stole them from Mom. I look at them every once in a while when I don't know what to do. But look at us. In the pictures. Then look at us right now, look at us. And see how we look now."

Jessa studied each picture individually, taking her time. She couldn't avoid studying their father, but she did eventually get herself to focus on herself and Rik.

"We were happier. No, it's more than that. We were different then. You think we were happier with him, before Meph and Gary got to us?"

"Do you know anyone our age, anyone in our old school or at Paradise, who faces the world like we did then?"

Her first reaction was, of course not. She thought. "There was Regina, that Down's girl, in the class between us."

"And she was the only one."

"She saw a different universe than we did." Jessa looked again at the pictures, one by one. She closed her eyes every few seconds to soften the hurt. "Remember when Mom sent us to Sunday School?"

"Only the boredom."

"Well, the only thing I remember from that whole deal was something Jesus said about becoming like children. You wouldn't know the kingdom of heaven unless you became like children. I thought that was stupid. I just wanted to grow up and be an adult. Maybe the guy was on to something."

They felt a presence.

They looked up.

An elderly black woman with dark eyes sat in a rocker watching them. She'd wrapped herself in blankets and only her face was visible. The three looked at each other as if they were passengers on two trains running in opposite directions and this would be the only glimpse of each other they'd ever get. Then she was gone.

*　　　*　　　*

Evelyn made certain her family was busy upstairs, then, carrying a small plastic bag, the kind a store would give you for a half dozen small purchases, she sneaked down to the kitchen.

At the table, she laid out the two daggers, a couple of soft cloths and two jars of cleaning and restoring products, one for leather and the second for metal.

She went to work.

*　　　*　　　*

Jessa studied her sketch of the ghost she'd first seen. She'd finished it. She knew it was done by staring into those eyes, the eyes that told her he knew her better than she did.

CHAPTER EIGHT
Monday

G ary lacked the guts to tell the drivers about Paul. They'd find out soon enough. He was sure they'd blame him. When the drivers had driven off for their deliveries, he returned to his office, told the office manager he wasn't to be disturbed and closed the door.

He sat at his desk. Ten minutes passed before he opened the lower drawer and took out two 1.75-liter bottles of whiskey. Some store would later find out it'd been charged for a full case it didn't receive. They would blame the driver.

Gary poured his first glass.

He sniffed it.

He drank it.

He proceeded.

*   *   *

"Haluuuuuu-o!"

Evelyn flushed the toilet, not because it needed to be flushed, but because she happened to be in the bathroom and the flush best expressed her emotional response to Annie's appearance.

"Ev-e-lyn!"

"Come in, Annie. I'll be down in a moment."

When she came downstairs to the kitchen, she found Annie pouring herself a cup of coffee and cutting a piece of the blueberry cake Evelyn had made the day before, which no one had eaten. Apparently, she'd lost her concern about her weight.

Her mouth full, Annie greeted Evelyn with an "Ummph."

"Good morning, Annie. Since you're making yourself at home, pour me a cup and cut me a piece while you're there, will you?" Evelyn plumped herself down on a chair. "My family won't eat my cooking, so I will."

"Most," Annie swallowed a bit of the cake, "happy to."

Evelyn thanked her when she brought the coffee and snack.
"So," Annie asked, "what do you think?"

"About living with ghosts? Just two little kids. Scared as hell of me though."

"I bet. But you know, they grow up and then we have to watch them very carefully. Oh, but I'm so glad for you! Evelyn, now you're one of us!"

Evelyn didn't find that encouraging.

"Oh," Annie said with a swish of her hand, "you'll see more soon enough, I'm sure." Though she held a coffee cup to her mouth, her eyebrows went up, as did an index finger. "I almost forgot to tell you what happened yesterday." She stopped. "Today's Monday, right? So, yes, it was yesterday. Sandy, poor Sandy, he's got this lawnmower that he likes to ride around on? It's like his favorite thing in the world, next to, well, you know what. Well, he took Sunday afternoon off to mow his lawn, but wouldn't you know it? Well, he keeps the mower machine of his in this toolshed out in his backyard. And he couldn't get the mower out all day! Would you believe it? And you know why? Because three of those awful ghosts were out there doing something. They just wouldn't go away! Like they were doing work or something. He said they were bending and straightening, bending and straightening all day. They didn't even take a break so Sandy could get his mower! What an awful day he had!"

Evelyn did not even try to sound sympathetic. "That's too bad." Gary would have slipped the ghosts twenty each to stay out there.

"You won't believe what I had to do to help poor Sandy deal with his frustration."

Evelyn's radar detected incoming. "I don't want to know."

"I..."

"Really, I don't want to know!"

"I was only going to say that I think we have to stand by our men in difficult times. Don't you agree?"

160

Evelyn managed to say, "Yes. I agree."

Annie sipped her coffee while watching Evelyn's face. "What's wrong, Evie? Come on, baby, tell mama."

"Nothing."

"Come on, Evelyn. We're friends. Tell me."

"Something upset him."

"Him? Who him?"

"My husband."

"How do you know?"

Evelyn glanced at Annie. "You have to know him. He's a sports addict. He watches everything that's a sport. He didn't watch any of the games yesterday. He went upstairs and stayed there. Didn't come down for supper."

Annie bit her tongue for two seconds. "Well, I bet I know." Very levelly, she said again, "I bet I know."

"You know?" Evelyn wanted to ask who Annie was fucking and in what position and exactly how long it took and did she orgasm and would she share the video of it at the time she learned this bit of information about her husband, but she held back. Extreme dislike slid ever faster and faster down the slippery slope toward outright disgust.

"One of your husband's employees, well, no, they're not employees anymore, one of your husband's whatevers tried to kill him on Friday."

"What?"

Annie waved Evelyn back into her seat. "No, Gary was never in any real danger because the police were there. Well, this attempted murderer offed himself in the jail." She cocked her head to one side and used a hand to indicate a noose. "Gary seemed very upset when Clint gave him the news. I suppose he wanted to bring him to trial to see him get his just desserts. I can understand. Not to mention, he's probably not recovered from the shock of, you know, finding out black ghost-men are lurking around his woman. That can be very disturbing." She giggled.

Evelyn was shocked, by the arrest, by the suicide, and by the fact that Gary had kept this all to himself.

"Oh, come on, Evie, it can't be that bad. He'll cope. He's a strong guy. He can handle it."

Evelyn wondered how Annie might know that. "Maybe you're right."

*   *   *

At 1:10 p.m. Evelyn received the call. She phoned the school. The principal pulled Jessa and Rik out of class and provided transportation to the hospital.

*   *   *

The doctor said, "Alcohol poisoning. See it all the time in high-school- and college-age kids. He passed out at work. How long has he had an alcohol problem?"

Evelyn stared at the doctor. Jessa and Rik stood behind her. "Today?"

The doctor frowned. "Today what?"

"His drinking problem. It began today."

"How often does he drink?"

"Every day. Something, anyway. Wine or whiskey."

"Has he gone on a binge like this before?"

Evelyn shook her head no.

The doctor visualized the word "denial" written across her forehead in capital letters: bold, underlined and in italics.

He closed the chart in his hands and said, "Follow me."

*   *   *

"If I was stronger, I'd be able to do this. I'm not strong enough. I'm not...enough."

Gary couldn't believe what he'd said.

"Of course I'm strong enough. It's nothing. I feel better already."

162

Gary was trying to sit up to greet his family. The clock on the hospital room wall showed past two thirty.

Jessa said, "It'll be okay, Dad." She bent over the bed and hugged him. She smelled the whiskey.

"How do you feel, Mr. Hollie?"

He turned his head. A nurse came into his view.

"Great," he said.

"That's pretty good, considering what you've gone through. You looked like a blue baby when they brought you in and you had hypothermia. Your signs and tests show you've had a bad time, but you're most likely going to pull through."

Gary felt almost disappointed to hear that. Being alive didn't mean much when you were incapable of doing your job.

*   *   *

Gordie Sands was the kind of man Clint respected even if he couldn't bring himself to like him. Gordie got things done. Gordie sipped the drink his woman had brought him and thought.

"So, you want to do this on Friday. That should work."

"Let me tell you, the neighborhood's ready. And that's when this shaman can make it."

Gordie frowned. "Don't know why you've got to complicate matters with some clown."

"I want the neighbors to know I did my best to get them out of this predicament without having to move."

Gordie shook his head. "Fucking witch doctors. I had to deal with them in the Amazon. You want to build something and all they can say is 'sacred land.' Fine, so what's the going rate on Amazonian sacred land?"

The woman came back with a tray of snacks. Gordie's taste ran to the slutty side of tall, thin redheads with British accents.

"I've got the church basement for the meeting."

163

Gordie laughed, then leaned forward over the food. "You gotta try these. She makes them herself. Something unbelievable."

Clint put down his drink. He knew when to be polite. He took a gold-edged plate, speared a couple of what looked to be something a bottom-feeding fish would think was a delicacy, and returned to his seat.

The woman sat opposite Clint. He could almost see her panties. He didn't hide where he looked. He thought she smirked at him, as if to say, "Too good for you."

Clint ate one of the things.

"Ain't they great? Evangeline here, she's a genius."

"You're right." He didn't gag on the whore's name. "They're great. So we're on?"

"Right. I'll have the attorneys draw the papers tomorrow. The bank should cut all the checks within twenty-four hours of my request. I'll even sign the paperwork ahead of time. It's a go for Friday."

Clint breathed a sigh of content.

Evelyn, Rik and Jessa arrived home close to nine in the evening. Evelyn poured herself a glass of wine, said good night, and went upstairs to their bedroom.

Rik and Jessa got snacks and drinks and carried everything up to Rik's bedroom.

Before she began to eat, Jessa checked her phone.

"Celisa called. Must have been while we were at the hospital." She put the phone on speaker and played the message.

"Hey, guys, why'd you leave school so early? I hope everything's alright. I wanted to tell you my mom does know someone you might want to talk to. She had a history teacher she really liked. They're still in touch. She's been over for dinner a bunch of times. I kind of like her. Mom asked if she could come over for dinner to meet you guys. She's actually coming but it has to be tomorrow, Tuesday. It's the only day she could come this week. Mom says you're both invited. I know that's short notice, but let me know if you can come. Otherwise, you can meet her later."

Jessa said, "We took all these precautions about communicating with Steve and Dr. Dreier and forgot about Celisa. I hope our favorite neighbor isn't checking our phone calls."

"Point. I hadn't thought about that. What do you think about tomorrow?"

"Let's do it."

"What about Dad?"

"We can see him after school. We can say we're meeting with a study group."

Rik added, "And if Mom needs the car, we could walk to Celisa's."

"Call her."

"Me? She's your friend."

"You."

"Give me your phone."

She slid it over to him. "Put her number on your phone, will ya?"

*   *   *

Jessa sat with her red sketchbook open at the page she'd begun to draw the girl they'd seen, the girl who'd been kidnapped and chained.

She placed pencil to paper and the lines came as if they'd existed from the beginning, when the page had seemed blank. That's how Jessa knew she was getting the sketch right: when the lines appeared not to have needed her to draw them.

She thought about letting Dr. Dreier know the medication switch had worked.

Once, twice she used a gentle eraser, but, carefully, she drew her ghost out of the paper.

When she understood she was finished for the night, she raised her head and pulled back. The girl strained against the chains and the man holding her. Her eyes held the wildness of a tigress. The man snarled. They lived, breathed, fought on the page. Though it still needed a bit of finishing, she felt satisfied.

She looked at the clock. Three-fifteen. She already felt more relaxed than had she slept a whole night.

CHAPTER NINE
TUESDAY

The nurse's aide had just laid the breakfast tray over Gary's lap when the phone rang. The aide frowned. "It's probably my wife. Can you hand it to me, please."

"Hello."

"Gary, how are you doing?"

"Hi, Art."

"You've got us worried about you. What's going on?"

"I don't know exactly. I had some kind of episode at the office yesterday. Passed out, so they brought me here."

"Scary, I bet. When are they going to let you go?"

"They want to do some tests. Tomorrow, maybe the day after. I'm guessing."

"Whoa. Well, I'm not telling you to leave before you feel well and the doctors say you're okay, but we need you at work. You're my key man, the one guy we can't do without. You get what I'm saying?"

"Yeah. Thanks for noticing. Look, I'll be back day after tomorrow."

"Yeah, that's fine. I mean, I have to think about the company, you know, Gary? If the company goes then everyone loses. Maybe I should start a search for your replacement, just in case, you know? This is the second time you've been out in just the last two weeks. I'm not talking about getting rid of you because I need you to train your replacement..."

"Art, I'll be in as soon as I can."

"When is that, Gary?"

Gary knew in his bones that Art could fire him. He knew that if Art asked him to stay long enough to train his replacement, he would. Art could outsource his job as well as the drivers'. Art could do whatever he wanted. It was his business.

"Today."

"Great. I'm real happy to hear that." Art hung up.

You did your job. Whatever the boss told you, you did it. If you didn't, they cut you. Without your job you were lost and alone. You couldn't support your family. That was the one thing he had to do, Gary knew. He knew it in his brain, in his stomach, in his balls. He had to support his family, even if they didn't appreciate what he had to go through. Someday, he hoped, they'd understand. Someday they'd appreciate him. He wasn't a quitter. He was too tough for that. Too tough.

Gary lifted the tray away and swung his legs over the edge of the bed. Getting the needles out of his arm wasn't as hard or painful as he'd feared. He quickly found his clothes in the bedside stand. By the time the nurse's aide returned, he'd showered, dressed and left.

*   *   *

Evelyn, Rik and Jessa arrived at the ward a few minutes before ten to learn Gary had discharged himself against medical advice.

Evelyn called him on her cell.

"Gary, where the fuck are you, you bastard?"

"I'm at work. Where I'm supposed to be."

"No, damn it. You're supposed to be in the hospital. Which is where we are looking for you. How can you do this to us?"

"Evelyn, you don't know what the world's like. You think..."

"I don't care what the world's like. I care what you're like and I don't know who you even are!"

She threw the phone the length of the ward. Had it been a baseball, it would have beaten the runner home.

Doctors, nurses and aides turned to watch her.

*   *   *

Gary called Art from the office number as soon as he arrived at work and left the message that he had returned to work.

He decided he could not leave the phone in case Art called back.

Work had piled up on his desk. Miriam, the office manager, brought him checks and letters to be signed.

He sat, took a breath and opened the top file. He frowned, blinked and stared, unable to make sense of the papers in front of him. He saw the papers and knew he had seen similar papers before, but holding the meaning of words in his mind long enough to complete reading a sentence proved impossible. The meaning and intent of any document lay beyond his comprehension.

He sat. Too much rattling around in his head: Paul, ghosts, and a wife who was angry because he went to work.

After a while, he felt hungry.

He called Miriam and asked her to run out for his lunch.

"It's only ten thirty."

"Is it? I guess I had breakfast early."

He tried to remember when he'd had breakfast, picturing himself at home at the kitchen table. Then he realized he hadn't been home, and that he'd left the hospital before eating.

When Miriam returned, he ate, his mind full of impenetrable clouds.

Finished, he tossed the wrappings in the trash and called Miriam again. He asked her to come in.

With her standing beside him, he said, "I guess I'm out of sorts today. Can you tell me what I'm supposed to do here?"

He recognized some of the papers after she explained them to him.

*   *   *

Evelyn answered the phone.

"Mrs. Hollie?"

"Yes."

"This is Dr. Gregoire. Your husband's treating physician ran several cardiac tests on him before he signed himself out. He asked me to review the test results. I'm a cardiologist. It's important that your husband come see me."

"Why? What's wrong?"

"Some of his test results require follow-up work."

"Alright. I'll have him call."

She stood by the phone.

*　　　　*　　　　*

Evelyn sat at the table in her new kitchen staring at the grounds in the bottom of her coffee cup. She tried to remember if people claimed to be able to read coffee grounds or tea leaves or both and wondered what the ones in her cup might have to say. Nothing in her life made sense and she would have found it comforting if grounds or leaves or anything else did.

She wasn't crying properly, but when she looked up the water in her eyes blurred her sight. Three people stood in front of her. She startled.

"Evelyn, I'm sorry. The door was open. I called your name but you didn't answer. I thought maybe you'd left the door open when you went out, or someone was in here."

"Hi, Annie."

"You don't look good, Evelyn. These are my daughters: Sophia and her younger sister Issa. Can I get you something?"

Evelyn managed to wave and greet the children. For all her distress, she did register their blank stares. They looked like those failed plastic surgery patients who lost the ability to move their facial muscles. "Would you like some lemonade?"

Annie answered, "They would."

"Annie, what would you like?"

"Tea, if you have some?"

"Sure."

Evelyn put the water on and set the glasses of lemonade in front of the children.

Sophia asked, "Are you sad because of Ellen?"

Evelyn looked at Annie. "Who's Ellen?"

"Oh, she used to live here. She was friends with these two."

To the children, Evelyn said, "I didn't know her."

She poured out two cups of tea and joined the others at the table.

Annie asked again, "So what's wrong?"

"Gary was in the hospital. He, uh, they said he passed out at work. Then he signed himself out this morning and went to work. The doctor wants to see him. He won't take care of himself."

"Is he feeling better?"

"How would I know?" She knew immediately she'd spoken too loudly and too angrily. "Sorry. I'm upset. He never called. He just went to work. I took the kids to the hospital and he had gone. I was never so embarrassed."

Sophia asked, "Is that why you're sad?"

"Yes, dear." That and having a daughter who's depressed, a son who wants to write poetry and a house that is supposedly haunted. "Don't you want your lemonade?"

Two small heads shook no.

"I want Ellen," said Issa.

Annie tried to shush her.

Evelyn said, "She doesn't live here anymore."

Sophie said, "She's in hell."

Annie put down her cup. "Okay, girls. We're going. You're upsetting Mrs. Hollie, and she's already upset enough."

Sophie said, "Well, Mom, Sister Marie said people who kill themselves go to hell."

"Come on, say goodbye to Mrs. Hollie."

*　　　*　　　*

Jessa, centered on her anger at her father for acting like a teenager, had trouble focusing during their walk to Celisa's house. When her emotions got stirred together, she found it beyond her means to unstir them.

Rik had decided they would walk to Celisa's and leave the car for their mother, just in case. Rik felt guilty leaving her alone after the call from the doctor.

After fifteen minutes they arrived at Celisa's.

Celisa's house and property stood on one of the first notable hills north of the Mystic. The house looked as if it had been repaired, updated and painted ten years before and since then regularly swept and tidied. Inside, the walls appeared sturdy, the windows and doorways framed with carved wood, the wood floors polished. The furniture and upholstery were uniformly colorful and worn to the edge of threadbare. Lightly colored, framed sketches hung wherever space permitted.

More than from its structure or contents, the feel of the house rose from the intensity of the occupants.

Celisa greeted the brother and sister at the door. They brightened as soon as they saw her.

"Mom! Rik and Jessa are here." She stepped back. "Come in!"

Celisa's mother greeted her guests warmly. She wore an early-fall dress and copper jewelry that complemented her midsized figure and mahogany skin. She carried herself with an earned and humble dignity. In her early forties, she'd accumulated enough life experiences with whites to know that some hated her and her family to the point of doing them bodily injury because of their race, and that some others, who thought of themselves as well-meaning, could do as much damage as the racists. She worried that her less-experienced daughter might be too appreciative of the wrong kind of white person. The best-intentioned white teen would likely have no idea what he was getting into by showing affection for a black girl.

Jessa noticed that Celisa stood beside Rik, her eyes wide and focused on her mother as she introduced them. Celisa practically bled, "Mom, what do you think of him?" But Jessa knew Rik. The turtle had already begun to retreat beneath his shell. Too many people; too much small talk. Jessa figured at some point she'd have to coax him out or he'd go through the whole evening silent. Meanwhile, she marveled at Celisa's mother's clothes.

Celisa's mother, Sona, introduced the children to Christine Kinney. "Christine taught me history in high school. You taught there, was it...?"

"Twenty-three years."

"And before that, she was a nun working in Central America." Ms. Kinney narrowed her sharp, bright eyes and shook each of their hands deliberately. Her parchment complexion lent her an air of fragility, but her alertness and bearing required respect.

Celisa asked, "How's your dad doing?"

After the high schoolers had a brief discussion to bring everyone up to date, Celisa's mother said, "Well, dinner is ready. Let's sit down and enjoy."

The women did their best to include the young people in the conversation, and with Jessa and Celisa they earned some success. But however many times the talk circled the table, it never drew Rik in. He sat, eyes always following whoever was speaking. He showed more interest in the talk than the food.

Sona had kept at least one eye on the boy at all times, reading his facial reactions to the conversation. This mound of silence was her only daughter's first love interest. Time, she thought, to attack. "So, Rik, Celisa tells me that you are a very good listener but you don't talk much."

Jessa nearly gagged laughing. She dropped her fork and covered her face with both hands.

Celisa looked sideways at her mother in horror.

Rik blushed.

Ms. Kinney said, "There's a lot to be said for introverts."

"I'm sorry. Besides," said Celisa's mother, "we're not playing fair. We've got you outnumbered four to one." She held a wineglass in her hand. "Perhaps this will help. Rik, what is it about Paradise's history that you're interested in?"

Rik immediately focused. "Jessa and I just moved in. We're interested particularly in the history of the part of the city that we live in."

Ms. Kinney asked, "Where is that?"

"Not far from here. Toward the river."

Jessa added, "Antigua Avenue."

Ms. Kinney's eyebrows elevated. "Interesting. I mean, interesting place and interesting that you're interested in it. Is there something that led to your asking?"

Rik took in a breath. "Yes."

"That may be the most pregnant 'yes' I've heard in my life!" Ms. Kinney frowned. "Fair enough. Well, have you tried the library?"

"Yes."

"And?"

"All the books on Paradise's history are missing. In both the school and main libraries."

Silence followed.

Sona put her wineglass on the table and left her fork and knife on the plate. She became all attention.

Ms. Kinney said, "That's strange. Why would...?" She gave a split-second glance at Sona.

Jessa decided not to repeat the mistake she'd made with Dr. Dreier. "I...we...Rik and I...don't want to mislead you. There's a problem that we can't explain because our parents made us promise not to tell anyone about it. We don't want to break our promise. It's not just a family problem, in case that's what you were thinking.

174

"I'm afraid to say much more. But understanding Paradise's history may help us understand the problem. Does that make sense to you?"

Sona said, "Some. And thank you for being up-front with us about your promise. Of course we won't ask you to break a promise to your parents." She thought carefully about her next words. "If this is the type of problem in which someone may be in danger, have you thought about notifying the police?"

Rik spoke. "No. It's not the type of thing where we'd call the police." Once again, the truth was a lie.

Sona looked relieved. "Well, then, perhaps our history teacher can help you. Since she didn't flunk me when I was in her class, we've remained friends."

"Sona, you were never in danger of flunking anything." Ms. Kinney turned toward Jessa and asked, "Where would you like me to start?"

Jessa said, "Well, we don't really know...so probably from the start."

Rik interjected, "I think we mean from when Paradise was first settled by Europeans."

Ms. Kinney nodded. "I'll try to provide a quick summary. Stop me anytime you have a question.

"Paradise is one of the places on this continent where the history of Europeans goes back to the beginning of European settlement in North America.

"In 1628, a group of financially fortunate men in London founded the Massachusetts Bay Company. Let's call that the MBC. They were Puritans, a Protestant sect very out of favor with the king. The plan was for the Puritans to immigrate to the New World.

"One of those men was John Winthrop. He's important for a number of reasons, which we will get to. He eventually was elected governor of the MBC.

"Two years later—this is 1630 now—Mr. Winthrop commanded a fleet of four ships that sailed from England for Salem, just up the coast here.

"On the way over Winthrop gave a very important sermon in which he wrote that they should found the City on the Hill. That was a biblical reference to a city dedicated to God that would lead, at least by example, the world. This idea later came to be called American Exceptionalism, the idea that we were different from and better than all other nations, that we were God's new chosen people."

Ms. Kinney reached for her flex, tapped a few times, then resumed.

"More telling was Winthrop's opening to his sermon. His first words were: 'God Almighty in His most holy and wise providence, hath so disposed of the condition of mankind, as in all times some must be rich, some poor, some high and eminent in power and dignity; others mean and in submission.'

"Not exactly 'love your neighbors' or 'blessed are the poor.' In the hands of the rich, the crucifix became a knife.

"From the beginning, the City on the Hill possessed a dark underside that included exterminating Native Americans, exploiting poor European immigrants, and slavery.

"From Salem they sailed south and found where the Mystic River flowed into the ocean. They sailed up the river to about where we are now.

"In a letter to his wife back in England, Mr. Winthrop called this area paradise, referring to what is now Paradise, Somerville, Medford and Malden. Yes, well, smile and chuckle as you will: this place was very different then. Picture it in your mind if you can: no roads, no bridges, no homes, no buildings at all, just the river, the land, the animals, birds and the fish. And the Native Americans. We humans can take credit for the changes that now make us laugh when we think someone once named where we live Paradise.

"Winthrop claimed six hundred acres under the MBC charter: two hundred for himself and fifty each for his eight servants. Not that his servants got any land. Winthrop got more land because he had servants. Free. Affirmative action for rich people.

"Winthrop and his followers believed that God had cleared the land of those they called Indians. A disease, probably brought by earlier arrivals in Gloucester, we think, eventually killed more than ninety percent of the Native Americans in North America. Thus the English claimed to have taken title to the land directly from God.

"Winthrop named his land Ten Hills Farm. You live on part of it.

"The colonists didn't have a good time of it at the beginning, especially during the winters, but by seven years later they'd established themselves well enough to make war against the remaining Pequots. The British leaders made captives of the Native survivors and distributed them amongst themselves as slaves.

"As Columbus had discovered, Native Americans didn't make good slaves. They hated being slaves, they refused to work, they did anything to escape, and they knew the land so well that the English had little chance of catching them.

"The English traded their Native slaves for African slaves. "Now, where did they find African slaves?

"Two years after Winthrop discovered his paradise, other British entrepreneurs established a colony in Antigua."

Jessa sucked in a breath.

"Yes. The street you live on is named for that same Antigua. The Brits used African slaves there to grow sugar."

Rik asked, "In Antigua?"

"Yes. At first, John Winthrop traded Pequots for Africans. He quickly expanded this trade: ships with products from Boston sailed to the Canary Islands, where those products were traded for slaves. The ships delivered some of those slaves to the West Indies and took on wine, sugar, salt and tobacco, then sailed back to Boston with their new cargo and the remaining slaves.

177

"Winthrop was no slouch. He also realized that the plantations in the Caribbean grew sugar, not food. The plantations needed food and equipment. He started up a Boston to Antigua trade, sending food and manufactured goods south and taking sugar north. What did the New Englanders do with sugar? Make rum.

"Paradise became one of the great rum producers of the world.

"But John Winthrop died an unhappy man. He saw corruption in the society he'd helped found, the love of money coming before God, undermining the glory of the city on a hill.

"Winthrop himself sowed the seeds of those evils in the institutions of class and race.

"Now let's jump ahead to 1698. Isaac Royall, the son of a Boston sailmaker, inherited considerable wealth when his first wife died in childbirth. He moved to Antigua, set up his own plantation and got into the slave trade. He sold slaves to the Governor of Massachusetts, among others.

"Isaac had long hoped to return to Boston. After a slave revolt in Antigua, he determined on it.

"In July of 1737, Royall, with his new wife and family, returned to Massachusetts with twenty-seven slaves and settled into the newly refurbished Ten Hills Farm, again right back where you two live."

Rik said, "So the slaves came with them."

"Right. Royall, along with many other gentlemen around here, made a fortune off the slave, sugar, and rum trade. The Royalls were noted for their high-minded Christian ways, commitment to the community, and parties.

"When Royall died, his son, also named Isaac, took over.

"Second Isaac's luck, or judgment, was not so good. He tried to split the difference when his friends vowed that they would not be Britain's slaves—that was their choice of words—and tensions between the colonies and the mother country grew. In the end, he chose the wrong side. On the night of Paul Revere's ride, he dined with the captain on board a British vessel anchored in the harbor.

"He fled to Canada shortly after that, while the rebels made Ten Hills Farm an encampment.

"After Independence, the state courts put an end to slavery here. The state constitution reads, 'All men are born free and equal,' and the courts ruled that it meant what it said."

Rik said, "Excuse me. You're saying that these people, I mean the colonists, who lived on this land right here, kept slaves? Here. On this land."

"Yes. Is that important?"

Rik nodded.

Jessa said, "Very."

"Good." Ms. Kinney continued. "But that's only the first part of how we in Massachusetts, New England and New York became rich off of slaves.

"The economy continued to depend overwhelmingly on slaves. We made rum from Antigua's sugarcane, grown and harvested by slaves. We sold food grown here to Antigua for owners and their slaves. Our earliest manufactured goods also went to the Caribbean and later to the slave South. Carriages, carriage whips, tools, belt buckles, chains, shackles, and the cloth for the slaves' clothing. And rum."

"Slavery disappeared in the North, but something very different had happened in the South.

"In the mid-seventeenth century, Britain began exporting the Irish to the colonies in the thousands. At this time, a favorite British and Colonial theme was to compare Native Americans and Africans to the Irish.

"Troops who had served in Ireland and then in the Colonies said the Irish and Native Americans had the same faults: they held land in common, the women had too much power, and they bathed every day."

179

Jessa said, "Yeesh. They looked down on people who bathed daily?"

"Customs, even those we hold near and dear, come and go. Bathing daily was deemed a sign of sin here and in Britain, but to rape an Irish woman or an African woman was not rape. To kill an Irishman or an African was not murder.

"In 1676, a hundred years before the American Revolution, Bacon's Rebellion erupted in Georgia. Irish and African bondsmen joined together in a violent uprising to end the bondsmen labor system. The revolt was defeated, but the alliance of Irish and Africans fighting together struck fear into English hearts.

"The English knew they had to separate the Irish and the African-Americans. They did it by laws that allowed the Irish to work off their bonds, become free, and earn very low wages. These same laws made blacks and their children, not only slaves forever, but property.

"That law created a legal white race, which included the Irish, with some of the rights of being human allowed even to the lowliest, and a black race, who had no rights and who were property. Africans had no rights as living beings. Yes, there had been many versions of slavery before, but this was the first time in human history that a person's value was completely determined by the market."

Ms. Kinney continued. "Southern agriculture came to depend on, and require, slaves. Most slaves worked on plantations growing tobacco and later cotton. Massive amounts of cotton. At first, most of it was shipped to Europe, particularly England, where first individuals and later machines turned the cotton into clothing. Profits from the slave trade financed British textile mills, and, in turn, that nation's whole industrialization.

"In 1789, a British fellow stole some of Britain's mill secrets and brought them to the US. Ten years later, US cotton production had increased sixty times.

"During the War of 1812, a man named Francis Cabot Lowell, an American, made off with more secrets from England. The Lowells, the Cabots, the Lawrences, and several other wealthy families, most of whom had made fortunes directly or indirectly off the slave trade, joined together and opened a mill in Waltham. Once that proved successful, they opened other mills, including the one in Paradise that is now a shopping center. The cotton once sent to England came north, here.

"In 1822, mills began opening in the town of Lowell. In 1847, Lawrence was founded specifically as a mill town. The Irish begin arriving in Lawrence. Cotton became king of agriculture in the South and king of industry in Massachusetts, all of New England and New York. No-wage slaves grew the cotton and next-to-no-wage workers turned it into cloth. Much of the cloth went back South as clothing for owners and slaves. Other industries sprang up making everything from shoes to walking canes to horse-drawn carriages, all manufactured up here and sold down South for slave-produced money. Fortunes were made.

"In 1808 the slave trade became illegal in the US. This meant that, to meet the needs of the Southern economy, slaves needed to be bred to have as many children as possible. Bred, like horses or cattle, breeding the large and strong together so the next generation would be larger and stronger. They forced men and women to have sex and breed. Or, the owners raped the slave women.

"The owners regularly raped the female slaves, which confused the whole system of black and white. After four or so genera-tions of owner-slave interbreeding, a population of white-skinned, blonde-haired, blue-eyed slaves was created. The white female slaves were particularly valuable, as they were sold into sex slavery for exceptionally high prices."

Sona interrupted. "Jessa?"

The girl looked frozen, as if her spirit had flown to another time and place.

181

"Jessa? Are you alright?"

She blinked and seemed surprised to see the others around the table. In a voice thin as lace, she said, "Yes. I'm fine."

Rik refilled her water glass.

Christina continued. "Well, the Civil War comes and goes, the slaves are technically freed, but for practical purposes, after the failure of Reconstruction, nothing much changed. The freed slaves were trapped by laws, customs and police forces to continue working for nothing or virtually nothing. The Black Codes, the Jim Crow laws, were slavery under a different name.

"The Irish invasion diminished, but the Germans, Italians, Poles, Norwegians, Finns, Scots, Lithuanians, Syrians—who have I left out?—immigrated to Lowell and Lawrence to work the cotton mills. The beat goes on.

"In 1912, thirty thousand workers in Lawrence walk off their mill jobs. It's the Bread and Roses Strike. Peoples of a dozen nationalities who can hardly speak to each other unify against the owners. The strikers demanded a fifteen percent raise in their six-dollar-per-week salary. The owners answered that such a raise would destroy their businesses. Not many believed that argument, because mill stocks at the time were going for more than three thousand dollars per share, and one mill had reported an eleven-million-dollar profit the year before.

"And that's the way things went until World War II, when the owners moved their businesses south, closer to the source of their raw materials The labor was even cheaper, mostly poor whites and the children of freed slaves. They didn't stay there long. Soon they moved to Asia, where there was even cheaper labor.

"So, there it is, in a nutshell. The history of Paradise—specifically, the area that you live in now."

Ms. Adebayo thanked her.

Rik felt exhausted by so much new information. He wasn't able to bring it all into focus. It was terrifying, but he couldn't yet understand why.

Jessa felt stunned and shaken. She'd hardly heard any of what Ms. Kinney said after her description of breeding slaves through rape. Her mind rebelled at the thought of living like that. The women had to have been crushed in body and spirit. Jessa thought back to the ghost woman Rik had seen and the story about the twelve-year-old who had given birth. She hugged herself like she wanted to hug the girl.

Everyone sat silently for a nearly a minute. During the silence, a tortoiseshell cat appeared. It jumped up and settled onto Celisa's lap. "Hey, Josie, how are you doing?" Celisa smiled at her friend and began stroking her head.

Rik said, "Thank you. That explains an awful lot. I didn't understand that people here had slaves. Or that slavery was so important to...who we are and how we live."

Jessa pulled herself together a bit. She said, "I'm sorry. I feel... Sometimes the things you don't know can make you feel real creepy when you get to know them." She rubbed her arms and asked, "Are we saying that if it wasn't for slavery, people like Rik and I might not be here now? That our ancestors' opportunity to come to America was created by slave labor?"

Ms. Kinney frowned. "We can't know what the world would be like now if people hadn't decided to kidnap people in Africa and bring them to the Americas as slaves. But there wouldn't have been paying jobs for our ancestors here, certainly not in such numbers, had it not been for slavery and the domination of blacks by whites after slavery ended.

"So much of our economy got its start with slave profits: banks, insurance companies, you name it. The cities of Lowell and Lawrence wouldn't exist as they do today if it hadn't been for slavery."

Tentatively, Jessa said, "It feels like a trap...everything... I don't know what to say."

Sona said, "You're just starting, Jessa, Rik." She glanced at Celisa. "You've got time to figure it out for yourself." She looked at Jessa, then Rik. "My only advice is: if you pray, don't pray for justice. Pray for mercy. Pray that we all—African, European, Hispanic and Asian—can be merciful." She folded her napkin and placed it on the table. With a bittersweet smile, she said, "That was quite a discussion. Thank you, Christine. All of you."

"Mom, why don't you play something?"

Everyone at the table looked at Ms. Adebayo.

Jessa asked, "What do you play?"

Celisa answered. "She's first violin for the BSO. She plays the piano and other instruments too." To her mother, she said, "Play something on the piano!"

"Well, I can't play the kind of music that your friends listen to."

Jessa said, "We'd love to hear you play!"

"Alright. How about Chopin?"

She rose, walked into the living room, then stopped before the piano.

"My great-grandmother bought this piano. It's been passed down to me. The keys are actual ivory. Elephant ivory. The ivory was carried by African slaves to the coast of Zanzibar, where it was shipped to Connecticut to be turned into piano keys." She looked at her guests. "It's so sad, isn't it. Sad and strange." She took a breath. She sat and held her hands over the keys. "For the African elephants, now extinct; for the slaves that carried the ivory, now deceased; for the men who built the piano and their families, also deceased; for you, my guests, and for Chopin, Nocturne Number 2, in E flat."

Rik checked Jessa to see if she was holding up, then slouched a bit in his chair to listen. The notes flowed, joy and sorrow wrapping around each other, he thought, like words in a sentence with multiple meanings. Could he ever write as exact as Chopin?

With each note Jessa heard a bell and felt a hammer. The conflict shook her. She steeled herself. It would end. Everything did.

*   *   *

"So, Mom, what did you think?"

"About what?"

"Mom! Stop it! You know who I'm talking about!"

Sona sighed. "You're right, Celisa. I do know who you're talking about."

"So what did you think?"

Sona realized this conversation was a road marker on a trip of hundreds of miles. Still, she regretted it. She felt like refusing her motherly duty in order to hold on to her daughter longer, longer, even forever. She had white friends who had raised teenagers. Sona was under no illusion that parenting a teenager wasn't always a high-wire act, regardless of race. Yet she knew that her daughter faced more hazards than their daughters. Their daughters would not have risked being called a whore by students and a school official if they walked along a street with Rik. She hoped Celisa would find a college where there were more black men, men who understood what it would be like to build a black family, another fortress with vigilant guards against surprise attacks. Or, better yet, her daughter could just skip the college and go to a nunnery, a place that would protect her from...life. The regret of all parents: to raise an open, loving, inquisitive child and introduce her to a world occupied by evil and endless disappointments.

"Mom, what's wrong? I thought you'd like him."

"I do like him, Celisa. He's a fine boy. Smart. Deep. Both of them are. He's a bit quiet. You kind of have to wind him up to get him to talk, but then he's fine. He felt comfortable here and I felt comfortable having him here.

"And it's your choice who you date, if anyone; who, if anyone, you marry; and who you have children with, if you have any. Did I leave all your options open?"

"Yes, Mom."

"Yes, until I became your mother I never thought much of arranged marriages. Now I'm not so sure. But it is your choice. You get to make it. All I can ask is that you find someone you love and trust. And you're not going to like this, and never repeat this to a white friend because they won't understand it, but, as husbands of black women, white men are not as trustworthy as black men. It's not hard to see why, is it?"

"Mom, you do realize we're not engaged?"

Sona smiled. "Of course. I have no problem with you seeing him, dating, or whatever it's called these days. But before something becomes serious, you have to think. Rik said he will testify for you at the school hearing. After meeting him tonight, I'm confident he will. Not many white boys his age would do that. But there will be a next time, and a time after that, and another time, on and on as long as the two of you are together. And if you have children, they will face those situations long after you're dead. A black man won't run away from you or your children for that reason. He can't. He's black. For a white man, this is all voluntary. He can walk out any time and leave the problem behind. He's bound by his vows but not by his skin.

"I know your father told you how the forces in this society work to turn families into economic machines, as if we were tiny corporations concerned only with producing and consuming. There's so little security, so little left to rely upon, nothing really, and mentally every moment of every day can become consumed with worry about money. We have to fight that. Even the people with money are consumed with worrying about it. It's no surprise that men and women who lose their jobs kill themselves at a high rate. They've already given up being husbands and fathers and

186

EDWARD J. SANTELLA

wives and mothers because, working sixty or more hours a week, they've had no time for it. They've become a single-dimension thing, a breadwinner, and now they feel they've failed at that, the only role they have, and their family is about to lose everything.

"And there are others who cannot get enough hours to work, who cannot support themselves or their families.

"Can Rik handle that kind of pressure and the pressure of an interracial family?"

Celisa fought back. "We'll learn to live a different way, a better way. We don't have to do things the way you and Dad did them."

"Well, I wish you luck on that. I do. And if you find such a way, you let us and everybody else in this world know, because we'll be right there with you. It's just that so far, no one has figured out how to do that."

"But, Mom, you make it sound like...like love is stupid. Like I should move into a cave somewhere and never come out. Why are you like this? I thought you'd be happy I found someone I... like. Isn't life worth living? Why did you tell me all that stuff about sex if I should never have it? Why did you tell me about how to have children if I should never have any? Why do you want me to go to college and learn something if it's all a dead-end trap? Why are you setting me up like this? I want to live!"

Sona felt tears coming. "Because I want you to know what you're facing. I need to warn you, to tell you how hard it can be. I want you to have a meaningful life. I want you to have love and a life you love because I love you, only child of mine. I love you so much and I'm so afraid for us all."

*   *   *

"Cthulhu."

Jessa had settled back onto the bed. The word came out of nowhere. She rolled onto her side, crawled to the foot of the bed, and looked over the edge. Her brother lay on his sleeping bag, eyes staring upward. "What?" she asked.

"Cthulhu," he said. "H. P. Lovecraft's Cthulhu."

"Duh! I know who wrote the story. I'm asking what made you think of his monster, of all things?"

"The monster: a thing, part human, part octopus, part dragon. So self-involved it's prepared to destroy the universe."

"Funny. I was just thinking about local history. That's painful enough. I know he was sort of local, too, but why drag in Cthulhu?"

"That's what I'm talking about. Remember after they closed the state borders and the n'okies kept trying to come across? And the police or army killed a hundred of them in this suburb somewhere in Pennsylvania? And the people who lived there were so upset that they and their kids had to see all the dead bodies on their lawns that they sued the government?"

"Yeah. I remember."

"That's what I'm like."

"I don't get it."

"The people weren't upset that all those people had been killed. That was no big deal. They were upset because the bodies were left where they could see them. Right now I feel angry at Ms. Kinney for telling us about all the horrors of slavery. I'm not so much bothered that it happened. I'm angry because she told me about it."

"You aren't upset by how we treated Africans?"

"Of course I am. Being angry at Ms. Kinney and the ghosts for leaving the bodies on my lawn is just my way of avoiding the real issue."

Jessa probed her mind. When she spoke, it was softly. "I hate the men who raped the slave women. I...I can't even describe how I hate them."

Rik said, "It gets worse."

"What do you mean?"

"This is where Cthulhu comes in. I know it sounds terrible, but I think this is important. Don't think I don't care about the slaves, but..."

Jessa said, "How nice of you to care."

"Shut up. Listen. What did owning slaves, what did breeding and raping slaves do to white people? What does that do to you? Who do you have to become to be able to live that way? How many lies do you have to tell yourself and believe? How many screams do you have to learn not to hear? What does building a super-successful business on the basis of slave or unpaid labor do to you? What does living as a well-dressed, educated, cultured monster do to your soul?"

Jessa began to speak, but Rik said, "Wait. Not only that, but how crippled did white people have to be to begin with, to believe that owning slaves, using them to do the work they were too delicate to do themselves, raping them as if...as if I don't know what? What had to be wrong with them to begin with?"

Jessa's voice rose with anger. "Wait. You want me to feel sorry for the slave owners? Those poor rich people who destroyed millions of lives? You want me to feel sorry for them?"

"No. Not feel sorry for them. I want you to look at them and tell me what you see. I see Cthulhu, the most horrible monster ever imagined. And we are its children."

As if a window had opened, the slightest of breezes entered the room.

Jessa sat up on the bed.

Rik sat cross-legged on the sleeping bag.

As if she'd been listening, waiting for her opportunity, the woman in the rocking chair had returned.

Untamed gray hair framed her thin, lined black face. She wore a worn and faded flowered dress with a white collar and trim. Thin, arthritis-twisted fingers draped over the chair's arms. She sat in a rocker with a shawl over her shoulders and a knitted blanket on her lap. Though her body appeared content to sit and gently rock, her eyes blazed like brown garnets. Those eyes studied the brother and sister, searching for a way of understanding, of trusting.

"They named me Belinda. Some called me Belinda Royall, others Belinda Sutton. None were the names my parents gave me. You saw them slavers take me from my family, you did, didn't you?"

"Yes."

"Yes, ma'am."

She dropped her head for a moment, then ran a hand over her face. "I can't never forget. Nobody forget something like that. What happened to my mother, my father? What happened to my brothers and sisters, my grandparents, my friends? What happened to my home?" Her hands reached out, holding nothing. Her knuckles stretched her skin like some species of large brown nuts. The bones between were thin. "Each day I ask and I get no answer. My wondering become a prayer. A great unanswered prayer.

"Prayers, maybe most of them, go unanswered. You two, you're too young, too fortunate, to know that. You will. Prayers go unanswered. Not God's fault. People keep getting in His way.

"You see these old hands? Every move is pain. I can't do work no more. Lucky for me the court passed a law saying slave owners got to provide for slaves too old or too ill to work. A kind law, do you not agree? The gentlemen got tired of seeing our dead bodies tossed out by their owners along the roadsides. Unsightly, they claimed. Lucky for me, too, that Master Royall obeyed the law and provided for me in his will. Course, Master Royall's execu-tor paid me nothing. I had to petition the general court. Phillis Wheatley and Prince Hall wrote what needed to be wrote for me. You look those two good people up in your books and you'll learn something.

"So Samuel Adams and John Hancock ruled in my favor. They paid me. One year. Next year, had to sue again. I won again. But no one paid me. After all, how can two freedom-loving gentle-men such as Mr. Adams and Mr. Hancock have time for a lost black soul such as myself? Despite the white man's law, I died homeless, hungry, sick and thirsty. You see, the law sets different on different people.

"But, Rik, you know that, don't you?

"They do what they can get away with. It ain't about progress and it ain't about no people. With them it's about their money and their property and how important and saved they feel.

"They got the money and the property alright, and they do feel so important, and they feel saved, but, by God Almighty as my witness, they ain't saved. They ain't loved. They ain't even liked. They just the center of attention for a while. A bit of wayside entertainment. By my soul, they got the blood of the children of God on their hands and they ain't saved.

"This I know. The story ain't yet writ. The story go on. I believe the story go on somehow because of who you are. And your brother. I'm sorry, Rik. I talk like you wasn't here. That's cause I'm partial toward Jessa here, like she my daughter. I seen what he did to her, that fool devil you call Meph. Suffering brings people close.

"Celisa, she my real daughter. Great-a-dozen-times-over-grand-daughter. Yep.

"You must bring here her. She must be with you, be part of you, regardless of what they say, before we can even begin to hope.

"Oh, my, I'm a ghost that tears up. I can't wait to meet her!

"Ms. Belinda...Ms. Sutton?"

"Yes, child?"

"I'm sorry."

"Oh, don't be sorry."

"We...we've been wondering why you and the other ghosts are here. I mean, we can't figure out what you want. From us."

Belinda nodded her head. "Why we here now?

"Cause this our home, child. White people made this our home. They brought the first of us here and here was where most of us born, where we loved, where our children born, where we died and buried. This where our descendants live to this day. We're home here. You don't ask why people in their home live there, now do you?

"But, now? Why now?"

Somewhere inside the folds of her blankets, Belinda's body shifted, straightened as much as old bones are able. Her ghost face hardened, like the face of a sentencing judge, but her eyes became terrified. "We here out of suffering. Our suffering. The work we forced to do? Being owned? Laughed at? Insulted? Whipped? Raped? What, with all that and the lynchings? Paul Revere. Take that man. He famous for riding and warning all the white folks the redcoats coming. Yeah. He ride right by the bird-eaten body of a dead slave man hanging from a tree.

"Some of us once talked of reparations, that white people should pay black people for all they've stolen from us, or all the misery they inflicted.

"It ain't going to happen. That time gone.

"Too much time, too much stolen, too much pride been done to us, the First Peoples, the whole of the earth.

"It ain't going to happen because white folks about to get as poor and oppressed as black folks. White folks ain't going to have any money to pay us, even if they wanted.

"Nope.

"It's coming full circle. We gathered here to watch, and many more coming. We here to watch you die, and those don't die gonna wish they was slaves. The world lost its balance the way you been kicking it. It fighting back.

"Next time bring Celisa. I'm so worried about her."

Jessa asked, "Isn't there some way to stop this?"

Belinda looked at Jessa. The older woman's mouth set firm. "One way, only one way, maybe, who knows? We need our souls back, our whole souls." She pulled the ends of her shawl apart, revealing a gaping hole where her left breast should have been, a hole like those all the ghosts seemed to have. A few stones had been set in place of the missing flesh and bone. "This what happen when they make you a thing to own. We need back what they stole. Children, you listening? What they stole. Our souls. Not just our souls. Everybody's souls. The whole earth's souls."

*   *   *

Rik's insides seethed. He glanced at Jessa several times, trying to read her. She ignored him as she paged through some homework. Finally, he asked, "What are you thinking?"

Her fingers stopped moving pages. She closed the book, pushed it away. Still looking away from him, she said, "We live in hell and we created it. Been creating it for centuries. This isn't civilization. It's an excuse for powerful people to use everyone else. For money, for power. For sex. And so they can still think well of themselves."

Rik frowned. "Oh. I wasn't thinking that."

She turned sharply to him. "What?"

"I was thinking about being...white."

"Well, that's what I'm talking about too!"

Rik exhaled, exasperated with his own slowness in pulling his thoughts together. "There are three groups, really. Not just blacks and whites, but blacks, whites and white whites."

"White whites?"

"Yeah. The white whites are the ones who owned the slaves and the cotton factories. The whites are people the white whites used, use, just like they used slaves, to make their fortunes. The whites have very little power but they, ah, um, sort of win the booby prize because at least they have white skin like the white whites and are better than blacks."

"Consolation prize, maybe?"

"Right. Thank you.

"The question I've been asking myself about how to be a man is really how to be a white man. That's the wrong question. I don't want that. I don't want to let myself be used by other people, rich people, any people. I'm not going to spend my life being obedient like some good little boy, getting through it all by telling myself, 'well, hey, could be worse. It's not like I'm black.' Being white is a fucking consolation prize for having your life ripped off. At least black people figured it out."

"That's how I feel," Jessa said. "Exactly."

*   *   *

Sona lay in bed awake, unable to stop her mind from racing. She remembered. Celisa had been ten at the time. Like now, her husband had been away.

She had noticed, by chance, a man walking past their house, first from her dining room window, and again, within half an hour, from her upstairs study. He wouldn't have registered in her mind except both times he stopped directly in front and turned to look at their house. The second time he stayed long enough to finish his cigarette and toss it, still burning, onto their lawn.

She continued to watch, and he returned twice more, pausing in front both times, depositing another cigarette on the grass.

With a knot in her throat, almost against her better judgment, she called the police. She explained the multiple appearances, the staring, and the cigarettes. The officer informed her that the man had done nothing illegal. "Walking on a sidewalk isn't against the law." He chuckled, as if to suggest, "silly woman."

Of course it wasn't.

Four months earlier, her husband had gone out for a walk just as spring had managed to clear the walks of ice and snow. Two Paradise police cars, each with two officers, pulled up and stopped him. Someone had phoned in a "black man walking" report. They'd interrogated him until one of the officers, going through his wallet, recognized his Massachusetts Bar card. Without an apology, they quickly retreated and left the lawyer to his walk.

As for the white man in front of their house, Sona had retrieved her firearm, walked downstairs, opened the front door and stood on the porch holding the gun in plain view.

This time the man left with his cigarette. She never saw the man again. The white man.

*   *   *

Gary sat on the bed beside his sleeping wife. She'd taken more sleeping pills than recommended to make sure she slept. He listened to her breathing. When, he asked himself, had they turned into a machine, two pistons driving side by side, a well-oiled, mechanical, economic unit? When was the last time they had made love, as she insisted on calling it, not, as he would, having sex? Nothing felt farther beyond him. He could never love a woman after what happened to Paul; he felt dirty, corrupt, though he struggled to believe he'd only done his job.

There had been a time. So much time had passed, had disappeared.

They'd lived a dream that now smelled more of vinegar than wine, of bank balances than flowers, of fear than hope.

He didn't want to be in bed with his wife. He didn't want to be in their bedroom, so he left. He walked down the hall, down the stairs, to the living room. He fell into his chair and used the remote to switch on the TV.

The game had ended and the post-game show had devolved into the usual string of a dozen or so commercials. This commercial was, in fact, quite beautiful. The first scene took place in a swanky bar filled with finely dressed and very sleek retirees, drinking, smiling and laughing. Young, scantily dressed stewards served them. One whole wall of the bar was a window through which the earth could be seen in all the splendor distance could achieve. Viewers would recognize this as the new orbital retirement community. "People who demand the best..." The screen changed to a nonagenarian woman wearing a two-piece without need for embarrassment floating off a diving board and, in the low gravity that supposedly added decades to one's life, gliding into a pool. "...plan the best." Now two retirees welcomed children, grandchildren and great-grandchildren coming off a shuttle. "You may not be able to retire to the Star Community..." A beautiful naked couple received massages from two beautiful naked stewards. "...where even your most personal pleasures are planned for..." The screen faded into a sign on an office door which said Calvin Zwingli Investments, FEPC. "...but you can invest your money with those who will. Call now." Shot of gyrating people on a dance floor. The dancers may have been wearing clothing, but the camera found mostly flesh pressing against flesh. The dancers sang, or shouted, a repeating single line backed by drums and horns. "Let your money mingle!"

For once Gary felt neither entertained nor titillated. He felt shamed. Angry tears filled his eyes. He threw the remote and hit the screen dead center. The remote bounced off and fell to the floor. The screen remained undamaged, having moved along to the next commercial. A beautiful, smiling, naked-above-the-waist, very young woman rode a horse bareback along a beach as morning sunlight sparkled off rolling blue and white ocean waves. A long-forgotten rock group sang, "You can't always get what you want..." A racy red convertible pursued the woman along the beach, but fell hopelessly farther and farther behind. "...but if you try sometime you find..." The driver, his face healthily suntanned, his graying hair combed smartly back and undisturbed by the wind, slowed to a stop on the beach, having given up his pursuit, and caressed the steering wheel and dash as if it were a...you know. "...you get what you need!"

Gary obediently bent over, retrieved the remote, turned the TV off, and replaced the remote on the lamp table where the family had, after energetic discussion, agreed it should be kept.

He didn't stop in the kitchen or at his usual place, the shelf of liquor. Not hungry. Not even thirsty. He wanted to be someplace new.

He walked out onto the back porch, not someplace new exactly, but someplace he felt he hadn't really been, certainly not in his pajamas and not at night.

Out the back door, down the four wooden steps.

The air was warm, muggy. The birds made a racket. He could see their dark forms fluttering among tree branches.

He stood in the shadows at the side of his house.

A deep, expressive voice spoke out of the shadows. "The stars used to sweep across the whole sky, horizon to horizon, millions and millions of them, on a night like this. You white people covered them up, hid them behind your lights. I miss them."

Gary's eyes took half a minute to make out the collapsed shadow sitting with its back against the porch struts. He surprised himself with his lack of outrage at discovering someone, something, some ghost on his property. He didn't have words for how he felt, but he might have used words like "comforted" or "pleased." He simply thought himself confused.

"I know what you mean. I saw them once. Some friends and I had gone north, up into Quebec, hunting. Two nights I think we were there. The stars, I remember the stars. I would like to see them again."

"You not a bad man, Mr. Gary. Maybe they ain't no bad men. Just fucked-up men. You one of the fucked-up men."

Gary rolled his eyes and shook his head. He even smiled a little, though it was far too dark for anyone to notice. That was about the most complimentary thing anyone had said to him since...birth.

"You're not so bad yourself." Gary sat down on the ground, his own back against the porch struts, five or so feet from the ghost.

"Oh, Mr. Gary, you don't know the half of what I done. Some bad things. Not bad in white men's eyes; bad things in my eyes. They's what counts." He paused. "Some good things, too. Some good things."

"Birds sure are noisy."

"And at night. They know things we don't. That's why. The last time I heard birds like this at night I was home. In Africa. A child. They was warning us. Then the white men came and took me. The birds, they know."

"What... what do you think they know?" Gary became uncomfortable. He didn't like things happening. He was supposed to make things happen.

The ghost laughed. "Not me. I sure don't know. Ask the crow. Ask the raven. They the smart ones. They know. They tell all the other birds."

"You have a name?"

"Two. My Africa name and the name the first Mr. Royall gave me. That name George."

"George. Where did you live?"

"Here."

"Here?"

"First Africa. Then Antigua. Then here."

"What here? I mean, there weren't any..."

"Oh, we was slaves and we was here. I had children here. Then grandchildren. One great-grandchild on the way. Then I killed myself."

"Wha...why?"

"Um. The way things were. Old Mr. Royall die. A man die, they give away his things. The ones they don't give away, they sell. They couldn't sell an old man like me. But they gonna sell my children, one son one place, another a different place, my

198

daughter a third place. Same with my grandchildren. Places I even never heard of. They advertise them. They sell them and I never see them again. No life worth living. I hung me."

Gary sat quietly, his body making involuntary small movements. He wanted to stay and he wanted to leave. After a while, he stood.

"George, I'm going in. You can sit here. Anyone give you any trouble, you say I said you can sit here. Any time you want."

Gary climbed the stairs and went into the kitchen.

George sat there, shaking his head in disbelief. Only a white man like Mr. Gary would be dumb enough to think another white man would take the word of a black ghost.

*   *   *

Rik lay awake trying to figure out how to be a free human being when you've got white skin, a soul, a penis between your legs, and a need to write.

CHAPTER TEN
WEDNESDAY

"Tah dahhh!" Annie announced her arrival. "I bring news!" Evelyn had sent two unusually subdued children off to school and taken two headache pills. Even the promise of five more days of sun and heat didn't improve her spirits.

"Hi, Annie. What news is that?"

"He's coming tomorrow! Tomorrow!"

"Who might that be?"

"Big Tom! Big Bad Tom!"

Evelyn found it almost painful to look at the woman. "Am I supposed to know who Big Bad Tom is?"

"Why, he's the Christian preacher and shaman and exorcist we hired to get rid of all our ghosts. Yes! He'll be here tomorrow. And the neighborhood meeting is Friday night!"

"That's wonderful. Do you think he can get my husband to go to a doctor?"

"Oh, Evelyn." Annie sat like a collapse. "What's wrong?"

"He won't go to see the heart doctor."

"Still? Why not?"

"He can't take time away from work."

"Well, that's good that he's busy."

"Not if he drops dead of a heart attack."

"Does he have life insurance?"

Evelyn stared at the woman. "Annie, please leave."

"Oh, I thought so. You've got a headache. So early, too. Not good."

"How did you know I had a headache?"

"The box of Aspirin on your counter over there. The flap is still open."

*   *   *

Jessa recognized him right away. He was one of the few boys who paid attention in class. He'd made a few comments that had made the class laugh. Even the teacher appreciated his humor. Almost always with a smile, he seemed friendly with everyone.

He didn't stand that close when he came up to her at her locker. He kept his weight on his back foot, and, in an attempted offhand manner, asked her if she'd think about going to the coffee shop with him after school.

Paralysis set in. Her body, her real body, the body she felt inside her body, became twisted like the victim of some horrible disease. She was too panicked to do anything but freeze. She felt the remains of her lunch rise in her stomach.

Her eyes filled and more than a few tears ran down her cheeks. She fought hard to keep from bursting out sobbing. She shook her head no.

That was the only response she could manage.

The boy lost his smile. "I didn't mean anything by it. I just thought..." He turned and left.

Jessa pushed her face into the locker to hide it. She wiped her eyes, took a breath, rearranged her books.

She remembered a movie in which a high school girl had dozed during class. When she woke, she found everyone was gone. The implication was that everyone in the world had disappeared and she was alone. It was a movie, so the audience knew there had to be at least one other person in the world, who doubled as love interest. Jessa remembered joking that it would be horrible to be alone on earth with one other person. Who could they talk about? But she felt alone now, like that girl had been at first.

Being corrupted and unlovable meant being alone. You can't respond to "hey, how are you doing?" by answering, "I'm recovering from being sexually abused by my mother's boyfriend." That was the truth, though the word "recovery" seemed optimistic. She couldn't tell the truth of who she felt herself to be. She had to learn to be normal. To pretend.

She was too broken to pull it off. She was a ghost of herself.

After lunch, Gary told the office manager he was going to the bank to run a few errands. She probably thought he was going to a bar to get drunk.

He drove to Medford, a trip of less than five miles, chosing an alternate route off the main roads and into West Medford. He pulled into a parking lot.

He sat for a minute in his car trying to comprehend what he was about to do.

Finally, his eyes heavy, he slipped out of the car.

He nodded to a family, blacks all dressed in black, and walked past without lifting his eyes to theirs.

Another suited black man opened the front door for him.

Gary glanced at the sign pointing people in the correct direction and walked off to the right.

He'd come early to avoid the drivers, in case they would think of coming. Now they'd all still be working.

He swallowed. He was the only white person. Every one of the perhaps three dozen people was black. He felt naked, like he sometimes did in dreams, lost somewhere and having forgotten his clothing.

A man in a collar approached him.

Gary felt rain began to fall. He couldn't see it. He felt and heard it. In the funeral parlor. A moderate rain. The rain's sound obscured the reverend's words.

Gary leaned closer to hear.

The reverend raised his voice to help the man who seemed both a little lost and hard of hearing. "Thank you for coming. You knew Paul?"

Gary nodded.

The reverend ushered him toward the front of the room and the receiving line.

Gary nodded and thanked him. He stood naked in the rain—when he looked down at himself he saw his nakedness—waiting in line, as if there were nothing more natural than for a man to forget to wear clothes to a wake. He let his eyes wander everywhere but the faces.

The line moved a few steps.

Gary looked at the back of the woman in front of him, then his eyes drifted forward, to Paul's family. Again he looked away. He began to feel soaked by the rain.

Time skipped ahead and he faced a man that looked too much like Paul. Too much. A brother. A twin. That close. The man squeezed his hand. Gary's hand had no strength. The man, tears flowing one by one down his cheeks, insisted on looking Gary in the eye. "I'm Peter. Paul's brother."

Gary said, "I'm sorry for your loss." He'd never seen a grown black man cry before. He felt a bit surprised and embarrassed by it.

"Thank you for coming. Did you work with Paul?"

"Yes."

The man squeezed his hand again.

Next was a young boy, perhaps twelve. Gary had always had difficulty judging the ages of black people. Another handshake.

"Sorry for your loss. Your father...?"

Tears in his eyes, the boy nodded. He said something that Gary couldn't hear above the patter of drops.

Another boy. Gary guessed fifteen, this one a bereaved stoic, staring off into space. Like his brother, he had a soft handshake.

The widow used a tissue to wipe away her tears, then took Gary's hands and said a few words. Because she tilted her head as if asking a question, Gary assumed she'd asked if he'd worked with Paul. He nodded. The woman threw her arms around him. He had to put his arms around her. The rain fell over them but because her mouth was now beside his ear he heard her say, "Thank you so much for coming. Paul loved his job. He always said how fortunate he was. Thank you so, so much."

They released each other. The widow wiped her tears. Gary looked toward the floor, nodded a goodbye and shuffled on.

Gary knew he should kneel at the casket and say a prayer. Everyone who went through the reception line did. He didn't want to, but knew he had to. He knelt. The casket was closed, of course. It would have been an impossible task for the undertaker to hide everything. Gary managed a single-word prayer.

"God."

If there was a God—an unlikely possibility in his mind—God would know what his prayer meant. He certainly didn't. He stood.

Rows of chairs held family and friends. Gary knew he should sit, even for a short time, but his panic had begun to rise. He couldn't stop himself from making for the door.

"Sir! Sir!"

Gary stopped.

The reverend held out an open hand directing Gary toward a stand with a book. "You haven't signed the guest book."

Gary went to the book, took the pen in his hand. Amazing how the rain ran off the paper without damaging it. He wrote, "John Franklin," and an address that he hoped didn't exist. He put the pen down, nodded to the reverend and walked out into the sun.

The reverend watched him walk away, wondering whether the man had been real or a ghost.

*　　　*　　　*

Two minutes after Gary returned to his office, Miriam buzzed him with an incoming phone call.

"Hello?"

"Gary, damn you, this is Clint." The voice was unmistakable. "Look, I thought you understood. I must have not made myself clear. You went to that thug's wake today."

Clint's voice had a way of making Gary feel like garbage. "How did you know that?"

"It's my job to know things. It's what I get paid for. That's not the point. You're not supposed to do that. You shouldn't have anything to do with those people. Nothing. At all. Do you understand?"

"Yes. Yes, I do. I'm sorry..."

"Don't let this kind of thing happen again."

"I won't."

"Order, Gary, we need to keep order! Some people are getting nervous. Shape up."

Confused, Gary turned the call off. For a moment he thought about calling Clint back. He wanted to know who "some people" were. He knew he shouldn't.

*   *   *

For fifteen minutes the three teenagers stood at the intersection where Rik and Jessa turned to go to their home and Celisa continued on to hers. Rik glanced up and down the street to check if any cars carrying harassers were coming. None were. Celisa repeated how glad she was that they had come for dinner and the discussion with Christine. Jessa kept a suspicious eye on Rik. She didn't care about his furtive looks up and down the street. It was the way he leaned, like the Leaning Tower of Pisa, always in Celisa's direction.

Her suspicions were confirmed. Rik asked Celisa if he could walk her home. Then he asked Jessa if it was okay with her. Polite to a fault. She felt a flash of hatred toward her brother, but pretended it was fine with her.

Jessa turned down the street and didn't look back. Without Rik, she felt the day hotter, the streets narrower, her backpack heavier, and her future more despairing.

When she arrived home, she grunted some greeting to her mother, who was in the kitchen, and went upstairs to her—Rik's—bedroom. She threw her backpack on the floor and threw herself on the bed. At least it was cool inside.

She stared at the ceiling. She wished she were dead. She didn't want to kill herself, but she wished she were already dead. Or never born. Another thing to blame her mother for.

There. She'd thought of suicide. She had to call Dr. Dreier. She was forbidden from calling Dr. Dreier. A properly brought-up young lady would, of course, know how to do both simultaneously. It was one of those tricks proper young ladies knew.

But why kill yourself if all that got you was becoming a ghost who remembered everything and was still caught up in the same feelings? Why...?

She sat up. She felt the sudden shock of discovery. Exactly. Why had Ellen done such a brainless thing?

*   *   *

They walked past Celisa's house as if they had discussed the idea and voted to do so. Rather, it was an issue of inertia: bodies in motion tend to stay in motion. Together they were moving on to somewhere, though they didn't know yet where.

Rik was about to ask where they were headed when Celisa said, "There's a bit of a park down the street here, a half block, along the river. My dad said there used to be a park along both sides of the river that went for miles. Most of it's gone."

The park appeared as predicted, along with an unkempt dock that stretched about twenty feet into the water. They walked out and sat side by side on the edge.

Rik's brain exploded with rocketing thoughts and cannonball emotions that left him unable to form a meaningful two-word sentence. Celisa did her part by remaining silent. Gradually, the rippling water, catching and shattering sunlight into millions of sparkles, worked to calm and center Rik's mind.

"It's kind of nice sitting here."

"I come here sometimes when I want to be alone."

Rik blinked. "You mean, being here with me is a lot like being alone?"

Celisa laughed. "You would think that! No, I mean I like being alone with you."

Rik blushed. Having no words, he put his arm around Celisa. For her part, she leaned against him, hip to hip, head to head.

*　　　*　　　*

Rik thought Jessa was asleep when he returned to his room. She was still dressed from school, lying on her side, a pillow under her head. Quietly, he removed his backpack and laid it on the floor.

"You still a virgin?"

He closed his eyes. He had expected Jessa would be upset. "Yes, Jessa. Your brother is still a virgin."

"Damn. I was hoping you two fucked."

"Why?" He sat on the foot of the bed, looking away from her.

"So you could tell me what it's like to do it and like it. So, what happened, then?"

He told her about the park, the pier, sitting together.

"That all? Come on! There has to be more than that!"

"We kissed."

"How many times? What kind of kisses? Where did you kiss her?"

"Geez, Jessa. Leave me alone."

"You have to tell me!" She pushed herself up so she was sitting. Her eyes were puffy and red. "Really. What happened?"

Rik heard a small bit of curiosity in her voice and a good deal more desperation.

"It will only make you feel bad."

"That's my purpose in life: feeling bad. Tell me. I have to know."

"We kissed. A lot, I guess. I wasn't counting. On the lips and, you know..."

"Open mouth?"

"Yeah."

"Sitting or standing?"

"Both."

208

"Lying down?"

"No."

"You get a boner?"

"Jessa!"

"Did you?"

"Of course."

"The boy says 'of course.' Did she feel it?"

"Not with her hand."

"What does that mean? She have a foot fetish or something?"

"No. We were standing."

"In a clutch. Pressed together. She had to feel it."

"If you say so."

"She didn't vomit her lunch all over you?"

He answered quietly. "No, Jessa, she didn't."

"I hate women who don't throw up when they feel a boner. I hate them. I hate them!"

Rik had no answer for her despair. Quietly, he asked, "Are we going to go through this every time I see her?"

"What? Aren't you enough of a man to deal with your corrupted little sister? You can't handle the way she's all fucked up? Does she embarrass you?"

Jessa jumped off the bed.

"Well, you can fuck anyone any time you want. You can just ignore me!"

She ran out the door. Rik heard her run down the stairs.

He continued to sit on the bed, wishing they'd never met Celisa and never moved to Paradise. It wasn't his fault Meph had raped his sister. It wasn't fair to him. But life hadn't been fair to her, either.

He heard Jessa's steps coming slowly up the stairs.

She came back into the room. She closed the door and leaned her back against it. She looked up at the ceiling.

"Mom's downstairs. She looked at me like she'd seen a fiend.

Annie's two kids are sitting on our front steps. I can't get away. There's no place for me."

Rik stood. "You stay here. I'll go downstairs and do some reading or something."

"No. That's not right."

Rik walked over to her and hugged her. "It's okay. You can be by yourself."

"It's not okay." She had to tell him. "This nice kid, this guy, came up to me at my locker. He didn't even come that close. He... he asked if we could go to the coffee shop. My stomach... I thought I was going to throw up on him. I even felt it coming up to the back of my throat. I think I shook my head no. He looked at me. I can't imagine what he saw in my face. He looked totally confused. Maybe horrified. He just left. I hid my face in my locker till I calmed down."

Rik thought it through before he spoke. "I'll take care of you. I'm not going to leave you alone." He realized what he was promising: that his life would be bent to his sister's needs, as if he were her parent.

"No. You don't understand. I'm not done. When he asked me... to go...and I thought I was going to be sick, I felt other things, too. My therapist said many girls who get raped feel this, but I never told you. Besides wanting to run, I also want...I wanted to go with him. I wanted him to touch me. I wanted to touch him. I wanted to make him take me. If I could have, I would have jumped him right there, in school."

"I know."

"It's awful. These... What do you mean, 'you know'?"

"I read about it. When I was in counseling, we talked about it. The therapist gave me some things to read about what it's like after."

"What things? I never saw you reading anything about being raped?"

210

"A couple of books. I went to the library, picked them off the shelves and read them there. I didn't want you to know. I thought you'd be embarrassed. Anyway, it makes sense when you think about it: that you should feel that way."

Jessa squeezed him. "You really do try to take care of me, don't you?"

"I try."

"I was lying on the bed."

"Yeah. I know."

"I was fantasizing."

"I don't think I want to hear this."

"You have to. And that boy was lying beside me and I bit him on the neck and injected him with my paralyzing vampire venom. And when he couldn't move, I undressed him and touched him all over. But gently. I was very gentle."

"Sounds like rape to me."

Jessa let him go and sat on the bed. "Yeah. I thought of that, too. But I felt fine. I didn't throw up. I was in control. That's what made it bearable. I was in control. If I'm ever going to fuck anyone I'll have to knock them unconscious first."

Rik heard Jessa's labored breathing.

"Don't worry about me. Do your thing. Get married. Have kids. I'll take care of myself." She leaned forward, hugged herself and cried.

Rik sat and put his arm around her. "I'll be there for you."

Jessa exploded. "No, you can't! No one can!"

Something gray and formless inside her made Jessa need to be hard on herself. She found it easy to be hard on herself. She calmed down the way a foreshock passes to a returned stability just before the volcano rends itself to fire and ash.

She remembered her thoughts of suicide and the question of how someone who knew that the pain continued after death could kill herself. It was a way of reopening contact with her brother. She looked at Rik.

"Yes, sister?"

"I lied."

"About?"

"About whether I wanted to kill myself. Since Meph...I've thought about killing myself a lot. Almost every time I think about what he did. But... Listen to me. Stop looking like you're going to put me behind bars to keep me from committing suicide. I do want to kill myself, but it's the self I've become since Meph. I want to kill that self, but not the self I was, the person I used to be. I want to crawl out of the skin of Meph-me and be me again. I mean, I know I can't make it unhappen, that it will always be part of me. It's just right now it seems to be all of me."

"You're a brave woman."

"No, that's not true. I didn't choose this...whatever it is. Someone made it happen to me."

"You're brave to feel it, to know it, to know what needs to happen, to still hope it can happen. I respect you. A lot."

"You understand what I mean, right?"

"I think so."

"Good. Thanks."

"You're welcome."

"There's something else that I can't tell you because it's too crazy."

"You don't have to tell me all your sexual fan..."

She shook her head. "Not that. Remember that Poe story, 'The Purloined Letter,' where the missing letter is in plain sight?"

"Yeah."

"It's like that."

"Tell me."

Jessa paused. "You did listen to me. Okay. So Ellen, we think, knew about the ghosts."

"Yeah. Hard to imagine she didn't."

"Okay. So, she knew that at least some people, or part of them, can become ghosts after they die. And that if they do, they suffer almost as bad as they did when they were alive."

"Yeah."

"So, if you knew that, why would you kill yourself?"

*   *   *

Rik rummaged in the freezer in hopes of finding some frozen pizza for a bedtime snack. His parents were upstairs sleeping, as far as he knew. He had done his best all evening to give Jessa space.

The best the freezer had to offer was a couple of frozen donuts, the sight of which made his hunger recede.

He ate a frozen donut without thawing it and gnawed on the problem Jessa had put to him.

The landline rang.

He thought about letting the call go to the answering machine, then decided to answer.

"Damn you, Gary! This is the second time...the second time you've made me call you today. If it isn't you, it's one of your dumb kids! That son of yours is a piece of work. You know he's all lovey-dovey with some black chick, don't you? Well, if you don't, you should. And if you do know, you need to do something to stop it! Who's in charge in your house anyway? They've even caused an uproar at school. You'd better get control of your family, or the neighborhood is going to have to take drastic action! Do you understand? This is serious!"

Rik allowed a few seconds to pass.

"Gary, are you listening to me?"

"Actually, he's not. But I'll be sure to let him know what you said. Your concerns are very important to us."

*   *   *

Jessa had exhausted herself on homework but fought against sleep. Rik slept on his sleeping bag on the floor, his copy of his new assignment, Huxley's The Island, beside his head. She sat at her desk, which they'd dragged in from her bedroom, along with her dresser, into Rik's now-very-crowded room. She decided to sketch a bit, nothing serious, just to try a couple of ideas that had occurred to her. She wanted to use the scraps of paper still in her room.

She turned on the light in her room and grabbed the paper from a shelf just inside the door. The room remained relatively shadowed despite the ceiling bulbs burning. She saw her bed, and, sitting on it, a figure, a ghost girl. The child seemed a few inches shorter than herself, younger, but weighed down by a burden. She sobbed and rubbed her eyes.

Jessa wasn't one to leave someone in tears without trying to help. Slowly she closed the door behind her and approached the girl.

The girl lifted her face. She looked at Jessa through red eyes. A single tear ran down her cheek. Her hair barely curled, and her skin looked paler than either Celisa's or her mother's. The child had a hole gouged out of her body from her heart to her crotch. It had been stuffed with dirt. Soil. Particles scattered when she moved.

"What's wrong?" Jessa whispered to avoid waking anyone, to maintain their privacy.

The girl pushed against the hair that had fallen in her face. She stood.

Brown eyes and gray eyes gazed into each other.

"I'm Nan."

"Jessa." She remembered the name. This was the twelve-year-old that Rik had told her about, the one who had given birth to the dead child.

Nan raised a hand and touched Jessa's face, beginning with the outline of her mouth, then across her cheeks, then around her eyes. The ghost said, "You're sad. You're like me; you're sad."

Jessa let go a breath. "I'm sorry you lost your child."

214

Nan cocked her head. Her eyes widened. "No. No. Didn't lose the poor thing. I sent her away! I sent her away so she wouldn't suffer, so no man would whip her or use her. I know! And I know what you're asking. Why didn't I send myself away?" Her face grew serious. "I'm frightened. They forgave me, my mom and sister did, for sending my baby away; the master would whip me for stealing if he knew, but I don't care about him. Ain't no forgiveness for sending yourself away. Just Hell, they say. I afraid I not see my baby again.

"You been used by men. I been used by men. We almost sisters, though our skin...our skin..."

Jessa licked her lips. "There's something you might know that I want to ask."

"I know."

"You know?"

Nan looked into Jessa's eyes. "I want to draw."

Jessa wondered at what she thought was a sudden change of subject. But she felt excited. "Have you tried?"

Nan looked at Jessa as if the older girl was crazy. "They don't let me have paper or pens."

"But you want to try? You'd like me to help you try?"

"I need to draw."

"I know what you mean. I feel that need, too."

"No! I need to draw to show you what happened! You have to know what happened, what I saw happen."

Now Jessa understood. "How... What should I do?"

Nan spread her arms.

Not having any idea what else to do, Jessa spread hers.

The girl walked up to Jessa and stopped. Nan looked into her eyes. "You ready?"

"Yeah." Jessa wondered, ready for what.

Nan walked into Jessa, ghost flesh and bone against living flesh and bone.

215

Jessa felt Nan alive inside her own body.

Jessa felt a flowing, a mixing, a joining, a closeness both sexual and spiritual.

She felt Nan's wound merge with her own.

Jessa felt the girl's mind within her own mind, her eyes behind her own eyes, her hands and arms and legs and feet inside her own. Jessa felt the girl's torn womb and knew she would never become pregnant again. She understood Nan's contentment with that. She felt what it was like to be African; to be a person, but despised by power; to be property and yet know you are more; to have killed your own child to save it; to regret everything, to hate your life, and to still want to love the world.

"Walk us into your brother's room."

Jessa turned out the light and closed the door behind them.

Rik remained asleep.

"Sit."

Jessa sat.

"Take a sheet of paper and your pencil. I will draw. I will show you what I saw."

After several minutes of practice, Jessa learned to surrender her arm and hand to Nan's guidance. It was a ballet of two arms and hands. The young girl possessed a good eye for detail, a good sense of arranging the elements of a picture. What Jessa experienced as a sure hand became unsteady as the sketch subject became visible. The eraser got a number of calls. The more the drawing progressed, the more Jessa found herself overcome by fear...and by rage.

"Please," Nan said, "don't shake."

Jessa steeled herself.

When Nan had finished, Jessa stared.

"This is what I saw."

Jessa made no reply.

"Thank you." Nan shook. "Please let me go now."

Jessa stood, arms again spread.

Nan stepped out of Jessa.

Jessa felt alone, deserted.

"I must go back to your room. I live there now. I hope you don't mind. I need to be alone. I don't like people. I don't like being with anyone at all."

Nan turned and walked through the wall that separated Rik and Jessa's bedrooms.

Jessa never thought of thanking the girl. It wasn't the sort of thing one felt thankful for.

"Rik!" Rooted to where she stood, Jessa whispered harshly. "Rik!" She kicked him in the ribs. Tears fell. "Wake up! Get up! I need you!"

Rik's eyes cracked open. "Stop! That hurt!"

"Get up. I've got to show you."

"Can't you say you're sorry?" He sat up.

Jessa held the paper against herself, the drawing hidden.

Rik stood and rubbed his face. He said, "Damn. What's going on?"

"That girl who had that baby you saw buried? Nan?"

"Yeah."

"She lives in my room."

Rik frowned. "Oh?"

"She asked me if she could draw something she saw."

"Ghosts draw?" Rik was not the best person to wake in the middle of the night.

"She walked inside of me, she...inhabited me, and we drew what she saw." Jessa held the paper toward him. "This is what she saw."

Rik held the picture. His hands began to shake. His teeth pressed on his tongue to keep him from screaming. Tears came.

By the placement of the windows, it appeared to be Jessa's room. The bed had been pushed back against the far wall. A hook had been screwed through the ceiling plaster, probably into a beam.

217

A rope had been passed through the hook.

A man he didn't recognize held one end of the rope, leaning back, legs spread, bracing himself against the weight that hung from the noose at other end.

The person in the noose was Ellen Scarpacia.

A second man appeared to be restraining her hands behind her, but the view of what exactly it was he was doing was blocked by Ellen's body. His face was not.

The second man was Clint Adams.

A third person wrapped arms around Ellen's legs, pulling her down, adding to the weight that was stretching and bending the girl's neck, choking the life out of her.

Annie Jessop.

Jessa said what didn't need to be said. "Ellen Scarpacia was murdered."

CHAPTER ELEVEN
THURSDAY

Rik wanted to crawl out of his skin. "Fuck!" The would-be writer found no other words. "Fuck!" Jessa whispered, "Calm down, Rik." She put her arm around him. With her free hand, she touched his arm and pointed. A drone whizzed past them on its merry, snooping way.

Neither had slept during the remainder of the night. It wasn't exhaustion that made Rick want to collapse on the ground, dig a hole and hide in it rather than continue on their way to school. It was despair at the world. Who wanted to be part of a world in which police officers and neighbors murdered a high school student because...because why? Because she'd seen black ghosts? A scream of obscenity was the only possible rational response.

Jessa hadn't slept at all but felt surprisingly, if somewhat numbingly, awake. She needed to cry, but needed even more to be in rational fighting mode. Calm reason, she told herself, was her goal.

She said, "We can't tell Steve, we can't show him Nan's drawing before school."

Rik agreed. "He'd leave school looking to kill Clint and Annie. We'd have to follow him and stop him. For some reason. Explain that to me again."

"You know why! And we can't tell him until school is over. And we should have a group of us to help calm him down. Or restrain him."

"A group of us? Us and who else?"

"Celisa."

"Sure. And Zach?"

"I guess."

Rik said, "We're going to have to tell them everything. No secrets anymore."

"We don't owe that murdering bastard Clint fuck."

"Fuck: that's my word of the morning. You can't use it."

"You're a sick fucking bastard, Rik, you know that?"

They laughed. Briefly.

*　　　*　　　*

Dr. Dreier, running a few minutes late, got off the elevator and found her office door not only unlocked but open. The security system box by the door showed no signs of being activated.

She took several seconds to think the situation through.

Gently, she pushed the door fully open.

She saw that no one was in the waiting room.

She called, "Charlie!" She didn't expect a response and got none. Charlie was hardly ever there before she arrived.

The door to her office was off to the right of the waiting room. It stood open.

Quickly, she stepped to the door.

She sighed as she realized her desk and files had been rifled.

She went to her desk and pulled open the top right drawer. Her gun was missing. The leg iron remained.

She dropped her briefcase and bag on the desk and picked up the leg iron. Just in case.

She went into Charlie's office. That too had been rifled.

She knew where to look. No surprise to find the two files missing and no others.

Psychiatrists had to protect themselves. Clients and clients' significant others could be violent. Dr. Dreier knew her security system. She knew who would have had the knowledge and access to turn her system off.

She decided not to notify the police of the break-in.

*　　　*　　　*

Tom Morton, the man Clint Adams had hired to rid Paradise of ghosts, loaded his luggage into a rental van at Logan

Airport. This was not a matter of simply counting the four pieces of luggage in front of him. One piece contained his clothing. That piece he ignored.

The other three he opened one by one and painstakingly accounted for each item inside using a checklist. Too many times during his travels security people had pilfered some of the contents "for further study." Much of what he carried with him was not only necessary but irreplaceable and incomprehensible to most citizens.

Two things bothered him and lingered in his mind.

Assignments in which the clients wanted Tom to rid them of ghosts without wanting to understand the reasons behind the haunting rarely ended well. He had already begun to learn more than his client wanted him to know about the ghosts of Paradise.

Tom's second concern was the pain in his right leg. His leg had never been wrong since it was broken twelve years before in a Christchurch earthquake. Pain in his right leg meant rain. Of course he had checked the weather before he'd left. The predictions had been unanimous: sun, heat and humidity. However, as he was loading his luggage, a sharp pain ran up and then down his right leg, deeper and more persistent than he could remember. The weather app on his phone continued to project sun and nineties. He looked skyward. Just blue. Not a wisp. Something was up.

*   *   *

Gary sat at his desk thinking until Miriam came in. He told her "Good morning," then resumed thinking. He remembered that, as a young teen, he had been excited about a career he'd dreamed of having. He remembered the energy he'd felt working toward it. But he couldn't remember what that career had been. Nor did he have any idea why his plans hadn't worked out.

As crazy as it was, he felt he was standing in his way to remembering.

221

It puzzled him, too, that he should feel so reluctant to work. Disinterested, he decided, was a better word. But he knew, he always seemed to have known, that work was what everything was about. He searched his mind for reasons. Gary knew that, if he kept this up, Art would find out and fire him, but he couldn't rouse any feeling of concern. He felt in the front halls of his mind that it did matter, but he knew it wasn't enough. He wanted to explore the back halls, the small rooms he'd forgotten about, places he might learn why he had let the police take Paul, why he had visited him in jail, why he had attended his funeral—and why the first of those demanded repentance and the latter two respect. When he continued to ask himself why, his only answer was that, somewhere below his heart and above his gut, sat a knife-edged emptiness he hadn't been aware of before.

The emptiness made everything—the paperwork, his desk, the floor, the walls, Miriam—irrelevant. He wasn't tired, but he felt like sleeping. Suddenly he needed a smoke. He hadn't smoked in years, hadn't even thought about it for years. He rummaged through his desk drawers, though he knew he had quit long before his promotion got him this office and desk. Then he thought about getting a drink, but decided not to make the same mistake twice in one week. Dope. Anything that would gloss over the pain. Did his kids keep dope in the house? But he couldn't ask them. That would lead to problems. Besides, they were at school. Perhaps Miriam knew where...no. Not a good idea either.

What stupid things: feelings.

He decided that the only option was sleep. For that he needed a bed. He had no bed at work. He had a bed at home.

Simple computation.

Then he decided to make a stop on the way home to visit Paul's grave. Yes, he'd do that. To hell with Clint. Then go home to sleep.

"Miriam, I have meetings all day with customers. I won't be back till after you leave. Take messages. Got that?"

"Yes, Mr. Hollie."

"Thanks. You're a sweetie."

Miriam lost her smile. He'd never said that before. In fact, no one had called her "sweetie" in years. She remembered the last time. It had been a Saturday evening in the spring of...

*   *   *

Clint kept his house dark and cool. His living room was no exception. Three-layered curtains, regularly cleaned but nevertheless decades old and faded; ivory venetian blinds; and green pull-down shades barred the sun. The two low-wattage bulbs of the end-table lamps were the only light Clint allowed. Except for wear and tear and fading brought on by time, Clint had changed little in the living room for more than a decade.

Indeed, he kept the whole house dark, and repaired or replaced only out of necessity: appliances that died or flooring that broke through. His only improvement to the house had been a necessity: to have the central air conditioning upgraded.

The living room wasn't large, not nearly as large as the dining room, and Clint crossed it with three large steps. Back and forth, three steps each way, repeated over the course of more than an hour, Clint kept walking and waiting.

His damn phone wouldn't ring. It refused. He'd set it on the coffee table and it lay there, blank and innocent, like a smug criminal taking the Fifth.

Clint had taken the day off. It was an important day, the day his alleged Christian Shaman Witch Doctor, whatever-he-called-himself, was due to arrive. He'd even sent the man a down payment as demanded. Now his calls went unanswered.

To a more rational mind, this would have been less disturbing. Clint had a Plan B. In fact, whether or not this witch doctor showed up, and no matter what, if anything, happened if he did, Clint intended to go to Plan B. Plan A was solely a deception.

But Clint needed events to occur in good order. He disliked leaving decisions to others, any others, pretty much all of whom he believed to be unreliable if not untrustworthy. This included most of his fellow officers and pretty much all of law enforcement everywhere. It included his neighbors Steve, Pat, Nick and Gary. This judgment did not include Mr. Sands, whom Clint needed to make his plan work. People did not get as wealthy as Sands had, or as connected with the men who ran the world, by being unreliable or untrustworthy. The richest of the rich, Clint believed, still held to a code of honor.

So Clint paced around the cluttered room, waiting, sweating, sometimes discovering his hands shaking uncontrollably. Once in a while he glanced at his wife, perched, as, always, on her pedestal.

How slowly time moves when we're waiting in a dark room!

The phone lit. It sang its merry little marching tune.

Clint grabbed it.

The person on the other end wasn't a witch doctor.

It was Sergeant Bellihue.

"Clint."

"Yeah, what do you want. I'm off today."

"I know, but you'd better come down here. We've a...gentleman in custody claims he knows you."

"The whole town knows me. Handle it."

Clint knew that was the thing about police. They loved authority. They loved to suck up to authority. Authority gave them their jobs and protected them. You got your voice into that command tone and they'd do whatever you told them.

Clint ended the call. The phone lit again.

"Jesus, what now?"

"Listen, Clint, I wouldn't be calling you if I didn't think this was something you needed to know."

"What?" His voice had a cutting edge. "Tell me!"

"We picked him up driving through downtown in a rental van. He was driving and the only person in the car. The reason we picked him up was we read his GPS. He was heading for your house. And we recovered some stuff from his vehicle that appears to be drugs. We're sending them to the lab."

Clint glanced at his wife. "Holy shit. You assholes. I'll be down." He threw his wife a kiss.

*   *   *

Zach figured out where they could meet. He played alto sax for the jazz band. He created an excuse to call off rehearsal that afternoon, and the music room the band had reserved became free. It was soundproof. It was also windowless and pretty much airless. It could be uncomfortable.

*   *   *

The booking officer asked Tom what he did for a living.

"Well, I'm a doctor."

"You from the Midwest?"

"Sure am."

"Could tell by your accent."

"You're sharp. I haven't been there for years."

"We have to keep a lookout for n'okies."

Tom frowned. "How do you know I'm not one?"

The officer appeared pained. "You don't have the look."

Remembering his childhood and high school, Tom asked, "I don't look like I'm from the Midwest?"

"No. You don't look like a n'okie. And they don't have valid credit cards."

"Interesting."

"So you're an MD?"

"Yes. Psychiatrist, actually. I also have an undergraduate degree in botany and doctorates in theology and ethnology."

225

"What's that mean?"

"Nothing."

"So, you practice medicine?"

"Sure. That will do."

"Alright. We're going to hold you until Officer Adams gets here." Under his breath and somehow without moving his lips, the booking officer said, "Lucky you."

Tom asked the man walking him back toward the cells, "So Officer Adams is an important figure in the police department?"

"Everything that happens here is recorded."

"Ahh! And is Officer Adams chief among those who believe in his importance?"

"I would never say that." The policeman smiled involuntarily as he locked the cell door.

Tom found himself sitting on a steel bench beside a chipped and stained toilet in a single cell painted in what could only be described as "depression green." The paint, he sensed, was depressed both because of its color and because of what it had seen.

He closed his eyes and paid deep attention and didn't lift that attention back to the "real world" until he heard his name. He opened his eyes to see another police officer.

The man repeated, "Tom Morton?"

"Yes. Officer Adams?"

"The same," Clint said. "My apologies for the misunderstanding."

Tom replied, "No apologies needed." He stood and shook Clint's hand through the bars. The only thing faster than Tom's instinctive sizing up of an individual was the speed of light. It was as if Tom could see Clint covered with levers, buttons, switches, things here to pull, there to push. That is to say, easily manipulable. Tom also understood that Clint was both intelligent and unforgiving. Once Clint realized he was being manipulated, and he would sooner rather than later, then, hell.

"Your officers acted as any duty-bound law enforcement officers would act when they discover a strange rental van bearing out-of-state license plates driven by an unknown individual heading to the address of a local police officer."

Clint looked into the swimming blue of Tom's eyes and the open credulity of the man's face and decided he must be like those geniuses he'd read about who could solve impossible scientific riddles but couldn't figure out how to eat with knife, fork and spoon. "Well, I'll have the duty officer return your clothes and we can get going."

"Yes, we can. And my van, luggage, the tools of my various professions and those packages that your officers described as 'suspected drugs.' I do thank you. Oh, and my black bag. My doctor's bag. Need that."

As they left the police station, Tom, dressed and in possession of all his possessions, turned to Clint and said, "Clint—can I call you that?—I'm really so appreciative of you coming and getting me out of that cell. Despite the dedicated kindness of your fellow officers, based on what had happened there before, I'd begun to fear for my life."

Clint turned sharply toward the man. "Nothing happened there before! What the hell are you talking about?"

"Clint! Clint! Calm down. Don't be upset. Clint! What did you expect? Didn't you just hire me to deal with ghosts?"

*　　　*　　　*

An impulse made Evelyn stop outside of Jessa's door. Former door. Evelyn wanted to rest for a few minutes before starting dinner. Against her judgment, and with the feeling that she had lost an argument to someone who wasn't there, she opened the door.

The darkness brought about by the pulled blinds surprised her. So did the ghost of the little black girl with eyes swollen from crying sitting on Jessa's bed. The girl looked at her, surprised and

227

disappointed. Her expression carried an accusation that Evelyn understood the child to be making against her. She, Evelyn, had no business interrupting the poor child's four-hundred-year-long misery.

Evelyn backed up two steps and closed the door.

Dinner.

She clutched the word firmly in her mind.

She forgot about resting.

Dinner, God damn it.

She started down the stairs and nearly missed the first step. She lost her balance but recovered quickly. She didn't go headfirst down the stairs, but rather sat back on the top step with a thud.

She shook.

Everything felt wrong.

She could clean and clean and clean that room now, but it would always be that little ghost girl's room. Always.

Evelyn felt defeated by a ghost.

That hateful little ghost.

She really did need to lie down and rest a few minutes. She went into the bedroom. That was when she discovered Gary asleep in their bed.

*   *   *

Jessa, who stood through the meeting with her back against the door, underestimated the time it would take to fill Zach, Steve and Celisa in on what she and Rik knew. Part of the problem stemmed from her inability to hold to a straight story line. She backtracked and circled as she remembered details. Rik routinely broke in with comments that fleshed out her ramblings. Questions tested their memories. Rik commented that he wished he had written everything down right after it happened. And lastly, despite Zach's best efforts in getting fans for the room, the space quickly became stuffy and uncomfortably warm.

EDWARD J. SANTELLA

Celisa had understood from the moment she'd been invited to the meeting that something important was up. She was there because Rik and Jessa trusted her. Being experienced at ferreting out others' feelings and intentions, Celisa soon noticed Jessa and Rik's frequent glances at Steve. She figured they were gauging his reaction. She sighed as she decided that the point of this meeting had to do with Ellen.

Celisa hadn't anticipated a more personal connection. She held her breath, her mouth open, when Jessa told her that Belinda was her ancestor and wanted to meet her. She felt the world had unexpectedly opened to her.

As Jessa started recounting the events of the previous evening, Celisa leaned forward and pulled her knees toward her, as if she were hugging her legs. She, too, now watched Steve.

Steve's hopes had been denied too often in the past months for him to get excited by the meeting. That Rik and Jessa hadn't told him everything only reminded him that Ellen hadn't told him everything either. The sting of not being trusted, or of being protected, hurt. In any event, he hadn't expected ghosts. He tried to imagine Ellen's reaction to discovering her neighborhood was haunted, how that had caused her to...

Jessa took the paper she and Nan had drawn from her backpack. "All of you should see this at the same time." Her voice, already tired from talking so long, broke. She took a swallow of water and a deep breath. She began again. "It's awful. Horrible. But most likely the truth."

Zach, Celisa and Steve stood and approached her.

"Steve, please..." She couldn't finish.

She placed the sketch in front of them and closed her eyes.

Zach saw, looked quickly away and sat back down.

Celisa sat, covered her eyes with her palms and sobbed.

Steve turned to plaster, fragile, immobile, feeling nothing. Rik put his arms around him and felt the boy shudder. A low moan

229

came from the place that existed before words. Tears welled like a flood but he held them back. He did not cry. In a voice that wasn't his own, as if a ghost had possessed him, he asked, "Who are they?"

Jessa pointed. "Clint Adams. Police Officer and our next-door neighbor. Annie Jessop, our next-door neighbor on the other side. We don't know who the other man is."

Zach and Celisa shook their heads.

"Jesus, they murdered her," Steve growled. "They fucking murdered her. They murdered her and told everyone she'd killed herself." He felt his breaths coming harsher and easier. No more self-questioning. No more guilt. Just pure, roaring rage burning though a storm of tears.

Rik held him tightly, quite aware that Steve was bigger and stronger than he was.

"It's okay, Rik. I'm not going anywhere."

Rik let the young man go.

Steve walked to Jessa, threw his arms around her, and said, "Thank you." Jessa controlled herself long enough to return the hug. Steve was giving her a different kind of hug. The not-wrong kind. After several seconds during which he looked at Jessa, he turned and walked back to Rik. They shook hands. Steve said, "You, too. Thank you." He looked around. "I guess we have to do this together. No one can do this alone."

*   *   *

Evelyn sat at the dining room table, head resting between her hands, with a plate of food in front of her. Gary had woken just before four p.m. As if it were morning, he had showered, gotten dressed and went off to work.

More than three times as much food as she needed sat in pans and on an oven tray on the stove cooling. Evelyn said to herself, "A husband and two children and I have dinner alone." She said

it again. "A husband and two children and I have dinner alone."
She'd said it. She'd heard it. Now it was real.

She refused to put on the monitor or play music. She ate aggressively but slowly, spearing each green bean, each chunk of glazed potato, each slice of marinated chicken as if taking revenge. She tore each item off the fork with her teeth.

When done, she took her plate and utensils and slam-dunked them into the dishwasher. She covered the leftovers and shoved them into the fridge. When the door wouldn't close because the green beans hung over the shelf, she slammed the door and forced it to close. To hell with the green beans.

She could hardly keep up with her feet as she went upstairs. Without second-guessing herself, she walked straight into Jessa's bedroom and pushed the door closed behind her.

The room was blindingly dark.

The ghosts were all she could see. Three of them: the young girl who still sat on the bed looking sad and put-upon, an elderly woman wrapped against the chill night air rocking in her chair, and a man of barn-sized dimensions who had frozen mid-fiddle.

The ghosts appeared more surprised by Evelyn's appearance than she was by theirs.

"Alright," she said, "since you're the only people who will stay home with me, one of you is going to tell me what the hell is going on around here!"

The man laid the fiddle and bow across his legs and said, "Well, I guess the best person for that that would be my ma, Missus Belinda here, ma'am."

*   *   *

Clint had a glass of wine in his right hand. With a motion of his index finger, he indicated he wanted Tom to join him. Tom excused himself from his conversation with Pat.

Clint had invited the neighborhood committee over to meet and greet Tom.

"Hey, Tom, how you doing?"

"Good. Good. Nice neighbors you got."

"Hey, uh I just wanted to sort of explain, you know? I mean, you probably think, you being a psychiatrist and all, it's kind of strange that, uh, I mean, like maybe you think I'm cracked. Or something like that, you know? I'm not. Really, I'm not."

Tom put on his best quizzical face. "No. Of course, you're not." He switched to his seriously interested face. "Why would you think I'd think what you think I think?"

Clint nodded his head toward his wife.

You could say that, in a personal setting, Tom had a way of getting people to open their lives and souls to him, to confess and feel, if not forgiven, at least accepted back into the ranks of the human simply because he had listened. Tom took no action to inspire such revelations. It was who he was. People looked into his eyes and saw a grandparent willing to hear without judgment. Perhaps it was the color or expression in his eyes or the way he bent toward you with complete attention when he listened. Whatever it was, it worked. People regularly exhausted Tom with their confessions.

Tom raised his head as if struck with sudden understanding. "Your wife. Well, I should say she's quite beautiful. Really. Unusually beautiful. You're a very lucky man to have a wife as beautiful as that."

"Thank you." Clint dropped his head. "They don't make women like her anymore."

"I should say not."

"She has class. She has dignity. Good taste. She deserves respect. She knows her role in life. She knows how to dress and how to act. She knows how a real woman behaves, especially with her man. Now women drop their panties and spread for anyone."

Tom nodded seriously. "I've heard that, too."

"You're not married, are you?"

"Oh, no, no, no." Tom put up his hand as if to say, "I absolutely refuse to join the mine-defusing unit."

"She means everything to me."

Tom noted the present tense. "I can see she would. You have been a very fortunate man to have known and loved a woman such as her." He saw Clint was verging on tears. "That's a wonderful way to honor her. Not many husbands would have done that. Impressive. Really. Very impressive."

"Thank you."

"No, I don't think you're cracked, Clint. You're in love with someone who can't be here. You've memorialized your love in the best way you can. No woman could ask for more. I'm sure she's truly honored. Truly honored." Tom did respect Clint for this. The man was clearly twisted in ways Tom as yet didn't fully understand, but you had to admit that Clint tried. Far beyond the call of duty, Clint tried.

Tom deposited his empty wine glass on the tray held by Clint's wife. Because she stood on a pedestal, he had to reach a bit. He took a full glass from the tray, looked the woman in the eye, nodded, and said, "Thank you. Very good wine." Tom continued, "Amazing work. I mean, I didn't know her when she was alive, but she is very lifelike. Madame Tussaud's people?"

"Actually from the Musée Conti in New Orleans. Yes. Yes. Amazing what they can do. I, uh, hired some people right after New Orleans...you know. They were unemployed."

"New Orleans. Right. Terrible. Terrible. No one saw that coming."

"No, no one. Terrible." Clint wet his lips. "Tom?"

"Clint?"

Clint glanced furtively around. He licked his lips. "I've never...seriously, I've never"—he swallowed—"ever told"—he

233

coughed—"this to anyone...before...but somehow I feel...uh, I feel I must tell you."

"Clint, don't. Really. I appreciate your confidences, but, really, we only met today."

"No. No, Tom, I really, really feel I have to do this. I don't know why. Maybe Scarlet is talking to me from where she is. That must be it. She wants me to tell you. I really feel I have to."

"Okay, Clint. I'm so honored."

"I've got another one upstairs."

Tom reissued his surprised face. "My God! Just like this?"

Clint's head bobbed up and down. "Yes. Yes. Yes! I mean almost...almost the same."

Tom waited.

"She's in our bed."

Tom released a long, long sigh of knowingness. "Clint, you dirty old man."

"I know!"

"That is genius!"

Clint leaned in a little closer. "She's got no clothes on."

Tom placed an arm around the officer. "Clint, you are one of the world's greatest lovers. Ever. In all of history. Oh, my. I'm so honored, I'm so amazed to meet a gentleman like you."

"Thank you. I feel so much better now that I've told you."

"May I ask how long it's been since she passed away?"

Clint cocked his head. "Oh, no." He bit his tongue. "No. She's not dead. No."

Tom returned to quizzical amazement. "Where is she, then?"

"Toronto."

"Toronto? I don't understand."

"She's on ice."

"Ice?"

"Ice. Cryogenics."

234

"Ahhhh!"

"She had terminal cancer."

"Oh, no!"

"When we found out, well, I did some research about cryogenics. You know Ted Williams had himself frozen?"

"The baseball player? No. I didn't know that."

"Yeah. That's how I heard about it. So when I looked into it, I mean, no guarantees or anything, but it looked promising."

"Amazing."

"So we decided together. She was nervous. You can understand that.

"Of course."

"But we did it. First they froze her and then they took out all the cancer."

"While she was frozen?"

"Yes, while she was frozen. And then they kept her. Until they think they've got the technology to bring her back."

"Oh, when will that be, do you think?"

"Now."

"Now?"

"Right now."

"Oh, my Lord!"

"All I got to do is come up with the money."

"I can't ask if you've got the money. That would be an invasion of privacy. I have no right to do that."

"Not yet. Let me tell you, it's a lot."

"Not yet? But soon?"

Clint grinned. "I got a plan! Pretty soon! I can feel it." He shaped and moved his hand as if rolling dice. "I can feel it!"

*　　　*　　　*

Steve sat on the floor in a corner, his back wedged against the angles of two walls. Rik had run out to buy iced tea and coffee. Zach and Celisa sat on chairs, the former spread out like a letter X, the latter bent forward, hands joined over the back of her head. Jessa sat on the floor, her back still against the door.

There was a soft kick against the door.

Jessa let her brother in. His hands were full of caffeinated drinks.

Rik said, "Jessa and I have a couple of ideas—actually I think it's only one—but first, do any of you have any thoughts on what we might do?"

"I want to find out who that guy is," said Steve. "I'd like to scan Jessa and Nan's sketch and see if we can find a match online. I wouldn't be really hopeful, but it's worth a try."

Jessa said, "Good idea."

Celisa sighed. Her eyes looked in, and when they looked out again, her face was stern, determined. "I've got some invest-ment in this deal. I want to meet her, Belinda, my great-what-ever grandmother." She waved Rik silent. "But I think we should all meet the ghosts, or as many who might be willing to meet with us. They set this all in motion. We can't know what to do until we know what they're about."

Rik nodded. Of course, it was only fair to Belinda and Celisa. "We'll do it."

Jessa looked at him, her expression asking, "Really? How?"

"We'll do it."

*　　*　　*

Once he was alone, Clint felt embarrassed by what he'd told Tom. That wasn't him. He wasn't the kind of guy who went around "sharing," as they liked to call it. In fact, the meeting had gone much like that. One after another, he, Pat, Nick, and Sandy had opened their souls to this stranger. For the first time in his life, Clint felt he knew too much about his neighbors.

236

Clint hadn't believed that anyone like Tom existed before. He'd expected a fraud. But now he'd seen him. He'd talked to him. He'd spilled his soul to him and watched three other grown men do the same.

Now he almost believed. Soon, he feared, he would see.

Should Tom do what he'd been hired to do, meaning get rid of the ghosts, Clint's plan would collapse. He'd achieve nothing.

He'd never hold his flesh-and-blood Scarlet again.

He couldn't take chances.

"Scarlet, I'm doing this for us."

He locked the house, got in his car and drove. He thought about going to the station and taking his patrol vehicle, but a Para dise police car outside of Paradise might attract attention.

*　　　*　　　*

Jessa spoke. "Mom, you don't drink whiskey!"

"I can damn well drink what I want to drink! Wine and weather aren't enough tonight."

Evelyn sat at the kitchen table, glass in hand beside the remains of the bottle. She looked at her children and smiled, not a pleasant smile, but a pleasantly inebriated smile. She raised her glass to them and said, "In the absence of my loving family, I spent ninety minutes talking to three intelligent ghosts. Black ghosts, at that." Her tipsy relationship with the world was evident. "And where have my children been?"

Rik straddled a chair. "Who did you see?"

Evelyn swallowed. "Sit," she said, motioning to her daughter. "Who did I see? Hmm. Who did I see?"

"Mom!"

"Hmm? I met Mrs. Belinda Sutton, a wonderful woman, reminds me of my grandmother, bless her; the little girl Nan, oh, how horrible, I can't..." She couldn't. She looked at her daughter.

237

Jessa saw her mother's face red with shame, her eyes tearing, red from rubbing, and pleading for some kind of sense to come from it all. "And I met Belinda's son and Nan's father, Joseph." She brushed tears away. For the smallest sliver of a second her mouth managed a smile. "How can someone so angry play the fiddle like he does!"

Jessa said, "He's damn scary when he wants to be."

"And," Evelyn said, drawing the three-letter word out to six syllables, "I could hardly contain my enthusiasm when I learned that poor girl Ellen was murdered in your bedroom, Jessa, by our two next-door neighbors." She wrinkled her nose. "Of course, you two knew that already, so that wouldn't be news to you." She made an angry face, then looked hurt. "You could have told me!"

"Mom, calm down." Rik continued, "If we'd told you, you probably wouldn't have believed us. Besides, we're still putting stuff together ourselves."

"Well, you'd better be putting stuff together fast because Big Tom is in town."

Rik narrowed his eyes.

Jessa asked, "Who?"

"Big Tom. The Christian Indian Shaman and Exorcisor."

"Exorcisor?"

"I think she means exorcist."

"They're having a meeting over at Clint's. By invitation only. I don't know what's big about him but I can hope."

"Mom!"

"Where's Dad?"

"Work. He came home sometime, I don't know when, he didn't tell me, and took a nap. Then he went back to work. He didn't tell me that either. I need to hire a detective to tell me when my husband is home."

"Mom, it's going to be alright."

"Really? We should ask Big Tom so we can be sure."

Jessa looked at Rik. "Mom, we think you should go upstairs and take a nap. You look very tired."

"Oh, really, I'll just sit here and..."

"Jessa's right, Mom. You need a nap." Rik closed his eyes and said, "You can bring the bottle upstairs with you if you want."

Evelyn's face lit slightly. "Well, that's a good idea. I think I'll do that."

Jessa walked her mother upstairs, carrying the whiskey for her, while Rik opened the back door to let their friends in.

Only Celisa stood at the door.

"Where are...?"

"We saw a guy pulling out of the driveway next door." She pointed. "Is that where Clint lives?"

"Yeah."

Celisa texted a confirmation to Zach. Then she said, "They're off following him."

*   *   *

Zach's phone chimed. "Celisa says that's him. We're probably following him to the police station."

"That's not the way he's heading." Steve sat up straight in the driver's seat, his eyes wide, trying to memorize the pattern of tail- and brake lights on the car ahead. Extraordinary, he thought to himself: here he was, tailing one of Ellen's murderers.

They fell into silence as Steve did his best to keep what they hoped was Clint's car in sight.

Steve's headlights picked out a shiny, squat traffic robot ahead, yellow and red lights flashing. "Shit."

Zach said, "What?"

"There's a robbie up ahead."

"We're busted."

"Just get your head down so it doesn't see you."

239

"We left our IDs back at home!" Zach folded himself up so that he couldn't be seen. "It'll wonder how the car is driving itself with no one in it."

"I took my dad's ID just in case this happened. Just stay down so it won't detect two people with one ID."

A few seconds passed. "It's okay," Steve murmured. "It gave us permission to pass. Just stay down until it's out of sight."

They followed Clint's car into Medford, where he turned left onto Route 60. The officer stayed on that road through Arlington and into Belmont, past two stoplights. Then he slowed.

Steve said, "He must be looking for something."

After another quarter of a mile, Clint's car's brake lights flared and the car suddenly stopped. The back-up lights came on. Then the brake lights again. The car turned right.

Steve drove quickly to the intersection and stopped. "The GPS doesn't have a name for this street. Must be a private way. You see a street sign?"

Zach got out of the car and flashed a light around. "Nothing."

"Damn." As soon as Zach was strapped in, Steve turned down the unknown road. He turned off his headlights and drove slowly, using the light of the infrequent streetlamps to drive by.

They'd lost sight of the taillights. The houses, few and far between, looked like cruise ships in the night, surrounded by gracious grounds and manicured lawns.

"You think we lost him?"

"Check the driveways as we go by. Maybe we'll recognize his car."

Most of the houses they passed were dark.

"What the hell is he doing out here anyway? Wait. There."

"I saw it." They'd caught the flash of brake lights as someone got out of a car. The house sat at the end of a moderately long drive that wound up a slight hill. The lights above the garage illuminated two cars parked side by side. One was Clint's. The other's trunk stood open. What appeared to be two suitcases sat on the ground beside the trunk.

"I think that's him. Look, there's someone else."

"Looks like someone else just got here. Or maybe was just leaving."

Beneath the light, two men shook hands.

Steve put the car in reverse until he'd backed up out of sight of the house. "Come on."

"What are we going to do?"

"How would I know?"

Steve turned the engine off. "Let's go." They ran up to the edge of the bushes that lined the front of the property. The front door was just closing.

The house appeared to be one of the larger ones on the road. The center entrance was bookended by two large, brightly lit rooms. One of the upstairs rooms was also lit.

Zach said, "That thing is so big we could move in and they'd never know."

"Look," Steve said, "you approach the house on the right and I'll come from the left."

The lights in the upstairs room flickered out.

"There's at least three people. What do you think?"

"What do we do if we get up to the house?"

Steve said, "Try to get in, or at least try to hear what they're saying."

Zach, not having a better idea, agreed.

He moved down the edge of the tree line closest to the driveway. He did his best to mimic the elbows-and-knees crawl of soldiers in movies. It went slowly. Every ten feet or so, he stopped to listen. He heard nothing. Why didn't they have security or dogs or something to guard the property?

He reached the trees closest to the house. He began moving toward the front.

Meanwhile, Steve used the bushes by the road as cover, confident that no one in the house would be able to see him. It was a different story when he reached the corner of the property. It was too dark to look for a path through the thicket of trees, so he crouched and moved quickly toward the house.

He stopped beneath the corner of the front room's window. He took a few deep breaths to calm himself, then slowly raised his head. The window had curtains along both sides and his view was obscured, though not blocked. He could see inside the room, and he hoped the curtain hid him from the inside.

Two men, their backs to him, stood in front of the mantel over a large fireplace. One of the men appeared to be showing an object to the other. Steve couldn't recognize either of them.

He saw movement on the other side of the front steps and hoped, then became sure, it was Zach. The boy crawled beneath the window of the front room on the other side, made a quick waving gesture to Steve, then went up to the door. Slowly, he tried the handle. No noise, no movement. He looked at Steve and shook his head no.

Steve motioned to him that he'd meet him around back.

Zach and Steve circled the house and met at the back deck, which included a barbecue area, a pool and a hot tub. The deck led to a glassed-in porch. There were two doors: the first led onto the porch, the second from the porch to the interior.

Through the window they saw a woman dressed for a night out in a skimpy black dress working in the kitchen, pouring wine. She carried three glasses on a tray toward the front of the house. Zach and Steve's eyes met: not the style of woman they'd associate with Clint.

Zach tried the porch door. Locked. He looked to Steve and shrugged his shoulders. They weren't going to be able to get in, at least not unnoticed.

Suddenly the door from the house onto the porch opened. Steve and Zach dove into the shadows.

Light flooded the yard for a moment. Two poodles preceded the woman outside. She hooked the dogs' leashes to a wire that allowed the dogs to run the yard.

The woman returned inside. She walked out of the kitchen.

The dogs sniffed around and quickly found Steve and Zach to bum a couple of head pats. Then they ran off.

Zach tried the door again. Open.

Steve said, "Go."

The nob on the inner door turned and the door opened. Zach went to the left. The kitchen had two doors. The woman had gone through the one on the right both times. Apparently that led to the front room where the men were.

The second kitchen door led into a front dining room that gave access to the front hall and the second front room.

The boys settled behind a stuffed armchair by the door to the hallway. The room where the three adults sat drinking wine lay across the hall.

The voices came across the hallway muffled but under-standable. One voice, loud and burly, sounded used to giving commands. The other voice was more conversational, but no less authoritative.

Male #1: "I can't believe an obvious fraud like this Morton has you shaking in your boots."

Male #2: "You haven't met him."

Male #1: "No. And I don't need to. You need to be careful. Too may dead bodies create suspicions."

Male #2: "I know how to take care of things. No suspicion. He simply won't show up."

Male #1: "You can handle that?"

Male #2: "Of course. And when he doesn't show, that's when I announce your offer."

Male #1: (After a pause.) "Tomorrow night?"

Male #2: "Of course. That's always been our plan. I'm here to pick up the documents."

243

Male #1: "I was going to call you. It's too early."

Male #2: "What? What do you mean 'too early'? Have you given up on the casino? We planned it this way. Don't tell me the paperwork's not ready!"

Male #1: "No. Of course I haven't given up. Everything's ready. The deeds and checks are all there. All that's needed are the homeowners' signatures. But, look. We're going away for a few days. We'll finalize when I get back."

Male #2: "I'll have them all together tomorrow. I don't know when I'll be able to do that again. We do it and you can announce the new casino the day you come back."

Zach became aware of the sound first. Steve's concentration had focused on the discussion.

Zach turned his head slowly. His eyes met eyes, suspicious eyes in a head held low to the ground, as was the tail. Not one of the poodles, this was a larger animal. The dog growled low.

Male #1: "I said no. There are other factors. That's it. We'll review the situation when I return. There will be no discussion."

Zach smiled at the dog and held his hand, palm out, toward it. The dog stretched its neck and sniffed. Not a guard dog, Zach concluded. A good-looking dog. Perhaps a show dog.

Male #2: "What other factors?"

Male #1: "I said no further discussion."

Zack touched Steve, who had remained oblivious and jumped when he saw the dog.

The dog backed up and growled.

Male #2: "And I said what other factors."

Woman: "Clancy, is that you? What are you up to?"

Male #1: "Tax factors. Things you don't know about."

The dog took a step to leave the room but stopped. It seemed undecided. Zach waved it away. It left.

Male #2: "Alright. Fine. I'll play. Where are you going?"

Woman: "Hey, Clancy, I thought that was you. How are you, boy?"

Male #1: "Monte Carlo. We're going to have some fun, right, dear?"

Woman: "Looking forward to it."

The dog whined, then barked.

Woman: "You wait, Clancy. I'll feed you in a minute."

Male #2: "Taking your jet?"

Male #1: "Of course."

Male #2: "Then where are the deeds and checks?"

Male #1: "Upstairs in my office."

Woman: "Clancy, where are you going?"

Male #2: "Well, go get them and then you can be on your way."

Male #1: "You don't understand."

Male #2: "I don't understand what?"

Zach saw Clancy enter the room again. Clancy walked up to him and licked his face.

Male #1: "You don't understand...why we're going away...why we have to go away...this weekend. Look, I'll make you a deal. You come with us."

Steve tried to shush the dog away, but Clancy thought he had a new friend.

Male #2: "Come with you? Why? You're crazy."

Zach quietly led the dog from the room into the kitchen. Where would the dog food be? Too many cabinets.

Woman: "Listen up, cop. He's offering to save your ass."

Male #1: "Shut up! I'm doing the talking! Clint, listen. Trust me. Come with us. You'll be better off."

Zach headed for the fridge, opened it and found a drawer labeled "cold cuts." Inside was a packet of roast beef.

Male #2: "Why? What's going to happen if I stay?"

Male #1: "Shit. You're not supposed to know."

Zach began unwrapping the packet.

Male #2: "Know what?"

Male #1: "Jesus, man! Put that thing away! You think this is some barroom squabble you can settle with a gun? You can't get away with killing me like you get away with everyone else. Point that thing somewhere else, will ya?"

Zach heard the words and understood immediately. Jarred by the announcement of the gun, he fumbled and dropped the packet. Its contents spilled over the floor. Clancy thought it an act of love.

*   *   *

Gary drove home late even by his own standards. Not that he'd been working. He'd read the paper the way people read signs while waiting for a bus, listened absently to a game on the radio without knowing the score, and ordered a sandwich delivered from a local deli. He tossed the sandwich in the trash half-eaten. He was beginning to think no one would notice if he never did any work. The company seemed to run along fine without his attention.

Thoughts whirled around his mind, amazing thoughts that he would never have harbored two weeks before, but there were too many of them to hold at one time.

He didn't want to go home. Home was a box with problems labeled "family" and "ghosts." Not to mention the "Clint" problem next door. Not that he wanted to be in the "work" box either. As alternatives, his mind careened through options: a hermit's cabin in the woods; a cave in some undefined mountain range; and, lastly, sitting alone in his grave waiting for burial. The final option most appealed to him, as it seemed more just, a concept he'd begun to worry over lately.

The windows of almost all businesses and most homes had long gone dark by the time he got back to the neighborhood. Even Clint's house lay in darkness. Gary noticed Clint's car was missing, but, other than a mental sigh of relief, thought nothing of it. Police worked odd hours.

He pressed on his brakes and stopped. His car hadn't quite made it past Clint's house. Several lights in his own house burned, but it was the figure standing on the sidewalk in front that had gotten his attention.

Gary squinted into the shadows his headlights threw across his front walkway.

A ghost? George?

Slowly, he eased his vehicle into the driveway.

The figure didn't seem to notice him.

He set the parking brake and turned off the ignition. Keeping his eye on whatever it was in front of his house, he walked around the rear of his car and toward what he was coming to believe to be a flesh-and-blood man.

Gary was, in fact, in the middle of a desperate attempt to come up with something to say other than "may I help you" or "get away from my property or I'll call the police," when, without turning, the man spoke.

"Something hopeful is going on in this house."

Gary stopped a good ten feet away. "You're talking to me?"

The man turned a full circle, as if looking to see if there were someone else he might be speaking to, then half again, stopping when he faced Gary. "Yes, I believe I am talking to you."

Gary shifted his weight from left foot to right. "What makes you think something hopeful is happening? In there?"

"Well," the man said, "I hope I'm not being presumptuous, but the voices, the three of them, their tones are concerned, yes, actually deeply concerned, but there's even a bit of wisdom about them, and hope."

"My wife and stepchildren are hopeful?"

"Ah, no. The voices are of three children. Teens, I should say. Not an adult among them."

Gary, perplexed, answered, "You're wrong. I, I mean we, only have two children."

The man strode up to Gary. "Let me introduce myself. I am Thomas Morton. Your neighbor Officer Adams asked me here to help rid your neighborhood of ghosts. You can call me Tom."

"Oh." Gary glanced over his shoulder at Clint's house. "I'm Gary Hollie. You can call..."

"I see you distrust your neighbor."

"I didn't say that."

"You have a very expressive face."

"I do?"

"Would you introduce me to your family? I find them very interesting."

Gary was undecided about inviting an agent of the neighborhood into his house.

Tom said, "You have the most exceptional stepchildren, a son and a daughter I believe, and their friend."

"No, they're not allowed to have friends over. And how did you know I had a stepson and daughter?"

"I do my homework. And I have a very good sense of hearing. I can almost hear their words. Well, I am most anxious to meet them."

Gary found it impossible to refuse hospitality to a man who flattered him through his stepkids. Though he disagreed with the man's assessment, he said, "Certainly. Follow me."

*   *   *

Steve rubbed his aching knee. His frame was too large to comfortably fold up behind the armchair.

Male #2: "I trusted you. You gave me your word. I'm not letting you back out on me now."

Male #1: "You're not supposed to know about the storm."

Male #2: "What storm?"

Male #1: "Shit. Look. There's a Category Seven hurricane going to hit New York Friday and grind its way around Connecticut and Rhode Island. It'll be here late Friday night or Saturday morning. It's supposed to destroy pretty much everything from the coast to a hundred, hundred fifty miles inland. Certain people have been told and are getting out. We're among the lucky ones. You could be, too."

Zach returned and crouched again beside Steve.

Male #2: (After a pause.) "I don't believe it. I'd be one of the first ones to know if a hurricane was going to hit. We'd be..."

Male #1: "Only a few people know. Important people."

Male #2: "You're lying! They always notify the police. We have to prepare!"

Male #1: "It's Category Seven! Are you listening? It's too fucking huge to prepare for! The winds are up to two hundred ten miles per hour! It's hundreds of miles in diameter. I've seen pictures. It covers half the Atlantic. If it was announced, there'd be universal panic. You think there's a refugee crisis now with the n'okies? All of New England and half of New York would be flooding highways to get out! They decided to let the storm do whatever it's going to do. Better to have millions of drowned people than twenty-something million refugees doing whatever's necessary to get into upstate New York and Vermont. Even Pennsylvania and Ohio. God! Canada's already closed the border. Where would we put those people? They're better off dead. Now, are you coming?"

Male #2: "They decided to let the storm do what it's going to do?"

Male #1: "They're writing this place off. Just like those states in the Midwest."

Male #2: "We're too important.

Male #1: "When it comes to something like this, believe me, you've got to have a lot of something to be important. And you ain't got it, Clint."

Clint: "The fuck I don't! I put in my time! I worked hard! Long hours. I protected you and your billions. I never complained. I didn't ask how you got your money. I didn't ask questions. I forgot whatever I heard. I kept myself in check. I did what I was told! I lived with what I had to live with! You can't just write me off!"

Male #1: "I'm not writing you off. You're coming with us."

Clint: "No. No. You're not inviting me along because of the work I've done. You're only inviting me along because I'm holding a gun on you."

Male #1: "This isn't about work. It's about money. I've got it. You don't. Put the gun away and come with us."

Clint: "So you don't want to pay money for a casino in a disaster zone. I get it. I understand. Your word is only as good as the weather. Then we have to close the deal before the storm hits."

Male #1: "Clint, what the hell are you thinking!"

Clint: "I'll use this if I have to, so you better listen up. Hurricane or no hurricane, I'm doing the deal tomorrow. Call your pilot or whatever. Tell him you're postponing the flight till late tomorrow. Tell him I'm coming with you."

Male #1: "You crazy bastard!"

Clint: "Now! I mean now. Don't reach in your pocket. Your phone is on the coffee table. Now. Or both of you are dead."

Male #1: "Alright. Calm down." (Pause.) "Christ. I didn't hear the alarm go off. Did you? Something set off the security system. Something in the front and back yard."

Woman: "I put the dogs out."

Male #1: "They said they fixed that!"

Clint: "Forget your security system. Make the call! Now!"

Male #1: "Karl! Yeah, it's me. Look, we've had a change of plans. We decided not to go to Monte Carlo till tomorrow night." Pause. "No, I'm not joking. Really. We're staying here until then. About midnight. I know it's cutting it close. We'll have one passenger coming with us. Clint Adams. An associate of mine. Yeah. Thanks." (Pause.) "Okay, Clint, you got what you want?"

Clint: "Not yet. Almost, but not yet. This is about more than money but you two wouldn't understand. Well, I'm sorry to see you two go like this, but I have to do what I have to do."

Two gunshots. A scream. Two more.

Steve and Zach jerked with the sounds.

A bark, the sound of four feet running. Teeth penetrated flesh. A human scream. Another shot. A whimper. Silence.

*　　　*　　　*

Clint said, "Fucking dog." He paused. "Well, that wasn't so hard, was it? Yeah. Killing gets easier the more..."

But his hands were shaking, seemed removed some distance from his body, though one still held the murder weapon, the gun he'd taken from that psychiatrist's office. He'd had his fill of staring at the bodies. His eyes scanned the room, lurching from item to item, as if he'd come to rob the house. His vision settled on an odd mirror, hanging in a frame and no more than a foot on each side. The glass had been cut to distort its reflection.

"You tell me I'm not important enough to save? Really. Officer Clint Adams, American! If I'm not important enough to save you aren't either! Fuck you, you're dead! You and that bloody whore of yours. This deal is going through on time. I'm getting my money. Maybe I'll even ride your rich little airplane to Toronto."

Steve and Zach heard the sound of footsteps running upstairs, the opening of a door, a few minutes of no sounds and then footsteps descending. The lights in the kitchen went out. The rest of the lights went out.

Footsteps.

The front door opened and closed.

Zach ran to the window. "It's Clint. He's getting in his car."

Steve said, "Don't touch anything! Fingerprints."

"Okay."

"Is he gone?"

"Yeah. He just backed out and drove back toward Paradise."

"I'm going to turn the lights on."

"You said don't touch..."

"I'm using my handkerchief."

The lights returned.

Three dead bodies, two human, one canine, their blood still pooling. No. The woman opened her eyes and looked pleadingly at Steve. Then her eyes closed. Steve took pulses. "Nothing." He swallowed. "Look."

Zach, too, recognized the face.

The other man in Jessa's drawing.

A gun lay beside the dead man's right hand. Steve looked at Zach. "To make it look like a murder-suicide?"

Again using his handkerchief, Steve turned the lights out.

Zach said, "Wait! I touched the fridge."

Steve turned the lights back on so Zach could wipe the appliance clean.

They left by the front door.

They were about to get in the car when Steve said, "We still don't know who that guy is. Was."

"I'm not going back in there! I've never seen anybody die before."

"Me neither. Ask Clint about it. Apparently it gets easier."

"Wait," said Zach. "The mailbox."

"They probably picked it up hours ago."

"But out here I bet they leave mail they're sending in the boxes for the mailman."

Using Steve's handkerchief, Zach brought back an envelope. Steve put the name and return address onto his phone.

Zach replaced the mail and they drove off.

They'd gone a quarter mile when Zach asked Steve to stop. Zach opened the door and vomited.

When Zach closed the door, Steve said, "There're tissues in the glove compartment." A bit later, he added, "Here's some mints if you want them."

"Thanks." Zach glanced at Steve. He could see no reaction to what had happened. "I've sweated through everything, even my jacket."

Steve didn't look at him. He said, "Me, too. I'm soaked. But I'm cold. Freezing." It was some, a little, satisfaction that one of Ellen's killers was dead.

He breathed her name.

*   *   *

Gary opened the front door and saw Evelyn descending the stairs with the not-totally-unfamiliar, frantic, slightly flushed expression that meant she'd been drinking and had many important things to tell him immediately. She stopped in her tracks. She stared past him. Her mouth closed, her eyes narrowed, and she asked, "Gary, who is that behind you?"

"Tom...er, Tom..."

Tom gracefully danced past Gary. "Tom Morton. Hello."

"Are you allowed here?" she asked.

"I believe I am."

She exclaimed, "Oh, you must be Tom the Exorcisor! Annie told me about you."

Tom hesitated, a frown curling his face, trying to figure out what Evelyn meant. "Well, yes, not...I...am glad to meet you."

"Can I, uh, can I get you something?"

"A cup of coffee, if it isn't too late? You can reheat what you've got for me. You two might also want some."

"How did you know?"

"There was coffee? I have an extremely sensitive sense of smell."

"Yeah," Gary said, having second thoughts about letting the man in. "Get yourself one too, Evie. You need it. And one for me."

Evelyn didn't think there was enough for three, so she put on a new pot.

Tom sat. "I'd love to meet your kids."

"Oh, right." Gary disappeared. From the bottom of the stairs he called, "Jessa? Rik? Come down. Someone wants to meet you."

Seconds later, the sound of four feet cautiously descending echoed from the stairs.

Gary brought another chair from the dining room, put it at a corner of the table and sat.

"See? There are only two."

Tom nodded at the brother and sister.

Jessa and Rik stood sizing the stranger up.

Evelyn made the introductions. "Rik. Jessa. This is Mr. Tom Morton from, uh, I forget."

Rik searched the man's face for clues.

Jessa glanced at Rik, forced a smile and sighed. She knew what was coming.

Tom said, "Very nice to meet you. Why don't we all just have a seat?" He poured a bit of milk into his coffee. "Now, Rik and Jessa, I know you've gone through this recently and it's tiring, but, please, tell me, and don't mind if I interrupt you along the way with questions, everything you know about the ghosts haunting this neighborhood."

"Wait." That was Jessa. "First of all, why ask us? Why not ask our parents? And what makes you think we did this recently?"

"Well, I noticed a few things. As you entered, each of your parents looked at you two, back and forth, one to the other, wide-eyed and with very firm mouths, indicating to me that your parents were concerned about what you'd have to say. Jessa, you and your brother both looked, not at your parents, but at me. Clearly, among the four of you, you and your brother have the most to say.

"And as for knowing you'd gone through this recently, well, the look you gave Rik along with that soul-weary sigh"—here he mimicked her—"were as good as saying 'again?'"

Jessa squinted at him. "You're good."

"Thank you. So are you. And your brother."

Jessa said, "Before we answer your questions, if we do, aren't you working for the, uh, neighborhood? For Officer Adams?"

"Ah, I see you share your father's opinion of your next-door neighbor. Funny, I got the feeling this afternoon that some of his brothers in blue also see him as somewhat of a problem."

"The question I asked is: do you work for him?"

Tom squinted at the girl. "How old are you?"

"Fifteen. Answer the...I mean, please, answer the question."

"Well, I'm here because Clint invited me and because he sent a deposit on my fee. As I understand it, I'm supposed to try to get rid of ghosts. Is that a goal you all agree with?"

Rik frowned. He said, "We don't know yet."

Tom's eyebrows went up.

Jessa said, "Rik's right. We don't know enough yet."

Tom nodded his head. "Do the ghosts want to leave or stay?"

"The ghosts are here to watch our destruction," Rik said.

Tom bit his lip. "Whoa. You'd better tell me the whole story."

Jessa colored. "There's something you might want to know first."

"I know," said Tom. "It's up to you whether you want the others to know."

Jessa sighed and looked at Rik.

Tom added, "She might have contributions to make."

Rik said, "Okay. Should I bring her down here or should we go upstairs?"

"Who her?" demanded Gary. "Who's upstairs?"

Jessa said, "A friend."

Gary, face flushed, came half out of his seat. "You know you're not supposed to bring anyone here! Clint will..."

255

"Gary, calm down." Welcome back to life, Gary, Evelyn thought. "Let's find out what's going on before we...we..."

Tom said, "Before we anything. Very on point, Mrs. Hollie."

"Evelyn," she replied.

Jessa said, "Let's go upstairs. The ghosts seem to feel more comfortable in our bedrooms."

Gary's mouth opened, but Evelyn again placed a hand on his arm before he could say anything.

Rik said, "We should bring some chairs up."

"Wait, I'm going to bring the coffee."

Upstairs they went, four each carrying a chair and Evelyn carrying a tray with coffee and cups.

On the way, Gary noticed Tom favoring his leg.

"Problem with your leg?"

"Yes. It's telling me very strongly that we are going to have rain, and a lot of it, very soon."

Evelyn, who was behind them, said, "The weather today said sunny through Monday."

Gary said, "I never trusted those weather forecasters."

Evelyn recognized the black girl who'd been with Jessa when she picked her daughter up from school, the one who, last she'd heard, wasn't supposed to be her son's girlfriend.

Jessa made introductions.

"Mom, Dad, Mr. Morton, this is our friend Celisa."

Celisa said, "Good to meet you."

Gary scowled.

"Oh," the girl said, trying to justify her presence, "And the, uh, the reason I'm not wearing my ID is I left it at my home so Clint, I mean Officer Adams, wouldn't know I'm here. My mom, though, she knows I'm here."

Evelyn tried to remember what she'd said about the girl to Jessa, but she felt she had a more pressing question. "Rik, why do you have a girl in your bedroom?"

Rik said, "She came with two other guys, but they're not back yet."
Evelyn was sure that wasn't an answer but she somehow felt comforted.

Rik and Celisa sat on the bed. The others took chairs, leaving one chair open. Evelyn squinted suspiciously at the narrow-to-invisible space separating Celisa from her son.

Jessa began. The story came easier this round. Jessa had her facts lined up and Rik and Celisa freely contributed.

Tom listened mostly. He asked a few questions, but Jessa and Rik were good with details, so he didn't have many. Celisa's comments caused him to smile. She understood that she could become the center of the conversation, but she refused that role. She persisted, instead, in being part of the discussion. Celisa understood she was descended from ghosts. But then again, Tom thought, aren't we all?

*   *   *

You couldn't trust anyone anymore, Clint thought as he drove back toward Paradise. Not even rich people. The country, the whole fucking world, was falling apart because everyone was in it only for themselves.

He had a handkerchief wrapped around his left hand. He would be fine. The stupid dog had got just enough teeth in him to open a wound. Already the bleeding had stopped.

Category Seven! What did that even mean? Men had survived worse, he was certain.

In Clint's mind, everything was clear. In this world, a man protected his family. A man kept his family together and safe. Scarlet was his family. By protecting his family he protected civilization, because civilization was founded on the family. At least American civilization was. If that meant executing a lying gambling magnate and his slutty girlfriend, so be it. A man did what he had to do. God, the way she had sat, the way she thrust out her

257

breasts, the way she crossed her legs, he knew she had been provoking him. Her entire being had proclaimed that he wasn't good enough or important enough or rich enough to have someone like her. It was as if she bled superiority through her pores.

She bled. He laughed at his pun.

A man became what he had to be to be a man.

They'd shamed him. Not just her. Both of them. Shamed him because he wasn't good enough, not even good enough to be warned to get out of the way of a hurricane. He'd settled that right away.

Maybe this was the end the Christians were always talking about. The end of the world. Apocalypse. The Second Coming. He hadn't gone much to church, not at all since his wife had been frozen, but he read the paper and watched the news, so he knew what Christians were up to. But he'd fought the good fight for law, order and civilization. Wouldn't God bring Scarlet back to him? He would. He had to. Clint loved her too much. God was fair. Just.

A black leather briefcase lay on the shotgun seat. It contained signed and notarized documents providing that the company founded and owned by the recently deceased had purchased each and every house in the haunted zone. The briefcase also contained a check from that company to Clint Adams, his "broker's fee," in an amount more than sufficient to have Scarlet resurrected. A good woman, a woman who not only understood her role and her place, but who filled that role perfectly.

He had to go by the police station before he went home. He had to destroy any electronic surveillance record of his car being on this road tonight.

Then he'd stop by Annie's. He need not worry about the time; Annie was on call. She knew how to help a man understand what he'd done. She'd have bandages for his hand, too.

If only she'd put on some weight, she'd be half sexy.

Jessa unfolded the drawing of Ellen's murder.

Three heads lowered over the drawing. Rik nudged Jessa and, having got her attention, looked at their father. Jessa's eyes followed.

Gary had seen enough. He sat back in his chair, his eyes grown small, his face fiery red and his jaw locked.

Evelyn, who knew, still had emotions to swallow.

Gary's face had hardened into a mask. He turned toward Tom with zombie-like unsteadiness. "He killed him, right? That lying Clint fucking killed him."

Tom asked, "Paul Lasxeau? That's a hard question. Clint didn't take him into custody, but when he discovered the case had something to do with you, Gary, he took it over. Clint made it very hard for Paul, physically and mentally, so hard that suicide seemed the right choice. Clint was not disappointed."

"Paul. I knew it."

Evelyn frowned. "Gary, who is this Paul person? What are you talking about?" But then she remembered. Annie had told her about the man who had tried to kill her husband.

"I...the boss...we...made some changes to the way our drivers would be paid. I had to tell them. They didn't like it. It meant a cut in pay. Steep. Twenty-seven percent. Art—that's the boss—arranged to have a lawyer and some police there when I told them. Four of them. Police, I mean. They singled Paul out for some reason. Probably because... Beat him. Maced him. Dragged him off to jail. Where he killed himself.

"I sat there. I saw it. I didn't do anything. Now he's dead. And I'm thinking I could have saved him. Maybe...maybe I don't need this job as much as I thought."

Tom's eyes flashed from one family member to the next.

Evelyn moved her left hand slowly until her fingers wrapped around her husband's hand.

259

Jessa said, "We'll be okay if that's what you decide."

Gary nodded his acknowledgement. His eyes were wet.

Rik looked at Gary. He swallowed. His voice came out somewhat garbled, but everyone understood what he said. "You should quit, Gary. Nobody should have to take shit like that."

Gary's eyes came up and met Rik's, just for a second. Then his head dropped again.

Celisa's eyes teared a bit. She put an arm around Rik and smiled, as if she'd discovered the source of Rik's strengths.

Someone banged on a downstairs door.

The group looked at each other.

Celisa said, "Steve and Zach?"

Rik said, "We hope."

Gary said, "It better not be Clint."

Rik followed Gary down the stairs.

* * *

Clint took the elevator up to his office. Erasing the surveillance evidence of a trip was a process he had performed several times before. It came naturally now, like a new driver who'd learned to turn a corner correctly. But his eyes spotted something worrisome on the videos. A car had followed the same route behind him, had stopped near where he had stopped, and returned after he had returned. He called for the driver's ID: Lars Ostrum. The name meant nothing to him at first. He scanned the address, occupation, Social Security number, driver's license number, education, employment and the remaining information. Only when he came to the names of family members did his memory click. Steve Ostrum.

"Shit."

Where was that car now? The computer took a few seconds to find the target. At first Clint thought the car's location made no sense, but then he saw the car had been parked four blocks over from Antigua Street.

Like Gordie had said, the more dead bodies, the more likely they'll find you. But Clint knew that you do what you have to do.

Besides, time was short. That worked in his favor.

But Tom, where was Tom? Clint located Tom's car. So. The fool was actually trying to talk to ghosts.

*   *   *

Rik peeked through the door and told his father it was alright. Gary opened the door. Rik said, "This is Steve and Zach." Gary closed the door. The arrivals forgot to say hello. They stood at the door, one paler than the other.

Rik led the way upstairs.

Steve described following Clint to the home in Belmont, overhearing the officer's intention to kill Tom, the vague outlines of a plot to purchase the houses in the neighborhood to allow the construction of a casino, the couple's plan to get away, and the double murder.

No one spoke. Everyone understood that Clint was capable of killing any or all of them. Jessa shivered with cold, the kind of cold that brings clarity. Rik's adrenaline spiked. Evelyn felt as if she'd turned on the news and she was on it. Celisa, who had been in threatening situations before, alone and with her family, pushed aside the fear and focused on the problem. For God's sake, she thought, there are monsters next door. Steve couldn't move his focus off the fact that Ellen had been murdered in the next room. Zach wondered whether he was up to facing such a world. Gary felt as if he'd been living with his eyes closed his whole life.

Tom interrupted the silence. "Clint is a very interesting fellow. He loved what he mistook for good so much that he became evil."

Celisa said, "Good way to put it."

"Thank you."

Rik asked, "If he killed the guy who was supposed to buy our houses, how can Clint get his money?"

Zach said, "They said the checks were cut and signed and the documents were all ready. After Clint killed them, he took the checks. By the way, we got his name."

"We never got the woman's full name. His was," Steve checked his phone, "Gordie Sands."

People shook their heads.

Steve explained. "We looked him up. When he came to the US as a child his name was Lavero Gauschi. He made a fortune from casinos in places like Macau and Goa and he seems to practically own Cuba. He was a big political supporter of the president."

Zach spoke up. "But that's not all the bad news."

Gary asked, "What?"

"The reason Mr. Sands and his..." Zach stopped. He had to get the image of the bodies out of his mind before he could continue. "The reason they were leaving is there's a huge hurricane going to hit us Friday night."

Steve added, "Or early Saturday. A Category Seven."

Tom sucked in a breath and held it. Rik and Jessa exchanged glances.

She said, "That must be what Mrs. Sutton meant."

In a subdued voice, Evelyn asked, "What does that mean? A Category Seven hurricane?"

Steve said, "Yeah. I looked that up, too. Remember Houston two years ago? Everything leveled. Nothing much left standing. No place to hide. That was a Category Six."

Gary erupted, "We just bought the house! Now it's going to get washed away! Damn hell!"

Evelyn shot back, "It's not just the house I'm worried about, Gary!"

Gary looked at her, blinked, realized his mistake. He took her hand.

Evelyn pushed herself to ask, "Are we...all going to...drown?"

Tom rubbed his leg. "We don't know enough to answer that question." After a second, he added, "No. It's very bad."

Tom exhaled. He slouched. He said, "If we only had more time."

Rik asked, "What do you mean?"

Tom looked at Rik with tired eyes. "I'm a trained shaman. What we are most called on to do is soul retrieval. You all saw the holes the ghosts suffered from. Well, when a person is seriously mistreated or even suffers a serious accident, it rips out part of their soul. Being a slave must have destroyed much of their souls. Mrs. Sutton said the ghosts wanted to be made whole, that they wanted to heal the holes they suffer from."

Rik frowned.

Celisa asked, "There's a way you can do that?"

"Shamans and soul-loss sounds, I know, primitive. It is. It began with our ancestors—most all of them, it appears, whether we trace to Africa, Asia, Europe or the Americas—when they were hunter-gatherers. Before farming took hold.

"For at least five thousand years, shamans worked to recover and heal souls. The word wasn't spread over the internet or by newsletters or news broadcasts. It was discovered by different people, far removed from each other by distance and time, over and over again. The particulars differed from one place to another. So did the rituals involved. But they all learned the same lessons because they all had similar experiences. There is an underworld, a middle world and an upper world, all connected by a central Tree of Life. We live in the middle world. Broken and lost souls live in the underworld. Shamans learned how to 'travel' between these worlds.

"Is it real? That is my experience, but personal experience isn't necessarily true. It's also been the experience of my patients, and of shamans and patients over thousands of years. From my patients' perspectives, it works.

263

"A number of shamans and some neuroscientists and I now suspect the basis for these experiences lies in the mind and body of each individual. A kind of universal and interconnected deeper world packed away in our selves. Perhaps the process involves touching one of the other seven dimensions some physicists claim we live among."

Evelyn swallowed. "Tom, you're not...Annie said you were a Christian shaman. But you're not Christian, are you?"

"Is the Christian god a god of all peoples and cultures or is the Christian god just another tribal god?"

Evelyn felt an uncomfortable shift in her mind and body. "Oh."

Rik said, "Tom, no offense, but I wouldn't believe a word of this if we hadn't met Mrs. Sutton and the other ghosts and seen how they had lost parts of themselves."

Jessa said, "Felt it, too. I felt it when Nan joined me to draw that picture. I felt her missing places, her longing to be whole. I know it sounds insane, but I'm beginning to think I feel mine."

"I haven't seen a ghost so part of me thinks...I won't believe it till I see it." Celisa looked a bit frightened by all this. "But think of it: what would it do to you to be a slave? Every day. Every time you wake. All day, every day, to know you were..." She shook her head. "You'd lose something. They took something away. They stole! If it wasn't part of your soul, it had to be something important. And nothing is more important than your soul."

Rik asked Tom, "Do you think Mrs. Sutton knew you were coming? She said the ghosts needed healing and then you come saying you can heal them."

Tom thought it over. "Could be you're right. Wouldn't surprise me. So I may have something to offer the ghosts, if they are interested. It would be helpful if the ghosts held some power over the storm."

Rik heard Tom's careful choice of words. "What do you mean by 'if the ghosts held power over the storm'? Do they or don't they?"

264

"I don't know. If they did, we might be able to make a deal."

Jessa said, "We could ask."

"The problem is we don't have time to recover their souls before the storm hits. I'd have to promise to journey after the storm. We'd be asking them to help us first. We'd be asking them to trust us."

Rik asked, "Why wouldn't they trust..." Then he remembered. "Yeah."

"I think Jessa's right," Celisa said. "We should ask." She held her words for a few seconds. "I could ask. Maybe because..."

"One more thing," Tom said. "It's not just victims who lose parts of their souls; the victimizers also lose parts of their souls."

Rik's eyes widened at that. He swallowed. He'd been terribly right.

Tom explained, "Think of Newton's Third Law."

Zach raised his hand as if he were in class. "I know: every action has an equal and opposite reaction."

Steve smiled and gave Zach a two-fingered victory sign.

Tom said, "Zach's right. And just as Newton made observations from which he concluded that every action has an equal and opposite reaction, we observe the law of the universe that the soul that kills or maims is itself killed or maimed."

"So the slave owners...?"

"Right, Celisa. The slave owners and the neighbors. All of us."

"Huh."

Gary spoke up. "What do you mean our neighbors? We don't own slaves. That was a long time ago!"

Tom nodded. He caught Gary's eyes. "But we deny them. We push their historical memory into a dumpster and hope the garbage people come and take it away. We deny we live on land they worked. We deny that the wealth of our country was founded massively on slave labor. And we continue to treat their descendants as less than our equals. We refuse to listen to them, pretending we know in advance that what they have to say isn't worth listening to. And we hate them because their presence reminds us of who we are. Our souls have missing pieces."

Gary thought of Paul. He glanced briefly at Celisa, then looked away.

Rik said, "So, should we try to call Mrs. Sutton?"

Tom surveyed the group. He saw several nods. Then he said, "Good. Let's do it."

Jessa went to the window. "Clint's not home yet."

Evelyn frowned. "Just a minute." She walked down the hallway to her bedroom, which overlooked the other side of the house. She returned and said, "His car is parked out front at Annie's. I'm sure he needs an extra good fuck after murdering two people. And a dog."

Gary looked at his wife, blinked, then blinked again. She never talked like that.

The doorbell rang, rang again, then again.

Jessa said, "Sounds like..."

Everyone finished. "Clint."

Gary said, "Let me."

Evelyn followed her husband to the top of the stairs, where she stopped to listen. Gary walked down the stairs and answered the door.

The voices quickly rose in volume so that everyone upstairs heard every word.

Tom walked as quickly and quietly as he could to Evelyn's side.

Evelyn glanced at him.

Gary wanted to keep Clint out. Clint wanted in—to search for Tom.

Then everyone upstairs heard Gary exclaim, "Put that away! You don't need a gun!"

Tom muttered to Evelyn, "I'd better put a stop to this."

He descended the stairs as noisily and jauntily as his weather-forecasting leg allowed. "Clint! Clint! Why are you always so angry? And loud? Calm down. Say, did you get the money for your wife yet?"

Tom's question hit Clint like a judo move. The officer's fury tripped over itself and became frustrated confusion. "Maybe." His right hand seemed unable to hold the gun steady. The muzzle hole wandered like a blind eye.

Tom brightened. "Well, congratulations! You're going to do it! That's great! Hey, what's wrong with your hand?"

The firearm made its way back into its holster. "What are you talking about?"

"Your hand. It's all wrapped up. Nice job. Who did it?"

"My hand's fine. Nothing's wrong with it. What are you talking about to these people?"

"Clint, do you remember earlier this evening when we talked about how I was going to help the good people of this neighborhood deal with their ghost problem?"

"Yeah?"

"That's what I'm doing here."

"All I know is I walk out of...I mean, come home, I was driving home from work and I see all the lights on in this house at this time of night and I think something must be going on."

"It's all okay, Clint. I'm doing what you paid me to do. That's all."

"Where's that Ostrum boy? I know he's here. He's another troublemaker."

Tom and Gary exchanged glances. Gary said, "I don't know anyone named Ostrum. What kind of name is that, anyway?" He stared at Clint with wide eyes.

After a nasty glance at Gary, Clint turned his attention to Tom. "Why are you doing your work here?"

"Nobody else's lights are on. You weren't home. I went to the house where the people were still awake to ask them about their experiences with ghosts."

"So why did Gary lie to me? Why did he say you weren't here?"

267

Tom looked the officer straight in the eye. "Probably because you were so angry, Gary thought you might try to kill me."

Clint's eyes walked back and forth between Tom and Gary several times. "I know what you are up to. I know which side you're on. Don't think for a moment you're going to get away with it." Then he stepped back, performed a military-like turn with his feet and walked down the porch steps.

Tom called after him. "Clint, why is your car parked in front of Annie's?"

Gary closed the door and took a breath of relief.

Tom said, "Gary, I think Clint is worried about us. I so hate it when Clint is worried. He's such a frightened man."

Gary asked, "Who's Ostrum?"

Tom shrugged.

*   *   *

Celisa stood in front of the group of the living. Her eyes fixed on a bare wall.

Rik's room was unrecognizable. His bookcases and Jessa's desk had been pushed up against the inner wall. The mattress, box spring and frame all stood on edge, leaning against the bookcases.

The eight of them stood facing the same wall that had revealed to Rik the woman burying Nan's child. A single lamp remained on, and that was turned against a wall to provide only the most necessary light.

Celisa stood as straight and tall as she was able. She felt frail, a strand of grass trying to stand against an impending storm.

"Grandmother Belinda? Please, could you visit us again? It's me, Celisa, your great-granddaughter. I'm here as you asked. I'm with some of my friends. We would like to talk to you."

A clock would scarcely have ticked off two seconds before the wall lapsed into a moving cloud.

Celisa's wide eyes probed the vanishing wall for signs of her ancestor.

268

A patch of grassy earth appeared beneath Celisa's feet and spread until it included those behind her and perhaps ten feet beyond the wall in front of her, where it disappeared in the haze.

Tattered human shapes emerged at the far end of the clearing. An elderly woman came first, assisted by a younger man and trailed by a young girl. The man held the woman's arm, steadying her.

The appearance of the ghosts drew Celisa forward. She took a half step toward them, then another, hardly realizing what she'd done. She smiled expectantly. "Grandmother?" she whispered.

Belinda's eyes met her own, and then the woman smiled, too. Celisa felt the warmth of homecoming.

The three stopped less than ten feet away. Another ghost brought up a wicker chair and placed it behind Belinda. She sat. The man helped her wrap a knitted shawl about her shoulders.

Belinda said, "Child, to see you stand there free, my mind tricked me when I saw you. I thought I felt my heart—the one they took—again." She motioned with her hand. "Joseph here, my son, your great-grandfather, so many greats back. And little Nan, Joseph's daughter, your great-aunt."

Celisa swallowed. Great-grandmother. Great-grandfather. So far back. And Nan: poor, strong Nan. Celisa's eyes slipped over the three like a caressing hand. "I...I feel...I can't even say how I feel, Grandmother." She stood solid, tears cascading down her cheeks, simultaneously emotional and stoic. "Can I call you Grandma? Grandfather? Grandpa? Aunt?"

"You may. The rest of you may call me Mrs. Sutton. Like their hymns say, 'I feel joy.'" Belinda's hands returned to her lap. She sighed sadly. Her eyes met her grandchild's eyes. "Glad, so deeply glad...so much time gone, my child. So many changes. I prayed to see you, and this time, this time 'yes' came the answer. Grateful. I am happy. But I fear for your young life. I fear for you, your mother, your father, your friends...I fear what comes."

"Grandma, you mean the storm?"

"Yes, child. The storm and what comes after."

"I don't care, Grandma. What will happen will happen. I'm so happy to know you. I'm glad all these people with me can meet you. I'm proud of you. I'm proud to be your child."

"Proud to be the child of slaves? Child, think!"

Celisa rejected her great-grandmother's words. "Better than being the child of slave owners!"

"Umm." Almost involuntarily, Belinda smiled. "Your spirit is strong, child. I can't but be proud of you! Tell me. I've met Jessa, Rik, and their mother. Who are these others?"

Celisa made the introductions.

"That one, the one you call Morton, I can see he likes trouble, what's he want?"

Celisa tossed a glance over her shoulder, making sure Tom hadn't abandoned her. "He thinks he may be able to help you. I think we all want the same, Grandma. We want to help all of you."

"Hmm? The living offer to help the dead! What a day this is." She looked behind Celisa. "Mr. Morton, come closer. Now I see you better. I've seen your likes. I remember a healer when I was a child in Africa. Strange man. I saw him save a child once when the midwife couldn't get it from its mother's womb. He tried to help the sick. Sometimes they got better. Sometimes they died. Most of the time he was a cranky old fool. The moon faces killed him."

"Mrs. Sutton, I am honored to meet you. I spent seven years in Africa..."

"Mercy, Mr. Morton. The years have worn me. I am a ghost. Charm and flattery do nothing for me. Tell me. What do you want?"

Tom, flushed, cleared his throat. "Of course. All of you have lost pieces of yourselves, of your souls. I would try to recover them so you would be whole."

"Generous of you."

"There may be some help we might request from you."

"May be?"

"Uh, there is, actually."

"So you're not generous! You're selfish!"

"For those who understand, as do you and I, there is no difference."

"Hmm. And what might we do for you?"

"The hurricane..."

Belinda exclaimed, "The hurricane!" She laughed. The laugh subsided. She looked at the man with concern. "What makes you believe ghosts can save you from a hurricane?"

Seconds of silence ended with a small, breaking voice from the rear of the crowd of the living. Evelyn said, "But you left things for us. You moved the daggers."

Jessa spoke with less fear. "And you left leg irons for Ellen! They were heavy. You must have some power to move matter."

Belinda said, "Um. That we did. But the universe move itself, my children. We are just its most fragile parts. We might nudge it one direction or another, ask it to release its goodness or fury in a better place or time for us, but we do not control. We do not control."

With as much steel in her voice as her respect for Belinda would allow, Celisa asked, "Would you try to help us?"

Belinda glanced toward Celisa. Then she refocused on Tom. "We ghosts come—and many more be here by tomorrow night— to see your," she chewed the next word, "arrogance die of its own wounds. Why should we want to help?"

Tom said, "History doesn't end with this storm. Life, even here, will go on. It will please you that after four centuries the life that goes forward will be whole."

"Whole! Ah! Mr. Morton, what words you choose. I would describe it as some of the racial elitists got dragged kicking and screaming to the admission that their own declaration that all peoples are created equal is true.

"But haven't you skipped something important? Don't you have to convince these people to look at their own souls? Don't they have to admit the reasons their souls broke? You can't heal those who deny their sickness!"

"No. Of course not."

"And how you going to convince them? With your pretty words? Come, Mr. Morton."

"We will offer them safety through the hurricane and healing for their wounds."

"Sounds like a favorable deal. What's the downside for them?"

"To be healed they need to give up being white."

"Hah! They won't do it! I know these people. If they can't pretend to be better than somebody else, they won't know who they are. They ain't going to do it."

"We need to try."

"We? Why 'we'? Why do 'we' need to 'try'?"

"To stop the hate, the pain, the suffering from continuing to add up for generations more."

Belinda stared. "Arrogance!"

Tom answered, "Celisa."

The ghost woman had known from the beginning where this discussion would end. She loved this child of hers of so many generations, and to love this child was to love her friends, even if they be white and descended from the likes of her own slavers. She addressed the girl. "Is this what you want?"

Celisa said, "Yes, Grandma. I don't know if it will work and, if it works, I don't know if it will matter much, but, yes, I want to try."

"Alright." Belinda sighed.

"Thank you, Grandma." Celisa wanted to dance, but she felt she was too old for that now.

Belinda asked Morton, "You have done this before? You've helped heal souls?"

"For the living, yes."

"You could fail?"

"Yes. But we might succeed."

"There another problem. You know what I mean?"

"Of course. I will do all I can to prepare someone else."

"With us, then, how might it be done?"

*   *   *

When Tom was leaving, Gary followed him out the door.

"I know it's late, but I was wondering if you had time for a question."

"Sure."

"I went." Gary stopped as if he'd asked his question. He pulled himself back together. "I went to Paul's wake. Early. In the afternoon. There were a lot of people there but I was the only... you know."

"White guy."

"Right. And the sun was out, okay?"

Tom frowned. "Okay."

"But then I went in. Inside the funeral place." Gary shrugged. "Well, I got inside and, well, I was naked. And it was pouring rain."

"Did anyone say anything about you being naked or the rain?"

"No."

"And when you left?"

"I had my clothes on. And the sun was still out. No rain."

Tom thought for a moment. "Well, Gary, it's hard to make a determination on a single incident, but, you might, just might, have some talent for being a shaman."

Gary nodded. "I was wondering that."

Tom placed his hand on Gary's shoulder. "You're a good man, Gary. You are. But people put in a lot of hard work hiding it from you."

274

CHAPTER TWELVE
FRIDAY

U nlike most of his fellow officers, Clint took the time to thoroughly learn the working details of each new piece of police technology. For anyone not in law enforcement, the piece of tech in his hand was illegal to own or even possess. It unlocked doors. Technically, but only technically, Clint's use of it this early morning was also illegal. He wore civvies, lacked a warrant, and wasn't engaged in law enforcement.

He'd watched from his window until Tom left the Hollie residence, then given him an hour to get to sleep. It was two hours before sunrise.

Clint stood between a dumpster and a decrepit metal door. His flashlight showed chipped, peeling layers of paint, burnt red over green over white. He pressed the activating button on the instrument. A few seconds passed before a green light came on.

All commercial locks were digital. The instrument analyzed the mechanism in any one of them, found the unlocking code, applied it, and opened the lock. Standard police equipment.

Clint pressed the start button. In less than two seconds, he heard the lock's mechanism click.

He walked into the basement of the Riverside Hotel. He wore plastic gloves and a black mask that covered his face from hairline to chin, revealing only his eyes.

Clint had studied the building's blueprints. He knew which room Tom Morton stayed in. His device would unlock a hotel room door quite easily.

Clint found the service elevator and took it to the sixth floor. He followed the arrow that pointed to rooms 620–632. He stopped at Room 627.

He used his device on the lock. Silently, he opened the door. The room, as he expected, was pitch dark. So was the bathroom. Morton must be in bed. Clint knew from the blueprints where the light switches were, but he followed the narrow beam of his light. It found the foot of the bed. The sheet, blanket and bedspread lay on the floor at the foot of the bed.

Slowly, holding the light in his left hand and that psychiatrist's firearm in his right, he moved the beam to the head of the bed.

The bed was empty.

"Shit." The word sounded like a sneeze.

Clint turned on the room lights.

He searched under the bed. He threw open the closets. He looked in the bath and tore down the shower curtain.

Nothing.

Empty.

He stood at the foot of the bed for half a minute thinking about what to do next. He kicked the pile of bedclothes on the floor, turned out the lights, and left the room.

He walked around the hotel and, not seeing Tom's vehicle, entered by the front door. He walked up to the desk. A smiling clerk, whose face, skin and thinness spoke of far foreign origins, emerged from a side office.

"Yes, sir. May I help you?"

"Yes. I'm here to pick up a friend. Could you buzz him for me?"

"Certainly, sir. His name?" The clerk posed his fingers over the computer keyboard.

"Thomas or Tom Morton."

The clerk's fingers remained stationary and his face lost its smile. "Oh, sir, I am so sorry. Mr. Morton checked out about an hour ago." He typed something and turned the screen so Clint could see. "Here." The clerk pointed. "Mr. Morton checked out... oh, dear, it's almost two hours ago. Time flies."

Clint pretended concern. "I see. I hope nothing's wrong. Did he say anything?"

"No, sir. I personally checked him out. But, yes, he did say one thing. I remember now. He said he had an early flight. He also said 'thank you' to me. He was very polite."

"Oh. Well, it could have been a family emergency. He may have left a message at my work. Thank you."

"Thank you, sir. You, too, are very polite. Not many people here are. I deeply regret I couldn't help more."

Clint marched to his car. He knew from the arrest records where Tom had rented his vehicle. He drove into town and out to the airport through the tunnel. At this hour, there was little traffic.

He'd worked it through in his mind. Whatever happened after the storm hit, he would have his money and be gone. He'd ride Sands' airplane to Toronto and return to Paradise after the storm passed to pick up the pieces. The land of opportunity, that's what this would be.

The car rental attendant sat behind a small desk in a swivel chair, his head back, snoring. A small laptop, a dirty coffee cup and an ashtray overflowing with half-smoked cigarettes sat on the desk.

"Hello?" Clint tried again, louder. "Hello?"

The attendant shuddered awake. "Oh, man. Oh. I must have fallen asleep. Give me your stub." He reached a hand out.

Clint ignored the hand and shoved his police ID in front of the attendant's face.

The man's eyes widened. "What... What?"

"It's not concerned with you. A man, Thomas Morton, rented a car from you. I need to know if he returned it this morning."

The attendant, relieved, fumbled with his computer. "That name, it seems familiar. Here it is. Yes, Mr. Tom Morton returned the van forty-five minutes ago. He took one of our shuttles to Logan."

"He say anything about where he was going?"

"No. Nothing. I had several customers just then. There're a few early flights."

"Thanks." Clint glanced again at the ashtray. "You really should stop smoking. Bad for your health."

"I know! I try not to, then I light one like I'm not even thinking about it. I feel all guilty and I quit halfway through. Then I light another one. It's hard!"

Clint climbed back into his car. The sky was still dark. No hint of light lay over the eastern horizon.

He decided not to go to the airport, but to go to the station. He could check the flights and passenger lists from there and get any records of his own travels this morning erased.

He headed north on 1A, saw a stopped vehicle in the break-down lane and pulled over. A woman who had just come into Logan had a flat tire. Clint identified himself as an officer and changed her tire. She thanked him profusely. He told her his parents had raised him to be helpful.

By the time he got to the station, the eastern sky had begun to brighten.

*   *   *

Rik opened his eyes. The sunlight struck the upper part of the bedroom wall, just below the ceiling, and sent photons dancing into his eyes. The sun promised another beautiful day. The sun lied.

He sat up and checked the time. Six ten. He'd barely had three hours of sleep to prepare himself for what could be his last full day alive. He leaned forward, head between his hands. His mind spun out of control, searching for someone to blame. The answer didn't come as a thought so much as in a feeling: everyone. Everyone who lived the past four-hundred-plus years. And everyone alive today, including himself, who hadn't done anything about it. Four hundred years. He wanted to sleep at least that long. Let someone else deal with the garbage left by history.

Quietly, he stood. He could run, take Gary's car and drive for the next eighteen hours. He had enough money for gas. He didn't

278

have to tell anyone. He could save himself and laugh at those he left behind. That's what it was all about, wasn't it? Every man for himself.

"I'm awake." Jessa had the covers pulled over her head.

Rik didn't answer. How could he leave if she was awake?

"Rik? That's you, right?"

Already his plan had failed. He was a coward. He was going to die. "Did you sleep?"

"A bit." She sounded defeated. She felt all the symptoms Meph had left her to live with, the ones her medications had helped counter, rise up again.

"You want to shower first or should I go." He could hear fate laughing at him: the world is ending; who should shower first?

"You go." The energy to get up hadn't come to her yet. She felt helpless, which is to say, useless. Her feelings had died and been replaced by dried mud. That's how she felt. That's what she believed. Her future appeared as harrowing and destructive as her past, but much, much shorter.

Rik gathered his clothes and walked to the bathroom for his last shower here. Ever. Apparently. Short of a major miracle. Go through the motions because it's better than doing nothing and thinking. The future had disappeared. Every decision he had worried about making, every hope he'd harbored, every lousy outcome he'd imagined, all had become inoperative. Writer? Would the future have computers and flexes, let alone paper and pencils? Options had been reduced to two: drown or survive and live like a Neanderthal.

He shook. His hands shook. He decided not to shave.

When he returned to the bedroom, he asked, "You still awake?"

"Course."

"Bathroom's free."

"So?"

"I mean, Mom's already downstairs and Gary isn't up yet."

Jessa kept silent.

"I was thinking we should pack some things, you know, toothbrush, toothpaste, razor, stuff we won't be able to get."

She had a retort but lacked the interest to say it.

"You know, your meds and stuff."

No response.

"Jessa?"

She grunted.

"Look, your meds are here. I'll get you some water." He quickly returned with a small plastic glass. "Sit up. Take your pills."

"Right. You're absolutely right." Jessa pulled the covers off her head and sat up. She took the pills and drank the water. "Now all we need are two years' worth of food and water, a couple of flush toilets, a refrigerator, and a dozen table settings. Just the necessary stuff. Oh, and how's Noah coming along with his ark?"

"That's not funny," he snapped. "It's stupid."

Jessa hugged herself.

"Sorry."

"Sure."

Rik said, "Look, I don't know why this is happening to us, but we've got to try to stop it, or..."

"Why?"

Rik was about to put gel in his hair when he realized how absurd an act that was. "Why? I don't know. I have no idea why. But we do. I know we do." He rubbed the glop into his hair.

"Well, there's no reason and that's good enough of a reason. So I guess I'd better shower."

"I'll wait for you."

She stopped in the doorway to look at her brother. Life, she thought, was a trap, and inside that large trap were legions of smaller traps, and inside those traps were...

Evelyn had woken before her alarm sounded. She'd lain on her back in bed feeling a bit breathless and confused. She'd dreamt the memory of the first ghosts she'd seen: the two chil-dren, not as dark as some of the ghosts but not pale enough to be mistaken for white, dashing into her kitchen. Except in the dream these children had been her grandchildren. In her dream and now, in bed looking up at the ceiling, she smiled. She wanted to hold them. They were hers.

When she got out of bed, she looked out her bedroom window to see if any clouds had shown up. None. Yet. A person could hope.

She opened the bottom drawer of her dresser and reached beneath an old comforter where she'd hidden two objects wrap-ped in white cloth napkins. When she left the bedroom for the kitchen, she carried them with her, one in each hand. After some thought, she chose one to lay beside Jessa's place; the other she placed beside Rik's. Then she prepared their breakfasts.

The kids were less than fifteen minutes behind her.

Jessa asked, "Cloth napkins?" Well, she thought, maybe cloth napkins were not a bad idea on the morning of the apocalypse, so to speak. She picked her napkin up and felt an object wrapped inside. Jessa undid the napkin. A sheathed knife slid onto the table. Jessa had to clear her head to deal with this appearance. She swallowed and gently picked it up. She drew the dagger from its sheath. The blade gleamed in the morning light. "Oh, my God! Mom? Oh, my God! Where did you get this?"

"Where did she get what?" Rik had just entered the kitchen; he saw what Jessa was holding. "Whoa!"

Evelyn finally acknowledged the surprise she had sprung. "There. Right beside your plate, Rik. You've got your own."

When both napkins lay open and flat on the table, framing the impossible vision of centuries-old daggers, Rik reprised Jessa's question. "Mom? Where did you get these?" He followed the handle's art with the tips of his fingers.

"Just a minute. I'm flipping the eggs."

"Mom!" In stereo.

She turned the burners down. "The ghosts left them for me. To find. For you."

Rik asked, "How do you know? I mean, that they left them for us?" The sight of the weapon had shaken him awake. He kept his hands away from it. The gift of a weapon to a boy presented all kinds of expectations, demands really. Nothing was simple anymore. Everything came with layers of questions and alternate meanings for Rik. "It's beautiful. In its own way."

Evelyn hadn't considered the possibility that the daggers hadn't been meant for her children. "I just knew. Who else could they have been for?" She returned to the eggs.

Jessa examined the blade, the handle, tried to determine how the blade had been fixed. She felt a surge of excitement. The ghosts thought she could help. The ghosts believed in her. She felt proud.

Evelyn said as she carried the pan of eggs to the table, "Jessa, I read you're supposed to carry it in your boot. Rik, yours goes inside your slacks."

Rik felt humbled. Evelyn trusted him with a knife he could use to protect or kill. So did the ghosts. So, then, did Belinda and Joseph and Nan. Life and death. Could he truly make such decisions? They thought so. He discovered he respected their opinions. They had given him a new view of himself. He traced the artwork on the hilt and wondered where it had first come from. "How can a thing made to kill be beautiful?"

Jessa paused. She looked at her brother. "Maybe it's just to scare someone?"

Brother and sister's eyes met. They trusted each other.

Rik muttered, "Thanks, Mom. Thanks, ghosts."

Jessa said, "Right." She pushed the blade into its sheath, then slid the assemblage into her boot. It fit like a "sold-separately" accessory.

When they left, Evelyn called the high school to tell them her children were home sick. Then she made her own breakfast. Before she sat to eat, she turned the TV on. She'd left it on the weather station, so, of course, that's what came on.

Evelyn changed the channel. She refused to sit through a series of lies. Briefly, a flash of indignation warmed her.

She didn't turn the second channel off, at least not right away. She watched as a reporter, a bouncy blonde-haired young woman wearing combat gear, explained the landscape of dead bodies. The uncountables had attempted to break out of one of the reservations only to be met with the full force of infantry and armor of the US Army. Once again, good had defeated evil.

Evelyn wondered for two or three seconds whether Jessa and Rik would end up on a reservation. She was sure she and Gary would never live long enough to make it there. She hoped Rik would protect Jessa. By that time her arm and hand had reacted to her subconscious orders to turn the damn machine off.

She ate, then poured herself a second, then third cup of coffee. The sound of the screen door closing focused her.

"Evelyn! Evelyn! Where are you?"

"Right here, Annie, in the kitchen. Where the hell did you think I'd be?"

Annie stopped in the entrance to the kitchen, spread her arms wide, and announced, "It's tonight, Evelyn! Tonight! We get rid of the ghosts tonight!"

"We do?"

"Yes, we do!"

"Would you like some coffee. Although you don't sound like you need caffeine."

"Oh, I'd love a cup! You know I love your coffee."

Evelyn poured.

Annie sat, elbows on the table, hands in the air, fists clenched. "We're going to do this!"

"So did this Tom person show up?"

"Yes, he did. Wow, is he something special!"

"Did you meet him?"

"Oh, no. I heard. But tonight I will meet him. We all will."

"Where and when is this supposed to happen?"

"At St. Benedict's. In the church basement. Eight o'clock."

"I didn't think St. Benedict's was in the, um, affected area."

"It isn't. Not really. But it's very close. And we needed to have a place big enough for everyone. I convinced Father Vic to let us use it. He knew about the ghosts already because he tried the first exorcism." She giggled.

"Well, we were all planning on being there, but Rik and Jessa have come down with something. They're home sick. We'll see how they feel later." She felt she'd pulled that off like a seasoned spy. Evelyn had no idea where the kids actually were or what they were doing. All she knew was that Tom needed them. "Hopefully, we'll all be there tonight. Gary is coming home early."

"I'm so glad to hear that! Once Tom gets rid of the ghosts we'll have our homes back again! It'll be wonderful!"

Evelyn thought for a moment before saying, "Yes, it will."

"Oh, don't worry! I'll still come over. We'll still be friends!"

"Oh, good."

Annie put her hand on Evelyn's arm. "How's Gary doing?"

"Good. Better. He still hasn't seen the doctor, but he seems better."

"See! Everything works out. And so will tonight."

"I hope you're right, Annie."

"What's the weekend weather?"

"Sunny, sunny, sunny."

"Good. I like it better when the kids can play outside."

* * *

284

Clint sat at one of the research cubicles in the Paradise Intelligence and Surveillance Unit. The PISU took up most of the fourth floor of the Paradise Safety and Security Building. Nothing on any of the screens or data feeds showed the slightest hint of a pending emergency.

He ran possible scenarios through his mind.

That Morton had checked out of his room so early, had returned his rental car and taken a shuttle to the airport, certainly indicated the man had bolted. But why? Clint would have felt better if Morton's name had been on a passenger list, but they were not available for some reason. Probably because... He frowned. Probably because so many familiar names were fleeing the Northeast. The plane should have been booked. How had Tom gotten a seat? Or had he?

Interestingly, the early-morning international flights included one destined for Monte Carlo via Paris. Were Morton and Sands in cahoots? Had Morton gone out and discovered the bodies?

The feeling swept over him, the nightmare sense of having been cut off, of drifting on the wind, of being abandoned by the world. If the storm was really coming, it meant that they didn't need him, that he'd been read out of the United States of America as not worthy. That Detective Clint Adams was expendable. That... He began shaking and crying, but fought it back. He could take. He would take. He'd fight back. He'd win. Silently, he said, "Scarlet, I'm coming to get you."

He'd show them who was expendable.

He pushed his feelings away to somewhere outside himself. He had to think now.

The best Clint could figure was to assume that Morton had removed himself from the picture for whatever reason and to proceed with his plans for tonight. He had to convince his neighbors to sell, deposit his own payment, and then commandeer Sands' plane to go to Toronto.

Scarlet.

He was very close.

Evelyn answered the phone. The voice on the line introduced herself as Sona Adebayo, Celisa's mother. She told Evelyn she hadn't been able to contact her husband, who was working in Europe for a few months. Cross-Atlantic communications had become nearly impossible. Sun spots, they'd told her. She and her daughter would be home alone when the storm hit. Their house was up a hill and nearly surrounded by rock ledges, and therefore more like to survive any storm surges or floods. She offered an invitation.

Evelyn looked around her new kitchen; mentally, she walked through her whole new house. Her spirit faded some.

She accepted.

"Thank you. You're awfully kind to think of us."

"Oh, I wish I had thought of it. I'm embarrassed not to have. It was Celisa. Kids in love think of everything."

*   *   *

Jessa and Rik waited on a corner several blocks from their house for their ride. Tom showed up several minutes behind schedule driving a van.

Tom offered, "Good morning!"

Neither answered. They took two of the three third-row seats. Rik asked if Tom would stop at a pharmacy. He did.

Rik and Jessa went in. Jessa tried her best to resemble a happy high school sophomore. She told the pharmacist that she was going away on a school trip to Japan for three months and that she needed enough medication to last that long.

As he prepared the prescriptions, the pharmacist asked, "Tokyo?"

"Yes." Jessa used her mother's credit card to pay. Then she waited for Rik to finish his purchase at the front of the store.

"What did you get?"

"Some stuff."

She slid into the seat beside her brother. "What do you mean 'stuff'?"

Tom pulled out of the parking lot.

"Nothing."

"I'm not your mother." She grabbed the bag.

"Hey! Wait!"

"Oh, my God! How many..?" She rummaged through the bag. "How many did you get?"

"A dozen."

"And each box contains, uh, a dozen. That's a hundred and forty-four condoms. Are you sure that's enough?"

"Give me the bag. Look, there's Celisa. Come on. I don't want her to see them."

"The thing about condoms is the woman is supposed to see them." Jessa handed him the bag.

When the van stopped, Jessa began getting out so that Celisa could sit next to Rik. Both Rik and Celisa protested. Jessa, as an act of self-martyrdom, insisted Celisa and Rik sit together.

Celisa couldn't figure how to be close to Rik and not come between him and his sister. The whole world teetered and she couldn't handle...she was going to think 'easy stuff' but nothing was easy. Nothing at all.

They picked up Zack and finally Steve.

Father Vic was waiting for them in St. Benedict's basement when they arrived.

Tom followed Father Vic around asking questions as if he were the building inspector. When he'd collected all the answers he needed, Tom stood at the front of the room and said, "This will have to do."

*   *   *

At noon, the Paradise police received an order from FEMA to cancel all vacations and days off and to call all regular and supplementary forces to duty. All or parts of seven states went into lockdown. Train traffic and shipping came to a halt. All national or interstate turnpikes, thruways and highways were shut. People were instructed to fend for themselves. The order contained no explanation.

As far as Clint was concerned, that settled it. FEMA always described and graded the threat. Any hope that the storm wasn't real dissolved. All illusions that the people who mattered considered him essential vanished. They considered him a nobody.

*   *   *

Why was it so hard to figure out a way to convince people to save themselves and their families? Why should they believe Tom's claims? Why should they believe the ghosts would help? How could they expect the neighbors to think clearly after they learned of the hurricane? Why shouldn't they give in to fear and strike out thoughtlessly at those offering help?

Even Tom's amazing plan couldn't raise Rik and Jessa's spirits.

Celisa looked at her friends and said, "Look, guys, I know this has got you two down. It's got me down too, but we have to do this. We have to save as many people as we can."

Rik countered, "Easy for you to say. You're practically up on a mountain where you live. We're at sea level. Remember us when we're gone, okay?"

"Oh, no! Wait, wait." Celisa grabbed her head. "What a dummy I am! I'm sorry. It's my fault. I forgot! My mom called your mom to say your family could stay with us because we're a bit higher. I was supposed to tell you as soon as I saw you. Actually, I checked the geologic map last night on the internet. We're almost sixty feet higher. And besides, if the ghosts are going to help keep anyone safe it will be us. I'm sorry. I forgot to tell you."

Of course, Jessa thought. That's what friends do. "Thanks."

Rik felt caught between his surrender to circumstances and Celisa's offer. He'd begun thinking of hope as a betrayal of reality. Yet, he'd tried to give Jessa reason to keep going. Now Celisa was holding hope out to him. What good would it do if they all ended up dead by tomorrow morning? What would it mean? Nothing. He felt Celisa's eyes on him. It meant nothing but it was something. Not giving in, being true to something lurking inside him, inside them, was something. "Thanks."

He thought, But everyone else?

Tom wanted each of them to have something to say to the neighbors if circumstances came up. Jessa and Celisa wanted to work together. Rik felt off-center and needed to be alone. But something had been bothering him. As he stood to find a place, he asked, "Celisa, how could you access geologic maps?" That was government information. Even the school computers couldn't access that level. A license was required and it cost.

"My father has government permits. He's working for the International Criminal Court in Geneva for a year. That's why you haven't met him." She added with sad anger, "We haven't been able to get in contact with him for several days."

Half seeking more quiet and half trying to get away from himself, on impulse Rik headed up into the church. The day was sunny and the church was warm and alive with stained-glass colors. More importantly, it was quiet. The church seemed like a forgotten castle, a sanctuary. The pews were as comfortable as rocks, so he walked onto the altar and sat in one of the plush red-upholstered chairs. A dozen feet from the altar, he smelled the flowers that had been arranged there.

He was alone with the quiet, the flowers, and the red, gold, green, blue and purple sunlight. From his seat he had a clear view of the front right window, the main subject of which was the tall, angular, blond, blue-eyed Middle Eastern Jew called Jesus Christ. A disconnect he had never noticed, much less thought about, now carried multiple important meanings. Apparently even Jesus Christ was required to meet white standards.

He asked himself what he knew. First, he knew that he had been raised to believe that he and Jesus were white, which was to say, normal. And while he couldn't remember hearing the words "whites are superior to blacks," he had learned that blacks were not whites, which was to say, at best, not normal.

He had learned that there were questions blacks must answer that could not be asked of whites. Blacks had to justify their presence by answering those questions. They had the burden of proof. Whites didn't have to prove themselves to blacks.

Celisa had told him that she often felt white men didn't listen to her but cut her off and acted as if anything she had to say was, because she said it, dismissible. She couldn't tell whether this was because she was a woman or because she was black. Probably both, she thought.

Eventually Rik's list of what he knew ran to three pages but the unifying concept of what this all meant eluded him.

Rik had begun sliding toward a doze when his eyes again found the window Christ. Invisibly connected hands from heaven were placing a crown on his head. Christ the King. Rik's mind cleared. He pulled himself up in the chair. The Massachusetts family that had owned the most slaves had been the Royall family. Ms. Kinney had said that had not been the original family name. It had been Ryall. Isaac Royall the First had decided the added "o" would aid his drive to join the Boston aristocracy.

To be white, Rik understood, was to be royalty. To be white was to belong to the tribe that held dominion over the earth, all plants and animals, and all non-white peoples. People with white skin had invented the white race so they could live like royalty, or at least share in the glow of royalty.

The earth, all plants and animals and all non-white peoples owed white people, especially white men, fealty and gratitude.

The Divine Right of White Males.

290

Clearly, the patron saint of white males had to be Marie Antoinette.

Hopefully no one believed all those things now. But people had believed all those things, and still did believe some of those things, or even all those things if only somewhat. The war went on.

Everyone and everything resisted. Women resisted; blacks resisted; Asians resisted; Latinxs resisted; Native Americans resisted; plants resisted; animals resisted; the earth resisted. Everyone and everything white men ordered into a category resisted.

Then he had the answer.

*   *   *

Celisa watched as Rik wandered away. He seemed different today, not so much a different person as a different version of himself. She assumed it was the same fears and pressure they all felt. She wondered if Rik and Jessa were seeing a different version of herself.

Jessa said, "He likes to be alone."

Celisa turned toward the girl. "An introvert."

"More like a recluse."

Celisa flinched at the words. "What do you mean?"

Jessa felt like crying but she didn't want to wallow in front of Rik's girlfriend. "Nothing."

"The pressure's getting to all of us."

Jessa said nothing.

"We're trying to stay busy mostly to avoid thinking about..."

Jessa smiled coldly. "You can't even say what we're avoiding thinking about."

"No. Guess I can't. What's bothering you, Jessa? I mean besides...what we're here for?"

"You wouldn't understand."

"I probably wouldn't but I'd listen."

"God, you sound like my therapist."

"But I don't charge a co-pay."

Jessa felt trapped and relieved. "I'm afraid Rik will leave me. It seems everyone has left or betrayed me except him, and now...?"

"How did people betray you?"

Jessa told her story in a cool, fact-by-fact, narrative. Her facial expressions and body movements became jerky and mechanical as the emotions she tried to hide fought back.

When Jessa finished, Celisa breathed, "I'm sorry." She paused. "I don't know..."

"What to say? No one does." Jessa stared off.

Celisa looked at Jessa's face. She bit her lip. "Jessa?"

"Yeah?"

"Would it help if I just took your hand?"

Jessa's shoulders jerked as if indicating she didn't care.

Celisa took the girl's right hand in her own left and held it.

Jessa glanced down at the two hands together. Somehow it did help, though she fought back tears. Wrong day for tears, she thought. "You listened. That's something. A lot. Tell me something about you."

"Sure." Celisa felt guilty feeling relieved she could change the subject. "This goes way back. On the first day of fifth grade, our new teacher, Mrs. Akerley, caught me. The boy sitting behind me had been touching my hair and first I whispered to him to stop. Then he began pulling my hair. I told him to stop. Mrs. Akerley heard me. She looked at me and said, "Is there something you would like to tell the rest of the class?" I said, "No, Mrs. Akerley." Then that kid really yanked my hair. I yelped, then I stood up and punched him twice in the face. Knocked him half out of his chair. Mrs. Akerley shrieked and ran over to where I was standing. I've never seen such a red face. I'll credit her though. She didn't hit me. She yelled, 'Girls don't hit!' At least she lived by her own rule. "I was still pissed. I told her, 'He pulled my hair.' She said, 'And girls don't talk back! That's the kind of behavior that gets people like you thrown in jail.' Yeah, I got it then. Don't know to this day whether she was warning me or threatening me. Whatever—she was working on a whole different basis than I was. I said I was sorry. She said she'd let it go this time because I was a girl but if I ever did anything like that again in her class she'd haul me to the principal's office and get me thrown out of school. Then she looked at the kid I'd hit with a mean face and said, 'Boys!'

"Didn't threaten to expel him though. The other kids looked at me, like they were examining...a bug or something. No one else laughed. I was an exhibit. A few of the kids sneered and mouthed the N-word. I was too afraid to move. It was open season on me after that. Fifth grade was miserable."

"That's awful."

"You don't get used to stuff like that. You know what people will be thinking when they see us together, I mean, you, Rik and me? 'Oh, look, there's Rik and Jessa and that black friend of theirs.'"

"Geez."

"So what do you want to say tonight if there's the chance?"

Jessa looked away. "I don't want to say anything." She took her hand from Celisa's. "You listened. Rik listens. They won't. I hate being mocked and I hate being pitied. Really, I'd hate to have to speak."

*   *   *

Tom spent the day reminding everyone that there were no guarantees, that, in fact, this was a chewing gum-and-chicken-wire operation. Deeper forces would determine whether his plan came off. Still, Tom's streak of perfectionism came out in his directions.

When he stopped to check the time, he muttered, "Damn!" Father Vic, Celisa, Jessa and Rik stopped what they'd been doing and turned to listen as he called out to the others. "It's almost seven! Let's clean this place up and take positions before Clint gets here."

293

The group worked even faster now, testing all things electric one last time.

Father Vic walked up to Tom. "So, everything's ready?"

"Hope so. But I have to thank you for letting us in here to prepare."

"No problem. I like to be helpful."

"I can see that. How long have you been a priest?"

"Eighteen years."

"Does it seem longer or shorter?"

Father Vic smiled. "Both."

"You enjoy it?"

"Sometimes."

"You don't strike me as a priest. No, I don't mean that. I apologize. I guess I think most priests, ministers, rabbis, imams, monks, shamans even, what have you, are like, well, they remind me of zookeepers. They work really hard to care for the spirit, but they always remember to lock the cage. I think you don't always lock the cage."

Father Vic stared at Tom.

* * *

At seven thirty, a half hour before the meeting was to begin, Clint, in uniform, with his firearm on his hip and the recently deceased Gordie Sands' briefcase in his hand, approached the basement of St. Benedict's Church.

Clint had the documents and checks in his possession. All he needed were the signatures of his neighbors—that, and to deposit the checks made out to him. He'd wait until Toronto to do that. And to get out before the storm hit. He pulled open the basement door. Only a few hours remained, but he understood exactly how he needed to fill them. Perfectly straightforward. But he could not forget that he had been left behind by his supriors. He'd been judged not worthy. His identity and self respect depended on their need for him, the trust they placed in him, trust justified by the indisputable fact that he was one of them. And not like those others.

They'd acted as if he were one of those others.

He struggled to hold his head up. Only the anger rising from his sense of having been dealt with unfairly provided energy sufficient to continue. Could he be an important person if they believed he was unimportant?

No. He couldn't allow himself to think this way. It was all a mistake. Mistakes always happened. They just weren't supposed to happen to him.

It would be alright.

He still had the means. He had his authority, his gun and his neighborhood for a few more hours. After that, all he would have would be his gun and more than enough money.

And Scarlet.

He was what he was. Still.

With Scarlet.

Except he discovered, standing in the church basement, none other than Tom Morton. The memory of the preceding night, of Tom wheedling the story of his wife from him, of discovering the traitor in the Hollie home, blotted Clint's thinking process. He steeled himself. He touched his gun for reassurance. He removed his cap.

The basement could have been set up for a meeting of the Ancient Order of Hibernians, the Sons of Italy or AA. All the lights were on, leaving no place for a poor shadow to hide. More than enough folding chairs had been set out to provide seating for the neighborhood. Clint assumed that the large table at the front of the room with a single chair was for him.

Tom smiled broadly and waved.

Annie and Father Vic, who had been talking to Tom, turned and also smiled and waved. Annie's kids had moved a couple of chairs in a half circle about them. They used the chair seats as tables to color books.

Clint gritted out a smile and strode toward the group.

"Didn't expect others to be here before me." It was a complaint, but he managed a friendly tone.

Tom asked, "You like how we've set it up? We can change it if you want."

Clint looked around and said, "It's fine. Thanks for saving me the work."

"Say, Clint, how's your hand doing?" Tom pointed at the gauze bandage.

"Ah, nothing. Just a scratch."

"As long as it was just a scratch and not a bite. Bites get infected very easily."

Clint squinted at Tom.

Tom asked, "Clint, could we talk privately for a moment?"

The officer shrugged. "Sure."

Tom said, "Excuse us."

Clint smiled again, nodded at Annie and Father Vic and walked slowly away, following Tom. He thought Annie was screwing the priest. Not that it bothered him. But he knew it would bother them if other people found out. Another tool for his tool kit.

Clint followed Tom into a corner. The officer eyed an old confessional that had been propped up against the wall. He looked as if he might be considering kicking it in the kidneys.

Tom, noticing, asked "You ever get caught in one of these things?"

Clint sniffed. "Last time was when the priest screamed out, 'Clint Adams, what the hell did you do that for?' Fucking embarrassing. Never went back."

"Don't blame you. Wasn't Father Vic, was it?"

"Nah. Long time ago. Priest's dead now."

Tom blinked. After two seconds ticked by, he licked his lips and asked, "You didn't kill him, did you?"

"No, but, oh, my God, I wanted to!" He laughed.

Tom breathed a sigh of relief. "Good. So, what are your plans for tonight?"

Clint shrugged and smiled. "Make my friends the offers that will get their homes off their backs and give them some money."

"Why bother? You know what's going to happen tonight. Why not take your money and run?"

"Who told you?"

"About the storm?"

"Yeah."

"My leg. Why are you still here?"

"I have to finish the job. I haven't earned my fee yet."

Tom blinked. He leaned toward the officer and whispered, "But you killed..."

"Who? What about it?" Clint stopped. He smiled. "I see what you're getting at. Makes sense you wouldn't understand. A man does what he has to, to defend himself and his family. Whatever it takes. That doesn't mean I'm a cheat. I earn my money."

Tom got that he hadn't got it. Clint was right. He hadn't understood. For Clint, cheating someone was worse than killing them. "Well, speaking of murder, I was wondering, why you are trying to kill me?"

Clint feigned amazement. "Now who told you that?"

"The ghosts."

"You take the word of ghosts above the word of a law enforcement official?" Clint had a wonderful way of acting unjustly wounded. He could also swagger without moving his feet. "You believe them more than me? You find ghosts more trustworthy than me?"

Tom smiled gently. "Amazing. You're so detached from your feelings that you have to feign the feelings you actually have. Clint, you did break into my hotel room this morning. You didn't stop by the desk first or just knock on my door. You broke in. That's not something law enforcement officers are expected to do."

"How the hell do you know all this?"

"Clint, we've had this discussion before. You hired me to get rid of ghosts. Then you seemed surprised that I talk to ghosts. Why is there such a disconnect in your mind? You want to hire someone who doesn't talk to ghosts to get rid of ghosts? I'll admit, those people are cheaper, though I hear they aren't very good."

Clint sniffed. "To be honest, I thought you, sir, were frauding me."

"What? You mean just pretending I could do it?"

"Right. I thought you'd take your money and run."

"Which would work well with your plan. Am I correct?"

Clint's eyes narrowed. "Something like that."

"But now you think I will get rid of the ghosts, and that's what threatens you."

Clint made a you-might-be-right-you-might-be-wrong face.

"Well, I'm not saying I can get rid of the ghosts or I can't. It doesn't matter really. I still work for you. All you have to do is fire me and I'm gone."

Clint asked, "You offering me a deal?"

"You fire me and this stage is yours."

"You want the rest of your money?"

"No."

"Well, alright." Clint looked Tom in the eyes. "You're fired."

Tom put on a stern face. "No, I'm not. I quit."

Clint felt good about himself again as he watched Tom exit the church basement. He smiled toward the half dozen or so of people in line for coffee. None noticed him.

*   *   *

The room was small. The banks of switch boxes with their wires and tubes made the room feel even smaller. Unlike in the church basement, there was no air conditioning, and the afternoon's heat lingered. The room's best feature, other than that it was one concrete block wall away from the church basement, was its separate entrance from the rear of the church, intended to provide easy access for electricians and other repair people.

The occupants shoved closer together when Tom entered.

He whispered, "Everything okay?"

The others nodded.

Tom tapped Rik on the shoulder and motioned him to follow outside. When the door closed behind them, Tom held out a ring of keys.

Without taking the keys, Rik asked, "What?"

"These are duplicates for my rental van, that's this big one here, and keys to my luggage and stuff. In case something happens to me."

"In case..?" Rik didn't like this talk. "You don't need to do this."

"I don't know which of you it is, but it has to be at least one of you: you, Jessa or Celisa. Maybe more than one of you. I think I know but I can't be sure so I won't say. I know you will be able to figure it out."

Rik took the keys. "I'll give these back to you later."

"Anything is possible."

They hugged, hard and long, and both cried.

*   *   *

Clint watched the people from the neighborhood come in, the Hollies among them. He walked over to greet them.

"Hey, hey, looks like a great turnout! Good to see you. Where are the kids?"

Evelyn waved her hand, as if to say, "You know how they are." She said, "Sick like dogs. Stayed home from school and spent the day moaning and groaning."

"Well, that's too bad. I'd hoped they would be here. Gary, looking good, old guy." He slapped the man on the back.

"Yeah, thanks. You, too." Gary wasn't as good or gracious an actor as his wife. Being uncertain who he was, he was unable to tell when he was being himself and when he was playing a role.

299

"Oh, say, getting to be time. Get yourselves a seat."

As if they'd come to hear a sermon by Father Vic, most people filled in the seats starting from the back, near the doors, and moving only as far forward as necessary. But Clint caught the Hollies and led them to the front row, where Sandy, Pat and Nick had already taken seats with their wives. Annie reached over two other people to tap Evelyn on the shoulder and wave hi.

Once they took their seats, Evelyn leaned toward Gary and said, "Seems like a hundred years have passed since we met them."

*   *   *

Clint gave the sign.

Sandy and Father Vic ushered those who remained standing into seats.

When the priest closed the doors, Clint began.

"Well, thanks for coming. Good to see everyone. We've been through a lot together and we've become family, really. I consider each and every one of you family. I do. We've had a few disappointments together and we're having another one tonight. But I promise you that by the end of the evening you won't feel disappointed. You'll feel relieved. A great weight will be lifted from you. And me.

"Our Christian shaman, whatever he claimed to be, punked out. Couldn't perform when the time came. Performance anxiety. You all know the type.

"Let's consider our options. They're limited. The shaman option is gone. We can't continue to live in our neighborhood with these ghosts and we won't be able to sell our houses for any decent price once the world outside finds out about our infestation."

He waited until he felt every eye on him.

"But I've been working long and hard for your interests. It took time. It took a good deal of convincing. But I took the time and I did the convincing and I'm here tonight to tell you that we have, we do have...one...final...option."

Everyone leaned a bit forward.

"I found a man...actually, I found a company willing to buy the whole neighborhood.

"Yes, I hear you all silently asking: does he know about the ghosts?

"Yes, he does. The company does. The company wants to build a new casino on our land. Would you believe, he's thinking of working our ghosts into his marketing plan!

"And like any good businessman, he did his due diligence and came up with figures to offer each and every one of you for your haunted home.

"But I said, 'Show me those figures. I need to see them before I can recommend your offers to my friends and neighbors.' And he showed them to me.

"I went over each and every one.

"I told him to forget it. The money was too little. I told him people needed real money, they needed money they..."

That was when Clint noticed the wheelchair half hidden in shadows at the back of the room.

"...We...they needed money..."

No one in the neighborhood used a wheelchair.

"...Money for, uh, so they could buy a new place where they could get on with their lives."

Clint looked away from the puzzling figure in the wheelchair. He didn't want to draw other people's attention to it.

"He...this guy, the one with the money, he frowned. You know how rich people frown, right? He frowned as if frowning cost him money. He said he couldn't offer any more.

"So I said, 'Thanks for your time.' And I began to walk away."

Against his will, Clint's eyes returned to the back of the room. He squinted. A woman sat beside the person in the wheelchair. Must be homeless people who crashed receptions and the like for the free coffee, he figured. He decided not to interrupt his presentation to arrest them.

"He said, the man with the money said, 'Wait!' He said, 'Let me think about this again.' And he got a pencil and a pad and he began writing and figuring. It took him maybe twenty minutes. And at the end of that, he pushed the pad across the table to me.

"I sat there comparing the numbers. They were better, no doubt about that. But I shook my head. I shoved the pad back at him.

"He didn't touch the pad. Don't know what he was thinking, but after a few minutes I said, 'Let me have the pad back.'

"He pushed it back at me across the table.

"I studied the figures. One by one I crossed each one out and wrote in a new, higher figure. I pushed it back at him. Like we were playing ping-pong, you know?

"He looked at my figures. He studied them. He didn't pick up his pencil again. He just looked at me and said, 'Alright. I'll pay it.'"

Clint felt the electricity of the crowd.

"Friends and neighbors, I've got all the paperwork right here." He pointed at the briefcase on the table. "The buyer has already signed." Louder, he said, "I've got the bank-certified checks made out to you. You can take it. Or you can leave it. If you leave it, you'll live in that house with those..." He paused. "You know what word I'm thinking of, right? I'm not supposed to say it, but we're all thinking it, right?" Laughter swept the room. "Those 'ghosts' till your dying day, because no one is ever going to buy it for what is being offered for it tonight.

"Here's the deal: for those of you who still have mortgages, the buyer pays off the mortgage and then pays you the remaining value of your home. If you don't have a mortgage, then the check represents the full value of your home. It's simple as that.

"If you sign tonight, you can stay in your house until January fifteenth of next year, four months, plenty of time so you can find a new place.

"But before I show any of you the offers for your houses, I'm going to sign mine. To show how much I like this deal, I'm going first. Because this is a great deal for sellers in our position.

"So!"

Clint pulled out the chair and sat at the table. He unlocked the briefcase and removed the top folder. He read, "'Clint Adams.' Sounds like me, right?" He unfolded the legal-sized papers, took a pen, and studied the papers briefly.

"Kinda sad, you know? This is where Scarlet and I spent our years together. Lots of memories.

"Alright! Here goes!" He signed once. "You gotta sign two places. You used to have to sign a hundred times. Remember those days? We finally got the government out of our business."

He signed the second time.

"There it is!" He pointed at the two signatures. "And here's my check!" He waved the check like a flag. "I'm free!

"Who wants to be liberated next?"

The lights went out.

In the dark, Clint reached for his gun.

*   *   *

When the lights went out, the adults hunched, as if they hoped to make themselves smaller targets for what dangers might lurk in the dark. A few exclamations of "what the..." were heard. Everyone concentrated on listening for the slightest clues about what had happened. Those with children reached, quickly found their young, encircled them with their arms. Those with significant others found the other's hand.

Some of the neighbors noticed the timing. Just when Clint reached his high point, the curtain dropped. Maybe, they wondered, Clint had arranged it.

Then a deep, fatherly voice, calming as a fluffy blanket, said, "Be not afraid."

No one mistook that voice for Clint's.

"Be not afraid," the voice repeated.

The neighbors' feet grew heavy, at first as if they'd worn multiple pairs of wool socks, then as if their legs were sending roots into the floor.

"You have been invited on a journey back in time, a journey of discovery and possibility. You have nothing to fear until you return. Be not afraid."

Those who tried lifting a leg couldn't. They were trapped.

Someone leaned toward his wife and asked, "Do you feel...?"

She whispered, "Yes."

A child worriedly said, "Mom, something's wrong with my feet."

The voice said, "Changes are happening. You are being made secure to protect you. Everyone is safe here. Be not afraid."

Some people thought their reply, get us the fuck out of here! For others, the hidden speaker's words acted like a shot of Novocain. Most began calling out objections, questions, threats. They hung on the verge.

"Wait!" the voice said. "Now! See!"

Pinpricks of light, scattered and drifting, grew out of the dark. Several of the neighbors closed their eyes, then, after counting to five or so, opened them. Others merely blinked. When they opened their eyes, the tiny lights were still there. A child held by her father reached out her hand to grab one. It slipped away like a firefly.

That's when the neighbors realized they were standing. No one remembered having stood, but sure as hell, everyone had. And the chairs had disappeared.

"Light is returning. Be not afraid."

The pinpricks of light grew larger and brighter, turned into sparks. Gradually, the light grew till they could almost see.

Then, yes, hallelujah!

Eyes became able to make out the structures of the church basement, the walls, the floor, the ceiling.

"There are good reasons for these changes. Be not afraid."

The neighbors, most of them, took some reassurance in the reappearance of the building. Everything was where it was supposed to be.

Not to last. Things drained away. The walls lost substance, leaving them flimsy, filmy objects, ready to be blown away by the slightest breeze.

Through the walls the neighbors looked into a more substantial darkness outside.

A child's voice suggested, "It's all special effects, right, Dad?"

Beneath their feet, the tile floor silently shattered into splinters and fell away, disappearing into the void beneath. People floated. What could their feet be rooted in?

A child clasped in her father's arms looked at him and said, "Daddy." As the father turned his head and looked into his two-year-old's eyes, she disappeared. The man felt he continued to hold her but he could no longer see her. He couldn't see his own hands or arms or anything or anyone else. He clung to his daughter. There was no such thing as visible solid. Just space.

"Be not afraid."

Then the air began to give birth to solid beings.

From the dark, a new ground assembled itself. People had something to stand on again. Ground. Earth. They were outdoors, standing in a ring of uneven soil more than a hundred feet across, sparsely covered by low grasses. Inside that ring a rough circle of exposed earth formed, perhaps thirty feet across. Dirt.

The neighbors could tell they stood on dirt and grass without looking. Their feet were bare, though no longer rooted. They'd lost their shoes.

People became visible. First, a crease or fold or patch of brown cloth might appear. Outlines constructed themselves, patches grew and connected, then filled in to become wholes. Bit by bit existence became visible.

As if they were penitent monks, everyone wore hooded, ground-length brown cloaks. Round masks that were all apiece with the robes hid their faces. The masks were white, full moon faces with mouths like slashes of agony.

As strange and disconcerting as that was, their attention turned to something worse. Each individual felt they'd been maimed, that, as if a large animal had torn pieces of flesh and bone with its teeth, they had suffered multiple injuries that left them with gaping holes. Chunks of themselves had gone missing. The voids ached and yearned. Some realized they'd felt this loss all along but hadn't been conscious of it. Everyone felt compelled to stuff anything that might fit into those gaps, but their cloaks and masks prevented it.

Now they became thankful for the cloaks. No one wanted to be exposed in such an embarrassing condition. Everyone feared others hadn't suffered, or that they had more lost pieces than everyone else.

Instinctively, they felt shamed, and pulled their cloaks more tightly about them.

The walls had thoroughly vanished now, and the outside was a night free of electric lights. The neighbors stood along the edge of a well-trodden clearing surrounded by seven great trees with leafy branches.

Moon faces faced moon faces. No one recognized any other, except parents who recognized their children, and then only by height. Most people didn't want to be recognized.

Young children, overcome by the sight of their parents' masks, screamed and cried. Some pushed their parents away.

The ceiling, too, had thinned, as its molecules drifted off like smoke. And there, in the sky, within the frame of the leafy, overhanging branches, flowed the hundred billion stars of the Milky Way.

Beyond the trees to the south, perhaps a hundred yards behind where the neighbors stood, a river's rippled surface reflected starlight. On the left and right, shadowed forms of scattered bushes and clusters of trees could be seen. Opposite the river, at the top of a hill, a two-storied wooden house stood in all its glory, its upstairs windows lit discreetly with candles, the downstairs rooms ablaze.

306

Three coaches, each with its own lantern and a pair of handsome horses, stood idle before the house.

Beside the grand house was a smaller, unpainted, unkempt house.

The air was cool. A breeze ruffled the leaves and smaller branches.

Turning heads and craning necks, the neighbors situated themselves in this new landscape. But they did their best not to look at each other, not wanting to be reminded of what they, too, looked like in and beneath their cloaks.

The neighbors might have been forgiven for feeling they'd been dropped into a museum diorama. Countering the terror of the transformation, the tableau provided a sense of peace and quiet. But the seemingly calm landscape constituted a stage on which a tragedy would be performed. The stage was a mythic memory of some idyllic Eden for the Few. A few men had forced this Eden on the world by cunning and violence. At that point, already, all had been lost.

*   *   *

My kids got me through that. Emily and Lana. Fifteen and thirteen. Good kids. I'm so lucky. They knew as soon as it started what it would do to me. Disorientation. Fear. I can't describe what it's like when panic owns you, body and soul. They held me so I could feel them even when we couldn't see each other. Like my therapist said: the wars always come home. They follow you, sniffing at your footsteps like some giant lizard until they strike and dig their teeth into you. Rip you apart.

When things stabilized and I'd gotten my breath back, I asked, "You guys okay?"

"As good as can be expected under the circumstances." That was the answer they'd learned from me.

"Me, too," I said.

That bit of ritual helped.

There wasn't much of me left under this gown thing. Most of me was gone. Was surprised I could still move, breath, talk, think.

"I know where we are," I said. "I can smell it. This is a battle-field. Terrible things have been done here."

We held each other.

*   *   *

I'd slept in that smaller building, the slave house, when I was younger, with all of us slaves, each with a piece of the dirt floor. We had scraps for blankets. That's where I'd given birth, on that dirt floor. And where I'd...where I'd done what I had to do.

Most of my life I spent nights in the larger, grander building they called the Royall House after its owner. Our owner. They made me sit on a wooden chair in the second-floor hallway beside a door, prepared even as I dozed, no matter how deep or cold the night, to rise immediately at the mistress's call.

Tonight I wore a blue dress and Grandma had done my hair in braids for the meeting. Despite the aching holes in my soul, I felt fresh, almost new.

I stood among bushes, hidden from the neighbors, but I could see them.

I watched Clint. It was easy to tell which robed figure he was. He stood apart from the others and held a gun. With his other hand, the bandaged one, he'd pulled his robe tight around his body.

Clint shouted, "Quiet! Quiet! I know who's doing this!"

Another brown-robed, moon-faced figure stepped from a cluster of bushes. "You're right, Clint. It's me."

Clint snarled, "You lied to me!"

I feared Clint would shoot Tom then and there.

"Yes, but lies are the foundation of our relationship." The neighbors had to recognize the calm voice.

I felt Clint blink behind his mask. "What do you mean by that?"

308

"Doesn't matter. It really doesn't. Come on, Clint: put the gun away. If you shoot me, you and your neighbors will be stuck here forever. You'll never get back to the Paradise you know. You need me. Besides, it's my turn to speak. I haven't even introduced myself yet."

"What are you going to say?"

"Don't be afraid, Clint. I'm going to tell the truth."

Clint recognized the threat implied, but once again Tom had outmaneuvered him. Slowly and deliberately, he dropped the hand holding his weapon to his side. The truth, he knew, is double-edged.

I'd been watching Tom and Clint and hadn't paid attention to the neighbors, but they let out a sigh when Clint pointed his gun at the ground.

"Thank you, Clint. How's your left hand doing, by the way?"

Clint held up the bandaged hand as if in a victory salute. The pain had grown. "Fine."

"Good."

"Don't be afraid," Tom said to the neighbors. "At least not about what has just happened. We're here because we need some time and a place to talk. Actually, we haven't come far in terms of space. We're a few hundred feet from where St. Benedict's will be in another three hundred years or so. When we're done, we'll return to St. Benedict's basement. We'll arrive there at the same time we left, which is good.

"You're going to need all the time you can get when you return there."

Tom's voice carried like a preacher's: it could be heard clearly all the way back. "You are all the same people you were before I brought you here," he counseled the neighbors. "But you're seeing, well, no, feeling yourself, from a new angle, an angle from which we are our full selves, both body and soul. I provided cloaks and masks to save us all, including myself, severe embarrassment.

"It is amazing, isn't it? And a bit scary. Maybe a lot scary."

I had to admit Tom had a way with people. This white shaman spoke with authority, not the kind that comes from a uniform or a title, but that comes from presence.

Even I felt compelled to listen to him.

Still, I expected he had it figured all wrong. He expected the white people would understand. Really? After four hundred years, my God, how much time did they need? Generation after generation, they turned away, deciding not to free our people, which was to say, deciding not to free their own people.

I'd never heard anything so true as when the white preacher who served the slave masters talked about the Garden of Eden and how Adam and Eve got themselves evicted. Adam and Eve were white people. The original moon faces. Don't think so? Look at all the paintings. Ever see a black Adam or Eve? No. Adam and Eve were too important not to have been white. Why did they get thrown out of Eden? Because they wanted to be like God and get to decide who was good and who was evil. As in, white people are good and black people are evil.

God recognized what they were up to.

So I hoped, but with only a smidgen—a word Grandma often used—of hope.

"My name is Tom Morton. Clint invited me to come to Paradise to help rid the neighborhood of ghosts. Then he asked me to leave. I decided to stay to help."

"To help?" The male voice came from someone among the cloaked neighbors. "How is doing this to us going to help?"

"Good question. I must first explain our problem. Your problem. My problem. A big problem. One Clint didn't get around to telling you.

"You all ready? This is big. Listen carefully.

"There's a Category Seven hurricane going to hit Paradise tonight around midnight. Category Seven. That means near-total devastation. The reason you haven't heard of this is because the government that you've been loyal to, that you've paid taxes to, that some of you fought wars for, has written you off. They've written you off just like they wrote off the Native Americans, Africans and African-Americans, Hispanics, countless refugees from around the world, Puerto Rico, Louisiana, Florida, Houston, Nevada, Kansas, Nebraska, Oklahoma and all those other places.

"You are stateless.

"You are citizens of no country. You have no claim on any government agency for help.

"As of right now, legally you're all uncountables."

Of course, it was impossible for these people to take all this in. This was outside of their mental range of possible experiences. The neighbors stood in silence until someone gasped, "What?"

Tom repeated himself. As he spoke, murmurs, then protests, arose from the neighbors.

"That's insane!"

"I saw the weather forecast!"

More than a little desperation in all these shouts.

"You're lying!"

"They wouldn't do that to us!"

"Wait..."

"You fucking liar!"

"Get the hell out of here!"

"They'd never leave us behind!"

The white shaman shouted above the outrage. "Clint! Let Clint speak!"

The crowd dialed back. They looked to their neighbor.

"Clint, is what I just said the truth?"

Slowly, Clint turned toward his neighbors. "Yeah. He's right. Everything's shut down. The roads, trains, buses, air traffic, everything is shut down. They've cut us off. They decided we're not worth saving. The storm's going to hit in a few hours. I was going to tell you after you signed the papers. After you had the checks in your hands."

It got really hard for these people right then.

Yeah, they were stunned. It was like all of a sudden they found themselves on the other side of the television screen, the side where bad, bad things happened to people.

The kids bothered me. I remembered what it felt like to be lost. I even said a silent prayer for them. They picked up their parents' fear, began squirming, asking questions, crying. Of course, if this all never happened, if they grew up just like they'd expected to, they'd mostly become a reissue of their parents and nothing would ever change. Hell, it was totally possible this whole hurricane thing could go down and nothing would change for the better.

Next, Tom had to introduce the moon faces to their own history. He went over the whole John Winthrop, Ten Hills Farm, Isaac Royall-slave-trader-extraordinaire, Royall House thing. The neighbors must have understood that what Tom told them was connected to the hurricane because they listened without interrupting. I suppose they were hoping for a Hollywood ending.

"The ghosts who have been haunting you are the ghosts of slaves who worked the land here after John Winthrop arrived. Most of the ghosts were slaves to Mr. Royall or his son.

"The reason these ghosts have returned at this time is to watch everything built here since 1630 be destroyed."

"The ghosts are here to watch our destruction. Think of them as disaster tourists. The destruction will be done by the Category Seven hurricane."

The crowd began to move like heating water.

"Why would they do this to us?"

Someone shouted, "Destroy the ghosts!" Others quickly shortened the chant to, "Kill the ghosts!"

Tom's voice carried over the protests. "The ghosts did not create the hurricane. They are offering to help us."

"I don't want to be helped by any fucking ghost! I'll save myself!"

"That's right! Bring us back where we belong. We'll save ourselves!"

Yes, this was what I expected, nothing more. Still I was disappointed. I had too much at stake. These people were keeping me from being me.

There I was, stepping up to the center of the clearing as if I were taking charge from the shaman.

Guess they didn't expect a child. They went silent as I approached them. Took my time about it. Walked from one end of the monk's chorus to the other, examining them. I knew how to examine them, cause I'd seen it done so many times. No one examines like a slaver. You stand up straight, tall as you can, shoulders back, eyes wide and amused, you wear a grand smirk and you strut. They got themselves all into a shock at having a black twelve-year-old size them up.

"Those holes you feel? I got them, too. That's right. I know how you feel. I know all about you. So don't we all, us ghosts. We know all about your sins.

"Now I know most of you, maybe all of you, is pissed to have a black-child-slave-ghost explain life to you. But like you say, I'm just doing my job.

"You see, I got a lot riding on the decisions you all make tonight. You people have had four hundred years to get things right and you ain't. No, you ain't got it right yet. But tonight you got another chance.

"You got that chance because Tom here cut a deal with my grandma. That deal involves your futures. We ghosts can do what we came here to do which is to watch you all and your cities drown. Or you and Tom and us can work something out.

"You ain't got to listen. That's right. You can cover your ears or stick your head up you-know-where. You can drown not even knowing what it was we proposed to do.

"It's up to you.

"I'll say one more thing. Those of you who got children: it's a sin, a grave sin to send them to their deaths without listening. You know what they want you to do."

Then I turned around and sashayed, slowly and steadily,

taking my four-hundred-year-old time about it, back into the bushes.

Silence. Then a woman said cautiously, "Well, let's let them explain at least."

A few cries of opposition erupted but mostly there were muttered assents. The neighbors had decided. I felt exhausted.

Tom said, "Alright. We will now explain what you need to know to make your decision."

That's when the rest of us came out from where we'd been hidden. I walked behind my father. He helped Grandma make it to the center of the clearing.

We ghosts outnumbered the neighbors, filling more than half the clearing. More stood in shadows beneath the trees and unseen among the bushes and still others crowded in behind the neighbors.

I heard murmurs: They've got us surrounded.

We had more than us slaves. There were Massachusett, Pequot, Narragansett, Penacook, Natick and people from a dozen other tribes. Celisa stood a few feet behind us, flanked by Jessa and Rik.

George brought Belinda her chair. With my father's help, she sat. I helped her wrap herself in her blanket.

The neighbors had gotten past their first fright. I could smell the adrenaline.

*   *   *

"It's a beautiful night," Belinda said in greeting. She glanced up. "Ain't it?

"But cool. A nice cool.

"Thank you for being here. Though you been kidnapped a bit by Mr. Morton, I thank you anyway. It's scary, ain't it, to be plucked from a familiar place and brought against your will to somewhere strange?

"Like to thank my granddaughter, too, for helping settle things down so we can talk.

"To be truthful, as Mr. Morton said, we came to your time, we ghosts, first off to observe your destruction. Your predecessors destroyed our lives and now the come-around is going to get you. You see, you all are their successors. Not descendants necessarily, but successors. You got what they took because you put yourselves next in line.

"Watching your destruction would have been particularly sweet, I admit, since this hurricane is your own creation. You done it. It's like Professor Frankenstein created his monster and now you all created yours and here it comes. Think Mrs. Shelley was on to something? Hum?

"Till Mr. Morton shared his idea with us, we couldn't find reason to put our faith in you.

"So you find you all in a pickle, with a monster coming for you, a monster named Category Seven crawling out from beneath your beds to destroy everything, maybe even kill you, your loved ones, your children. That's the thing about monsters: they just kill and they don't care.

"And you all ain't got no way to defend yourself. Everyone else, all the good and just people, all your superheroes, well, they just wrote you off. That what Mr. Royall used to say when a slave died. 'Oh, well, I'll just write it off.'

"You ain't got no friends, no one to help. Hum? Been there myself. I feel for you.

"Mr. Morton here, he tells me he's being generous by being selfish. He thinks he can heal these wounds we ghosts have. He can heal us, so he says. I think he can. Maybe.

"He made us that offer, but he wants something in return.

"Mr. Morton wants us ghosts to protect you from the coming storm.

"Yes, Mr. Morton has your well-being at heart.

"We ghosts, well, we not so sure.

"You see, these holes we got were given to us by people like you, your predecessors who lived right here on this land. When one body wounds or kills another body, that body, the one that does the wounding or killing, wounds or severs the wounded person's soul. You get that?

"When you were a child, did grown-ups, people of authority tell you you were worthless and a failure? Worthless but for your market value? Anything like that? Remember how it stung? What if everybody told you that? How would you deal?

"When, say, one person makes another his slave, when one so-called race makes another so-called race all slaves, that owner person, that owner race mauls every slave person's soul. Grievously. You know that word? The soul is so maimed it must at all times grieve.

"That's why we slaves got all these holes in us. Most of them, anyway.

"What about you folks? Hmm? How'd you get your holes? Here's a clue. Those who cause suffering, they too suffer.

"My story simple. White men—we called them 'moon faces,' yes, your monk clothes were Mr. Morton's idea but your masks were mine—those 'moon faces' took me when I was a child, took me from my mother, my father, my two brothers and my sister, to name a few, from my home, from my people, from the place I belonged. They chained me to, well, it was night, but there must have been a hundred other African people and dragged us down to the ocean. There they put us in the bottom of a boat, in the dark, no lights, chained so we were shoulder to shoulder, hip to hip with no room to squirm. We peed in that position. We shat in that position. A good number of us died in that position.

"The sailors who came to carry out the dead wore covers over their noses and mouths because they couldn't stand the stench of us. We couldn't either. We didn't live that way. No one lived that way before the moon faces came.

"The next thing is we're standing on a stage, all of us naked, prospective buyers poking us wherever they felt like, talking business among themselves and laughing at us.

"Then we got bought and they marched us off to start working and building the white man's world cause he too weak and too lazy to do it himself. Um. Nowadays, you make the people in Asia, Africa, in South and Central America do your work cause you expect to be paid well and you claim you doing them all favors by paying them scraps.

"And yes, we slaves lived here in Paradise and in Boston. All around here. Every decent family had one or two. Humm? I'm one of them.

"And my soul is wounded!"

Belinda pulled back her blanket, opened her dress and exposed a breast, but instead of a breast there was a cave, an emptiness, a craving for wholeness, a prayer for redemption.

She covered herself once more.

"There are more. I have more. We all do.

"By we I mean more than just us ghosts, you got to know.

"It ain't just the victims that have their souls torn. Like a friend of a descendant of mine said, every action has an equal and opposite reaction.

"What you do to others, you do to yourself. The perpetrators tear their own souls when they do injustice.

"Yessum!

"So I got holes because of injustices done me and I got holes for injustices I done.

"Just like you. Except no one ever kept you as a slave. No one ever used you like a thing. I don't mean like an animal. Like a thing. No one ever told you you were too stupid to read and when you learned to read they passed laws saying they'll whip you for reading. No one ever told you to get married and then sold your husband south, your babies east and west and you north. No one ever told you, after they brought you here, to go back where you came from. No one told you you all lazy, stupid drunks cause of your skin. No one ever told you you ain't worth hiring cause of the color of your skin. No one sent you into poverty schools. No one hanged you by the neck till dead on the authority of malicious rumors. No one ever harassed you girls and women for walking on the street with a white boy. No one done those things to you.

"You see, we got holes for those things. Yeah, we got holes for those things. We do.

"How many them holes you got are cause what others done to you and how many due to what you done to others? You ask yourself that. Let your pain answer. Your pain knows.

"We going to help you understand some how you earned those holes in you, what you done to deserve them.

"We going to help you, too, if you want, if you grieve for what you done to others and the earth, we going to do what we can to help you to survive.

"So here's the deal. You all understand deals, don't you? Right? Mr. Morton offered to heal all us ghosts, all us slaves, all us tribal peoples, if we just nudge that storm a bit away from you. And we added a condition: that you agree to be healed too. That way we all be healed. We all be whole. We all be whole.

"It ain't as easy as you might want it to be. You see, you can't be healed if you deny you wounded. You got to listen to your wounds and to those you wounded. You got to listen to them explain. You got to admit. You got to be more honest than you ever wanted to be. You got to ask to be healed.

"And you got to diagnose your wound. You got to remember how you got that wound. That ain't easy. I know all about it. But we got some help for you, some ghosts and people to help you think it through."

*   *   *

All the things going wrong all at once! It felt like all three seasons of House on Horror Street wrapped up in one episode.

Everything was wrong. Everything.

Something had always stood between us and disaster, something like God or fate keeping us on the right side of things. People had to deserve what happened to them. I'd always felt superior to

318

the people hit by disasters. As if it was their own fault. Wasn't it? They deserved what they got. Didn't everyone? Wasn't there justice in the world? Or was it dumb luck and ours had run out?

And who wanted to be lectured by a black girl?

If Clint hadn't said Tom was right about the hurricane and everything, I wouldn't have believed it. But then, was Clint really on our side? How long had he known about this? Why hadn't he told us earlier when there was time to get out of here? What was he up to? Why didn't he put his fucking gun away?

I tried to understand what was happening, but, Jesus, I was scared. I mean, if there were a Cat Seven hurricane coming down on you, the government had sworn you off and the only people claiming to help you were a bunch of black ghosts, how would you feel?

I guess, when your life is at stake, you've got to take help where you can get it.

*　　　*　　　*

I ached with the need to draw that scene: the neighbors in their brown cloaks, hoods and white masks, their postures and movements exposing their thousand fears, gathered on one side; the ghosts in their worn period clothes, carrying their own pain, wary of the living, gathered on the other. And all framed by these grand trees, the hill topped by the house, and the dark and sparkling river below. Above it all hung the Milky Way and the moon that illuminated all. Could I get it on paper so others would see what I saw? Yes. I'd have to work at it hard, but I could, if I ever drew again.

*　　　*　　　*

I'd seen them, some of them, usually captives and from a distance, but I'd never known any Indians. That's what the whites called them. I couldn't take my eyes off Kutomá. She walked past Belinda and me to the center of the clearing as if she faced a headwind. You could tell she'd never been a slave. She walked like an American, straight, proud and poised. I tried to straighten

319

myself up to stand like her. Didn't work well. I shrank right away. We slave ghosts carry a cautious deference about us and a ready-to-shift defensive posture. We'd lived in constant fear. Kutomá never had a chance to learn that.

Kutomá had grown up learning to be free in a place. Her tribe was the Pequot. This land had been her place. To be here again, she'd had to be invited. How would you feel if Martians took over your town or city, totally changed it to their Martian needs and wants, then invited you back to tell them what it had been like before? Perhaps they'd ask you to make your mark as a memento they could have framed and hung in their equivalent of a living room. They could show their friends: this mark was made by one of the indigenous humans who lived here before we came. And their friends' eyes would open and they'd say, "Wow."

*   *   *

"Thank you," I said, "for asking me back. To my home."

No, where you lived, the place you would return to later this night, didn't look like my home. You'd changed the hills and even where the river flowed and cluttered the whole place with your box buildings. It didn't sound like my home either. Almost no bird cries, except the crows. No sounds of wind in trees. Just machine noises. It sure didn't smell like home. Or feel like it either. The land remained, hidden, its life drained. The spirit of the land remained. Even your civilization hasn't the power to kill the spirit.

"When I was sixteen, the whites warred against us. When they attacked, two Christian gentlemen took turns raping me and then cut me to death.

"On that same morning they killed my mother, my sister, my half-brother, my father and stepfather, my friends and most everyone I knew.

"But that's not what I came to tell you."

320

*   *   *

Listening to Kutomá I felt pressure in my chest and a shakiness through my whole body. Nan, Kutomá and me. Sisters of a kind. I remembered what Ms. Kinney had told us: there had been a time, Kutomá's time and a century or two after, in which it was not a crime for a white man to rape and kill a black woman, a native woman, or even, for a while, an Irish woman. Rape and kill. Now a white man could defend against a rape charge by arguing the woman's clothing, the time of night of the crime, where she had been, whether she was alone, and her state of inebriation. Except all that was no longer a defense against a murder charge. I and every woman in America could walk down a street at three a.m., naked, alone and drunk to the gills, and no one could legally murder us. Rape us, oh, sure. Murder us, no. I suppose this is progress of a kind.

Maybe this progress saved my life. How would I know? Who made this world? Who declared we need live like this? We did.

*   *   *

"The title you hold to your land descends from the war in which I died. Until now, you could have gone to your Registry of Deeds and traced your ownership all the way back to John Winthrop or the name of one of the people he led. It appears the storm may wipe that out.

"What violent, good luck you had. When you bought your home you received stolen property, but the blood had dried, the war forgotten, and it seemed your god himself had granted you this land.

"But I didn't come to tell you about that, either. You're smart. You all knew that. Right?

"Here's why I came.

"When the first European sailed up what you call the Mystic

River, we had lived here for thousands of years.

"When the first European sailed up what you call the Mystic River, he named this place Paradise.

"Your predecessors then set about, I believe you call it, making improvements. You have been making improvements for over four hundred years.

"I came here to tell you what you already know but refuse to think about: that if you arrived in your own time, in your own neighborhood, for the first time tonight, you would not imagine naming this place Paradise."

*   *   *

An image of a city built out of sand, on sand, formed in my mind. The City of Sand. And a hurricane was on its way.

I slipped out from behind Belinda, placed an arm around Kutomá and led her back to the edge of the shadows. Nan came over. My arms could go through them, but I circled my arms around them. The three of us hugged.

*   *   *

All my life all I'd ever done or wanted to do was to grow and sell plants. And that's all I had ever done: indoor plants, outdoor plants, flowering plants, non-flowering plants, bushes, small trees, cacti, moss, and all the stuff people could use to plant them and make them grow.

Now they said all that would be washed away in a storm.

There's nothing wrong with plants! And there's nothing wrong with running a business! It's hard work. Someone's always trying to take you out to help their own business. On top of that I had a wife and raised three kids. You don't get a lot of time for yourself. So now, why do I need to have done more than this just to be a good person? What are these fucking holes in me about? And who ever took time to care for me?

How do I stop this?

*   *   *

"So many times," Belinda said. Her voice lay low. It washed around each of us. You could tell a storm was coming. "So many, many times I hear white folks say, 'Black people don't feel pain the way we do. Indians don't feel pain. Asians don't feel pain. Those people don't feel sorrow the way we do. They don't love their families the way we do. You been hearing it all, right? With these wars in Africa? African people don't love their children like we do, don't love each other like we do, don't love freedom, their homes, their lives like we do.

"Don't white people have eyes? Don't white people have ears? I say white people do have eyes. And ears. White people just hiding from the pain and sorrow they caused.

"Now that would be something, wouldn't it, a real revolution: if white people could recognize our emotions are like theirs. Oh, you're right, some people hammer their feelings into tiny, dark boxes and hide them away and others let them out like Noah's flood. Most of us go somewhere in between. But that's people differences. That ain't about color differences. We all feel. Most of all, we all feel the hurt."

*   *   *

I didn't believe it. I was sitting here—not even knowing where 'here' was—and agreeing with this black ghost woman. And that Indian. Tribal person.

They'd made me remember some things I noticed over the years, some things that happened that I saw and couldn't understand. Now I understood.

When you have all the pieces, you see how they fit together.

Why didn't I understand them before?

Because I didn't have to.

Now I do.

*   *   *

AMERICAN GHOSTS

Jesus. Fuck.

If I'd said that instead of just thinking it, my wife would have been all over me about swearing in front of the kids. But seriously, fuck. Life was too fucking hard and fast to have time to deal with these people. I was fucking tired of it. It was always the same thing. They said it'd been four hundred years. Really? So what? So I yelled out, "Get over it! Move on! Take care of yourselves. That's what we do!"

But some asshole shouted back, "If we take such great care of ourselves, how come this hurricane is coming? How come they cut us off?"

How the hell should I know? But if it was a choice between ending it all and making myself equal to shit, then maybe the world should end. That's what I thought.

"Let it end! Let it end! Better dead than equality with...these ghosts!"

Another shouted, "Shut up! I don't want my kids to die!"

Well, fuck you. You think I do?

Now my wife was pissed at me.

I have a right to say what I think!

*   *   *

I hate those words: "Get over it."

I couldn't remember walking into the circle and stopping a few feet in front of Mrs. Sutton. I'd promised myself to remain silent. I'd told Celisa I didn't know what to say. The best-case scenario I could think of was I'd panic and flee the stage. Here I was. The panic didn't come. Tears came. Shaking came. But not panic. Instead I felt, deep inside, the calm steadiness of a rock.

I wanted everybody to hear.

"A man once told me to 'get over it.' I was a few years younger than I am now and he was a lot older. He'd raped me. He nearly always told me to 'get over it' when he raped me because I'd be shaking and crying. Like I am now."

I felt a presence at my side, felt an arm wrap around my waist. I looked down and saw Celisa's brown arm hugging me.

"No one just 'gets over' something like that. You don't understand because it hasn't happened to you. But have you even tried to imagine?

"I have one request.

"Ask yourself this: why would me not speaking about my rape make you feel more comfortable? Why are you uncomfortable? Why does my story make you uncomfortable? Ask yourself that."

*   *   *

We should be hiring lawyers to get an injunction! This is a terrible mistake. We've all seen video of the uncountables, their emaciated bodies, their dirty rags, their desperation. We're not like that. We're good people! The government needs to be made to understand. They hate to admit mistakes but they'll do it for us.

Let me see if I can get someone's attention.

What was she talking about rape for at a time like this?

*   *   *

"I like Jessa's question: why are so many of you uncomfortable?"

This was a situation I'd dreamed of only in nightmares: standing alone in front of a white crowd. What kind of black people do that? Stand-up comedians. Singers. Musicians. That's who. I'm flat out of jokes and songs. Be fair, I told myself, be just. Be kind. Kind. The word tasted like revenge. Kindness is revenge.

"I have a question, too. Actually, it's an invitation to imagine something. All my life, I've been told by white people how great it was my ancestors were brought here—to be slaves, sure, but to

325

be Christianized, to be given their freedom to live in the great United States of America. They asked, would you rather live in Africa?

"Well, imagine the United States of America without a single African ever being brought here. Imagine it. What great money-making industry would you have had to replace the slave trade? Would you have grown the cotton that turned this country into a force in the world market? If not cotton, then what would you have produced that brought about your industrialization? Who would you have gotten to work for you first for nothing, then for ten cents on the dollar? Who would have taken your jobs when you went off to fight wars and who would you have rioted against to make sure you got your jobs back when the war ended? Who would you have gotten to fight all your recent wars?

"Could you even be white if there were no African-Americans around?

"You can answer all those questions later.

"But this last question you must answer right now. You have to answer it because our survival depends on it.

"What would be left of you, who would you be, if your whiteness disappeared?"

*　　　*　　　*

Jesus, these people are fucking stupid! They think we have it so much better than them. They think our lives are so great? Well, if all happy means is doing whatever job you can latch onto and surviving long enough to get your kids into the same rut, then we're happy. We work, come home and get entertained by TV. What gets us through the over-and-over-again days and nights is knowing we're the cream. We're the ones who count. We work and we work hard. We make it happen. Even though they don't pay us like it, we're the ones. So don't give us crap about "history" or "feelings." We can do anything we want with these people because we're better than them and we're not letting them take what we've won.

"You're white. I'm white. We need to talk."

I'd had it written out on three pages. The closer it got to time for me to speak, the more I hated those pages. Those words weren't me; just me pretending to have it together. I tucked those pages into my pocket. All I could remember was the last line.

"You know we just moved here. The place we lived before didn't have black ghosts. We had mongols and n'okies. If I was walking down the street alone at night and I saw some n'okie guys coming my way, I'd be afraid. If it was mongol kids, yeah, I'd be afraid, too. I'd be thinking, 'They're not like us.'

"The first ghost my sister saw was Joseph." I turned a bit and pointed him out. "She screamed. You could say that Joseph really isn't like us cause he's a ghost.

"But what does it mean: 'they're not like us?'

"I've been trying to figure out who I am, who we all are, why the ghosts are here, why this hurricane is coming. Maybe some of you have asked yourselves those questions. I don't blame you if you've given up looking for answers.

"These are my thoughts. Okay? Just my thoughts.

"Maybe it all began when a group of people began thinking they were special, meaning, better than other people. They decided they could use other people however they wanted. It made their lives a lot easier: less work, more wealth. They could even buy and sell other people.

"Some of those same people also decided that men were special and could use women however they wanted.

"And then those same people decided they were so special they were entitled to use the earth any damn way they wanted. It was ours to destroy even if we destroyed ourselves in the process.

"That's it. People with a different skin color. People of a different sex. Earth with all its beings who aren't people at all. All of which is why we're here tonight.

"So, this is what I think I've learned.

"The difference between identifying as a white male and being a human being is the difference between owning a home and being home."

*   *   *

"Well, that's the single dumbest thing I ever heard in my life!" said the brown-cloaked, moon-faced man holding a gun. "It's fucking nonsense! Alright! Enough already!"

Clint walked to center stage. "I'm in charge here! You, Morton, get us back home! We've got papers to sign and work to do!" Home, he thought, what did these kids know about home?

The ground rolled like an uneasy sea.

Like many others, Clint nearly lost his balance. "Stop that!"

"I didn't do anything, Clint. This arrangement is a bit delicate. We're just about done. Give us two minutes."

"No. Bring us back now or you're dead."

"Clint, put the gun away. You kill me and you'll never get back."

"Then I'll kill the black whore and next I'll kill that Hollie slut and then her brother. Your choice. Three, two..."

"Clint, it's not time! Things aren't ready!"

Clint pointed his pistol at Celisa.

Rik moved in front of her.

The neighbors stood frozen.

Clint laughed. "Well, I'll get two with one shot! How's that?"

Tom said, "I'll do it. Stop. Point the gun down and I'll do it. Anything goes wrong, it'll be on you."

"Then do it!"

"Alright! Easy. Here we go."

"Stop!"

"What, Clint."

"I feel my legs doing that thing like they're part of the ground. Stop it!"

328

"That's how we get back, Clint! Remember that's how we got here? We can't get back without that unless you want to lose people between here and there."

Clint went silent for several seconds. "Alright, we'll do it your way. No tricks!"

The scene began to dim.

Tom immediately realized the transpose had gone off track. Rather than repeating the stages of coming in reverse, events happened simultaneously or disconnectedly and jumped out of order. He felt that a deep boiling fear had invaded the connection between the worlds.

The world tipped. The neighbors now occupied the side of a larger hill; the house lay in a valley below them. Their rooted feet kept them from tumbling down. The lights in the house went out. The river faded to a silver-blue streak that flowed over the edge of the hill in a waterfall, drowning the house. Horses swam for their lives.

Tree trunks crackled, swayed, bowed as church basement walls grew between them.

The grass and dirt of the hillside morphed into distorted tile squares.

A low ceiling formed above them, but the stars shone through.

The chairs, or most of them, reappeared. Without moving, the neighbors who had chairs found themselves sitting. Without moving, the others sat or lay uncomfortably on the floor.

Their feet came free.

All was not well. The walls groaned and cracked because of trees' movements. Where one of the trees might have been, all that was left was a hole in the wall, the other side of which opened onto a void. Many of the floor tiles had come unglued from the floor. The Milky Way still reigned, but shone as if it was below the church ceiling.

Instead of the present replacing the past, they'd structurally incorporated each other. Time came to be neither here nor there.

Many of the capes worn by the neighbors dissolved into millions of threads. Masks floated in the air like balloons. For several seconds, the neighbors experienced the aching naked horror of their wounded souls. They couldn't stand the sight but they couldn't look away.

The ghosts didn't understand what had gone wrong but the botched transition hadn't disturbed them. Tom, Jessa, Celisa and Rik had thrown themselves on the ground as soon as it had tilted and risen.

"Clint," Tom cried, "We've got to stop, go back and start again!"

"No! Keep going!"

Clint didn't have it rougher than anyone else but he'd had more than he could handle. To be fair, the pain in his left hand had grown and extended up near his elbow and impaired his judgment. Time pressed down on him. He had a plane to catch. Worse, he wore only his uniform pants. His torso was naked and he was certain the neighbors were judging his cratered soul. He felt outed.

"This is my neighborhood!" He shouted as if he wanted the whole world to hear. He fired two shots into the sky.

Tom shouted, "Stop shooting!" He approached Clint. "Put that down. We need to get things back to normal."

Clint spread his legs to steady himself and fired his second two shots at Tom.

"This is my neighborhood!"

He looked up. The stars had not gone out.

Tom lay dead on the floor.

A cry went up. "Who will heal us now?"

*　　　*　　　*

Zach pushed the light switches to "on."

*　　　*　　　*

Gary stood, intending to head-tackle Clint from behind. He'd had enough, been pushed too far, understood too much. For once in his life...

He took two steps toward Clint.

Something pounded him in the chest. His arm went numb. His strength disappeared. He gasped for air. He placed his hand over his heart.

Too late. Clint had turned. Clint saw him. The man had the strangest look on his face. But Gary couldn't see anymore. He lost his balance. He fell.

He heard Evelyn scream his name.

He lost everything.

*　　　*　　　*

Clint smirked. Gary Hollie couldn't do anything right. The man was going to die from a heart attack while attacking a police officer. What a loser.

Clint fired. Two shots, of course. Like putting a dog down.

A few of the neighbors shouted to Clint to stop shooting.

Gary lay facedown, bleeding from his back and front over the floor.

People screamed for help. Someone shouted to call an ambulance.

Clint looked around. The floor and lower part of the walls had returned, but the willow branches still hung from now-invisible trees, and the inexpressible stars remained, pouring like inexplicable offers of grace across the sky.

He saw Evelyn screaming and rushing toward him.

Clint raised his gun.

Before Clint could shoot her, he was hit from behind. They were young, strong and quick.

He went down. His left knee buckled and flexed in a way it shouldn't.

331

AMERICAN GHOSTS

Clint felt one attacker smash the wrist of his gun hand with a foot, but he held on to his weapon. Another forced his face repeatedly into the floor. Someone kneed his back. The pain! Others punched him and twisted his arms.

Clint had never known such pain.

Someone pulled his head by his hair and held a knife to his neck.

The knife slid through the outermost layers of skin. He felt his own blood running down his throat. Then the knife wielder pressed a bit harder, near Clint's artery.

"Drop the gun. Now! Right now!"

A girl's voice. A fucking girl!

She wrenched his head back for emphasis.

Clint let his weapon go. Even that was excruciating. Someone kicked the gun away.

He thought she was going to just slit his throat. He didn't know how much she wanted to. He closed his eyes. She didn't.

Suddenly it all stopped. People stood absolutely still. The ones who'd attacked him got off. The church basement had gone silent.

Using his left hand, Clint struggled to stand. His right hand was useless, his arm in intense pain, and his left knee buckled. He looked at who had jumped him: Rik and Jessa and some other kids.

A tall blond teenager held the gun. Oh, yes, Clint told himself, the first one's boyfriend.

Jessa held her knife as if she longed to use it again.

Her brother held a knife, too, pointing it at him.

What kind of children were they raising these days?

The church remained a shambles. Trees and walls intertwined. The floor was dirt here and tile there. The whole church tilted, as if it had been constructed on an incline. Some light came from the church lights, the rest came from the stars.

Clint realized the girl and the boy weren't looking at him. No one was. He followed their eyes.

A ghost walked up the tilted aisle between the rows of neighbors. Clint licked his dry lips. This was unfair. But they always were. They always had to have it their way. This was not how the game was played. He backed away, slowly, limping, unbalanced.

The ghost of Ellen Scarpacia walked down the aisle, sober, determined, staring at him.

Annie choked on a scream.

Ellen looked at Annie. The ghost raised a hand and pointed a judgmental finger at the woman.

Losing all muscle control, Annie collapsed, fell on her knees, then crashed to the floor.

Her children recoiled, screamed, cried.

Father Vic fought his way through the crowd to reach her.

Ellen walked to the front of the hall and stood among the ghosts. Nan walked to her side. They put their arms around each other.

Ellen spoke. "I wanted to live." She raised her fist and shouted, "I want to be alive! I didn't want to die. I did not kill myself!" She held her left arm out, and, with her forefinger, pointed at Clint. She lifted her right arm and pointed at where Annie lay crumpled on the floor. "Clint and Annie and another murdered me. They murdered me because I listened to what Nan and her family and friends had to say and because I wanted all of you to listen, just listen."

The neighbors, some still in monk robes, some in street clothes and some naked, shifted, glancing at each other nervously.

Ellen let her arms fall slowly to her sides.

"My parents fled. They knew I hadn't killed myself. They worried someone would kill them, too.

"Steve, thank you for your faith in me. If I only had arms..."

Ellen cried. Steve cried.

Ellen shook her sadness off though her eyes remained wet. She had a long time ahead for sadness. She walked up to Jessa. Their eyes met. Jessa's lips trembled. Ellen spoke. "Thank you." She turned to Rik and Celisa. "All of you."

To Jessa she said, "Now that Tom is dead, you will be the healer. You are the one who heals souls."

The girl felt instant panic. She thought: I'm a mess, a psychiatric patient, I'm depressed, I'm on meds, I can't talk to a boy about a date without feeling like I'm going to throw up! I can't heal anyone!

Jessa shook her head no.

Ellen said, "You can if you will. Without you, the pain and violence will continue. I tell you once more: you are the one who heals souls."

A few tears straggled from Jessa's eyes. She shook. She felt everyone was looking at her, hoping she would accept. Everyone was.

Perhaps Ellen realized Jessa was incapable of speech. "If you accept, kneel."

Jessa looked at the floor. It seemed very far away. She felt a ghostly touch. More than a touch. Nan's hand intermingled with her own. She felt Nan's need for her to accept. She felt Nan's support. She felt Nan's faith in her.

Jessa realized it had already been decided.

Her hand still intertwined with Nan's, she knelt. Ellen placed a hand on Jessa's head. "In humility, bring grace and clarity to all. Heal all."

Jessa stood. Ellen's hand joined Nan's and Jessa's. Tears came to all of them, but they were tears of joy and power.

Clint could not tolerate tears.

"It's all your fault!" he screamed at Ellen's ghost. "If you hadn't tried to tell..."

Steve raised the gun, pointed it at Clint. Clint snarled, "You motherfucking son of a bitch. Go ahead! Shoot me. You don't have the balls."

Ellen turned. She said, "Don't, Steve. He's mine."

Clint backed away as Ellen matched him step for step. What did she mean, he was hers? Inch by inch, step by step, he retreated cautiously toward the church hall exit, all the while facing Ellen, watching her. He left wet red footprints and slide marks wherever he stepped and on whatever he touched. He half walked, bent, his bitten left hand trying to clutch his bruised right arm, struggling to keep his left leg under him.

Halfway to the exit, he turned and scampered like a broken rat out the door.

Someone shouted, "I called 911 and no one answered!"

The church filled with sounds of pain and mourning.

*   *   *

Clint consisted of one hundred percent will. He was going to do this. He would make it to Toronto. He would hold his wife again.

Using only his bandaged left hand and arm and his right foot, he could drive. He started the engine and turned on all lights and sirens.

He drove like the madman he'd become. The streets had long before emptied of traffic, pursuant to the FEMA order. His only obstacles were police blockades. His police vehicle, sirens, lights and all, got him through all the roadblocks without being stopped. Stupid police, he thought, still following orders. Were they so dumb they hadn't figured it out yet?

He arrived at the airport in less than fifteen minutes.

Following signs, he found the private jet terminal.

He abandoned the car in front of the terminal without turning off the lights or sirens. He screamed at someone who looked like they might know where Gordie Sands' plane was waiting. The woman yelled, "Seven."

Clint ran out the gate to the base of the mobile stairway. He turned, expecting nothing, but she was there, Scarpacia, still following, closing in on him a single step at a time.

He half climbed and half pulled himself up the stairs to the plane's door.

He turned again. She was gone.

The pilot sat in the cockpit. "Where the hell you been? Everyone's been waiting."

Clint stepped into the plane, then, barely inside, stopped.

"All the way in. I got to close the door. We're taking off."

Clint didn't move until the closing door hit him on his butt.

The plane began to taxi.

Clint tried to push the cabin door open.

The pilot screamed, "Get back in and sit down! We're taking off!"

Clint looked again into the passenger compartment.

Gordie Sands and his girl sat in the first two seats.

Gary and Paul sat in the second two.

Ellen sat in the third row, across from Tom.

The plane was a six-seater.

Clint collapsed and folded up in the aisle, like a spider playing dead. His shoulders shook uncontrollably, then his body. His face wrinkled into a revelation of pain. Tears came like a flash flood. He sobbed. He wanted to hold himself. He knew it was over. He didn't have words for the feelings that filled his body. Relief was close, but relief into what? Such strange feelings to last such a short time. Just before he screamed, he whispered, "Scarlet."

The nose lifted off the runway.

Clint flew. Nothing held him down.

*   *   *

The neighbors and the ghosts looked to Jessa.

She looked at the naked, potholed neighbors clutching the remnants of their cloaks and reappeared clothes. She looked back at Belinda and Nan and the rest of the ghosts, then at her brother and Celisa. She noticed Father Vic holding Annie. She looked at the twisted church trying to bridge two times. She did not know what to do and was afraid she would never know what to do.

What had Tom done to bring them back in time? What or who or where were the powers that could do such a thing?

She had to try. She looked for words. There had to be words. But Rik was better with them. She drew pictures. Perhaps there was a picture. She conjured an image of the church basement as it had existed in their time and on a wall she pictured a calendar with the day's date.

As if she had been directed, she looked at Father Vic.

"Father, do you ask that your church find its true time."

Father Vic, still holding a shaking Annie, said, "Please."

She placed Father Vic into her image. Something flowed through her mind and body, flowed out and then back in. The return began, but she found she needed to maintain the full image in her mind or the process stopped.

The trees groaned as they disappeared. The floor leveled and became all tile. The walls grew together. People found themselves dressed in their regular clothing.

Evelyn lay sobbing on the floor holding Gary's body. Dr. Dreier sat on the floor, an arm around Evelyn. Charlie sat in his wheelchair, his mouth searching for words that might make meaning, his face an icon of sorrow. Every several seconds, he shook his head, as if saying, "There's nothing to be done." Nothing to be done.

Steve and Zach knelt by Tom. They'd become numb. So many dead. Too much feeling.

Jessa, Rik and Celisa stood: Jessa with one arm across her breasts and her face buried in her opposite hand; Rik with his head bent, eyes closed, breathing as if air had become scarce; Celisa with her face raised as if looking toward heaven, but her eyes closed.

A single death can slow time; two deaths can stop it. Death can also slice the bonds between people, marooning each on their own

337

foreboding island. Celisa, who had lost the least, saw what needed to be done. She walked Jessa to her brother and hugged both. Slowly, Jessa and Rik emerged from their isolation and extended their arms around the others.

Father Vic touched each of the three gently and reminded them there was work that needed doing. Time had begun running again and was short.

The three slowly separated and realized they were surrounded by a group of neighbors.

A man in his forties cautiously stepped forward. Two girls in their mid-teens held his arms. He said, "Seems there is little of me that isn't a wound. My therapist, who for some reason is here tonight, told me that wars always come home. She's right. The wars against the tribes have come home. The war against the slaves has come home. Our war against the earth has come home. I brought the wars in Africa home with me. I understand. I wish to be healed if that is possible."

Others crowded in, hopeful, fearful, confused from having seen so deeply into reality. Others shouted derisively, as if they had seen nothing. "Shameful," some said bitterly. One angrily said, "Circus." The words "trick" and "fake" were shouted several times. Several asserted, "I'm nobody's fool."

Others, at a loss for words, indicated their choice by leaving or staying. A woman stepped toward Jessa, guiding her children in front of her as if saying: "Even if you won't accept me, take them." A family of four came forward, the woman's eyes staring, her forehead furrowed, the man looking uncertain and drawn. The two children, one each side of ten, looked at Jessa in awe, as if she were a superhero. She heard words like "heal," help," "I never knew." One man looked at Jessa with his mouth open for several seconds before saying, "I'm good with plants."

The man last out the door declared, "You're not going to make me no slave to no n---r ghosts!"

338

The line in time had arrived.

Jessa turned to Belinda. "The pact has been made."

Belinda said, "It is. Oh, Lord, it is."

The ghosts and neighbors mixed, greeted one another. Some of the living tried to shake hands, found that to be impossible and ended with slight bows that were returned. The two children who had invaded Evelyn's kitchen found her still kneeling and stood mournfully beside her.

Jessa cleared her throat. She raised her hand. "Just a minute. Please?"

People and ghosts relayed her request to those who hadn't heard.

In the second before she spoke, she felt the weight of all their expectations. She felt their acceptance of her leadership.

"After the storm, we shall meet here. We need each other now in order to survive. Survival means food, shelter, clothing and so many other things. Survival also means healing. I will keep my promise to Ellen and Tom."

The man with two daughters said, "Thank you." Others spoke their assent.

Father Vic approached the widow, touched her, helped her stand and withdraw to the embrace of her children.

"I will care for the dead," the priest said. "You all, go and make ready." He then said what he'd been too frightened to say just seconds before. "Make ready the way of the Lord." He seemed to feel himself most a priest at the oddest times.

After he hugged each of the others and saw them back to their vehicles, Father Vic carried each body to the upper church and laid it out, covered with his own vestments, before the altar. Then, trailed by her daughters, he carried Annie, whose knees had swollen to softball size. The pain wouldn't allow her to stand, let alone walk. He lay her down on the front pew, using one vestment to soften the hardness of the wood and another folded up as

339

her pillow. He ran to the rectory to get ice packs. He thought for a second and then packed a lunch: sandwiches, drinks and bags of chips, enough to get the four of them through the night and, he hoped, most of the following day. He put all the food and drinks in a picnic cooler and fully understood the irony.

Father Vic set the children to coloring on the pew beside him. After minutes of sobbing wordlessness, Annie spoke.

"Why don't you ask?" Her voice overflowed with tears and sniffles.

Father Vic looked at the woman. "You'll tell me when you're ready."

Her breaths came at the pace of a hard jog. "I...helped...I killed her."

"The ghost girl?"

Annie nodded.

Father Vic expelled a breath. He closed his eyes. His head tilted and he nodded. "Do you seek forgiveness?"

"No!"

Her words delivered a jolt. Where had such deeply felt words come from? Not from this frail woman? But they had.

"I don't deserve forgiveness! I will never forgive myself. There's nothing I can do to bring her back. I can't...her parents... I...I—" Annie screamed while tearing her hair, "I hate myself!"

Father Vic realized she was haunted by what she had done. There would be much penance. Only a real healer could lead the dead to forgive the living.

Annie's sobs and the rustling of paper and sliding of crayons were the only sounds inside the church. Outside, the winds began to stir.

Father Vic looked up at the vaulted ceiling. He thought it beautiful, artful, reassuring. Yet his mind wandered back to the vault of the Milky Way, the memory of which penetrated his spirit.

Perhaps, the priest thought, humans sitting beneath such a sky had been the ones who first understood grace.

Father Vic told God in prayer that if the waters began to take over the church, he'd carry the bodies and take Annie and her children up to the choir loft. There they'd wait out the judgment of heaven and earth.

*   *   *

Jessa, Rik and Celisa said goodbye to Steve and Zach. Great hugs were exchanged.

"See you in a couple of days," they said to each other, bucking their fears.

Rik faced Jessa. "You did right. I'm very proud to be your brother." He kissed her on her forehead, then handed her Tom's keys. "There was really no other choice." They hugged. He said, "We got lucky with Gary and Tom."

Jessa stood silent for several seconds. "They're hard, but good, examples to follow."

Rik and Jessa helped Evelyn into the car. She protested. She wanted to stay with Gary's body, or at least in Gary's house. They decided for her.

When Rik got in the car beside Evelyn, he said, "I'm going to miss Gary. You made a good choice."

Evelyn responded by sobbing. Celisa said, "Yeah. He ended up showing us we can change. Become more like..."

"Who we are."

"And Tom showed us who we are."

With Rik in the backseat holding his mother, Celisa drove the Hollie car. Jessa followed in Tom's rental. Dr. Dreier and Charlie brought up the rear in the chair van.

Celisa and Jessa carried Charlie up the steps while Rik carried the man's chair. Dr. Dreier helped Evelyn out of the car, then encouraged the woman, one step at a time, until Rik and Jessa returned to help their mother.

Sona opened the door. Hearing what had happened, with tears in her eyes, she welcomed them into her home.

EDWARD J. SANTELLA

CHAPTER THIRTEEN
SATURDAY

By midnight, high broken clouds moved in, illuminated by the quarter moon. Two hours later, the air had lost its freshness and wind rumbled through trees like a highspeed rail.

Birds screeched warnings. They couldn't keep the wind from tossing them about like tailless kites. Small mammals dug deeper into the protective shelter of their holes. Branches snapped off. Creaking and groaning sounds rose, but it was impossible to tell from where.

Leaves released their hold on branches as if it were late autumn. Thicker, darker clouds moved in. On-and-off spurts of sprinkles got caught in the wind and evaporated or rose in an up-draft before they reached the earth. Clouds covered the gibbous moon momentarily, then gathered closer, with fewer breaks, and the moon disappeared.

By three a.m., the wind became a howl.

By four, objects became weightless in the wind. Newspapers, blankets, small toys, clothes on clotheslines left the ground and danced in the air like crazed dervishes.

As the sky began to lighten, the light turned from gray to an unnatural, sickly yellow. Windows vibrated. The wind never died, but gusts came like reinforcements, slamming into buildings like heavyweight punches. Sirens sounded, first in the distance, then closer, then everywhere.

By six, the birds had disappeared. The lucky ones who had nests inside trees hunkered down. Those that had nests precariously rigged on branches learned to pray. Trees leaned first in one direction, then, as the wind shifted, in another. Branches were bare as late November.

No wolves lived near, but some animals, perhaps coyotes or coywolves, howled and howled again. The air grew darker and lighter at the same time. Was that the sun rising or the light of a fire? It flickered red and orange. Fire. On the horizon. More sirens rose and fell.

Blowing this way, then that, the wind exuded panic. Something gone terribly wrong. The air smelled poisoned, for not only was the building aflame, but so were tons of chemicals it contained. Even when the wind paused momentarily, objects continued to fly through the air as if fleeing disaster. The wind caused emergency vehicles bound for the fire to shift lanes involuntarily, violently. As if hammered, an ambulance rolled over and slid across the road, only to be struck by a police car following too closely behind. Raising a ladder proved impossible. Firemen failed to stand against the gusts of wind. First they knelt, then they simply lay on the ground holding the water hoses. Lasers of water bent, turned and fell where the winds took them. Somewhere an oil tank burst. Flaming oil rode on water, like the devil surfing. As oil spilled through the building, and into the streets the firemen abandoned their hoses and fled. Flames chased them, dancing and leaping, untamed and fearless.

Unseen above the clouds, the moon pulled at the ocean, dragging its watery massiveness higher toward the coast, raising waves above twenty feet, till beaches, roads and houses were swept away. Waters rose in the harbor and forced their way up the river to Paradise.

The river flowed backwards, swirled and rose over Antigua Avenue. Two oddly beautiful twin wax women waited to be taken. Cellars and first floors flooded. The unpretty debris of civilization littered the waters.

The ghosts remained, gathering among the branches of trees bending in the gales. The trees were flexible and strong, having grown from the graves of slaves.

Neither the waters, the wind, nor the driving rain disturbed the ghosts. Nan, standing like a sea captain in the upper branches, kept an eye on George, the old ghost who'd hanged himself after the owners took his grandchildren. He sat on the stairs of the Adebayo house, smoking and talking to the storm. Her father guarded another house and other ghosts stood sentry for others. The ghosts would do their best to protect those of the living who wanted to heal. The other ghosts murmured among themselves. Belinda's tears mixed with the storm.

The arc was long, she knew, and nothing was ever erased.

Acknowledgements

One of the great strokes of luck in my life was that, from a few days after birth until the age of ten or so, I lived next door to the city public library. The library and the librarians, especially Mrs. Darden, introduced me to the world and the universe. Thank you librarians!

Thank you, English teachers, especially Mr. D'Ambrosio! Thank you for teaching me to write and to value what I wrote.

Beginning a novel is an act of faith that leads to frequent episodes of panic and despair. I had help getting through.

Dennis Reilly and Bob Sullivan, true friends, read an early version of American Ghosts and provided comments, criticism and encouragement. They helped shape the story.

Carolyn Jenks, friend and agent, read different versions of this book. She offered enthusiasm and timely encouragement.

Phoenix Bunke, friend and editor, read everything, made incisive comments, asked thought-provoking questions, and pushed me past what I wrongly believed were my limits.

I would like to thank my wife Karen for reading each of the many drafts of this novel and providing comments and encouragement. I also thank her for her endless patience. I am certain somewhere in her mind is a picture of me totally motionless as I wait for the next word to fall from the sky. The picture is titled, "Still Life with Laptop."

Each of these people contributed to American Ghosts in their own unique ways. Without them, this story would not be what it is.

And thank you, readers. Thank you for understanding that stories about people you will never meet are important to the person you become.

EDWARD J. SANTELLA

Works Quoted and Used With Permission

Bradbury, Ray. Fahrenheit 451. Simon & Schuster, 2013.

Kafka, Franz. "The Metamorphosis." Franz Kafka: The Complete Stories, edited by Nahum N. Glatzer, Schocken Books, Inc., 1971.

Lessing, Doris. African Stories. Simon & Schuster, 2014.

Poe, Edgar Allen. Complete Tales & Poems. New York: Castle Books, 2002.

Wheatley, Phillis. Phillis Wheatley: Complete Writings. Edited by Vincent Carretta, Penguin Books, 2001.

EDWARD J. SANTELLA

Suggested Readings

Massachusetts and New England
Settlement and Slavery

❧☙Farrow, Anne, Joel Lang and Jenifer Frank. Complicity: How the North Promoted, Prolonged, and Profited from Slavery. Ballentine Books, 2006.

❧☙Manegold, C.S. Ten Hills Farm: The Forgotten History of Slavery in the North. Princeton University Press, 2010.

❧☙Warren, Wendy. New England Bound: Slavery and Colonization in Early America. W.W. Norton & Company, 2016.

❧☙Winbush, Raymond A. Belinda's Petition: A Concise History of Reparations for the Transatlantic Slave Trade. Xlibris, 2009.

North American Slavery Sublette

❧☙Ned and Constance. The American Slave Coast: A History of the Slave-Breeding Industry. Lawrence Hill Books, 2016.

❧☙Jim CrowBlackmon, Douglas A. Slavery by Another Name: The Re-Enslavement of Black Americans from the Civil War to World War II. Anchor Books, 2008.

❧☙Alexander, Michelle. The New Jim Crow: Mass Incarceration in the Age of Colorblindness. The New Press, 2011.

Being White

❧☙Baldwin, James. "On Being White...and Other Lies." The Cross of Redemption: Uncollected Writings, edited by Randall Kenan, Vintage Books, 2010.

❧☙Thandeka. Learning to Be White: Money, Race, and God in America. Continuum, 2000.

❧☙Wise, Tim. White Like Me: Reflections on Race from a Privileged Son. Counterpoint, 2011.

Printed in Great Britain
by Amazon